# SIXTEEN
# BRIDES

# Books by
# STEPHANIE GRACE WHITSON

---

# STEPHANIE GRACE
# WHITSON

## SIXTEEN
## BRIDES

BETHANYHOUSE
MINNEAPOLIS, MINNESOTA

Published by Bethany House Publishers
11400 Hampshire Avenue South
Bloomington, Minnesota 55438

Bethany House Publishers is a division of
Baker Publishing Group, Grand Rapids, Michigan.

Printed in the United States of America

Library of Congress Cataloging-in-Publication Data

Whitson, Stephanie Grace.
    Sixteen brides / Stephanie Grace Whitson.
       p.   cm.
    ISBN 978-0-7642-0513-2 (pbk.)
    1. War widows—Fiction. 2. Homestead law—Nebraska—Fiction. 3. Women pioneers—Fiction. 4. Frontier and pioneer life—Nebraska—Fiction. I. Title.
    PS3573.H555S59      2010
    813'.54—dc22

                                                                                    2009041266

the memory of
God's extraordinary women
in every place
in every time.


And to my Daniel,
the best creative consultant ever . . .
*mahalo nui loa* . . .
*aloha wau ia 'oe.*

## About the Author

A native of southern Illinois, Stephanie Grace Whitson has lived in Nebraska since 1975. She began what she calls "playing with imaginary friends" (writing fiction) when, as a result of teaching her four home-schooled children Nebraska history, she was personally encouraged and challenged by the lives of pioneer women in the West.

Since her first novel, *Walks the Fire,* was published in 1995, Stephanie's fiction titles have appeared on the ECPA bestseller list numerous times and been finalists for the Christy Award, the Inspirational Readers Choice Award, and ForeWord Magazine's Book of the Year. Her first nonfiction work, *How to Help a Grieving Friend: a Candid Guide for Those Who Care,* was released in 2005.

In addition to keeping up with her five grown children and two grandchildren, Stephanie enjoys motorcycle trips with her blended family (she was widowed in 2001 and remarried in 2003) and church friends, as well as volunteering at the International Quilt Study Center and Museum in Lincoln, Nebraska. She is currently in graduate school pursuing a Master of Historial Studies degree. Her passionate interests in pioneer women's history, antique quilts, and French, Italian, and Hawaiian language and culture provide endless storytelling possibilities.

Contact information: *www.stephaniewhitson.com*; stephanie@stephaniewhitson.com; Stephanie Grace Whitson, P.O. Box 6905, Lincoln, Nebraska 68506.

# ATTRACTIVE
# WIDOWS

*April 7, 1871* —Another cargo of war widows arrived in Plum Grove last Tuesday morning, sixteen in number, and filed upon claims adjacent to town. This was decidedly the best lot of widows that has arrived thus far.

*A man's heart deviseth his way:*
*but the Lord directeth his steps.*

PROVERBS 16:9

As the carriage pulled away from Union Station, Caroline Jamison almost panicked and called out to the driver, "Wait! Don't go! I've changed my mind! Take me home!" Her heart racing, Caroline forced herself to turn away. *St. Louis isn't home. And home doesn't want you. Daddy told you that in his last letter.* Still, there were times when she entertained a desperate few minutes of hope. *But what if I was standing right there on the veranda. Would he really turn me away? If I told him I was sorry . . . that he was right . . . if I begged . . . what then?*

For just a moment the possibility that her father might forget everything and pull her into his arms made Caroline feel almost dizzy with joy. But then she remembered. It had been five years since she'd opened that last envelope, and still she could recite the terse few lines of the last letter posted from General Harlan Sanford of Mulberry Plantation.

*Daughter.*

*We received word today. Langdon now joins his two brothers in glory. Your mother has taken to her bed. The idea that any—or all—of these deeds of war may have been committed by one their sister calls HUSBAND—*

The sentence wasn't finished. Caroline still remembered touching the spot where the ink trailed off toward the edge of the paper, a meandering line that wrenched her heart as she pictured Daddy seated at his desk, suddenly overcome by such a deep emotion he couldn't control his own hand.

*We are bereft of children now. May God have mercy on your soul.*

For a moment, as Caroline stood, frozen motionless by uncertainty here on the brick walkway leading up to Union Station, desperate regret and a renewed sense of just how completely alone she was rose up. Panic nearly swept her away. If she didn't get hold of herself she was going to faint. A few deep breaths would be helpful, but the corset ensuring her eighteen-inch waist wasn't going to allow for that. She closed her eyes in a vain attempt to hold back the tears. *You don't dare go home . . . and you don't dare stay here.*

An axle in need of grease squealed as another carriage pulled up to the curb, this one drawn by a perfectly matched team of black geldings. Their coats glistening, their manes plaited with red ribbons, the horses tossed their heads and stamped their great hooves. As the driver called out to calm the team, a coachman hopped down from his perch, but he was too late to open the door for his fare.

One glimpse of the wild-looking man emerging from the polished carriage and Caroline swiped at her tears, snapped open her gold silk parasol, and bent down to pick up her black traveling case. *You'll make a scene if you faint right now, and the ladies of Mulberry Plantation never make a scene.* The ladies of Mulberry Plantation didn't associate with the kind of men emerging from that carriage, either. Lifting her chin, Caroline headed toward the station lest one of them offer to escort her up the hill. The last thing she needed today was to have to extricate herself from the unwanted attentions of some dandy dressed up like a poor imitation of Wild Bill Hickok.

*Wild Bill Hickok* indeed. Grateful to be thinking about something besides home, she almost smiled at the memory of Thomas, one of the Jamisons' servants, and the ridiculous hat he'd sported for weeks after seeing Hickok and Buffalo Bill on stage. A hat just like the ones on the heads of the men climbing out of the newly arrived carriage. Only these men didn't look ridiculous. They looked . . . dangerous. Caroline peered back at them from beneath the edge of her parasol even as she made her way up the hill. The tall one had a certain appeal—if a woman liked that kind of man. Caroline did not.

With every step away from the street and toward the station, her doubt and fear receded. She could do this. After all, it was the only thing that made any sense. No one was coming to rescue her. It was time she rescued herself.

"Painting walls and hanging pictures don't make a barn into a home, Mama." Ella Barton looked away from her own face in the mirror just long enough to catch her mother's eye. "A barn is still a barn." Shaking her head, she untied the new bonnet. "I'm sorry. I just can't. You were sweet to buy it, but I look ridiculous." She put the stylish bonnet back into the open bandbox sitting atop the dresser. "We'll return it on the way to the station."

"We will *not* return it." Mama snatched it up and ran her hand along the upturned brim. She smoothed the nosegay of iridescent feathers just peeking out of the grosgrain ribbon that bordered the crown. "It's beautiful."

"Did I say it wasn't?" Ella turned her back on the mirror. "The problem is not the hat." Gently she extracted the bonnet from her mother's grasp and nestled it back into the box. "The old one is better. It suits me." She settled the lid on the bandbox. "What do I need with a new hat, anyway? I hardly think they parade the latest fashions up and down the street in Cayote, Nebraska."

"Maybe not," Mama said. "But you can bet there *will* be a parade when we all arrive. Everyone says women are in short supply out west. That means you can expect a parade of bachelors coming into Cayote as soon as word gets out about the Emigration Society's arrival."

Ella crossed the room to where their two traveling cases lay open on the lumpy mattress. "And they will see me as I am—and leave me be. Even if I were interested—which I am not—a new bonnet wouldn't change anything." She finished folding her white cotton nightgown into the case as she spoke, especially mindful of the wide border of handmade lace as she closed the lid. It had taken her over thirty hours to make that gown. She wanted it to last.

Mama joined her by the bed, closing and locking her own traveling case as she said, "You don't *know* what others see when they look at you, Ella. You have lovely eyes."

Ella snorted in disbelief. "I know what they see. Milton reminded me almost every day."

"Milton!" Mama spit the name out like spoiled meat. She made two fists and pummeled the air. "I wish I could get my hands on him. I'd teach him—"

"Mama." Ella's voice was weary. Mama's opinions about Milton had grown old long ago. "Let him rest in peace. It's over."

"Except that it *isn't*. What he did to you—what he made you feel about yourself—none of that is *over*."

Ella sighed. It was no use debating Milton Barton with Mama. Mothers looked at their daughters and saw the best, which was, in Ella's case, her eyes. But mothers tended to see *only* the things like beautiful hazel eyes. They ignored broad shoulders and strong frames, large hands and noses.

As Ella lifted her traveling case off the bed and set it on the floor so she could smooth the blanket into place, she glanced toward the mirror. She always had regretted that nose. But simple regret had evolved into something else, thanks to Milton. It was *her* fault he sought other beds. It was *her* fault he wandered. It was *her* fault they had no children. She wasn't pretty. She wasn't feminine. She wasn't—

*Stop. Stop the litany. Stop it now. Nothing good comes of it.* What was it Mama always said . . . *forget what lies behind. Press on to hope.* She must do that now, even if she did still hear Milton's voice at times. She was clumsy. She lumbered like a cow. Such a big nose. Such large hands. Such rough skin. She was *barren*. But of all the words Milton flung at her, the ones that hurt most were the ones Ella added to the list herself. She was *gullible*. Gullible and *stupid* to have believed a man could love a woman like her.

And so, after being widowed by the war, having lost her farm and much of herself in the process, Ella moved to town and rented a nondescript room on a nondescript street in St. Louis. She cooked and cleaned at a nice hotel nearby, and kept to herself. She was never asked to stay on, never promoted to serve in the dining room. After all, who would want a cow lumbering about with their fancy china and silver candlesticks? Dark thoughts hung over the widow Barton like a cloud. And then one day she saw Mr. Hamilton Drake's sign in a milliner's shop window.

*WANTED*, it said in large letters. *ONLY WOMEN NEED APPLY.* Smaller print said that Mr. Hamilton Drake of Dawson County, Nebraska, the organizer of the Ladies Emigration Society, was here in St. Louis to help women *TAKE CONTROL* of their own *DESTINY* by acquiring *LAND IN THEIR OWN NAME.* He invited *ALL INTER-ESTED LADIES* to meet with him in Parlor A of the Laclede Hotel on any one of three evenings listed. He promised that if women would *HURRY*, they could still acquire *FREE PRIME HOMESTEADS* in the most desirable portions of the county.

*Control of her own destiny . . . land in her own name . . . a prime homestead.* Ella stood looking at that sign for a long while. At the first meeting she attended, Mr. Drake produced an "official" copy of the homestead law President Lincoln had signed back in 1862. Ella read it and learned that what Drake said was right. As a single woman and therefore the head of her own "household," Ella could file on a homestead. And Ella knew land. She knew livestock and crops and plows. She knew when to plant and how to harvest. She also knew there was little, if any, chance a man would ever love her, and even if some fool tried, how would she ever know if it was sincere? But Ella knew something else, too. For the first time in a very long while, Ella knew hope.

Ella looked into the mirror and smiled. Mama was right. The simply dressed woman with the plain face did have rather nice eyes. She glanced at Mama in the mirror. Dear Mama, with her tiny waist and petite stature. Mama, with her lively sense of humor and youthful spirit. What, Ella thought, would she have ever done without Mama?

"Ella." Mama patted her shoulder. "Stop riding the clouds and come back to earth." When Ella blinked and looked at her, Mama put her hand atop the bandbox. "I asked if you're sure about the new hat."

"I'm sure." Ella reached for the old brown one hanging on a hook by the door.

With a dramatic sigh, Mama took the bandbox in hand and opened the door.

Ella picked up their two suitcases and followed her out into the hall and downstairs. As they headed toward the train station by way of the milliner's, neither woman looked back.

The resolve that had propelled Caroline Jamison up the hill and into Union Station faded the instant she lowered her parasol just inside the door. She hesitated, gazing at the scores of people buying tickets, hurrying toward the tracks, seated in the lunch room sipping tea, browsing at the newsstand. Her head hurt. Her kid leather gloves were growing damp. Perspiration trickled down her back. She was feeling shaky again.

The members of the Ladies Emigration Society were supposed to proceed through the station and gather on the siding near Track Number 2. Mr. Drake had said he expected almost a train-car full of women to join the Society. Caroline wasn't ready to meet all those strangers. She looked toward the tracks. *Oh no. Please no. Not the sisters.* Caroline had especially hoped those four would have talked each other out of heading west. At the thought of facing those four—and maybe a few dozen women just like them—Caroline found an empty bench and sat down.

Pulling her traveling case onto her lap, she clung to the handle with one hand and her parasol with the other even as she tried to calm herself. *Close your eyes. Think of something else. Think about . . . the rose garden. Remember how wonderful those yellow ones on the arbor smelled when they bloomed? Can you hear old James humming to himself while he trimmed the hedge?* Shutting out the sounds of the bustling train station and thinking about the garden helped. She stopped trembling. *There, now. That's better.*

She looked toward the tracks. Where were the dozens of women Mr. Drake talked about? What if the sisters decided they wouldn't have her today? What if they united the others against her and spoke to Mr. Drake and talked him into canceling her membership in the Society? *Laws o'massey*, what if she had to go *back*? Back to Basil's parents' home here in St. Louis. Back to—

With a little shudder, Caroline stood up. When all else failed, thinking about Basil's father would give her the determination she needed for this day and a hundred more like it. It had cost her everything when she ran off and married a Yankee. Those women had no idea. Had any of *them* spent their widowhood listening to a rattling doorknob and the mutterings of their very own father-in-law begging them to move a trunk away from the door? Using her parasol as a walking stick, Caroline stood back up. She had as much right as anyone to homestead land. Abraham Lincoln himself had said so, may the good Lord rest his soul.

A gangly blond-haired boy just now coming out of the diner looked Caroline's way, nodded, and tipped his cap. She smiled at him. He blushed and hurried to where a woman dressed in a black traveling suit waited just inside the door. The woman glared at Caroline, said something to the boy, and literally pulled him toward the tracks and the group of women waiting near Track Number 2. *Oh dear.* She'd apparently just offended another member of the Society, and this time she hadn't even opened her mouth.

All right. The only way to do this was to . . . just go and do it and never mind the rest of them. With one last glance toward the street, Caroline headed for the tracks.

"You goin' west, too?"

Caroline looked back toward the owner of the gravelly voice. She couldn't possibly be old enough to file on a homestead, could she? Mr. Drake said you had to be twenty-one. This girl didn't look a day past eighteen. Surely she wasn't widowed, either—but then, being a *widow* wasn't exactly a requirement for joining the Society. Some of the ladies at her meeting had appeared to be more interested in finding husbands than homesteads. Maybe that was the case with this girl.

Caroline didn't know hair that color existed in nature. It reminded her of the scarlet crepe myrtle growing around the gazebo at home in Tennessee. And that dress. It was a bad enough shade of yellow now. It would have been an absolute horror before it faded. Women with hair that shade of red should *never* wear that yellow. Especially if they had ivory skin. It made them look ill.

The girl coughed into the handkerchief she held balled up in one palm. "Sorry," she said and coughed again before extending a hand in greeting. "I'm Sally. Sally Grant. No relation to the general by that name. Although I got his autograph at the Sanitary Fair when I was little and he said my eyes reminded him of his daughter—" She rattled on as Caroline introduced herself and shook hands, but then the girl broke off abruptly. "Sorry," she said. "I tend to talk too much when I'm nervous." She pointed toward the group of women waiting outside. "You with them? *Us,* I guess I should say."

Caroline nodded.

"You as scared as I am?"

When the young woman coughed again, Caroline wondered if Sally Grant's pale complexion was more a result of ill health than anything else. How frightening it would be to have committed to something like this trip west and then be threatened with illness. That would be worse than a dozen attacks of nerves.

The girl misinterpreted Caroline's silence. "I can see you're a real lady," she said, motioning to Caroline's dark gold traveling suit and parasol even as she made a vain attempt to smooth the front of her wrinkled calico dress. She gave a little shrug. "You don't have to talk to me if you don't want to. I was just tryin' to be friendly." And with that, she brushed past Caroline and headed for the tracks.

"Wait!" When the girl turned back, Caroline hurried to catch up. "I'm sorry. I seem to have been rendered speechless this mornin', but it's got nothin' to do with you." Her voice wavered. "I didn't mean to be rude. It's just that—just that I'm—"

"—scared?" Sally Grant's smile revealed a missing front tooth.

Caroline shook her head. "No, ma'am. I'm not scared. I'm terrified." Only it sounded more like *ah'm not scairt, ah'm ter-ah-fide.* She glanced away, hating the knowledge that she was blushing, trying to cogitate on how she would handle it if Sally Grant—frayed dress, missing tooth and all—was a certain kind of Yankee.

"Memphis or Nashville?" Sally asked, eyeing Caroline closely.

Caroline stiffened. What did that matter? She was just as deserving as any other member of the Emigration Society. She'd sacrificed her way of life and her own family to marry Basil, and he'd died for the Union just as surely as if he'd been shot in battle. And hadn't she herself done her duty, too, nursing him faithfully until the day his body followed where his spirit had already flown? Caroline didn't even try to sound less southern as she drawled, "What's it mattuh? Ah'm the widda of Private Basil Richard Jamison of the Ninth Missourah Volunteers."

Sally's blue eyes stayed friendly. She nodded. "That so? Well, it don't really matter whether it's Memphis or Nashville. I was just wonderin'."

"Ah—ah see." Caroline cleared her throat. She nodded toward the waiting group of women. "*You* know any of 'em?"

Sally shook her head. "Naw. I only went to the one meetin' and they wasn't much for chitchat seeing as how I'm ..." She bit her lower lip. Her bony shoulders lifted in a shrug. "Seeing as how I'm me. And divorced. And I told 'em so." She tilted her head and eyed Caroline carefully. "What about you?"

"Me? Oh no—like I told you—my husband was—"

"No," Sally interrupted, "not are you divorced. I heard what you said about all that." She frowned as she pointed toward the tracks. "Seems like Mr. Drake said there'd be more of us. Do you know any of 'em?"

Caroline shook her head. "Those four off to the side were at the meetin' when I joined. But I don't recognize any of the others." She shrugged. "A-course they weren't much for chitchattin' with me. Least not after I opened my mouth and let the Tennessee out."

The girl grinned. "What d'ya say you 'n' me stick together for the ride out?"

Caroline had never met anyone as forthcoming as Sally Grant. Her dress was frayed and her thin hands and bony shoulders were evidence she probably hadn't been eating very well of late. There was a good chance that everything Sally Grant owned was inside the worn carpetbag clutched in her hands. And Caroline liked her. "If y'all don't mind travelin' with a southern gal, ah think that'd be fine."

"Way-el," Sally teased, mimicking the accent, "not only do ah not mind ... ah'd be on-uhed." And with that, she looped a thin arm through Caroline's.

A gaggle of ladies, one boy, and a man who seemed to be shepherding them all made their way toward the train sitting on Track Number 2. As she watched them climb aboard, Hettie Gates wondered where they were headed—and why. At the sound of footsteps she whirled around, her heart racing. *Calm down.* Another half dozen chattering ladies scurried through the station and followed the group boarding the train. Hettie watched them for a moment, wondering if those four always dressed alike. They were obviously sisters . . . maybe one pair of twins. But for them *all*—well. It was just odd. Glancing back toward the street, Hettie adjusted the veil attached to her hat and went to the ticket window.

"And how may I help you, ma'am?" The agent nodded toward the train. "Assuming, of course, that you aren't one of Mr. Drake's ladies. If you are, he's already purchased your ticket."

"I . . . I beg your pardon?"

"You aren't with the land agent who's been collecting ladies for Nebraska?"

Hettie frowned. "Nebraska?"

The agent removed his spectacles and wiped them with a cloth as he said, "Well, I'm glad to hear it." He shook his head. "If you ask me, Mr. Hamilton Drake's got something else in mind besides helping women get their own homesteads."

Hettie peered at him. "C-can they do that? Homestead, I mean . . . without a man?"

"Well, now," the agent said as he settled his glasses back on his nose, "that's just the thing, isn't it? How on earth could they? Can a woman plow? Can a woman grow crops? Can a woman defend herself?" The ticket agent shook his head again. "It wasn't but three years ago the Cheyenne derailed a handcar out that way and—" He broke off. Clucked his tongue. "I don't know what this world is coming to when women begin to think they can just step into a man's world like it was nothing. But I beg your pardon for my sermonizing, ma'am. What can I do for *you* this fine day?"

Hettie glanced at the train and then back at the agent. "California," she blurted out. California was as good a place as any, wasn't it? Or Denver. Denver might be far enough. She could stop in and visit Aunt Cora. No—that wouldn't be wise. Aunt Cora was a lovely woman, but she never had been able to keep a confidence.

"That's it right there," the ticket agent said, and pointed at the same train the group of ladies had just boarded. He peered at Hettie over pince-nez glasses. "One way or round trip?"

"I . . . I don't know about the return trip. The date, I mean. I might be gone a long—"

"One way, then," the man said. "That'll be six dollars."

Hettie counted out her money. Six greenbacks. Only two left. That was all right. She'd get a job washing dishes. Maybe cleaning houses. Something. A whistle blew.

Snatching the ticket, she grabbed her carpetbag from where she'd set it at her feet and ran for the train. It started to move. When she tossed the bag up, it landed with a thud just outside the door to the ladies' car. Grasping the railing, she hauled herself aboard. As the train picked up speed, she struggled to catch her breath. Finally, she climbed the three steps to the car door. Just as she opened it and stepped through, the train lurched. If the stern-faced-looking woman in the seat on the left hadn't ducked, she would have gotten Hettie's elbow in her ear. "E-excuse me," she gasped, and dropped into the empty seat on her right across from a petite elderly woman and a near-giantess. She'd barely regained her composure when the elderly woman spoke up.

"Well. So now we are sixteen."

"S-sixteen?"

The woman nodded. "Yes. I agree. Disappointing. Mr. Drake reserved the entire car." She gestured toward the empty benches at the back, then smiled. "But I don't suppose anyone will complain about having an entire double berth to themselves when it comes time to pull down the shades and go to sleep tonight."

Hettie glanced across the aisle. The woman she'd almost hit in the head had turned her back to them and was rummaging in a bag on the bench between her and a blond-haired boy looking out the window. The bench facing them was empty. As the train picked up speed, Hettie smoothed her frizzy blond hair and adjusted her hat.

The old woman smiled. "Zita Romano." She nodded at the woman seated beside her. "And my daughter, Ella." She hesitated, obviously waiting for Hettie to introduce herself.

"I'm Hettie. Hettie Ga—" She broke off. Didn't the Bible say something about shaking the dust off your feet and not looking back? She cleared her throat as she pushed her spectacles up on her nose. "Please call me Hettie." If they didn't care about last names, so much the better. It would give her time to think of a new one.

CHAPTER
TWO

*The Lord is nigh unto them that are of a broken heart;*
*and saveth such as be of a contrite spirit.*

PSALM 34:18

A preacher had once told Matthew Ransom that demons were meant to be cast out of a man's life never to return and that the power of the blood of Jesus could do it. Matthew allowed that the preacher might be mostly right, but then, the preacher didn't know the particulars. And in his own mind, he, Matthew Ransom of the First Nebraska, deserved the presence of demons. Whatever it might take to atone for and banish them completely, Matthew thought it had to be more than the death of one Jewish man some eighteen hundred and seventy-odd years ago.

Death was the thing that had earned Matthew the demons' presence in the first place, and failing at banishing them, he'd learned to live with them as best he could. Usually they stayed in the far reaches of the life he'd built in Nebraska, which brought more peace than he felt he deserved. Once in a while, though, they sallied forth and stayed a night or two. When that happened, buried memories became nightmares, and whispers crescendoed until Matthew woke soaked with sweat, his face streaming tears, his heart pounding, his eyes open as his mind stared into the past. And this was one of those times.

The girl he'd brought to the dugout a few days ago had to be awake, but she would be afraid to move. Likely he'd let out at least one of those God-awful rebel yells while the battle raged in his nightmare. Hopefully he hadn't called any names she would recognize. If he'd shouted names, the girl would likely be standing over him demanding explanations. She was getting old enough to recognize a few of those names. That was a new worry.

Matthew cast an eye toward what looked like a bundle of furs near the hearth. "Linney," he croaked. "Linney, you awake? I had a bad dream, but you don't need to be afraid."

The bundle shifted slightly, and for a brief moment a flash of ivory against the buffalo robe signaled the presence of the girl huddled there. She was awake, but she was either too frightened—or too angry that he'd frightened her again—to roll over and engage in conversation.

"All right," Matthew said. He cleared his throat. "It must have been a bad one, I guess." Reaching for his deerskin breeches, he pulled them up and over his narrow hips, feeling his way to the arranging of things before he threw back his own buffalo robe and stood. He shivered. "What d'ya think your old pa should wear today, Linney? The blue shirt . . . or the blue one?" He forced a soft laugh but the joke fell flat, and so he pulled on the only shirt he owned without further comment, waiting until he had it buttoned before crossing to where a battered kettle sat on the board resting atop two pegs he'd hammered into the dugout wall to construct a kitchen shelf.

"I'll get water. I understand you aren't talking to me right now, but I know you're awake. You willing to grind the coffee?" He watched the mound of buffalo robe and furs, wondering what he would do if the promise of coffee didn't work, relieved when first a hand and then a head of tangled auburn hair appeared. The girl sat up. As far as Matthew Ransom was concerned, his daughter was as beautiful wrapped in buffalo and coyote—her shoulders encased in a faded flannel nightgown—as any queen swathed in jewels and sable. His heart flip-flopped when she looked at him with her great, sad eyes. "I'm sorry I yelled," he said. "You know I'd help it if I could."

The girl sighed. Her chin trembled and finally Matthew got his first glimpse of the only thing that had ever proven a surefire way to send the demons back where they belonged. When Linea Delight Ransom's azure blue eyes lighted on him, demons fled. Pure and simple. If he could have bottled the way that girl made him feel in the morning to sell as a patent medicine, he would be a wealthy man.

"I just hate it," Linney said.

"I said I was sorry." Sometimes he felt like a schoolboy being sent to the corner for misbehaving.

Linney looked up at him then, tears glistening in her eyes as she said, "What I *hate*, Pa, is whatever it is that makes you have those dreams. I hate that it happened to *you*. To *my* pa. And I hate that it still hurts you . . . almost as much as you hurt over Ma's dying."

Matthew reached for the coffeepot lest she see how very near to tears he was himself, how grateful for her gentle love and the way it threatened to break open the burnt-out lump of coal that was his heart. For all God's failure to answer most of Matthew's prayers, at least he had done this. He had let Linney believe it was the war that caused the nightmares.

Clearing his throat, Matthew said, "I expect most of the boys that marched with me have similar dreams from time to time." He forced a smile. "Having you come for visits helps more than anything. But it's past time when I promised to have you back at Martha's. She'll be needing you to help her serve supper to Drake's carload of ladies when they arrive." *Women.* What on earth would possess a bunch of widows to climb on a train and follow a stranger west to meet and *marry* strangers Matthew could not imagine. *The Ladies Emigration Society* Drake called it. Matthew wondered what the women would think if they knew some had taken to calling it *The Ladies Desperation Society*.

"I wish you'd stay in town until the dance Friday," Linney said. She tilted her head and smiled. "You might *like* it, you know. Martha says you used to like to dance. She said you and Ma—" She broke off.

Matthew swallowed. And nodded. "We did like to dance," he

agreed. "Your ma was a sight to behold. Most graceful thing I ever saw." He hesitated, then decided to ignore the pain it would cause him to talk about Katie and give their daughter a gift only he could give. And so he forced a smile, hoping it wasn't a grimace. "Did I ever tell you about the first time I saw your ma?"

The girl's expression transformed itself into something like the look Matthew had seen on the faces of soldiers standing in line for rations. Hungry. Half starved. Eager. Her obvious need helped him ease past the pain and dust off the memory. *Make it shine, you sorry excuse for a father. Give her something to treasure.*

"Well," Matthew said, and he sat down next to her, right at the corner of the pelt that protected her against the chill of the spring morning. "The first time I saw your ma she was waltzing with a tall, square-jawed cadet, and I was instantly jealous of that man's hand pressed against the narrowest waist I'd ever seen. Her dress shimmered like a golden sunrise. And it made her eyes look even more blue than the azure sky." He paused, remembering the moment and realizing that he was taking joy in that memory. *Joy.* It was an odd feeling.

"And then what, Pa?"

Matthew looked across at his daughter, and it was like looking into Katie's eyes all over again. The pain returned. A more familiar emotion. An emotion he could embrace. He cleared his throat. "Well, she saw me. I don't know why she saw *me* in that crowded place. There were plenty of more handsome men—"

"Hunh-unh," Linney disagreed. "You were the handsomest. I just know it."

Matthew chuckled. She wanted a fairy tale. He would give her one. "Well . . . I wasn't the ugliest, anyway." He winked. "Nor was I the tallest. That cadet she was dancing with had me by inches." *Always did. Always won the girls, too. Except for Katie. At least for a while.* Bitterness rolled in as Matthew contemplated the other cadet and Katie. Together. He caught himself clenching his hands. Took a deep breath. "So I crossed that dance floor. When I got close enough I was almost afraid to speak. I thought your ma might just evaporate . . . like she really *was* a dream. But she didn't." He forced a smile. "And when I tapped that tall cadet on the shoulder, your ma smiled at me. Like she was glad I broke in. It was bad manners to do that, but I couldn't help myself."

"What did the other cadet do? Did he *fight* you?"

Matthew shook his head. "Nope. He bowed out."

"And then what?"

"Well . . . then . . . she never danced with anybody else the whole night. Waltz after waltz belonged to me."

Linney clasped her hands with joy. "Oh, Pa . . ." and then the magic was gone. Her eyes filled with tears and she threw her arms around his neck. "I wish she didn't die. I wish—"

Whatever she was saying was lost to emotion. Matthew closed his eyes and held her and hardened his heart against memory lest he cry, too. When next he spoke, he was in control again. "So do I. And I know about your other wishes, too, and I'm trying. I really am. A couple more good trapping seasons and I'll give you a proper home again."

Linney let go and sat back, brushing the tears off her cheeks with the back of her hand. She gazed around the dugout. "I wouldn't mind living here," she said. "I could make it homey."

"I know you could," Matthew agreed. "But *I'd* mind your living here. I promised myself I'd do right by you. And I will." He stood up. "Now get your duds on while I see to things outside. We'll have us a nice breakfast before we get back on the trail toward Plum Grove."

He'd pulled the door open when Linney called out. "Can we stop at ho—" She swallowed the last sound of the word *home* and replaced it with another question. "Can we stop by Ma's grave?"

Matthew kept his gaze on the horizon. "If you want."

"Maybe you could show me where the violets are blooming. The ones you said she liked so much."

If Linney knew how the thought of Katie picking wildflowers seared through him, she'd likely never mention violets again. But she didn't know. She was just a sweet girl longing to move home and wishing her ma was still alive. Matthew nodded and stepped outside.

As he headed for the spring where he'd get water to make coffee, he wondered anew how he was going to tell Linney he'd sold the homestead. The new owner would be coming into Plum Grove sometime this week. Linney probably wouldn't see the sale as anything but horrible when, in reality, it was progress, at least for Matthew. He'd faced the fact that he would never be able to live in Katie's house again, and was taking steps to move toward creating a new future for himself and their daughter. But Linney wouldn't see it that way. She'd likely be hurt and angry.

Maybe Martha Haywood would help her understand. *Martha.* If ever there was a living, breathing angel on this earth, it was her. Matthew shuddered to think what would have happened to Linney without that good woman agreeing to take the baby and "give Matthew some time." He often wondered if Martha would still have said yes had she known that "some time" would turn into years. Had she known she'd end up doing the better part of raising Katie's only living child. Something told Matthew it wouldn't have mattered. Every time he screamed at heaven that he just didn't believe there was anyone up there listening, anyone who cared, it was as if something whispered *Martha Haywood* back to him as proof he was wrong.

His coffeepot filled, Matthew returned to the dugout. As he opened the door, the aroma of ham frying made his mouth water. Linney was standing at the stove, her back to the door. When she turned toward him, something in the way she held the meat fork reminded him of Katie. His heart lurched. And the demons danced.

Ruth Dow looked up from her book to where Jackson lay sprawled across the empty seat opposite them, his rolled-up jacket for a pillow. He'd been reading the book he'd purchased at Union Station, but now he was staring at her with sad brown eyes. "Do you think Aunt Margaret will ever come and visit?" he asked.

"Did she say anything about visiting when you said good-bye this morning?"

Jackson sat up. With a shake of his head he closed the book and laid it next to him. "No, but—" He shrugged. "It might be nice if she did someday."

Ruth waved him over to sit beside her and, looping her arm through his, said, "Once we're settled in our own home I'll write." She forced a chuckle. "After all, they say that 'absence makes the heart grow fonder.'" Of course, unless absence was a force for miracle working, the chances the two sisters would ever so much as speak again were slim. But fourteen-year-old Jackson didn't need to know that.

"If she won't come to Nebraska, can I go back to St. Louis sometime and visit?"

"Good heavens, Jackson. We're barely out of the city. It's a bit early to be planning a visit, don't you think?"

"I don't see why we had to leave in the first place."

"I told you why. Margaret and Theo needed the room, and it's time we made our own way in the world." *And while your father's legacy is rich in character, he left us destitute.* Ruth pointed at the book he'd left on the bench. "Is it good?"

Jackson shrugged. "You wouldn't like it."

Ruth reached over and picked it up. *Texan Joe, or Life on the Prairie.* A dime novel. Not exactly the kind of reading material a general's son should—

Ruth caught herself. *You were going to turn over a new leaf, remember? Positive thoughts, positive words.* "Perhaps you'll learn something useful." She made a point of looking out the window. "Do you remember how far Mr. Drake said it was to the first station on the route? You might be thinking on what you'd like to eat." She handed *Texan Joe* back. Thankfully, Jackson dropped the subject of his aunt Margaret and returned to his book.

Looking at her son's profile, Ruth realized that the older Jackson got, the more he looked like his father. Unable to get her mind back into her own book, she pondered Jackson's bright future. He was George Washington Jackson Dow II, and someday, thanks to what his mother was doing right now, he would stride across a dais somewhere and receive a university diploma. It was a plan that would make the General proud, and Ruth was going to see to it. In five years she would prove up and sell her homestead at a profit. The money would enable her and Jackson to move wherever he wished to seek his degree, and she would keep house for him, taking in sewing to make ends meet.

As the train sputtered and clacked its way west, Ruth gazed out the window. The trees in this part of Missouri were beginning to leaf out. Mr. Drake said that tree planting was one of the first things most settlers in Nebraska did. He'd warned them not to expect trees. Ruth couldn't quite imagine a landscape without trees. They would plant oaks. She would have flower beds on either side of her front door. Perhaps she'd transplant some wildflowers at first. A trellis would be nice, too. With roses. Red ones. She would have to remember to ask Mr. Drake which merchant in Cayote stocked the very best rosebushes. Some might see such a purchase as excess, but a woman needed beauty.

Fear nudged its way into her plans. *What if the homesteads near town are already claimed? What if you have to live far out on the prairie . . . alone . . . just you and Jackson . . . ? What if . . .* The familiar knot returned to her stomach. She gazed about the car. No one had taken the initiative to begin any conversations at the station, and Mr. Drake had disappeared as soon as the train began to move, promising to return soon and "make introductions." She'd overheard the names of the ladies across the aisle. Zita. Ella. Hettie. For the most part, though, everyone was keeping to themselves.

Zita . . . Ella . . . Hettie . . . the four sisters . . . Double Chin and Rotund . . . Redhead and Rebel . . . Ruth took each woman's measure, feeling somewhat dismayed by the excess of calico and bonnets. Only three of the ladies wore silk, and Ruth was the only one dressed in mourning. And those *sisters*. Plaid might be fashionable this year, but really—one needn't use up an entire bolt. Plaid dresses and bows and cuffs and collars. They must be very close sisters to have planned coordinating traveling ensembles. What would that be like? she wondered.

*What if I could take it all back . . . apologize . . . accept Margaret's advice . . . avoid that awful scene . . . ? What if . . .* Sighing, Ruth leaned her head back and closed her eyes. She could still see the fine lines around Margaret's mouth deepen as she pursed her lips with displeasure at Ruth's refusal to see things her older sister's way. It wasn't the first time they'd spouted angry words at one another, but it proved to be the last.

"Cecil Grissom will make you a good husband and Jackson a good father."

"I disagree," Ruth protested. "He's insufferably strict."

"He's *firm*, and if you ask me, Jackson needs a firm hand. You don't even *try* to discipline him. He's spoiled rotten, and you know it."

"Well, I *didn't* ask. And since when are *you* the family expert on child rearing?" The instant the words were out, Ruth wished she could draw them back. Her voice faltered. "I'm sorry, Margaret. I shouldn't have said that. It was unkind. But—there's more to it than the way Cecil and Jackson get along. The General was my soul mate. I loved him with all my heart and—" She took a deep breath. "I can't just decide to 'move on.' It . . . it isn't that simple."

"I didn't say it was simple. But it's been four *years*, Ruth, and you still dress in full mourning. Couldn't you at least *try* to encourage Cecil?"

Ruth stamped her foot and snapped, "I am *not* going to marry Cecil Grissom!"

"Fine." After a brief moment Margaret sighed. When she continued, her voice was calm. Calm and dismissive. Her hand went to her midsection. "I didn't want to tell you this way, but the fact is I'm about to gain some experience in child rearing. We'll be needing your rooms.

Jackson's for the nurse Theo wants to hire, and yours—" Margaret's expression softened—"yours for the baby."

Ruth's stammered congratulations fell flat, as did her apology. And suddenly, one season of her life was over, and she was forced unwillingly into another. Where to live now? How to provide for Jackson? She'd saved so much by living with Theo and Margaret, but not nearly enough. What to do . . . and then she saw a flyer at the milliner's and discovered an answer that would require only five years instead of a life sentence of marriage to a man she merely liked.

As the train rumbled and the car rocked, Ruth's thoughts cycled back to her list of "what ifs," and once again her stomach roiled. *Oh, God . . . please, God . . . I know I haven't said much to you these past years. . . .* She broke off. God hadn't listened when she asked him to keep the General safe. Why would he listen today? With a sigh, Ruth gazed out the window at the greening countryside. It was up to her now. *Everything* was up to her.

*It is better to trust in the Lord*
*than to put confidence in man.*

PSALM 118:8

The train had belched and clacked its way halfway across Missouri before Caroline looked up from her worn copy of *Jane Eyre* and noticed that Sally Grant, her once pale cheeks bright red, was leaning against the window hugging herself as if she were cold.

"You feelin' poorly?" Caroline closed the book and laid it aside.

Sally didn't even open her eyes. "I'll be all right," she murmured. "I'm just real tired." She coughed into the handkerchief she held wadded up in one bare hand. "Didn't sleep worth anything last night. Too nervous."

"Let me see the conductor about getting you a blanket," Caroline said. She glanced behind them. A few passengers had come aboard since St. Louis, but there were still empty seats. "We could fold out a berth if you'd like. You might as well stretch out."

"You don't got to go to any trouble on my account," Sally murmured.

"It's no trouble. I'm glad to have somethin' to do besides readin'. In fact, once you're settled, how about if I fetch some tea?"

"Only first class is allowed in the dining car," Sally said. "Mr. Drake said so."

Where on earth was Mr. Drake, anyway? Caroline wondered. For all his talk about seeing to their every need and "facilitating introductions on the train," he hadn't shown his face since St. Louis. She smiled at Sally. "They'll make an exception for a lady." Reaching for her shawl, she headed up the aisle. No rule had been made that a gentleman wouldn't break for a determined southern belle.

Caroline peered through the dining car–door window to where Hamilton Drake lounged, his back to the door. It was annoying enough to discover the man had apparently bought himself a first-class ticket at the expense of the Emigration Society. But she felt a great deal more than annoyance when she saw whom Drake was lounging with. The stranger didn't look any less threatening without the wide-brimmed black hat he'd had on when he descended from that carriage at Union Station this morning. Cool gray eyes. Chiseled features. Broad shoulders. And something about the mouth—cruelty? No ... not that ... something more familiar. An expectant, self-assured smile that somehow rankled. When he nodded at Caroline and then spoke to Mr. Drake, the latter turned around and, laying a napkin atop the table, hurried to greet her.

The gray-eyed stranger and his two traveling companions stood up, too. "Don't tell me this is one of your ladies, Drake," he said, his gaze never leaving Caroline's.

Caroline looked away from the stranger to smile at the approaching waiter. "Now, I know my place, and it's not in the first-class dinin' car, but I am sincerely hopin' y'all will make an exception and make some tea for a passenger—a friend of mine—who is feelin' a mite poorly."

The stranger's gaze followed the contours of Caroline's body as he spoke. "It's obvious you are first class in every way that matters." He smiled at the waiter. "And I'm certain George, here, will agree and fetch anything you request."

The waiter gave a little bow. "Lemon and honey, as well, ma'am?"

"How kind of you to offer. And yes, please."

With another little bow, the waiter retreated toward the small kitchen at the opposite end of the dining car. When the gray-eyed stranger pulled out an empty chair so that Caroline could be seated, she remained standing. Looking Mr. Drake's way, she purred a gentle scolding. "We all been wonderin' where you were. Dare I hope you'll agree to escort me back to the emigrant car?"

"Watch out, Drake," the stranger chuckled. "When a belle's voice sounds like molasses, she's got you in her crosshairs. Careful she doesn't take aim and shoot." He snatched Drake's hat off the hook on the wall above their table and handed it over. "You'd best do whatever the lady wants. We can talk another time." Once again he looked Caroline up and down. Slowly. "Since Drake, here, seems to have forgotten his manners," he said, "allow me to introduce myself. Lucas Gray." He indicated the other two men standing beside him. "These boys are two of my ranch hands. Johnny True and Lowell Day. I make them travel with me so I can keep an eye on them." He winked.

The man's air of familiarity was unconscionable. She was itching to slap the leer right off his face. Why didn't Drake speak up? *Why don't you just handle it yourself? Mama would.* Mama could glide through social muck and remain untouched. Caroline had once seen her defuse a situation likely to end in a duel without batting an eye. If Mama could do all that, surely Caroline could resist the temptation to slap a stranger who didn't have the sense to stop staring at her *that way.* But land sakes, were all westerners this rude?

The waiter arrived with a basket into which he'd nestled a sturdy white teapot alongside slices of lemon, a delicate teacup and saucer, and a sugar bowl. As Drake fumbled with the coins to pay for the tea, Caroline shone her most charming smile and thanked the waiter. "*You,* sir, are a very kind gentleman." With barely a nod in Lucas Gray's direction, she pretended that Drake had offered his arm and took it. She managed a triumphant retreat for a few steps. But then she gave in to temptation. Wishing to bask in the idea that she'd handed the arrogant Mr. Lucas Gray a gentle but undeniable social defeat, she glanced back as she and Drake exited the car. Expecting to see the rancher sitting back down, hoping perhaps that his two ranch hands were taking pleasure in seeing their boss put in his place, Caroline was disappointed.

Lucas Gray was watching her. When she met his gaze, he didn't bow. Instead, he smiled and winked. Again. *Oh dear.* Feeling her cheeks warmed by a blush, Caroline looked away. She could almost see Mama shaking her head in disappointment. *In games of cat and mouse, there must be no doubt to either party as to which player has the claws. Using those claws, however, is always a lady's last resort.*

As she followed Mr. Drake toward the emigrant car, Caroline flexed her right hand, embarrassed by the knowledge that in this most recent game, she hadn't been the player with the claws. She'd been the prey.

When the southerner returned to the emigrant car with a tea basket–toting Hamilton Drake, Ruth couldn't help but smile to herself. Leave it to a southern belle to get her way, enlist a man's assistance, and transform him from absentee to solicitous escort in the process. Why, Drake actually sat down next to Rebel and Redhead and helped with the pouring and preparing of the tea. It was a wonder what a tiny waist and a winsome smile could accomplish.

A few minutes later as the train began to slow for the next stop, Drake made a little speech about how the Ladies Emigration Society was pleased to invite them all to dine together at the Society's expense. He begged their pardon for "absenting himself" for the first part of the journey and assured them that he had been "detained by business of the utmost importance" to the Society's membership.

Had Hamilton Drake always been this . . . pompous? Had her own sense of desperation made her overlook all the little things about the man that set Ruth's nerves on edge now? For the first time she noticed that he never quite looked any of them in the eye. He had a nervous habit of smoothing his beard when he spoke. And that pose, one hand on the back of a seat, the other in a loose fist poised at his waist at just the right angle—as if he were the subject of an artist's portrait. Why hadn't she noticed these things before? Ruth wondered.

But then the train screeched to a halt, and amidst the flurry of activity, Jackson bounded off the train ahead of her, and Ruth forgot her concern for anything else as she hurried to catch up to him.

Clearly Jackson had not listened to a thing his mother had told him about speaking with strangers, for by the time she got inside the station he was engaged in conversation with a tall stranger wearing a cowboy hat—and sporting a western-style holster *and a gun.* Jackson gave a little wave the minute he saw Ruth, but instead of coming over to her, he took the bag the candy-counter attendant was holding out to him and hurried back toward the train. Ruth frowned. The broad-shouldered cowboy walked her way.

Touching the brim of his hat, he introduced himself. "Lucas Gray, ma'am. Please forgive my being so forward, but the boy was in a hurry to take some lemon drops to someone—a Mrs. Grant, I believe, and her friend Mrs. Jamison—and as I've had the pleasure of making Mrs. Jamison's acquaintance and already knew Mr. Drake from Cayote— well"—he shrugged—"I told young Master Dow that I'd see to the tea he ordered for his mother." He smiled. "From what he said, I was expecting white hair and a cane, not one of the most attractive women on the train." He barely paused before adding, "You will allow me the pleasure of joining you, I hope."

Flustered by the man's forward ways, Ruth didn't answer. Instead, she began fishing in her bag for change to pay for the tea. When Mr. Gray slipped the waiter a coin she protested. "That isn't necessary."

"If it were necessary, it wouldn't be quite such a pleasure, now would it." As he was speaking, Mr. Gray was pulling one of the chairs away from a nearby table, clearly inviting her to sit down. "Thank you," she said, "but we've a Society meeting over lunch." She turned toward the table along the far wall, where the rest of the women in the group had found places.

Gray seemed not to notice her desire to end the conversation. "Your son seems quite taken with the idea of moving west," he said. "Of course, a large part of the fascination is those dime novels boys read these days. I hope you don't mind, but I told him that if he ever wants to see how a *real* ranch operates, he's welcome to visit my spread. It's the largest one in Dawson County." He did have a very nice smile. "Of course, I told him it would all depend on whether or not his mother— and perhaps a new father by then—gave their permission."

What on earth did that mean? A new father? What an inappropriate and unduly personal comment. Ruth lifted her chin. "Thank you for being kind to my son. I don't know that there will be time for him to go visiting for a while. There will be a long list of things for him to help me with before we think about socializing. And now, if you will excuse me—"

"Of course." Gray smiled. He touched the brim of his hat with one finger. "I'll look forward to seeing all you ladies again on Friday."

Ruth frowned. "I beg your pardon?"

"At the dance in Cayote."

"The dance?"

"Why, yes, ma'am. You can count on there being a long line of hopefuls just waiting for the chance to charm you." He leaned a little closer. "Now, there's no need to be defensive about it at all. Life can be difficult for unattached ladies. No one in Dawson County thinks badly of the Society members for being agreeable to Drake's idea."

"Drake's . . . idea?"

Mr. Gray nodded. "A mutual interest in a homestead is as good a reason as any to marry. In fact, to hear him tell it, Drake expects the bride business to provide the circuit rider coming through Cayote on Sunday with the most well-attended service on record."

*Bride business?! Circuit rider?!* Ruth set her teacup down on the table. Her hand went to the frill of lace at her neck. "Yes. Well. If you will excuse me." She hurried away.

As evening came on, first one, then another of the passengers rose and began preparations for the long night aboard the train, folding seats out to create berths, accepting pillows and blankets from the conductor, pulling down shades and closing shutters. With Jackson stretched out nearest to the window, Ruth lay on her back staring up at the paneled ceiling above her. The redhead's cough was worse. *Sally Grant.* That was her name. The southerner was Caroline Jamison. Ruth glanced across the aisle, smiling at the sight of little Zita Romano curled up in the space left after her daughter Ella stretched out diagonally across the berth. Hettie had insisted on moving to the back of the car for the night so Ella and her mother would have more room. Ruth couldn't remember ever meeting a woman as tall as Ella Barton before. It hadn't taken but a moment over lunch to realize that she knew the most about farming of any of the members.

By the time each of the sixteen women around the table had introduced herself, it was time to get back on the train. Ruth hadn't had a chance to draw Mr. Drake aside and inform him of Mr. Lucas Gray's misunderstanding about the Ladies Emigration Society. Now, as she lay in the twilight thinking about it, she wondered anew how Mr. Gray had come to associate the Ladies Emigration Society with such poppycock as some kind of "bride business."

Thinking about Lucas Gray made her wonder if all the men in Dawson County sported holsters and guns. Did they wear spurs that jangled when they walked? When she scolded Jackson—mildly—about speaking with a stranger, Jackson said that meeting Lucas Gray was like having Texan Joe step out of his book. The boy's eyes shone with wonder as he talked about Mr. Gray's invitation to visit "a real ranch."

Ruth had to admit that her first experience with a real cowboy had been . . . interesting. He might lack a sense of proper etiquette around ladies, but Gray exuded a certain kind of charm. Not the kind of charm she would ever find attractive, of course, but still . . . charm. Sadly, he did walk right along the edge of propriety in his dealings with ladies. He spoke without being properly introduced, invited himself to sit and have tea, and expounded on personal topics that any gentleman—

*Whatever happened to your plan to think positive thoughts? You were going to resist the habit of judging others so quickly, remember? For all your thinking of Mrs. Jamison as a rebel, hasn't she been kind to that poor Sally Grant? And they've all been wonderful to Jackson. You were going to stop being so suspicious. Hope for the best. Look toward the light.*

Brushing the back of her hand across her forehead, Ruth decided that perhaps she should exercise her new outlook in the matter of Mr. Lucas Gray. In fact, now that she thought about it, she wondered if he might have been having a little fun at her expense earlier today. Perhaps his mention of ordered brides and weddings and circuit riders was just another version of a tall tale. People initiated newcomers with things like that all the time. *Don't forget how the men at Fort Wise "welcomed" new recruits.*

The more she thought about it, the more certain Ruth was that that was exactly what had happened between her and Lucas Gray. In fact, the rascal would probably laugh when he recounted how he'd toyed with a "greenhorn." Ruth forced a chuckle of her own. If Lucas Gray thought he was going to fool General George Washington Jackson Dow's widow with wild talk about how westerners engaged in instant weddings, he was mistaken.

As for Jackson's visiting Mr. Gray's "spread," that would never happen. Jackson Dow was not going on any flights of fancy about life in the west. He was going to school in Cayote, where he would study hard and graduate with perfect grades. If he got bored, he would work at the general store—or the livery, if it came to that. He liked animals, although Ruth wasn't comfortable with the inherent dangers of working around horses. Be that as it may, in five years George Washington Jackson Dow II would be a freshman at Washington University in St. Louis, and this little trip into the west would be nothing more than fodder for stories to tell the General's grandchildren someday.

*Mail-order brides, indeed.* As night came on and murmurs gave way to snores, Ruth smiled to herself. Perhaps she'd entertain someone in St. Louis with her own tall tale about cowboys and such one day. Wouldn't that be amusing?

Hettie Gates had already awakened, freshened up, and returned to her temporary seat at the back of the emigrant car when the sun began to fade the indigo sky. Ella and Zita were still sleeping and Hettie was glad. She needed time to think. Chasing after the first train leaving St. Louis and falling—very literally—into the midst of something called the Ladies Emigration Society had opened entirely new possibilities. Dare she entertain them?

She'd expected to be found out at lunch, but as it turned out, Hamilton Drake wasn't a very organized man. Hettie wasn't the only woman he didn't seem to remember from whatever meetings it was he'd held in St. Louis, and as the ladies each stood in turn and introduced themselves, Hettie was able to gather enough information to do a convincing job of things when it was her turn to speak. "I'm Hettie Raines," she'd said without hesitation. Then, shoving her spectacles up, she'd looked away and said, "My husband is—was—a physician. And I . . . I really can't talk about it." With that, she'd sat down. The tears she shed at the mention of a husband were sincere enough. So was the comforting little pat on her arm and the smile from "the General's wife."

As the other women in the group began to stir, Zita looked Hettie's way and waved her back to sit up front. Smoothing her hair, Hettie rose to rejoin her new friends. All things considered, it had been very simple to do away with Hettie Gates.

"We can't be 'here.'" Hettie turned in the direction of Mavis Morris, who warbled, "There's no station. No town. There's nothing but—" She pointed toward the water and the wide plank they would each have to walk to board the ferry waiting to take them across the Missouri. "I can't possibly ride that little thing across that water." Both chins quivered as Mavis fought back tears.

Tiny Zita Romano hurried past them all. Placing both feet on the plank, she turned about and waved for them to follow. "It's nothing," she said, gesturing toward the pilot, who waited just at the far end of the plank. "He's done this a hundred times—perhaps a thousand—and it's really nothing. Only a little river. Now, an ocean? Crossing an ocean with no land in sight for weeks. *That* was something." After Zita nearly skipped up the plank, what could the others do but follow?

Still, Hettie lingered, not out of fear of the crossing, but because the river represented a final dividing line between her past and present. Behind her lay anguish and brokenness. Across the river with these ladies lay . . . oh, how she hoped something better. She glanced down the tracks toward Kansas City to the south. *There's nothing to go back to. Everything you worked for has been destroyed and can't be restored. You have to face that and move on. You've been given a second chance. Hope lies across that river.* With a last glance toward the south, Hettie went aboard the *Omaha Queen.*

*Good-bye, Forrest . . . good-bye.*

All beauty dwindled away. Oh, things stayed green, but after their next train left Omaha, meandering curves and gentle slopes gradually gave way to miles and miles of track headed due west atop an expanse of flat land that Ruth wouldn't have known how to describe even if she did write Margaret—and she wasn't certain she *would* write. At least not for a while. Being tossed out still stung. With a sigh, she leaned her head back and closed her eyes. It wasn't long before murmured protests made her open them again. Black earth stretched from horizon to horizon, somehow even more desolate juxtaposed against a cloudless blue sky.

Mr. Drake stepped through the door into the car. "Now, I know," he said, "that this looks bleak."

Mrs. Morris spoke first. "You will keep your promise, right? If we want a return ticket—"

"Of course." Drake nodded. "If, by Saturday of this week, any of you wishes to return, the Ladies Emigration Society has agreed to provide a ticket at no expense to you. Except, of course, a small fee for baggage and handling charges." He waited until the murmured objections to this new information died down before continuing. "But you must realize that what we see as destruction, nature looks upon as a gift. Look carefully and you'll see green shoots pushing their way through the charred grass." He gestured toward the landscape. "This, dear ladies, is *renewal*."

"That's all well and good," one of the sisters said. "But I think I speak for us all—" She glanced at the others, who nodded agreement. "I speak for us all when I say, Mr. Drake, that if Cayote has been similarly *renewed* this spring, we won't be staying."

"That is of course your right," Drake said as he gave a little bow. "But I think you'll find that Cayote holds many unexpected charms that will entice you to remain." And with that, he exited the car. Again.

Something about the way Drake said the words *unexpected* and *charms* made Ruth uncomfortable. She glanced around the car at the other women and then stared back out the window. Perhaps it was the landscape. Perhaps it was loneliness. Whatever the cause, Mrs.

General George Washington Jackson Dow felt small and bereft and foolish and, once again, a little afraid.

Neither witnessing the greening of the landscape nor finally coming out of the vast area that had been burned helped Ruth feel better. Western train stations were little more than unpainted shacks plopped down every ten miles or so at nondescript places marked by names painted with black letters on white boards. In some cases, the only sign of civilization was the station and the house the railroad provided for the stationmaster and his family—if he had one. Ruth comforted herself with the idea that at least she and Jackson would not be living that kind of life—alone in the only house on a desolate piece of land. They *would* settle near town. She would see to it.

Jackson had finished *Texan Joe* long ago and now sat peering out the window. When she patted his arm, he leaned close and rested his head on her shoulder in an uncharacteristic display of affection. "It's ... *big* land—isn't it, Mother?" He sighed.

When tears threatened, Ruth took herself in hand. For Jackson's sake, she must be brave. And so she reached across with her free arm and laid her gloved hand on his. "Yes," she said. "*Big* is certainly one word for it. It will be ... interesting ... to see more of the west than train tracks and stations. At least we have a nice supper awaiting us in Plum Creek."

"Plum *Grove*," Jackson corrected her.

"It was nice of Mr. Gray to invite you to visit, wasn't it? Think how amazed your aunt Margaret will be when you write about your adventures." She hadn't changed her mind about Lucas Gray, and even if Jackson did write his aunt Margaret, it was impossible to know whether she would be amazed or horrified, but right now it was important that Jackson feel better.

Mention of Lucas Gray and a ranch accomplished great things.

Jackson lifted his head from her shoulder and turned to look up at her. "You mean you really *would* let me visit? I thought you were just being polite."

*Oh dear.* She'd done it now. Backed herself into a corner from which there would be no escape. "Of course I was being polite," Ruth said. "Good manners is part of being a lady—or a gentleman, I might add." She forced the most sincere smile she could manage. "But just because I was being polite doesn't mean I don't really want to see Mr. Gray's cows. I'm sure it will be very informative."

Jackson hugged her so hard she had to straighten her hat when he finally let go. "Do you think we could get a horse?"

Ruth worded her reply as carefully as possible. "I think we could definitely entertain the idea of a horse." Ruth smiled to herself. If a general's wife knew anything, she knew to choose her battles carefully, and Jackson's wanting a horse was not one to be fought today. They couldn't afford a horse, and even if they could, she wasn't about to let her son risk his neck trying to be a cowboy. But Jackson could entertain the idea to his heart's content.

# CHAPTER
# FOUR

*Brethren, whatsoever things are true, whatsoever things are honest,*
*whatsoever things are just . . . think on these things.*

PHILIPPIANS 4:8

Linney was not going to give up. She set her bedroll down just inside the mercantile's back storeroom door and continued the plea. "I'm fourteen, Pa. And I know you don't like being around a lot of people, but it's just one dance and Martha says you're the best dancer in the county and . . . well . . . a girl needs to know how to dance and who should teach her if not her very own pa?"

When Matthew glanced to where Martha Haywood sat perched on a stool behind the mercantile counter, Martha took the pencil from behind her ear and wrote something in the ledger. She didn't even look up as she said, "She makes a good point, Matthew. It's not like that train car of ladies is staying here. They'll be on their way to Cayote before nightfall. Friday will be mostly folks you already know. Shoot, half the boys from around here will be over at Cayote anyway, chasing after those women. What better way to celebrate spring than a dance among old friends with your very own daughter?"

"Just one dance," Linney said. "It can be the *last* dance of the whole night if you want. And then you can hightail it back to your cave and hibernate again."

He should be ashamed of himself—and was, for many reasons— but making the girl beg like this was just flat-out wrong. From the expression on Martha Haywood's face, it appeared she thought the same. "All right," Matthew said. "I can't promise I'll stay the whole evening, but—"Whatever else he was going to say was smothered by Linney's squeal of delight and her arms around his neck. Before he knew it he'd promised not only to dance with her but to take her to supper at the dining hall beforehand, too. When Martha looked his way, Matthew steeled himself against the teasing he expected, but she said nothing. She just smiled and nodded approval. *Good for you.*

A few minutes later when the train whistle sounded from the east, Matthew was in the haymow over at the livery, forking fresh hay down into a couple of vacant stalls. He worked there occasionally in exchange for Otto Ermisch not charging Matthew to board his pinto mare when he visited town. Seconds after the train whistle sounded in the distance, Matthew heard a door slam and a chorus of shouts. Making his way to the edge of the haymow, he watched as men spilled out of the saloon and the dining hall, the mercantile and the implement store, all of them hurrying along as they straightened collars, brushed dust off their pants, smoothed beards, and spat wads of tobacco out into the grass. Obviously word had spread that the Ladies Desperation Society was on that train. Tossing a final forkful of hay into the stall below, Matthew walked back to the wide opening above the livery's double-wide doors. This, he had to see.

Mr. Drake hadn't shown his face in the ladies' emigration car since redefining the prairie fire as renewal. Now, as the train began to slow for the long stop at Plum Grove, he stuck his head in the door and directed them to "proceed to the Immigrant House," where they would have opportunity to "freshen up" before the supper that they would enjoy during the unloading of a couple of freight cars and the taking on of water and fuel. "I'll join you in the Plum Grove Dining Hall soon to discuss our arrival in Cayote later this evening. Until then, I trust you'll all enjoy taking the air here in Plum Grove." With that, he was gone.

Feeling rumpled and out of sorts, Ella stood up and stretched. When the train lurched unexpectedly, she nearly fell.

"Land sakes," Mrs. Morris exclaimed, "what are they doing now?!"

Ella straightened her bonnet as she said, "Mama, I'm going to make sure they don't unload our chickens by mistake. I should have been keeping closer watch at the last few stations. I hope they aren't sitting unclaimed on some siding east of here."

"Ella." Mama motioned for her to bend down and look.

Ella looked. And plopped back down beside Mama. *Men.* A long row of men waited just below the weathered sign that read Plum Grove.

"I told you there would be a parade of bachelors." Mama grinned. "And we aren't even to Cayote yet."

Ella was not amused. What were they doing there, anyway? Were they really there to meet the ladies? Apparently so, for that was Hamilton Drake talking to them, and whatever he was saying wasn't making them happy.

"I don't know why he's so upset. I think it's nice. And kind of . . . exciting."

That was the youngest of the sisters-in-plaid, and since, other than introducing herself at lunch yesterday, she hadn't said a word, everyone stared at her in surprise. She blinked. Glanced shyly at her three sisters. Shrugged. "Well . . . all I mean is . . . it's nice to feel . . . welcome." She turned back to peer out the window. "And the tall one in the plaid shirt is kind of . . . nice looking."

Ella adjusted her bonnet. None of it had a thing to do with her. She had chickens to check on. With a promise to meet Mama over at the Immigrant House, she hurried off the train. As she barreled past the men and toward the freight cars, one of them shoved Mr. Drake aside and stepped forward.

"I like a beefy gal," he said and, snatching his hat off his head, introduced himself as Ed Ostergaard.

*Beefy?!* Ella ignored him and marched to the far side of the platform to watch and wait for her chance to check on her birds. It was impossible not to be aware of the *tone* as the men teased Mr. Ostergaard about his "beefy gal."

Silence made her glance back at the men and from them to the train. Watching them all watch Caroline Jamison would have been amusing if it weren't also pathetic. *Men. All alike.* Their heads moved in unison, first up toward where Mrs. Jamison hesitated before descending, and then down as she took each step. Finally, all those heads moved from left to right as Mrs. Jamison glided across the platform to join Ella. Not a single one stepped forward to introduce himself to her. *Struck dumb by a vision of loveliness.* Ella scolded herself for the bitterness in that thought before Mrs. Jamison said something that turned her attention to Plum Grove.

"Not much of a town, is it?"

Ella pointed toward the framed outlines of three new buildings. "No, but it's growing." She indicated the grassy space between the train station and the buildings a short walk across the prairie. "Someday this will be a real road running alongside the tracks. And there"—she indicated the imaginary line running perpendicular to the tracks and toward the short row of half a dozen businesses—"that will be Main Street. I imagine they already call it that. See those red flags in the distance? Probably meant to stake out a town square."

Mrs. Jamison nodded toward the two-story log building next to the Immigrant House. "Where do you suppose a body gets logs for such an enterprise out here?"

Ella didn't know, but she intended to find out. Maybe she and Mama would have a log cabin.

"Why does there always have to be a saloon," Mrs. Jamison murmured, pointing to the one building "across Main" from the five false-fronted buildings identified as the Immigrant House, Haywood

Mercantile, Plum Grove Dining Hall, Pioneer News, Lux Implements, and Ermisch Livery. "Do you suppose Cayote will look this . . . way?"

"You mean this pathetic?" Ella said. "I hope not."

"And do you suppose we'll have to face a similar welcoming committee?"

For the first time Ella realized that Mrs. Jamison wasn't really using her ruffled parasol to keep the spring sun off her lily white face. She'd perched it on her shoulder to block her view of the men—and theirs of her. Ella chuckled. "I never did want to mess with a parasol. But I think you just showed me a new use." She glanced at the group of men and back down at Mrs. Jamison. "Varmint deflector?"

The southerner laughed softly and twirled the parasol. "Maybe a saber if those particular varmints don't disperse directly." She frowned. "How'd they know to gather?"

From his place in the haymow, Matthew saw a gold parasol open. He counted sixteen women and as many men, each group staying to themselves as if battle lines had been drawn on either side of an imaginary space into which no one dared step. When a few other passengers appeared from the direction of the dining car, Matthew's attention was drawn away from the women. He tensed. The swagger . . . the Stetson . . . and a wrangler riding up with three mounts in tow. Everyone in Dawson County recognized that gelding. Luke had been back east.

Another passenger stepped off the train. Even from this distance the man's size was impressive. *I'm easy to spot,* Cooper had written, *just like Joshua's giants in the land.* So. Jeb Cooper, the man who'd purchased the homestead, had come to Plum Grove on the same train as Luke and those women. It was good timing for Matthew. Linney would be busy helping Martha in the dining hall. That would give him a chance to meet Cooper without her wondering at her reclusive pa's interest in a new arrival.

A horse screamed. Matthew looked toward the tracks just in time to see Luke lead a dark gray horse off the freight car. Swiping his forehead with one sleeve, Matthew returned to forking fresh hay into the empty stalls below. He'd head over and introduce himself to Jeb Cooper a little later. After he was certain Linney was busy with the new arrivals—and after Luke and company were well out of town.

Caroline had been far too nervous at the river crossing to pay much attention to Lucas Gray's horse. All she really remembered was impressive size and spirit. But as the freight car doors screeched open and the creature whinnied and tossed its head, and as the afternoon sun glistened against the pewter-colored coat, she caught her breath. The stallion stomped and snorted.

"Wow." Jackson let out his breath in a low whistle.

"He sure is somethin'," Sally said. "And don't he know it."

Lucas Gray strode up the gangplank and into the freight car. While he was inside, a cowboy road up with three horses in tow—another gray and two bays. Johnny True and Lowell Day mounted the bays. Everyone watched as the stallion danced its way down the gangplank alongside its owner.

"Gorgeous," Ella murmured.

"The horse is nice, too," Zita joked.

"Mama!"

"I'm old, Ella. I'm not dead."

"Aw, you ain't so old," Sally laughed.

Gray handed the stallion's lead to one of his "boys," then leaped astride the gray gelding. He spent the next few minutes helping to herd livestock from the freight car into the sod enclosure behind the station. A burly stranger with a full beard and a floppy hat manned the gate to the corral. When Caroline noticed that one arm ended in a stump, she wondered at the brute strength on display as he easily handled the massive gate with one arm.

When Ella stepped down to check on her livestock, Caroline went with her. She might not be able to avoid another "cat and mouse" with Lucas Gray this way, but at least she wouldn't have to wade through an entire crowd of voyeurs.

Ruth stood inside the station alone, trembling with emotion. She'd ducked inside to get a drink of water. And to avoid Lucas Gray's little performance. Now—now she didn't know whether to cry or scream. For the moment, she did neither. Instead, she filled another dipper with lukewarm water from the stoneware crock in the corner. When that didn't help her calm down, she crossed to the window opposite the tracks. The men were obeying Mr. Drake, making their way off the platform and heading back toward town. As she watched, more than one unhitched a horse, mounted up, and galloped off toward the west. Toward Cayote. She took another drink and wondered what to do. Part of her wished she hadn't overheard. Part of her was glad she had. And all of her longed for the calendar to turn back and make everything since George's sudden death a bad dream from which she could awaken.

*I'm telling you, this trainload of brides is already promised to Cayote,* the man had said. *But I'm headed back to St. Louis next week. You have my word I'll bring the next load right here to Plum Grove. But only if you disperse immediately. I can't have you ruining things for the boys over at Cayote who paid to have first chance at a bride.*

She'd wanted to scream. If he'd said the word "bride" again, she might have. As it was, the best Ruth could do was sit down on the bench and try to gather her wits. Had the other ladies signed on with the notion of marriage? She hadn't exactly gotten to know them on the ride out. Maybe she was the only one—but no, she could not believe that. Mrs. Barton had spoken of nothing but land and a homestead. Sitting across from her all this way, Ruth had overheard enough to feel certain of Mrs. Barton's plans.

She needed to think. Taking a deep breath, she exited the train station—sadly, just as Lucas Gray rode around the back side of the sod corral and up to the platform. At least most of the other ladies were already on their way to the Immigrant House. Maybe without them looking on she could keep her wits about her and keep from blushing like a fool.

Removing his hat, he smiled up at her. "I wanted to say that I've enjoyed meeting you and repeat the invitation for you—" Just then Jackson and Mrs. Jamison came along, and Gray included them, "—*all of you* to visit my ranch."

When Ruth said nothing, Gray nodded at Jackson. "I have to get Hannibal back to the ranch and introduce him to his own ladies yet today, so I can't be part of the crowd over in Cayote. But I'll be at the dance on Friday, and we can make plans to turn you into a proper cowboy then." He glanced at Ruth. "With your approval, of course."

He put his hat back on and tugged on the brim, then grinned as he said to both Ruth and Mrs. Jamison, "I sincerely hope you will both decline any and all proposals of marriage at least until Friday." And with a little salute, he rode away.

Ruth's hand went to the frill of lace at her throat even as Mrs. Jamison muttered, "I never saw a man who thought so highly of himself. And what in tarnation was he talkin' about—proposals of marriage? And a dance? I don't remember anything about a dance on Friday night. And what did he mean by there bein' a crowd in Cayote?"

Out of the corner of her eye Ruth saw Hamilton Drake duck into the telegraph office. He was probably sending a telegram right now. *Promised brides arriving soon.* She cleared her throat, then spoke to Jackson. "I . . . I want to telegraph your aunt Margaret and let her know we're . . . here . . . almost. And . . ." She rummaged in her bag for a nickel. "Perhaps you'd want to check at the mercantile for some more lemon drops for Mrs. Grant? And something for yourself."

Mrs. Jamison produced a nickel of her own. "I'd be obliged if you'd get some peppermints for me, too." She thrust a coin into Jackson's palm, then glanced at Ruth.

"Tell Aunt Margaret I'm getting a horse!" Jackson said, and bounded down the stairs and toward the mercantile.

The moment he was out of earshot, Mrs. Jamison spoke up. "Are you gonna tell me what's goin' on—besides Lucas Gray's bein' rude— 'cause you are not the kind of woman who gets the vapors just because a man's mouth wanders along the edges of propriety."

Ruth shook her head. "It's—" she broke off—"so embarrassing. I don't know how I could have been so stupid. Not to see it for myself." Taking a deep breath, she told Mrs. Jamison what she'd heard Mr. Drake say to the group of men. She then repeated everything Lucas Gray had said during the lunch stop the day before, ending with, " . . . and I thought he was *teasing* me. Putting me through some silly western initiation." She gestured toward the station. "Drake is probably in there sending a telegram to Cayote right now so his 'welcoming committee' can be on hand to—" She shuddered, and then every emotion in her congealed into rage. Rage overcame every rule of etiquette she'd ever been taught, and while what she meant was that she was going to give Hamilton Drake a dressing down he'd never forget, what she said had a distinctly "military" vocabulary. The look on Mrs. Jamison's face when Ruth finally ran out of steam made her blush with embarrassment. "I'm sorry. If you came west to find a husband, that's fine. But I didn't. And I . . . I just . . ."

Mrs. Jamison chuckled. "It's all right, honey. I heard much worse when I was nursin' poor Basil at Jefferson Barracks, and no—I didn't come west on a huntin' party."

"Jefferson . . . Barracks?" Ruth couldn't keep the surprise from her voice.

Mrs. Jamison nodded. "Yes, ma'am. I may sound like molasses and corn bread, but my husband's uniform was every bit as blue as your general's." She nodded toward the telegraph office. "The thing is, if you walk in there and scorch his sideburns, I've a feelin' we'll never see Mr. Hamilton Drake again. He'll hightail it with his little bundle of cash and leave us all stranded right here in Plum Grove. He promised a return ticket to anyone who changed their minds. He should at least have to keep *that* promise."

"How do we get him to do that?"

"Oh, honey," Mrs. Jamison said, "you just leave that to li'l ole Caroline." And she fluttered her eyelashes.

# CHAPTER
# FIVE

*These six things doth the Lord hate . . .*

PROVERBS 6:16

Is everything all right?"

Caroline started as Drake's voice sounded from the direction of the combination train station and telegraph office. When he strode toward her and Mrs. Dow with a suspicious look on his face, Caroline twirled her parasol. "Left my sunshade here on the train. Just because a lady moves west doesn't mean she has to turn brown as a sharecropper." *Please don't let him have noticed I've had it all along. Please . . .*

Drake offered his arm. "May I escort you over to the Immigrant House?"

"I'd be delighted," Caroline said, "but I don't want to delay you. I need to send a telegram. My dear aunt Tillie insisted I do so once I'd arrived safely." She patted Drake's arm. "And I'm as safe as safe can be, so I thought—" Her heart began to hammer as she blathered nonsense. *How am I going to rescue myself out of this?*

Thankfully, Mrs. Dow did the rescuing as she took Drake's free arm and said, "Mrs. Jamison may not require an escort just now, but I'd welcome one." She made a show of looking around. "Jackson seems to have deserted me for the charms of Plum Grove."

"I'll be over directly," Caroline said. When Drake insisted they would wait, she sighed. "I surely do appreciate your kindness, but . . ." She dabbed at an imaginary tear. "The fact is, I'm feelin' rather . . .

emotional ... and ... homesick ... and ..." She feigned a great attempt to keep from bursting into tears. "I'd just like a little privacy, if y'all don't mind."

"We understand." Mrs. Dow patted her arm. "Even the bravest of us has had moments of undesired emotion on this journey. You'll be fine, Mrs. Jamison. You tell your family we've a champion we trust." She smiled at Drake.

Caroline looked toward the station so that Drake couldn't see her rolling her eyes. Mrs. Dow was laying it on a little thick. But then, like a bottom-feeding catfish taking bait off a wicked hook, Drake added his reassurances and proceeded to help her descend the stairs leading down off the platform. Caroline sailed toward the station, pausing just inside to peer through the far windows and make certain Drake didn't sneak back to eavesdrop.

When Drake and Mrs. Dow reached the Immigrant House, Caroline stepped into the telegraph office, where the balding operator—James McDonald, according to the engraved nameplate on his desk—sat hunkered over a piece of paper tapping out what had to be Drake's message to the men in Cayote. When Caroline cleared her throat, he jumped, then stammered, "C-can I help you, miss?"

She smiled. "You go right ahead and finish with that." She pointed to the message. "I'll just wait right here." The minute McDonald finished dot-dot-dashing his way through the note and set it aside, she shrieked, "A mouse!" Jumping back, she pressed herself against the wall, staring at the floor with what she hoped was a convincing level of feminine terror.

As a good gentleman should, McDonald jumped up and hurried to her rescue, muttering about mice and traps and nothing-to-fear and needing a good cat or two. When Caroline slumped against him in a near faint, he half carried her behind the counter to his own chair, then hurried to the waiting room and the water crock to retrieve "a bit of refreshment." In the seconds he was out of sight, Caroline read Mr. Drake's telegram. *Sixteen brides arrive 8 P.M. Southern belle. General's wife. Farm women. All lovely. Sixteen dance cards confirmed. First dance guaranteed. Cash due by noon Friday.*

There was no subterfuge involved in Caroline's subsequent need to fan herself to cool off. When McDonald returned and set a tin mug of water before her, she continued the fanning as she exclaimed with wonder that "all these wires and such can send a missive to loved ones far away. How *does* it all work?" Visibly relieved that her moment of hysteria had passed, McDonald set about explaining the finer points of telegraph wire.

Her bogus recovery complete, Caroline stood up. "Well, sir, I thank you very kindly for bein' such a gentleman. However, I believe I'll have to compose myself further before writin' dear Aunt Tillie. Perhaps I'll wait until I've reached Cayote." She hoped aloud the Cayote telegraph office wasn't overrun with vile rodents and such.

When Mr. McDonald offered to walk her to the Immigrant House, Caroline thanked him in her most syrupy voice. "But I wouldn't dream of takin' a man away from his duty." She took her leave, Drake's printed telegram crumpled in the palm of one gloved hand.

"Jeb Cooper?" Matthew called out. The stranger was leaning his *one arm* atop the sod enclosure behind the station while he looked over the milling livestock. "I'm Ransom." When the man straightened up, he was head and shoulders above Matthew—and Matthew was not a small man. The stranger said nothing, only nodded as his good hand swallowed Matthew's in a firm grasp. Between the scraggly beard and the hat pulled down on his forehead, about the only thing Jeb Cooper seemed to be willing to reveal to the world was intelligent blue eyes that looked right through Matthew in a clear, honest gaze.

"I hope you haven't been waiting long. I—" Matthew glanced toward the dining hall, where Linney was hard at work sweeping the front stoop. "My daughter—"

"You haven't told her yet." It was a statement, not a question.

Matthew shook his head, grateful for the distraction when the owner of the golden parasol he'd seen from the livery emerged from the other side of the sod corral and began to hurry across the prairie toward the Immigrant House. He couldn't imagine an elegant thing like her would have signed on with Hamilton Drake if she truly understood what was in store for her.

A gust of wind ripped the parasol out of the woman's hands and flung it out of reach. It tumbled across the prairie in spite of its owner's scampering attempts to catch up with it. Matthew went after it without thinking, moving in an easy lope that quickly retrieved the ridiculous thing, although by the time he did, the shimmering gold silk was much the worse for its encounter with various grasses and, Matthew saw as he bent to retrieve the parasol, a rusted can likely left by the encampment of soldiers who'd spent a few weeks here this spring.

He couldn't quite decipher the look on her face as he carried the parasol toward her. Was she afraid of him? He supposed he did look rather . . . beastly. Something emptied his brain of words, and he stood, parasol in hand, as dumb as the oxen Jeb Cooper was yoking up over by the corral.

"I don't know how to thank you," she said, in a lilting voice that spoke of gentility and privilege.

What on *earth* was she doing out here? Still at a loss for words, Matthew reacted as habit dictated—or as it had for the past few years of his life. With a nod, he handed over the parasol and strode away.

*Jubal A. Cooper—Plum Grove, Nebraska—1871.* Together Matthew and Jeb lowered the massive inscribed trunk into the wagon bed Cooper had parked alongside the train. Next came the smaller crates, nearly a dozen of them, stamped *Arbuckle Coffee, Lion Coffee, Paxton Coffee,*

and other brands Matthew had never encountered before. Finally, he joked, "You planning to open a dining hall?"

Cooper looked confused for a minute, but when Matthew pointed to the lettering stamped on one box, a chuckle rumbled from his thick chest. "It's not coffee," he said. He didn't explain, although he did continue to chuckle as he shouldered the last box and settled it on the wagon seat. This one he wrapped in a rubber sheet before tying it down and pointing to the pile of lumber in the corner of the freight car. "That's mine, too," he said. Together the men piled board after board atop the wagon load until Matthew began to wonder if the oxen would be able to manage it. Finally, Cooper said, "That's it," and tossed the end of a rope across the load.

Matthew helped him tie it in place. Seeing that Linney had finished sweeping and gone inside, he walked alongside as Cooper drove the oxen past the dry goods store in the direction of the homestead north of town. The aroma of fresh coffee wafting through the front door of the dining hall made Cooper "whoa" the oxen to a halt. "Don't mind if I have a cup," he said. "How about you?"

Matthew hesitated. He'd already been in Plum Grove longer than he wanted to be, and he didn't care to take a chance on having to explain to Linney—

"Pa!"

—and here she was, broom in hand. "I thought you were headed back to the—" She stopped short, instantly shy at the sight of Jeb Cooper standing next to the wagon.

Matthew introduced Cooper even as he cast a desperate expression the man's way. *Please don't let on.* "Mr. Cooper was unloading by himself. It seemed he could use a hand." He winced inwardly at the reference to hands, but Cooper didn't seem to take offense.

"Then you've seen the ladies," Linney said.

"Some of them."

"Your pa here rescued a parasol for one of 'em," Cooper offered.

"A gold one?" When Matthew nodded, she enthused, "Isn't it the prettiest thing you've ever seen? Mrs. Jamison's already come into the mercantile to see if Martha had anything suitable to mend the rip." Linney frowned. "Of course we don't carry silks and such. But Mrs. Jamison was so nice. Martha offered to special order for her and send the package over to Cayote. Martha said she wished they were staying here in Plum Grove. She doesn't like Mr. Drake very much, and—"

Just then a stream of customers started heading their way. "Believe I'll get that coffee now," Cooper said. He ducked inside.

"I gotta get inside," Linney said. "You won't leave without saying good-bye again, will you?"

"Of course not." With a quick peck on her cheek, Matthew made his escape around to the back door of the dining hall. Smelling Martha Haywood's roast beef dinner almost overcame his unease about being around a bunch of ladies. Almost. But not quite.

Caroline paused just inside the Immigrant House's double doors to collect herself. Laughter emanated from the other side of the doors on the right labeled *Women's Dormitory*. On the left, a door stood open. Jackson Dow had apparently been waiting on a cot just inside the men's dormitory, for when he saw Caroline, he jumped up and came to the door with a small white bag in hand.

"Your peppermints," he said, then blushed bright red as he relayed the message that his mother was "indisposed." "She wanted me to ask you to meet her in the kitchen." He frowned. "Something about meeting before a meeting?" He motioned toward the far end of the building. "It's back there. Through the dining room."

Caroline gave a little curtsey. "Why, thank you, Master George Washington Jackson Dow the Second."

He rolled his eyes. "I hate it when Mother does that . . . thing . . . like she did at lunch yesterday. It's like she's reading a proclamation . . . like she expects everyone to be so impressed."

"Well, as a matter of fact," Caroline said, "I am impressed. Your father was a great man."

"You knew my father?"

"Not personally. But I read about him during the war. He was beloved by his men. I didn't know he'd passed on until your mother told us at lunch yesterday. I am truly sorry about your father."

"I don't remember much about him." He sounded wistful. "I wish I did. Mother talks about him all the time, but it's not the same."

The poor child. Caroline had been so wrapped up in herself for all this way she hadn't given much thought to how it must feel to be the only boy in this bunch of women. The way he'd jumped up to bring her the peppermints took on a new poignancy as she thought about Jackson sitting in that huge dormitory all by himself listening to the women's voices echo through the building. She nodded toward the kitchen. "When my brothers were about your age, we used to sneak peppermints out of the candy jar and melt them in hot water. We called it Sweet-mint Tea. Want to try it before your mother gets back from the necessary?"

"There's something you all need to know before we go to supper," Ruth said to the fifteen women crowded into the Immigrant House kitchen. "I was in the train station getting a drink of water when I heard Mr. Drake—" She repeated what Drake had said as he dispersed the group of men who'd gathered to meet their train.

Caroline stood up to add her part. "So when we realized Mr. Drake was sendin' a telegram, we . . . well, I . . . managed to . . . borrow . . . a copy." She read aloud. " 'Sixteen brides arrive eight P.M. Southern belle. General's wife. Farm women. All lovely. Sixteen dance cards confirmed. First dance guaranteed. Cash due by noon Friday.' "

At first the women sat motionless staring at one another, their expressions ranging from disbelief to shock to anger. Sally Grant was the first to speak. "He didn't say nothin' about a dance or any of that other at the meetin' I went to."

"Nor at mine," Ruth said.

Ella Barton spoke up. "It was all about the land. That's what I've come for."

"And I," Ruth agreed. She glanced around the room. "We can speak freely, by the way. I've sent my son on an errand and told him to meet us at the dining hall."

One of the sisters spoke up. She didn't mind the idea so much, she said. "But I most certainly do mind it all being prearranged without our knowing about it." She glanced at her sisters, who nodded agreement. "And the idea of his collecting money for dances?" She shook her head. "That's not right."

"Well, what are we gonna do about it?" Sally asked.

"Tar and feathers come to mind," Mavis Morris said, and nervous laughter circled the table.

"What are *you* gonna do?" Sally asked Ruth.

"I only know what I'm not going to do."

"Which is?"

"My son and I are *not* getting back on that train. I am *not* going to allow Mr. Hamilton Drake to earn so much as one cent from *my* dance card." She glanced at Caroline. "Mrs. Jamison and I will be staying here in Plum Grove."

"You going back east?" Sally asked.

Ruth shrugged. "I don't know." *There's nothing back there for me.*

"What about you?" Sally nodded at Caroline.

"I've got nothin' to go back *to*," the southerner said.

"Me neither," Sally said. "But I got no interest in puttin' myself under a roof owned by a man ever again." She looked around the room. "You all probably got me figured for a whore 'cause I talk so rough. But I ain't." She cleared her throat. "I was married. It weren't no fun. He beat on me one too many times. When he broke my arm I divorced the b—" She broke off. "Sorry." She took a deep breath.

"So. I'm divorced. But I ain't no whore. Never was. Never will be. I'd die before I'd have to face my ma on Judgment Day with that on my account." She smiled. "Guess a body'd think I'd be most worried 'bout facin' Jesus with such as that on my account. But Jesus was way nicer to whores than my ma'd be if she was to catch me doin' such." She sniffed. "I'd-a never married old Ray Gosset if my ma'd stuck to this earth. But she just had to fly away when the angels took a notion to call her up."

For a while no one said anything. Then Ella Barton spoke up. "You know anything about chickens, Mrs. Grant?"

Sally frowned. "What's there to know? You get some hens and a rooster and keep the varmints out of the coop. Why?"

"Well," Ella said, "when I get a homestead I will be busy with plowing and cattle and crops. Mama will be busy with cooking and sewing. We could use someone for chickens—and maybe the garden."

A faint smile curled Sally's mouth up at the corners. "Chickens, huh?" She nodded. "I could tend me some chickens."

Ella Barton would always remember the look on Hamilton Drake's face when, after he'd taken a big bite of Martha Haywood's succulent roast beef, he was confronted by the reading of the telegram he'd sent. Mama actually giggled as the man's face flushed. He stopped chewing. Took a sip of water. Chewed some more. And then, when the ladies leaned forward and began to ask questions, he barely managed to get that roast beef down.

"What's this 'bride business' that rancher mentioned to Mrs. Dow?"

"Did you really arrange for a circuit rider to come through Cayote on Sunday?"

"You didn't tell us about a dance. You *sold* the first dance?"

"Is *anything* you said about Nebraska true?"

"Can we even *get* free land?"

God forgive her, Ella enjoyed watching the beads of sweat collect on Drake's brow. When he finally jumped to his feet, Ella thought he might be bent on fleeing, but the burly man leaning against the doorframe sipping coffee precluded that. And when she realized that Mrs. Haywood was standing in the kitchen doorway, her arms crossed, a butcher knife poised in one hand, Ella decided once and for all that Martha Haywood was a woman whose friendship would be worth earning.

"Ladies. *Please*, ladies." Drake held his hands up, palms out. He cleared his throat. "No matter what you might have heard, there *is* free homestead land available in—"

"No. There isn't. Not near Cayote." The scrape of Ella's chair legs across the bare wood floor was the only sound as she stood up to speak. "I paid a visit to the newspaper office just now. They have a copy of a very interesting map. It shows all the land the government gave the railroad. Land they can now sell to recover their costs for laying all that track. Millions of acres. As it happens, *all* of the acres around the town of Cayote are for sale." Ella paused. "There is *no* free land near Cayote, Mr. Drake."

Mama stood up beside her. "Shame on you. You must have known that. Why didn't you tell us?"

"Well, now"—Drake reached up to loosen his collar—" 'near to town' means something different out here than it does in St. Louis. Homesteaders out here think nothing of driving a dozen miles just to go to a dance." He glanced Mrs. Haywood's way. "Isn't that true, Mrs. Haywood?"

"True or not," Mrs. Haywood said, "we both know there isn't any *free* land around Cayote, and these ladies seem fairly certain you said there was."

Ella gestured around the table. "You promised *free* land *near* town. And you knew very well what we heard when you said that."

"Eighteen dollars in filing fees," Ruth Dow offered. "One

hundred and sixty acres free and clear in five years' time. That's what I heard."

"It's what the law says," Ella added.

Caroline spoke up. "But you never gave the law much thought, did you, Mr. Drake? You never expected the land to be a problem because you've assumed we'll all get married right away. In fact, you've all but *promised* that to the men who received this telegram, haven't you?" She waved the paper in the air.

Ruth's voice wavered as she said, "And you shooed those men off the platform today for fear they'd give away the real meaning behind the Ladies Emigration Society before you had a chance to collect even more money on Friday."

Drake's eyes darted around the table. He swallowed. "You have misunderstood my intentions."

Sally sat back and folded her arms. "I'm listening. You gonna explain?"

When Drake nodded and said he would "gladly" explain, Ella and Mama sat back down.

Drake cleared his throat. "The telegram was meant to provide a possible—and I emphasize that word 'possible'—alternative for those of you who might have been somewhat . . . daunted, shall we say, by the landscape as we came west. I well remember the look on your faces when we crossed the burned prairie. Why, I half expected some of you to have turned back by now. And who would blame you? It seemed only reasonable that having some unmarried gentlemen meet the train in Cayote might provide yet another alternative. One that might be attractive—"

"To who? To someone with an idea to sell first dances?" Sally's cheeks flushed red as she said, "I made it real clear at the meetin' I attended that I don't want no man, and you was wrong to bring me out here thinkin' you could change my mind." She paused. "And fer yer information, who I do and do not dance with is not up to any two-legged, low-down—"

Drake interruped. "I assure you, Mrs. Grant, that no one is going to force you to—"

"Well, at least you got one thing right," Sally snapped. "I'm not takin' one more step in any direction you got a thing to do with."

Mavis Morris warbled, "I want that return ticket."

"So do I." Mrs. Smith and three others spoke in unison.

Drake closed his eyes in a pose that made Ella think of the minister at Milton's church. She never had liked that man.

Taking a deep breath, he insisted, "You have misjudged both me and the fine citizens of Cayote. Especially considering that you haven't so much as *seen*—"

"I've seen," Mavis said. "Just like you said: burned prairie and flat land. I wouldn't leave a *dog* I didn't like out here."

"Even St. Louis had its beginning, Mrs. Morris. A few years from now—"

But Mavis wasn't having any of it. "St. Louis also had a navigable river and trees," she retorted even as she stretched her arms wide and motioned around them. "There's nothing outside these four walls but grass and sky."

"Actually . . ." The one-armed stranger blocking the doorway spoke up, his voice a gentle rumble. "You may not have seen it yet, but there is plenty besides grass and sky out here." When Ella looked his way, the stranger set his coffee mug down and took his hat off. He dipped his head in a half bow. "Jeb Cooper's my name. I just bought a pre-emption. Good house, spring-fed watering hole, rich land. If a man—or a woman—has time and determination, Dawson County has a lot to offer."

Mama thanked him "for filling that doorway at just the right time."

"Glad to be of help." Cooper put his hat back on and returned to lounging in the doorway.

One of the four sisters spoke up to ask Mr. Drake if he'd ever done anything like this before. When he said yes, she glanced at her siblings, who nodded back. "And did those ladies marry right away?"

"Some did. Yes."

Another sister asked, "And were they . . . satisfied . . . with their decision? Are they still in the area?"

Ella could hardly believe her ears. Were they actually thinking of going on to Cayote? Entertaining the idea of instant marriages? She had her answer when one of them wondered aloud if the "tall man in the plaid shirt" she'd seen today would be at the dance in Cayote.

"I'm just trying to be practical," she said, and glanced around the table with a little shrug.

"You don't have to explain yourself," another woman said. "Not all of us came to supper wanting to tar and feather Mr. Drake. At least not until after we see what Cayote has to offer."

Ella shook her head. Mama patted her arm, then leaned close to whisper, "You cannot make the decision for them, Ella. They are grown women."

Mama was right, of course. The same freedom that allowed her to come west allowed fools to follow the likes of Hamilton Drake, even after they had learned of his questionable integrity. It was none of her affair. She grabbed a biscuit and took a bite. But then Mr. Drake actually thanked Ruth and Caroline for "clearing the air," and Ella decided that she had had enough.

Standing up, she blurted out, "I want my things from the train. Mama and I will not be going on to Cayote." Ella glanced at Mrs. Haywood. "We can stay at the Immigrant House?"

Mrs. Haywood nodded. "Delighted to have you. Plum Grove is poised to become the county seat. There's plenty of homestead land near town—and in our case 'near' really does mean 'near.'" She directed her next comments to the rest of the ladies. "If anyone is interested in a job, I'm looking to hire cooks for the dining hall and at least two ladies—or a married couple—to move in over at the Immigrant House and keep things running there. Plum Grove is going to be growing fast. Stay here. Grow with us."

Jeb Cooper spoke up then. "I'll be happy to help anyone who decides to stay with their freight." He smiled at Sally. "I'm a terrible dancer, so you don't have to worry I'll come to collect on Friday."

Sally smiled. "Guess we'll pay you with fresh eggs, then."

"Those of us staying in Plum Grove tonight should probably get to the station and get our things," Ella said. Mrs. Haywood promised to meet them at the Immigrant House and help them get settled. Ella couldn't believe that in addition to herself and Mama and Sally, only five other ladies joined them. Ruth Dow. Caroline Jamison. Hettie Raines. Mavis Morris. Helen Smith. That was all. Mr. Drake would still arrive in Cayote with eight "prospective brides." The idea made her skin crawl.

CHAPTER
SIX

*And I will bring the blind by a way that they knew not;*
*I will lead them in paths that they have not known. . . .*

ISAIAH 42:16

Ella woke in the night shivering. Nothing was visible through the curtainless windows on the far wall of the women's dormitory. Mama slept on the next cot, her white hair surrounding her head like a halo. Presently the "angel" sat up and, pulling her comforter around her, trundled over to the window, where she stood transfixed. When Ella went to her side and looked out, she whispered, "It can't be." *Snow.* Blowing wildly across the little town. It had already accumulated enough that the expanse of prairie between the Immigrant House and the mercantile had nearly disappeared beneath a blanket of white.

Mama wondered aloud about how the women in Cayote were managing. "I wish they all would have stayed here with us."

"I'm sure they'll be fine," Ella murmured. Of course she wasn't really certain, but Mama shouldn't be losing sleep over eight foolish almost-strangers. *Be careful about calling other women fools. You married Milton Barton once, remember?* With a sigh, Ella padded back to the middle of the room and stoked the fire in the little stove and lit two lamps. Once the fire was going again she sat on the floor beside it, trying to warm both hands and feet while she listened to the wind moaning about the building. She wondered about that nice Mr. Cooper. It bothered her to think he might have been caught in the storm because he'd stayed long enough to help them unload their things from the train. What did a person out on the prairie do when weather roared in? Ella didn't like most of the answers that came to mind.

Sally sat up, her rumpled hair sticking out in all directions as she muttered, "Who sent the extra freight train through the building?" Laughter revealed that all eight women were wide awake. Presently most were clustered around the windows to peer outside.

"Do you think it's doing this over in Cayote?" Mavis Morris wondered aloud.

"When it's snowin' sideways a body can't hardly tell which way it's comin' from," Sally said. "But Cayote ain't all that far away. It's likely blowing there, too." She shivered and padded back to where Ella sat on the cot she'd pulled closer to the stove. Settling in, Sally resembled a stuffed sausage with only a few tufts of hair and the tip of her nose peeking out from the folds of the comforter.

"I suspected weather was coming," Mama said, groaning softly as she moved closer to the stove. "My joints were hurting all evening."

Ella frowned. "We should have brought in more wood." Opening her trunk, she pulled out extra stockings and two sweaters, one for herself and one for Mama. With Mama swaddled in several layers of clothing and a thick tied comforter, Ella accompanied a worried Ruth Dow across the hall to check on Jackson.

"Come with us before you freeze to death," Ruth said to her son. "The ladies won't mind."

"I'm fine," Jackson answered from inside a mountainous sandwich of feather beds. "In fact, I'm almost hot in here."

"Well, if you need anything—"

"I know, Mother."

"You aren't . . . frightened? The wind's powerful."

"It's *wind*. Unless it picks us up and blows us somewhere, I can't see it doing any harm as long as I stay in here. Just be sure to call me for breakfast."

Ella chuckled. "He must be fine. He's thinking about food." When the two crossed back to the ladies' dormitory, the others had pulled four cots into a square around the stove.

Mavis wondered aloud if the storm was worse in the west and if the eastbound train would make it through later today. "And I sure hope those baggage handlers did something to protect all our—"

"Chickens!" Ella leaped to her feet and raced out back, lamp in hand, her heart thumping. Mr. Cooper had hauled the birds around to the back of the Immigrant House, where Ella could keep an eye on them, but now—in this weather. Expecting the worst, Ella sighed with relief when she opened the back door and saw her live chickens huddled together in one corner of the crate. Blocking the door open with one foot, she hoisted the crate and carried the squawking birds to the dormitory.

Mavis was still grousing. About the weather, about Cayote, about the freight handlers, about myriad and sundry things. Finally, her friend Helen spoke up. "Don't think about all of that, Mavis. Think about something positive. Soon you'll be back home and all this will be just an interesting story to tell."

"If I wanted to be at home I would never have signed up for this . . . disaster." Mavis began to sniffle. "Maybe I should have stayed with the others and gone on over to Cayote. The one fellow—what was his name—that ranch hand with Mr. Gray? The clean-shaven one. I thought he had kind eyes."

"Lowell Day," Caroline said, "and the man's eyes are anything but kind."

"Mrs. Jamison's right, Mavis," Helen Smith said. "Those were *shifty* eyes. I didn't like the way he looked at us at all."

"Well, he might have had other nice qualities. But I'll never know, because now I won't *be* at the dance, will I?"

"Mrs. Haywood said there's a dance right here at the dining hall this Friday, Mavis. We could stay. Maybe talk to Mrs. Haywood about those jobs she mentioned."

Mavis sniffed. "Cleaning out slop pots for a bunch of strangers?"

"We wouldn't have to run this place for her. She said she needs help in the dining hall kitchen, too."

Ella bowed her head and closed her eyes, pretending to sleep. Mavis was a complainer and a fool, and having little patience with the former and having been the latter herself, Ella did not suffer either lightly. When Mrs. Smith continued to try—and fail—to comfort her friend, Ella finally broke in. "You can still go to the dance in Cayote if you want. I'm sure the stationmaster would honor your original ticket. Maybe there's a position you'd like better over there." *Or maybe you can get a man to propose, since that's really what you want.*

"Well, maybe I'll just do that," Mavis said. "Mr. Drake said he could still fill my dance card if I changed my mind."

"I'm sure he'd be very happy to try," Ella said.

"You don't think anyone would *want* to dance with me, do you? You think I'd be stupid to go to Cayote. You really think those women who went ahead with Mr. Drake are fools."

"I think," Ella said, "that what a woman does or doesn't do should be up to the woman, and she should make up her own mind and not change it when the wind starts to blow. I think a woman should be who she is, not what others expect her to be. And if she wants to go to a dance looking for a man, she should go and not feel like she has to explain herself. And if she wants to have her own farm, she should do that and not feel like she has to explain that, either. And," Ella said, hunkering down inside her comforter, "I think you should be quiet now."

Caroline Jamison spoke into the tension with a voice so soft Ella had to listen carefully to hear what she had to say. "We should *all* be thankful, for the storm's givin' us time to think about what we really want to do now." She paused. "I don't really know what I expected when I signed on with the Society. Now that I consider it, I wasn't thinkin' so much about the future out here as I was about gettin' away from . . ." She paused. ". . . about gettin' away. But after talkin' to y'all on the train—especially you, Ella—I'm thinkin' on a plan."

Mavis's laugh was harsh. "Did you have your eyes open when we got off the train today? Or were you so blinded by that rancher's attentions that the sun completely addled your brain?" She snorted. "You wouldn't last a month out here, little Miss Georgia, and it takes five *years* to prove up on a homestead."

Ruth Dow spoke up. "For your information, Mrs. Jamison is from Tennessee. And you just might be surprised at what she can handle."

The wind picked up. The building shuddered. The women shivered.

Hettie Raines joined the conversation. "My husband and I got caught in a storm like this once. A confinement. The mother had buried two babies and the husband insisted we come the minute she felt the very first pain. As it turned out, it was a good thing we did. We likely wouldn't have made it otherwise because of the storm. The poor thing was in labor for two days . . . and it snowed for three."

"Everything turn out all right?" Mama asked.

"Just fine." Hettie chuckled. "The farmer brought his prize bull inside. Said it was for the warmth. Although I think he was more worried about the bull than keeping the doctor and his assistant—or his wife and baby—warm."

"Guess his wife knew what was important to *him*," Ella said.

"Oh, he loved her," Hettie said with a giggle. "He just loved the bull a little more."

"Hello!"

Caroline opened her eyes. The wind had died down.

"Hello!"

Lifting her head she peered about the room, hoping someone else was going to get up and see who in the world was outside hollering. All she wanted to do was hunker back beneath her inadequate blankets and go back to sleep. She could see her own breath in the frigid morning air. It was too cold to get up.

"Hello." Someone rapped on the dormitory door. "Is everyone all right in there?"

"We would be if they'd hush." Sally coughed and turned over to look at Caroline. "Want me to tell 'em?"

"No," Caroline said as she sat up. "You stay covered up. I'll go." As she threw back the covers, she wrinkled her nose. Hopefully Ella's chickens could go back outside today. Mrs. Haywood would throw a fit if she saw what those hens—and the lone rooster—had done to the corner of the room. Ah, well, a floor could be cleaned. A woman couldn't just sacrifice her livestock to the snow, could she? Keeping one thin blanket wrapped around her, Caroline padded in her stocking feet toward the door.

A stage whisper sounded from the other side. "It's Martha Haywood. Is everyone all right?"

Caroline opened the door and stepped into the hall, pulling the door closed behind her. "Everything's fine. Although I will say if this is springtime in Dawson County, y'all could do better."

Mrs. Haywood chuckled. "Well, we frequently do. It's been known to blizzard in April. This was just a light dusting by comparison. A few inches at best. It won't take long to shovel a path to the necessaries this morning."

"Well, I guess there's always somethin' to be thankful for if a body looks close enough." Caroline smiled.

"I'd still love to hear that you're going to give Plum Grove a chance. My William's up on the Graystone Ranch helping with calving, but when he gets back, I know he'd be glad to help you all locate good homesteads. William knows Dawson County like few others—although he isn't a professional land agent like Mr. Drake."

"Well, thank heaven for that," Caroline said quickly. "In my considered opinion, the world's got no need whatsoever for a man like Hamilton Drake."

Mrs. Haywood smiled. "You'll get no argument from me in that regard. I'll tell you what, Mrs. Jamison. I've been feeling more than a little overwhelmed since my William left last week. How about I hire you to lend a hand at the mercantile until he gets back? Then you can ride out and see what Dawson County has to offer before you make your decision about going or staying. I really think you'll like us once you've given us a chance."

Caroline liked Mrs. Haywood already. She liked her well-kept store with its pristine shelves and the bolts of bright calico fabrics stacked on the shelf behind the counter. She liked the cards of jet buttons and the lace collars on the top shelf of the glass display unit, and she liked the sweet redheaded young girl named Linney, who had seemed so eager to help her yesterday. And so she nodded and said, "Why, thank you, ma'am. I'd like that. Very much."

As Mrs. Haywood made her way toward the back door with a promise to have breakfast served up in the dining hall within the hour, Caroline turned back toward the dormitory just as Jackson called her name.

"You're staying?"

"I'm stayin'. At least for a few days."

Jackson smiled. "I think we will, too. If Mother wanted to get married again we would have stayed in St. Louis. She really does want a homestead—although I don't think she was expecting things to be so . . . empty."

"I don't think any of us expected what we got," Caroline said as she smiled and gave a little shiver, "snow included."

Jackson's voice sounded wistful as he said, "If we don't settle here, it means we won't be able to visit Mr. Gray's ranch. And he said he'd teach me to ride—if I wanted to learn."

"Do you?"

"Well, sure." He chewed on his lower lip for a minute. "Do you think it's hard?"

Caroline shook her head. "Of course not. I used to ride all the time. I had a li'l ole mare named Shiloh. She was gentle as she could be. That's the kind of horse ya'll want to learn on."

"Do you think they'd have any horses like Shiloh on Mr. Gray's ranch? I've been reading that book *Texan Joe* and it sounds like all the horses out here are bucking broncos and wild mustangs."

"I don't know a single thing about what kind of horses Mr. Gray would have on a ranch," Caroline said. She really didn't want to pursue the topic of Lucas Gray. "But maybe we can go up to the livery and see what they have in the way of horses for hire. In fact—if you'll go ask Mrs. Haywood to lend us a couple of shovels, we'll shovel our way to breakfast at the dining hall and then maybe go on to the livery this very mornin'—depending, of course, on what your mama thinks of the idea."

"She won't like it," Jackson said. Finally, he opened the dormitory door all the way and stepped out into the hall. "She's always worrying about me getting hurt. And horses?" He shook his head.

"George Washington Jackson Dow," Caroline said with mock horror. "Did you sleep in your clothes?"

He licked the palms of both hands and smoothed his hair. "Don't tell Mother."

Caroline just shook her head. She pointed toward the front door. "You'd best get started shoveling so there'll be a good reason why you're so rumpled. The sons of generals have no call to look so raggedy. And besides that, you need to be in your mama's good graces when we ask her about your learning to ride."

Caroline had just bent to scoop her first shovelful of snow when a snowball glanced off her left shoulder. "Hey!" She brushed it off and shook a finger at Jackson. "You'd better watch out, Mr.—" Another snowball landed. Jackson laughed. Caroline made a show of standing her shovel in the snow, then bent down to make her own snowball.

Jackson had pelted her a third and a fourth time before she had a chance to scrape together enough snow to launch even one defense. It fell apart in midair. With a screech, she made another one, this time packing it firmly and sending out a victorious shout when it hit its target. Turning her back on Jackson, she slid her way around the corner of the Immigrant House.

"Hey," Jackson called. "I didn't hit you too hard, did I?" He sounded worried.

Instead of reassuring him, Caroline concentrated on making snowballs.

"Caroline?"

She stayed quiet and kept working.

"Don't be mad," he pleaded. "I was just—"

The frozen top layer of snow crunched as Jackson came toward her. As he rounded the corner, Caroline launched three snowballs in quick succession—and landed all three. The boy let out a whoop as he scooped snow with a cupped hand and sent a wave of white her way. As she dodged the crystalline shower, Caroline heard a door open.

"You two children hush," Ruth called. "You've awakened the entire dormitory!"

"It's all my fault," Caroline said, breathless as she hurried to retrieve her shovel and get back to work. "I was just—" She never got the words out.

Ruth launched a snowball that, while aimed at Caroline's shoulder, glanced off and hit her in the face. Ruth slung a second snowball at Jackson. "I win," she called, and ducked back inside.

Caroline and Jackson exchanged surprised smiles.

"I guess Nebraska agrees with Mother," Jackson said.

They shoveled furiously and ended up clearing a path across to the mercantile and then on past to the dining hall and toward the newspaper office, laughing and challenging each other to go faster and faster until, from behind them, Mrs. Haywood called out that she had fresh coffee ready. Up ahead, the livery doors slid open with a screech.

"Well, I declare," Caroline said. The ladies would be glad to learn there was no need to worry about that nice Mr. Cooper being trapped alone in a snowstorm. Here he was, pulling his suspenders up as, hatless, he looked up at the blue sky. Apparently he caught a whiff of Martha Haywood's coffee, because he inhaled deeply and, smiling, turned toward the dining hall. At first sight of Caroline, though, he hesitated. His hand went up to smooth his hair. He looked down at his mud-spattered work pants and went back inside.

Caroline sent Jackson to return the shovels and then headed toward breakfast in the dining hall. She would have made it, too . . . had it not been for the ice.

# CHAPTER
## SEVEN

*Let us walk honestly, as in the day; not in rioting and drunkenness,*
*not in chambering and wantonness, not in strife and envying.*

ROMANS 13:13

I'll be fine," Caroline muttered to the air. Feeling silly, she floundered her way off the ice to a spot where a thin crust of snow still granted some semblance of footing. She glanced around, grateful that Mr. Cooper had ducked out of sight and thus no one had seen her graceless fall. She planted her left foot to stand up. Pain shot up her leg. She tried again. This time, a wave of nausea made her sit back with a grunt and close her eyes. Someone swept her up in his arms. He smelled . . . musty. Embarrassed, she demanded to be put down and was ignored.

"Put me *down*." A combination of anger and humiliation brought on tears. Her nose began to run. "I said, put me *down*." As she swiped the tears out of her eyes, she realized she was already at the Immigrant House. Her rescuer loped up the stairs, down the wide hall between the dormitories, and into the kitchen. Finally, he plopped her into a chair just as Hettie Raines came in from the hall.

"What's happened?"

Sniffing and swiping at her tears, Caroline recognized the man who'd caught her parasol when it blew away yesterday. He wore a hide coat and breeches tucked into knee-high boots decorated with a wide strip of beading up the side. Long, unkempt hair and a thick black beard made him look half wild. And once again he just stood there, staring at her with those pale blue eyes of his and saying nothing. When he finally did speak it was to Hettie. "She fell," he said. Glancing down at Caroline, he muttered, "Hope it isn't broken." He retreated out the kitchen door without another word.

The last thing on earth Hettie wanted anything to do with was doctoring. Ladies like her, who knew about doctoring, were unusual and people tended to talk about things that were unusual. Hettie didn't want to be talked about. Talk had a way of traveling, and the past had a way of catching up with a person. If that happened, she didn't know what she would do. The idea sent a tremor of panic to the very tips of her toes. But here sat Caroline, white as a sheet and in pain. Habit and Forrest's training trumped fear.

"Where exactly does it hurt, Caroline?"

She pointed to her ankle.

"W-we'll need to get your boot off before your ankle swells any more," Hettie said. "I'll fetch a button hook and be right back." Button hook in hand, she sat down and lifted Caroline's foot into her lap, quickly unhooking each of the ten buttons running up the side of the stylish black leather boot. She pulled it off as quickly as possible, pleased when Caroline only grunted with pain. "That's a good sign."

"What's a good sign? That it hurts like the devil himself?"

"No, it's a good sign you didn't scream." With her palm flat against the ball of Caroline's foot, Hettie applied gentle pressure, flexing the foot so the toes pointed to the ceiling. She prodded the swollen tissue around the joint and had Caroline move it from side to side. Finally, she nodded. "It's only a sprain, and I don't think it's too bad." Lowering Caroline's foot to the floor, she went out back and filled a dishpan with snow. "Ice is the best thing I know," she said as she set the tub on the floor in front of Caroline.

"You want me to put my foot in there?" Caroline shivered.

"You'll only be able to stand it a little while, but it'll help keep the swelling down."

"It *hurts*." Caroline grimaced as she slipped her foot into the snow.

"Who was your knight in shining armor?"

"My what?"

"The man who carried you in."

"Someone from town. I don't know. He was over at the station yesterday. Helping Mr. Cooper load his wagon, I think." Caroline clenched her jaw against the cold. "I was supposed to help Mrs. Hayworth in the mercantile today. For a few days, actually. Could you go in for me?"

"No!" Hettie ducked her head. "I . . . I don't know anything about keeping a store."

"Neither do I. I pretty much figured it was smile and do what you're told. I imagine Linney knows everything a body'd need to know. She told me she practically grew up working there, and she's sweet as sweet can be. You'll be just fine."

A solution presented itself when Mavis and Helen exited the dormitory and headed for the front door. Hettie hurried after them, explaining what had happened to Caroline and what she'd promised Mrs. Haywood. "I know you were going to ask about work at the dining hall, but maybe one of you could help in the mercantile instead?"

By Thursday evening the last vestiges of the snow had melted. Hettie said she felt confident that if Caroline kept her ankle wrapped and if she elevated it when she was sitting down, it would likely be "almost back to normal" within a couple of days. "I doubt you'll be up to dancing tomorrow night, but with a little help you should be able to make your way to the dining hall and enjoy the music. Martha says they have a fiddler who's next to none."

Sally winked at Caroline. "She won't have no trouble gettin' to the dance. I reckon that guardian angel will check in just when you need him again and want a dance, too. Although he smells a bit rangy to be a member of the heavenly host, he makes up for it with all the rest."

"The rest of what?" Caroline frowned at Sally over the top of the most recent edition of the *Plum Grove News*.

"Did you hit yer head when you fell? Didn't you see those blue eyes?" Sally gave a little shiver.

Caroline pretended to concentrate on the newspaper. "I did not hit my head. And for your information I remember quite well that he definitely did *not* look like a man who spends time waltzing with the ladies."

Only a very tiny bit of her halfway hoped that whoever he was, the mountain man might reappear at the dance. After all, waltzing wasn't all that hard to learn.

The framework that would soon be three new buildings on Main Street looked like as many skeletons silhouetted against the sunset sky. From where he stood just inside the livery's wide double doors, Matthew Ransom took stock of how Plum Grove was growing. Linney said the three newest buildings would be another mercantile, a hotel, and, of all things, a photography studio run by some fellow who'd just come into town today and was rooming over in the station house. Oh yes, Plum Grove was growing.

Already wagons and carriages lined Main for tonight's dance. Laughter sounded from up the street, and Matthew imagined he could already hear the one-two-three as boots and slippers waltzed across the dining hall floor. Today he felt Katie's absence as if it were something new. She wasn't there to hear the laughter, to wonder at how on earth

Bill Toady got the sounds he did from a fiddle, to exclaim over this new baby and that toddler, to complain when Matthew stood with the group of men gathered outside the dining hall jawing about crops and livestock.

How Katie would have loved the new display of geegaws in the front window at the mercantile. Her blue eyes would have shone just like Linney's did when she showed him the jet buttons. Maybe he'd buy a card of them for Linney. Martha was planning to teach her to sew this spring.

*Jet buttons.* The pretty little thing he'd scooped up out of the snow a couple of days ago liked jet buttons, too. He felt a little guilty about his ability to remember how those buttons marched downward from the velvet-edged collar of her blue dress. Scratching his beard, Matthew tried and failed to suppress a smile remembering how angry she'd been when he scooped her up. She was light as a feather. And she smelled like spring. He wondered if she would be wearing that same dress tonight. And he hated himself for wondering. *I'm sorry, Katie.*

Old Bill Toady was already outdoing himself this evening. Matthew hadn't heard fiddle music that good in a long while. *You haven't heard ANY music in a long while. Unless you count Jeb Cooper's humming to himself when you helped him load his freight.* Folks seemed to be having a wonderful time. The music and laughter had an odd effect on Matthew. He didn't quite understand why, but instead of drawing him toward it, the sound of people enjoying themselves made part of him wish he hadn't promised Linney a dance. Made him wish he hadn't agreed to stay in town for a few days.

Already Vernon Lux was talking about how he needed a carpenter to fill the orders he was getting for new wagons over at the implement store, how there would likely be a rash of business once the new homesteaders started breaking ground, how good Matthew had always been at woodworking and such. "Why don't you think about it," Lux had said earlier today. "That back room would fix up nice. You could use it for as long as you wanted. I bet Linney would dance a jig to have her pa close by."

These were the things keeping Matthew up here in the livery. Pondering Plum Grove's expansion and Linney's growing up and Katie's absence. Realizing that Vernon Lux was right. And dreading what it all meant for Matthew Ransom.

"Oh, Mama." Ella looked down at Mama's open trunk and the familiar bandbox from a certain milliner's shop in St. Louis. How had she managed to sneak it onto the train? "How did you—"

Mama waved a hand in the air. "Where there is the will, Zita finds a way." She grinned. "You are so easy to fool sometimes." She pointed to the hatbox. "The hard part was keeping you from seeing it when I took it out of my traveling case last night." Mama chuckled. "I thought you'd never go to the necessary! Now—" She reached for the hat. "Hurry and put on your Sunday dress. It doesn't match exactly, but—"

"Mama." Ella glanced toward the hallway, mindful of how the other ladies had looked a few minutes ago as they helped Mrs. Jamison out the door and toward the dining hall. Multicolored songbirds fluttering up the street—that's what Ella had thought. Even Mrs. Dow had laid aside black in favor of indigo silk.

"Take it." Mama held out the new hat. "A new hat for a new life. Wear it to please *me*."

"I can't." Ella plopped down on the bed. How could she make Mama understand? It had taken so very much effort to grasp a new dream and new hope and to climb back into the light. But that light did not include womanly things like new bonnets and waltzes. Ella's new light shone on dreams of well-fed livestock and mountains of newly mown hay.

"Ella." Mama sat down beside her, the bonnet on her lap. "God promises to make all things new."

"I don't think he was talking about bonnets."

"Well, of course he wasn't. He was talking about things inside of us, and he's making you new inside, too. On Tuesday when Caroline said Plum Grove wasn't much, you pointed out the new buildings. When Ruth and Caroline told us what the Emigration Society really meant, already you were thinking how you would cope. How you would use it all to make your own place of light—your own new creation in partnership with the God who will send rain and crops and baby chicks and all good things for us to richly enjoy." Mama paused. "That's what I want for you, Ella. I want you to richly enjoy *all* good things." She traced one of the iridescent feathers. "The morning stars made music when God created the earth. Do you remember reading that? Why shouldn't we enjoy some music in celebration of your creating a home for us? Why shouldn't we dance and wear new bonnets and laugh with our new neighbors? If God meant for life to be all sorrow, he wouldn't have created laughter, Ella." Mama squeezed her hand.

Ella sighed. Such a little thing Mama was asking. Put on a new bonnet. Go to a dance. Enjoy. It had been so long since Ella enjoyed life, she wasn't certain she would know how. No one would ask her to dance, of course. *Unless they liked a beefy gal.* She looked down at the new hat. It really was lovely. Mama had such a good sense of fashion. She'd even selected a more conservative color. "All right, Mama." Ella reached for the hat. *At least it isn't red.*

He had slicked-back hair and a thin red line along his right cheekbone. The cuffs on his shirt were frayed but clean, and if her ankle weren't throbbing so, Caroline would have loved to have danced with this Bill. He was the third Bill to ask her to dance, and the other two . . . well. The other two just plain smelled bad, and Caroline was thankful for the ability to say, "I'm so sorry, but I cain't." She didn't dare lift her skirt to show them her bandaged ankle, of course, but when she rose and

hobbled over to get a cup of punch from the pass-through between
dining room and kitchen, Caroline allowed it was testimony enough
that she wasn't just making excuses. Thankfully, neither of the aromatic
Bills invited themselves to sit down next to her. This Bill, however,
seemed nice enough. And so she accepted his offer to refill her mug
and didn't mind at all when he asked her if he might "set a spell."

"Nice evening," he said, cupping his own coffee mug between both
hands and staring down at the contents as if they required inspection
before drinking. "I heard—I mean, folks are saying—"

"Please, Mr. Miller. Do tell me what folks are sayin'." Caroline
grinned. "I've been dyin' to overhear what folks are sayin', but this
ankle of mine has nailed me to the floor in a corner. I'm just dyin'
of curiosity, seein' as how it would normally be my habit to be in the
middle of every single dance, where I could overhear for myself. So
do tell. What are the good folks of Dawson County sayin' about me
and my friends?"

As it turned out, Bill might not be all that good at handling a
straight razor, but he excelled at information. City lots were going to
be available soon. The board was advertising back east for a doctor
and there'd be a school before the end of the year. The late snow had
caused problems for the ranchers. "That's why there aren't so many
people out tonight," he said. "That and the big doin's over at Cayote.
Most of the boys headed over there to see the bri—" He broke off.

Caroline finished the sentence for him. "To see the brides, I
expect."

"Yes, ma'am." He sat back then. "If it weren't for that, there'd
be dozens more here tonight." He nodded toward the fiddler. "Bill
Toady's the best in the county. Folks always turn out in droves when
they know he's playing."

*Another Bill.* Caroline smiled. She was just about to comment on
the number of Bills and Wills in Plum Grove when this Bill let out
a little "uh-oh." He was looking toward the door. All Caroline could
see above the dancers were two cowboy hats. Expecting to see Lucas

Gray sashay into the room, she was more than disappointed when the two hats proved to be on unfamiliar heads, although the look in the men's eyes was not unfamiliar to her. *Uh-oh* indeed.

They'd obviously started the evening at the saloon. They stood inside the door for a moment, watching the five couples on the dance floor, then scanning the room. Caroline followed their gaze, her heart pounding. She turned in her chair, ever so slightly toward Bill. Sally was on the dance floor—had been for every dance so far this evening, as had both Mavis and Helen. Ruth, Zita, and Ella were over by the kitchen chatting with two young couples. And yet, as she scanned the crowd, Caroline thought she detected more than one worried glance in the direction of the two newcomers. Even the fiddler seemed to have changed. Somehow the music was more frantic. As if he wanted to keep the dancers moving.

Caroline wished she could rise and slip through the kitchen door and momentarily out of sight. Something about those two—and then they saw her. Words passed between them and they left. *It's your imagination. They just happened to glance over here as they were deciding to leave. They could have been looking for anyone.*

Except they weren't. Moments later, with Bill Toady taking a well-earned break from fiddling and the seat next to her having been vacated, Caroline rose and hobbled to where Ella and Zita stood admiring the new baby in a beaming mother's arms. After being introduced, Caroline said, "I believe I'll retire a little early. My ankle's throbbing something awful and the resident doc says I should prop it up—or ice it." She shivered at the thought.

"Doc?" the young woman asked. "Does Plum Grove finally have a doctor?"

Caroline pulled on her gloves while Zita explained about Hettie, but just as she headed for the door, the cowboys returned with a friend in tow. Lucas Gray's hand from the train. *Lowell Day.*

*The only thing certain in life is that things aren't certain.* Matthew couldn't remember who'd said that, or if he even had it quite right, but it did apply to how today had gone so far. He'd been convinced that supper with Linney would be a bit awkward. She would press him about moving back to the homestead, and he would feel uncomfortable. Martha would appear to stay out of the discussion, but all the while she would be looking his way with an expression that made him feel he was being scolded by a facsimile of his long-dead mother.

Neither happened. Linney chattered away about the eight ladies now staying at the Immigrant House and how one of them had a son named Jackson. It seemed to Matthew that Linney spent more time on the boy than on the ladies. He didn't quite know how he felt about that. Either way, supper was grand. He'd excused himself to do a little more work for Otto, mostly because he liked working around the animals, liked working with his hands, and liked being aware of the comings and goings in town without having to directly engage in the hustle-bustle.

What with the snow challenging calving season on the ranches to the north and the whole county jabbering about the "brides" over at Cayote tonight, Matthew was surprised when a half dozen wranglers rode into town, and even more surprised when he realized three of their horses sported the Graystone brand. Maybe the snow hadn't caused Luke much trouble after all. But then why hadn't he come into town for the dance? Ordinarily the little southerner—Caroline, Linney said her name was—would have attracted Lucas Gray like a bee to a blossom. On the other hand, Linney said as far as she could tell, the eight ladies who had remained in Plum Grove were bent on homesteading instead of sparking. Luke wouldn't care for that. He liked women—

Whatever obsessive thoughts Matthew would have naturally entertained about Luke were interrupted by the sound of a wagon rumbling up to the open doors at the back of the barn. Matthew straightened up just in time to see Jeb Cooper climb down from his perch. When

Matthew called a greeting, Cooper smiled. "Just the man I wanted to see," he said as he used his teeth to pull the glove off his one hand.

Not normally a man to jump to conclusions about anything, Matthew did now. A myriad of things that could be wrong with the homestead flashed through his mind. The worst, he knew, for a newcomer, would be a leaky roof, and with the recent snow and the melting over the past few days—"I'll make it good," Matthew said. "Whatever's wrong. The roof—I should have checked it—"

"There's nothing wrong," Cooper said. "The place is exactly as you promised. A little better than what I expected, to be honest. But it's . . ." He paused. ". . . unchanged. I can live with it just as it is, of course. But won't your daughter want her mother's things?"

Of course she would. But first Matthew would have to tell her he'd sold the place. "I was just headed toward the dining hall—I owe Linney two dances tonight. Care to come along?"

Grateful that Jeb Cooper wasn't the kind of man who had to fill silence with talk, Matthew tried to plan what he would say to Linney. And when. Dance first . . . news last. Definitely last. How was it that a child could hold such power over a man? He could stand down a bear with less heart pounding than he felt right now. It wasn't as if he hadn't thought it all through before, but thinking it through and actually preparing to do it weren't the same. He was terrified.

When they came to the dining hall, Cooper stopped in the street. "I'm not much for dancing," he said. "You go on inside. I'll be right here when—" He broke off and stared through the windows into the dining hall. His jaw clenched. Matthew had never seen a man of any size move as fast as Jeb Cooper did to get inside.

Ella had just offered to walk back to the Immigrant House with Caroline when one of the cowboys from the train sauntered toward them. The man reeked. Ella was reminded of Milton falling into bed after being away all night, ostensibly playing cards.

"Came for my dance," he said to Caroline. "Rode all the way over to Cayote tonight but you weren't there." He looked around the room, wobbling as he took off his hat and gave a drunken little speech. "Ladies. You're the talk of Cayote tonight. Funny how that works, ain't it? The ladies who didn't go are causing more talk than the ones who are over there dancing up a storm with every man from miles around." He put his hat back on. "But Lowell Day's not interested in the ladies that stuck with Drake." He reached for Caroline's hand. "Lowell wants to dance with the gal he paid for."

When Caroline tried to pull away, Day grabbed her free hand as well and pulled her toward him. Her face went white and her ankle must have given way, because she fell forward with a little cry of pain. The man who caught her didn't reek of anything but soap and fresh air and maybe just a touch of horse. The man who caught her had, just a second before, grabbed the stinking cowboy by his collar and spun him around and away from Caroline before she lost her balance. Then, the instant he caught her and helped her regain her balance, he snatched Day's hat off the floor, clamped it on his head, grabbed him by the collar again, and shoved him out the door and into the street.

It all happened so fast that half the room probably saw little more than a slightly drunk cowboy being helped outside to sober up. But the three ladies, Caroline and Mama and Ella, saw it all, and tomorrow, and the next day, and the next it would be all Ella could do to sound sincere when she scolded Mama for going on so about Jeb Cooper. "After all," she would say, "he only did what any other good man in that room would have done."

"You think so?" Mama would say. "Because from what I've been hearing, a lot of people are afraid of Lowell Day."

"Well, Mr. Cooper wasn't. And why would he be? He's head and shoulders above that cowboy. Probably head and shoulders above any man I've ever known." All of which was true. Physically Jeb Cooper hadn't had a thing to worry about Friday night. Except—Lowell Day and his friends had guns. And Jeb Cooper had . . . one hand. And none of that had stopped him. Now, wasn't that something? A man who would actually risk danger to himself to protect a lady.

*And we know that all things work together for good to them
that love God, to them who are the called according to his purpose.*

ROMANS 8:28

Small and wiry, Will Haywood was barely as tall as his dumpling-shaped wife. He had to crank his neck to look up at Ella when Martha introduced her to him the Monday morning after the dance. The man's slight physique reminded Ella of all the things about herself she hated most. But when Will Haywood sat down with the ladies at the dining hall breakfast table and started telling stories, Ella forgot to feel uncomfortable, lost in the pure amazement that one man and one woman could have lived through some of the events the Haywoods had witnessed, could have thrived in the wilderness that was Nebraska Territory when they first arrived, and could still have the sparkle that shone in their eyes when they looked at each other. It was enough to give a woman hope about things Ella had long ago stopped hoping for.

"Martha and I were nothing but pups when we came down from Canada back in '56. We started in Kansas Territory, but then war broke out and the Kansas-Missouri border was no place to be in those days. I'd done a couple of freighting trips out this way, and seeing all the wagons headed west put me in a mind to start a way station on the trail." Will shrugged. "At the time what was to become Dawson County was populated by a couple of farmers, a dozen or so hunters, one trader, and a host of Sioux and Pawnee. Those last two were always fighting over the rich hunting lands along the Platte."

"Indians!" Jackson suddenly entered the conversation. "You've seen some? Real ones?"

Will laughed out loud. "Well, it would have been hard to avoid them, son, seeing as how they were here first and weren't always all that happy about the pale-skinned folks who seemed determined to stay."

Ella hadn't thought about Indians all that much. Now she wondered if she should have. "Should we be—are there precautions to be taken?"

"Yes, ma'am, there are."

Hettie spoke up. "Th-the ticket agent in St. Louis said something about . . . Cheyenne. And a massacre."

Will sighed. He looked around the table at each woman there. "In general, the newspapers seem to enjoy creating as much sensation as they can over every little incident. The Plum Creek Massacre was a terrible and tragic event. Over the years Martha and I have spent more than our share of time holed up at Fort Kearney waiting for Armageddon in war paint. On the other hand, I've always found that man-to-man and woman-to-woman things between us and the people go just fine as long as we extend a hand of friendship."

Ella noted that Jackson looked somewhat disappointed at the news. The other ladies—Ruth especially—looked relieved.

"I'll be taking you up to where there's other homesteaders nearby. And Lucas Gray's ranch cuts a wide swath across that part of the sandhills. If you choose a homestead up that way, you'll be all right. But yes, you may encounter Indians. I can help you know what to do when that happens."

Ruth spoke up. "I'd like that. I once had a rather harrowing experience with a party of Crow. I'll take all the advice you want to give."

"You've seen Indians?" Jackson stared at his mother as if she were a stranger. "You never told me."

Ruth lifted her chin. "I didn't see the need."

Mama spoke up with a dramatic sigh. "*Children!* They never seem to think their mothers know anything but cooking and sewing." She nudged Ella and shook a playful finger at Jackson. "We may be older, young man, but that doesn't mean we're ready to sit in a rocking chair all day."

"Mama . . ." Ella shook her head. "I only meant to be kind on Friday night. I was worried you would tire yourself dancing."

Mama raised both hands and looked around the table as if to say, "See what I have to deal with?" She leaned toward her daughter. "I'm not a child, Ella. What better way to die than in the arms of a handsome man waltzing to beautiful music?"

"All right, Mama. The next time there is a dance in Plum Grove, I won't say a word if you dance all night. You can *die* dancing. Would that make you happy?"

Mama fluttered her eyelashes. "I can only think of one other better way."

"Mama!" Ella could feel herself blushing, but when she risked a glance in Will Haywood's direction, he was smiling at his wife. In the next few minutes as they listened to Will, it became readily apparent that parting from Hamilton Drake was likely the best decision Ella and her friends could have made. Will's life experience included a mesmerizing list of accomplishments that left Ella speechless and Jackson staring at the little man with openmouthed wonder.

Will Haywood had hunted buffalo with William Cody. He'd traded with Sitting Bull and Red Cloud. After running a road ranch on the Oregon Trail, he and Martha had realized the railroad north of the Platte offered better business prospects, so they'd packed their goods and, when the Platte was frozen, crossed over to make their new home at Plum Grove.

"Martha finally got herself a wood house," Will said. "After all the years of living in dugouts and soddies, she earned it." He smiled toward the kitchen, where Martha was now showing Mavis and Helen a few things about how she wanted the dining hall kitchen run. "I'd build her a gold-plated mansion if I could. She is the hardest-working woman God ever created." Will's face beamed with pride. "Back when we ran the way station—the Pony Express stopped there, you know—back in those days Martha went through nigh onto a hundred pounds of flour a day. Sold bread for fifty cents a loaf. Some days she earned nearly thirty dollars." Will shook his head. "But if I had it to do over, I wouldn't let her work that hard."

He swallowed. "We lost three babies during those years. I'll never forgive myself for that. And I'll never stop thanking God he gave us Linney to help raise." He looked around the table. "No, Linney isn't ours. Not by blood, anyway." He put his open palm to his heart. "But she stole into our hearts the day her pa brought her into town and asked for help." He paused. "But that's a story for another day. You want to hear about the land."

He took a deep breath. "I've no interest in being a land agent and telling tall tales to get folks to buy. But I believe in Dawson County, and I can show you the places that are going to get snapped up first."

"When can you take us?" Ella asked.

Will smiled. "How's tomorrow morning at first light sound?"

"Exactly right."

Martha called from the kitchen doorway. "Show them Matthew's place first." She smiled at the ladies. "You all need to see that a soddy isn't all that bad. You might have heard some horror stories at the social Friday night about leaking roofs and varmints. The truth is, I felt snug as can be in our little house." She glanced at Will. "Will was the one who seemed to feel bad about it. More than me. Our old place is mostly washed away now, but the Ransoms' is fixed up real nice. You'll see what I mean."

She was not one to cause a ruckus, but as Will Haywood pulled his wagon to a halt in front of Jeb Cooper's place, Caroline wondered—almost aloud—if westerners really did have a different dictionary than the rest of the world. Folks seemed to agree that "near town" could mean as much as a day's drive away, and Martha had already said that "spring" could mean "snow." And yesterday she had used "cozy" to describe life in a soddy. That was not the word that came to mind as Caroline stared at the dead bits of grass sticking out between the mud-brick walls that were Jeb Cooper's house. "Interesting ornamentation," she muttered, and nodded toward the roof, where several rather impressive sets of antlers lay atop hand-hewn shingles. Well. At least the roof was decent. If it didn't leak.

Crumbling plaster was falling off the "entryway," where the front door hung a good two feet back into the wall. Someone had stuffed rags in the gaps between the sod wall and the warped wood frame around both sets of double-hung windows. From where Caroline sat nestled in the hay of Will Haywood's wagon bed, she could see a collection of barrels and boxes stacked against one side of the house. Just thinking about the creatures that might inhabit a trash pile like that made her thankful her tender ankle gave her an excuse for staying in the wagon. She exchanged glances with Ruth, admiring Ruth's ability to manage a smile, albeit a weak one.

Zita got up and perched behind the wagon seat where Ella sat beside Mr. Haywood. "Mr. Cooper has a windmill," she said. "That means fresh water near the house."

"He told me he had a spring, too," Ella said. "And a barn."

"The barn's back there," Zita said, pointing toward the back of the house as Mr. Haywood jumped to the ground and walked to the back of the wagon.

"He doesn't have a *barn*," Caroline muttered to Ruth. "He has a smaller mound of dirt near the big mound of dirt they're callin' a house."

"The barn was the original dugout," Mr. Haywood explained as he and Jackson helped Sally and Ruth off the wagon. "That's where the Ransoms were living when Linney was born. Matthew built the house the next spring."

"Linney?" Caroline spoke up. "Your Linney? I mean—the Linney you raised? I hadn't heard her last name."

Will nodded. "Linea Delight Ransom. My Martha was midwife when she was born. You never saw a happier couple than Matthew and Katie when that baby came into their world." He shook his head. "Time was Martha and I thought losing Katie just might kill Matthew. But selling this place seems to have done him some good." He sighed. "Linney will likely throw a pure fit when she finds out. But she'll come around. The way that girl loves her pa . . . she'll see it's for the best."

Will stared past Caroline at the soddy for a moment, then with a little shrug, he smiled. "It's too bad your ankle didn't let you stay a bit longer. You could have met Matthew. After he and Jeb escorted Lowell Day out of town and things quieted down, Matthew came back to dance with Linney. I'm not sure the girl's come back to earth yet. Last Friday was the first time her pa's been to a social since Katie died." He broke off.

"Anyway, this is their place, and it's seen love and heartbreak, and now it's got a new owner. And if I don't stop jawin', it'll be dark before I get everyone back to town and Martha will have my hide."

When Will offered to help her down, Caroline shook her head. "If you don't mind, I think I'll wait right here," she said, and motioned to where the others waited by the soddy door. "Hettie said I should be careful, and"—she stared pointedly at the deep ruts in the mud running alongside the house toward the barn—"I surely don't want to turn it again."

"Well, now, that's perfectly all right," Mr. Haywood said. "There's no doubt this kind of life isn't for everyone. Not everyone is cut out of hardy stock." He glanced quickly at Caroline. "Not that I was saying you— I mean, I meant no offense."

"And none was taken," Caroline said quickly. As Will hurried off to open the door so the ladies could go inside the soddy, Caroline glowered. "I'm hardy," she muttered. *Oh, really? Hardy women don't let a wall of earthen bricks scare them off. Hardy women don't stay in the wagon. Hardy women make a point NOT to be the southern belle everyone expects them to be. Hardy women—*

Caroline got out of the wagon and limped after the others.

It wasn't as bad as she thought it would be. The door opened onto a good-sized room with one set of double-hung windows next to the front door and another set into the wall on the right. The plastered walls had once been white, and even with the layer of dirt on them now, Caroline could imagine that on a sunny day this room might be almost cheerful.

When she said so, Ruth nodded toward the wide window ledge where half a dozen houseplants had once soaked up sunlight filtering through the now dingy lace curtains. "That one looks like it could have been the start of a rosebush," Ruth said, pointing at the tallest of the dead plants.

"My Martha favored geraniums," Will said. "You'll find that most of the soddy window ledges are crowded with one kind of plant or another. Martha started some of her garden seeds that way, too."

"Mrs. Ransom was right smart," Sally said, and crossed to where a collection of dry-goods boxes stacked atop one another served as a cupboard. "That's a good way to get yerself a pantry." She traced the scalloped edging tacked to the edge of each shelf. "And this here's pretty. It must have taken a while to cut that outta papers." She pointed down to the worn braided rug beneath the small table in the center of the room. "I could make us one of them," she said. "I don't know lace makin' and that other fancy stuff, but I'm right smart at rag rugs and braids and such."

"Martha was right," Zita declared. "It's all very cozy."

Ella nodded agreement even as she pushed a tattered quilt aside and peered into the back room.

Ruth pointed to the quilt that formed the makeshift door. "That was beautiful once," she said, running her hand over the surface of meandering vines and appliquéd flowers.

Sally moved from the cupboard toward a sewing machine sitting in front of one of the windows. "Don't imagine Mr. Cooper has much call for this," she said. "I wonder if he'd barter for it if I made him some shirts or new curtains or somethin'."

"If you can sew," Will said, "you'll be as busy as you want to be as soon as word gets out."

"Well, let's see if Mr. Cooper wants it first," Sally said. "And if he don't, then you can get word out all around these parts." She glanced over at Zita. "Chickens don't need all that much tendin', do they? I mean—I'll have time for sewin', too. Right?"

Zita nodded. "We'll see to it."

Hettie wondered aloud what use Mr. Cooper might make of the beautiful cradle.

"Well, I hope he don't turn it into a grain bin or somethin'," Sally said. "It's too pretty for that."

Sally was right. The cradle boasted graceful lines and a fine oiled finish. It made Caroline sad just to think about what it represented in the way of lost dreams. Something that well crafted was meant to be an heirloom, used and reused and then handed down to the next generation. As tears threatened, she looked away.

A framed bit of needlework hanging above the front door bore lettering stitched in deep red thread surrounded by clusters of pink and red roses. It advised the viewer to *Hope On ♦ Hope Ever*. A good sentiment. At that moment Caroline's hope was that sweet

Linney Ransom would have a good life in spite of the way things had started out.

What was it Zita had said on the train . . . something about forgetting what was behind and pressing on to hope. As Caroline looked around at the group of women, she realized that each one had chosen hope in her own way, and—

Ruth screeched and pointed down at a black snake as big around as Caroline's wrist emerging from the spot where the rough board floor met the wall.

"Wow!" Jackson exclaimed, and with a mixture of boyish curiosity, surprise, and what Caroline thought might be a bit of fear, he headed for the snake.

"Don't you dare!" Ruth gasped as she grabbed his arm. "It could be poisonous!"

Mr. Haywood spoke up. "Naw, that's just a big old bull snake. Probably spent the winter under the floor feasting on field mice. I imagine all the stomping above his head scared him out."

"Can snakes hear stomping?" Jackson asked.

"Well, now . . ." Will frowned. "I don't rightly know, I guess. But he probably *felt* it and decided to skedaddle."

Caroline might not be afraid of mice, but gigantic snakes were another matter entirely. Feeling shaky, she plopped down in a chair. Hettie ordered her to put her head down and laid a cool hand on the back of her neck.

Ruth gave a nervous little laugh. "I suppose the poor thing is as terrified as me. Will it freeze outside?"

"Hard to say," Will replied. "Weather can change fast this time of year—as you ladies have already seen."

When Ruth told Jackson to take the creature "down to the dugout and let it go," Caroline sat back up. "Are you serious? You're gonna just let it go?"

"Well, if snakes eat mice . . . why not? I *hate* rodents," Ruth said.

"I want to see the dugout too," Ella said, and opened the door for Jackson.

When the two had left, Ruth glanced at Mr. Haywood. "Can I impose on you to give him a snake lecture on the way back to town?"

Haywood nodded. "At yer service. The worst snake out this way is the rattlers. Good thing about them is they generally let you know where they are and what they're about to do." Raising his index finger, he wiggled it back and forth as he mimicked the sound of a rattle.

"Maybe Jackson ought to be learnin' to shoot," Caroline said.

Haywood laughed. "Well, if Mrs. Dow wants the boy to learn, I'd be pleased to show him a thing or two one of these days."

Caroline could show Jackson a thing or two about shooting, too. But she wasn't certain that was something to boast about just now. The other women might expect her to go out and kill a buffalo or something, and while Caroline might have decided to try and redefine herself according to the western dictionary, she didn't think she was ready to go that far. At least not yet. For now it was quite enough to work on things like *spring snow* and *near to town* and *cozy*. Perhaps even *hope*.

Hettie spoke up for the first time. "It's quiet in here," she said. "I like that."

Mr. Haywood smiled. "Soddies have their advantages. They're quiet. Cool in summer, warm in winter. Matthew told me once this place cost him a grand total of twelve dollars. The truth is, you ladies would have been a lot more comfortable if you would have been here instead of at the Immigrant House the other night when that storm blew through. Three-foot-thick walls keep out the wind."

Caroline stood up. "Well, then. I say it's high time you show us your ideas for where Ella's place ought to be."

*"Ella's place,"* Zita repeated. "I like the way that sounds."

Back outside, some of the ladies headed for the wagon while Caroline and Ruth went to look for Jackson and Ella. They found the two looking down at a weather-beaten cross marking a lone grave a short walk from the back of the house.

" 'Carissima,' " Jackson read aloud. "But there's no date. No last name." He frowned. "Why wouldn't they put up a proper marker?"

"I imagine it was proper to whoever did it," Ruth said as she came to stand beside them. " 'Carissima' means *beloved*. It's Latin."

"How do you know that?" Jackson asked.

Ruth smiled at him. "Just another one of those mysterious things your mother knows."

Mr. Haywood and the others came around the side of the house. "Well, I'll be . . ." He stared at the ornate iron fence surrounding the grave. "Where do you suppose Matthew got this?" He ran his hand along a cluster of iron oak leaves and acorns. "I've never seen such fine work." Before he could say any more, a booming baritone voice sounded from just the other side of the ridge running behind the house.

As Caroline and the others watched expectantly, first two oxen and then the hulking figure of a lone man came into view. He was singing at the top of his lungs, "My hope is built on nothing less than Jesus' blood and righteousness. I dare not trust the sweetest frame, but wholly lean on Jesus' name." After a brief pause filled by the lowing protest of oxen, the voice continued to sing, "On Christ the solid Rock I stand; all other ground is sinking sand . . . all other ground is sinking sand."

The singing stopped as Mr. Haywood raised his hand and hollered a greeting. While the ladies waited by the grave, Jeb Cooper drove the lumbering oxen down the hill and toward the sod enclosure beside the hovel he was using for a barn.

Leaving the oxen standing by the primitive corral, Cooper walked toward the group gathered by the grave. "I cannot seem to keep those beasts at home," he said. "I truly meant to be here all day." He turned toward the ladies. "I hope you went on in and saw the house. I apologize for the grime. I haven't had time to clean much yet." He looked around. "There's a lot to do."

"It's a good house," Ella said. "I hope I can do as well."

Will spoke up. "I'm taking them to the cottonwood spring from here. You've seen it, I imagine."

Jeb nodded. "Indeed. I even thought of buying it." He glanced Ella's way. "There's no doubt you'll want it."

Ella hesitated. "But if you want to buy it, perhaps—"

The only way to tell that Jeb Cooper was smiling was the crinkles at the corners of his eyes. Still, Caroline thought him a very pleasant-looking man if a lady concentrated on the eyes and forgot about his resemblance to a grizzly bear. His deep voice was gentle as he smiled at Ella and said, "Good neighbors are more important than amassing much land."

A faint blush on Ella's cheeks made Caroline smile. She looked back at Mr. Cooper to see if he'd noticed, but he was looking toward his broken corral gate.

"You got a right nice sewin' machine . . . and such," Sally said.

Cooper nodded. He studied Sally for a moment, then asked, "You wouldn't know anyone who'd be interested in taking it off my hands, would you? I'm such an ox, and the way that front room is set up I keep bumping into it. I want to move the table over by the window. It'd be a shame for a machine like that to end up out in the barn, but I don't have an inch of extra space in the back room, either."

Sally scratched the back of her neck and tugged on a strand of red hair, twisting it around a finger as she said, "Might be I could earn it from ya. Make some new curtains and shirts and such."

"We have a deal, Mrs. Grant. I'll bring it over as soon as you're settled." He looked Ella's way. "And I'll hope that's over at the cotton-wood spring."

Sally whooped with delight.

Jackson spoke up. "Mother said to be sure and tell you . . . a big bull snake crawled out from under the floor inside. I let it go down there." He pointed toward the dugout barn.

"Thank you." Cooper nodded. "Perhaps he'll have the rat that's been eating my seed corn for supper this evening."

Will spoke of the fence again. "I'm wondering how Matthew got something like this into Plum Grove without the whole town talking about it."

"I brought it." Jeb nodded toward his wagon. "Beneath a false bottom in my wagon." He ran his hand along the iron rope that formed a swag for each section of fence. His voice mellowed as one finger traced the outline of a leaf. "I had just enough to fence in the grave. It worked out well." Everyone was quiet for a moment, and then Jeb looked up with a smile. "Well, I really should get to repairing the corral gate. Again." He pulled his glove back on with his teeth and, wishing them a good day, headed back toward the corral.

As Will drove the wagon across Jeb Cooper's land toward what he was calling "the cottonwood spring," Ella pointed at the dugout barn and a wooden stake jutting above a tuft of tall grass. "Is that the official surveyor's stake?"

"Probably."

Ella pondered that for a moment. "You said Mr. Ransom's family started out in the dugout. If that stake marks the property line running north and south, doesn't that mean the house and the dugout are on two different claims?"

Will smiled. "You don't miss much, do you, Mrs. Barton?"

Ella blushed at the unexpected praise. If Will Haywood knew

how very much she had "missed" in the past, he wouldn't have that admiring look on his face right now. Still, it was nice to be complimented. She pressed her point. "But the Homestead Act specifically says that each head of household can claim exactly a hundred and sixty acres."

"Right again." Haywood nodded. "And so, to get around that limitation, family members sometimes file on adjoining homesteads. In the eyes of the law, the land belongs to two different people, but practically speaking, it's one big spread. That's what you see at Mr. Cooper's place. Technically, Mr. Cooper's barn isn't really on the homestead he purchased from Matthew Ransom."

Ella frowned. "So will Mr. Cooper have to build a new barn?"

"I haven't heard if that's going to be a problem or not." He shook his head. "It's a shame it didn't work out. Matthew and his cousin came out here together and filed on their places on the same day. The plan was for Matthew's place to supply the hay and crops and his cousin to run cattle. The plan was also for them both to be rich within ten years." Haywood paused. "It just might have worked, too."

"Why didn't it?" Sally called out from the back.

Ella glanced behind her. The ladies in the wagon bed were all looking at Will, waiting for him to answer Sally's question. To Ella's mind, Will looked like a man trying to formulate a partial answer. Thinking about something he shouldn't say. Or didn't want to. She'd seen that look on Milton's face a thousand times. Whatever Will said next, it wouldn't be the whole truth.

When Will finally answered Sally's question, all he said was, "Lots of things, I suppose. The main thing was Katie. When she died, all those plans died with her." He slapped the reins and told his team to "Giddap."

He wasn't rude about it, but it was clear Will Haywood didn't care to say any more about Matthew Ransom's past. Ella sighed. It was a shame when family couldn't get along. It happened far too often.

As the wagon trundled across the spring prairie, Ella pondered the idea that had begun to form in her mind. She glanced up at the sky and toward the horizon and took a deep breath of fresh air. Nebraska made her smile. Mr. Cooper was right. It was important to have good neighbors. If Ella's plan worked out, both she and Mr. Cooper would have several.

CHAPTER
NINE

*Two are better than one;*
*because they have a good reward for their labour.*

ECCLESIASTES 4:9

Ella and Zita stood arm in arm looking down on the sweeping prairie before them. Zita said the few spots of remaining snow reminded her of white sails on a sea of pale green grass. Ella nodded at the metaphor even as she bent down and thrust her fingers into the grass, marveling at the thickness of it, the softness of it, the incredible vision it must be waving in the wind against a blue summer sky. She stood back up and gazed into the distance at the miracle springing from the soil. Just where the rolling plain before her began to rise toward the far-off horizon stood one towering cottonwood tree, with a trunk that three long-armed men might have trouble circumventing with outstretched arms.

"No one really understands how it could still be here," Will said. "Obviously the spring is the water source, but it's still a pure miracle that it hasn't been cut down. Overlanders have taken every stick of available firewood for miles on either side of both trails west, and the Platte's not that far south of us. But that tree still stands. You can imagine it's a familiar landmark to everyone from around here. Foraging cattle have rubbed off some of the bark, but it just keeps growing."

The other ladies were just now climbing down from the wagon

behind them, and Ella was glad, for she was barely winning the battle to keep from weeping with joy. Mama squeezed her hand. Dear Mama. She knew. Together, they walked through the damp grass, and as they walked, Ella thought of her new friends, of the places they came from, and what they might be thinking now that Ella was about to claim a homestead. Perhaps it was misguided to put words into their mouths, but Ella almost felt that in these past few days she had come to know these women well enough to hear their thoughts.

Ruth would be especially glad for that tree. Ella had seen the way her hand had lingered over the remains of the flowers on Jeb's window ledge and heard her exclaim over the early spring wildflowers just beginning to bloom.

Nervous little Hettie would likely find the broad expanse of prairie and sky almost frightening. She might contest Ella's idea of building near the cottonwood tree. "Wh-what if a storm brings down one of those limbs onto the roof?" she would say. And she would have a point, Ella thought as she continued to stride alongside Mama toward the place where Will paced, his head down, intent on finding boundary markers.

Jackson ran past them, his cheeks flushed, his head thrown back as he hollered and whooped. When a rabbit bounded out in front of him from behind a tumbleweed, Jackson tried to swerve, but then tripped, rolled, and sprang up again, laughing and flailing his arms up and down, a youthful hawk soaring low across the earth.

If she wasn't already thinking on which of Martha Haywood's fabrics to use for Jeb Cooper's shirts, Sally was undoubtedly envisioning chicks everywhere, following their mother hens as they pecked and scratched. She might be thinking on wolves and coyotes, as well. It was easy to envision Sally, her feet planted, her apron blowing in the wind, raising a shotgun to her shoulder and pulling the trigger as she swore at some varmint that had the temerity to threaten her flock.

Caroline, who had climbed down with the rest but was lingering near the wagon nursing her sprained ankle, was the hardest one to predict in all of this. She was the one who still gave Ella pause. It was hard for a woman who looked in the mirror and hated what she saw to be friends with someone like Caroline. Men had nearly fallen over themselves at the dance last Friday night in their eagerness to serve her lemonade or coffee or to just sit beside her. Only Jeb Cooper paid Ella any mind, and that was only after she'd gone back to the dance after helping Caroline and Mama back to the Immigrant House, and only because he wanted to talk about homesteading.

Mama was right about Caroline, though. Underneath the pin tucks and lace there really was a backbone. What's more, a wide streak of true kindness ran beneath the flattering smiles and the charm. If for no other reason than Caroline's kindness to Sally and young Jackson, Ella would have liked her. In spite of the tiny waist and all the rest. So while Ella might not be quite sure what Caroline was thinking as she stood back there by the wagon, she was hoping the thoughts tended toward the positive.

As she watched the others and tried to predict their reactions to this place, Ella and Mama continued to walk toward the little spring bubbling up out of the grass and trickling toward a small clear watering hole. Suddenly Ella tripped. On a stake. When she looked down at it in disbelief, Mama scolded softly, "Don't look so shocked, *cara mia*. You don't think God could lead you to something he had made certain was pounded in the ground he created just so his Ella could find it?"

Ella shrugged. "It's not a matter of *could* he, Mama," she said, and once again the tears threatened. "I just didn't think he *would*."

"So," Mama said, looking up at her. "What do you think now?"

Ella's voice broke as she whispered, "I think I'm home."

Dawn was some time away, but Ella couldn't sleep. She'd been awake for what felt like hours, working things out in her mind. She wanted to make her plan sound simple for the others, but if she'd learned anything from her life with Milton, even running an established farm in Missouri wasn't ever simple. Creating one out here in Nebraska would be a daunting task involving challenges that would begin the day a body set foot on their own land and likely end only when that body followed in the way of Katie Ransom. Just contemplating the largeness of the challenge made Ella tremble. With joy.

*Joy. How about that?* She'd almost forgotten how it felt to be excited about life. To be happy. Of course, Will Haywood had thought she was a little crazy when she asked to visit with him over at the mercantile last night. He'd been polite about it, but Ella could tell from the minute she started asking questions that his initial thoughts were that she was a bit daft. After all, he'd just told her about a similar arrangement that didn't work out at all. And those folks had been related. Ella's plan involved several women who'd been strangers only a week ago.

"Well, now," Will had drawled, leaning back against the mercantile counter and considering her idea. "I suppose it *could* work." He repeated some of the figures he'd shared as they rode back to Plum Grove last evening. "A yoke of oxen will run you about two hundred dollars. A milk cow or two is another hundred. Shoats run five. Hens are fifty cents."

"I already have the hens," Ella reminded him.

"So you do."

"What if I don't buy oxen? Are there homesteaders who would hire out to do my plowing?"

Martha put her hand over Will's and said, "Most charge about five dollars an acre to cut sod. The house you saw today is about what you can expect to build from that acre. You'll need considerably more." She smiled. "You should ask Mr. Cooper if he'd be interested in hiring on to do the sod-busting."

Ella shook her head. "He has too much to do already. He said as much today."

"He said he was too busy to turn sod for you?"

"Well, not exactly."

Martha nodded. "Then you should ask. He might be offended if you made other arrangements when he's right there nearby—at least as we all define 'near.'" She glanced at Will. "You could ride up Luke's way, too. See if he could spare a few hands for a building bee."

Ella didn't care for that idea. First there was the notion that Lowell Day worked for the man. Second was Ella's firm belief that a man as beautiful as Lucas Gray could not be trusted. On the other hand, if he could spare some good men willing to do what they were told for fair pay, Ella supposed she could get past the square jaw and the swagger. Still, to her mind, one Jeb Cooper was worth a dozen Lucas Grays.

Finally, Ella gave up on sleeping. Rising and dressing in the dark, she made her way down the Immigrant House hallway toward the kitchen. Once there she lit a single lamp and sat down at the table. In the golden circle of lamplight she began to maneuver saltshakers, sugar cubes, and coffee mugs, placing them in a dozen different configurations until finally she realized that the simplest plan was probably the best. She glanced toward the dormitory. *Now, if only the others will agree.*

It would be dawn soon. Setting the saltshakers and other things aside, Ella rose and lit more lamps. They had been eating their meals over in Martha Haywood's dining hall, but this morning would be different. This morning they had business to discuss.

Ella had just mixed up the flapjack batter when Mama slipped into the kitchen, still in her wrapper. "I can't sleep, either." She reached for the coffeepot. "I'll get this started."

"You should be resting," Ella protested.

"I can rest when I'm dead. Now leave the door open so the

lamps light my way to the water pump." Ella followed Mama outside and collected an armful of firewood. "Isn't it wonderful to have a pump right here by the back door?" Mama said. "We'll have one, too. Oh! Maybe we can even have a pump *inside*. That would be even better!"

"If the water table allows for it," Ella agreed, "it *would* be wonderful." She couldn't help but smile. Already Mama was planning for indoor plumbing in the wilderness. Next she would want a water closet. Ella chuckled at the idea of such a thing attached to a sod house. That would have to wait for the next house. The farmhouse that was already dancing in her dreams. *Dreams for another day. Stop riding clouds and come back to earth, Ella.*

Jackson arrived first, rubbing his eyes as he stood in the kitchen doorway and stared at the table. "Breakfast is here today?"

"It is," Mama said, and waved him into a chair. "Wait until you taste my Ella's flapjacks." She leaned close. "Mrs. Morris's don't hold a candle to my Ella's. You'll see."

"Mama," Ella scolded gently. "Mrs. Morris's flapjacks taste fine."

"They do," Mama agreed. "As long as a person doesn't mind cutting their flapjacks with a sharp knife."

"Oh, Mama . . ." Ella shook her head. The truth was she'd heard complaints about Mavis's flapjacks. Martha had put Helen in charge of the griddle over at the dining hall. Ah, well, it gave Mavis something new to complain about, and everybody knew Mavis thrived on grousing.

A bleary-eyed Sally stumbled in next, going first to the stove and peering down at Ella's flapjacks before mumbling, "Thank goodness. I didn't think I could face another dining hall disaster."

Before long everyone was seated at the table laughing and joking about Ella's saving them from Mavis's cooking. When Mama elbowed her, Ella sat down at the head of the table.

"All right," Sally said, gesturing with her fork. "We all know you got somethin' up your sleeve. So let's hear what it is."

"I'll take over the griddle," Ruth said, heading for the stove even as Jackson cleared his plate—for the second time.

Looking around the table, Ella placed her palms on either side of her plate. "All right," she said. "I begin with this: I believe in my heart that it will work, but there will be no hard feelings if any one of you disagrees. Even if you agree that it will work, but you simply don't want to do it, that is fine, too." She hesitated.

"Hard to know if we want to do 'it' until we know what 'it' is." Sally yawned.

Ella nodded. "All right." She took her knife and fork and laid them at right angles in front of her plate. "Imagine the table is a section of land. The knife and the fork represent the imaginary lines established when Dawson County was surveyed. Four homesteads meet exactly here." She balanced a lump of sugar over the intersection of knife and fork. "And this—" she upended a small empty cracker tin and settled it over the lump of sugar—"this is a house. A sod house like the one we saw yesterday. But it's only the main room. Stove, table and chairs, cupboard"—she glanced at Sally—"perhaps a sewing machine by the window."

"Where's the chicken coop?" Sally joked, and the women chuckled.

"Now this," Ella said, and looked around the table, "is where each of you comes in." She added two more small tins, one to either end of the box in the center, balancing them on the knife. Putting one hand atop each of those small tins, she explained, "These are the bedroom wings added on either side of the living space. As you can see, someone who sleeps on this side of this bedroom"—she traced a line down the edge of one box—"would technically be sleeping on a different homestead than the person sleeping over here—" and she traced a line down the opposite side of the same box.

Ruth spoke up. "So this arrangement would allow four people to prove up on four different homesteads while they shared the main part of a house."

"Exactly." Ella nodded. She sat back and waited for the others to ponder the idea.

Mama spoke up as she reached between Caroline and Sally to refill their coffee mugs. " 'Two are better than one; because they have a good reward for their labour.' The wisest man who ever lived said that. If two are better than one, what could six accomplish if they worked together?"

"But Ella's plan only allows for four," Ruth said.

"I told Ella I'd rather we all stay together than to have my own land," Mama said.

Hettie spoke up. "I . . . I don't want my own land." She dropped her voice. "I . . . I didn't really plan this trip. It was sort of . . . well . . . sort of a fast decision." She gave a nervous little laugh. "I imagine you've all figured that out by now. I didn't even have my own trunk when we unloaded." She cleared her throat. "I know I said the railroad lost it." She looked down at her lap. "I lied. I'm sorry." She nodded at Ella's model on the table. "I'd work hard just for room and board. If you'd have me."

"I have to have land in my name," Ruth said. "Maybe I could get something nearby, but—"

Caroline smiled. "Well, I think it's obvious to all of us that you're one of the four." She grinned. "After all, we aren't about to give up Jackson."

"Does that mean *you* want to do this?"

"Now, don't ya'll sound so surprised," Caroline said. "Just because I didn't run about Jeb Cooper's place shoutin' glory hallelujah doesn't mean I want to spend my life sellin' geegaws to the ladies who come into Martha's mercantile." She chuckled. "Even though I *am* very good at it." She gestured toward the model. "It's brilliant, Ella." She glanced around the table. "But we need sleepin' quarters for *seven*."

"What about a loft over the two bedrooms?" Hettie suggested. "One side for Jackson, one for me"—she glanced around—"if th-that's all right with everyone."

"All right, then," Ella said, and pointed to the parts of the model. "Sally here, Caroline across from her. Ruth here with Jackson in the loft above, and—" She glanced Ruth's way. "Do you think you can put up with me?"

"What about Zita?"

"Zita," Mama said quickly, "wants a dressing screen around her cot in the corner of the kitchen near the stove, where her old bones can stay warm. And a rocking chair. And indoor plumbing. And plastered walls like Mr. Cooper had. And a window right by her cot so she can smell blooming flowers every morning when she wakes up." She clasped her hands together and made a show of inhaling deeply.

"Is there anything else you'd like, Mama?" Ella laughed.

Mama twitched both eyebrows. "I want to be young for just one dance with that handsome rancher. Or an evening." She grinned wickedly. "Or perhaps even a very long evening."

"Mama!" Ella scolded.

"You don't want to know, don't ask." With a flick of her wrist toward Ella, Mama brought the subject back to the house by pointing at the model. "So. Tell us how we build it."

"First a breaking plow slices the sod and lays it over." Ella gestured as she spoke.

"And where do we get such a plow? And who uses it?"

"Martha suggested we ask Mr. Cooper. She said the plow that was used to build that house is probably still in the barn. She seemed to think he might be offended if we didn't ask his help." Ella frowned. "But after he spoke of all he has to do—"

"We could offer to clean up the house for him," Sally said. "Then he wouldn't have so much to do."

"I'd be happy to help with that," Caroline said. "I'm not gonna be much use with the buildin' until this ankle heals."

"I'll do whatever needs doing," Ruth said from her place at the stove. "But please, Ella. Explain the process. Just how, exactly, does one build a sod house?"

Ella described how the cutting plow laid over strips of sod. "Those we cut into three-foot lengths and then we lay up the walls like so many bricks. We fill the seams between the sod strips with more dirt. The windows and doorways are set in place and the walls rise around them. We hammer pegs through the door and window frames into the sod to keep them in place."

"And stuff rags around them," Caroline muttered.

"No," Ella said firmly. "No rags. With no offense to anyone, I thought that looked . . . shabby. *We* will seal things tight and keep them in good repair. And we will plaster our walls. At least the inside ones. But that comes later—after the roof. Once the walls are up, a ridgepole is laid at the top and then the roof is added. And we'll want shingles if we can find someone to make them." She sat back. "I can plow and haul sod bricks and do almost everything else, but I don't know how to make shingles and I don't know how to put on a roof."

"H-how long will it all take?" Hettie asked.

"Will said that if we file on the land right away, we could be moved in by the end of the month."

"That soon?" Several said it at once. Laughter rippled around the table and then everyone began talking at once.

"We'll want to make a list of everything each of us brought with us," Ruth said.

"Teapots," Caroline said. "We have enough teapots to host a county-wide tea party."

"What about a lean-to on the back of the main room?" Ruth said. "To keep our firewood out of the weather. And I've two pair of lace curtains. Did anyone else bring curtains?"

"What we gonna cook on?" Sally asked. She nodded at Mama. "Zita said she makes good soup. Looks like she'll be makin' a lot of it."

"We need a big stove," Ruth said. "And a good-sized table."

"We should go over to Haywoods' as soon as they open and order a stove," Mama said.

"How m-much is that going to cost?" Hettie frowned.

"I can buy the stove," Ruth said, "if it isn't too expensive."

"We need to keep an account book," Caroline said, "but I've got no idea how to make that work."

"You'uns figure out how to make it work," Sally said, and stood up. "I told Mavis and Helen I'd help serve breakfast over at the dining hall."

"But . . . don't you have more questions?" Ella asked.

"Probably. But none I gotta ask right now." Sally pointed around the table. "We've got sewing, cooking, knitting, doctoring, livestock, plowing, and"—she put her hand over her heart—"a first-rate henhouse tender. The way I see it, we got everything we need for our human henhouse, too. And a boy thrown in for good measure." Sally headed for the door. "Just tell me when to climb on the wagon." And with that, she took her leave.

"A wagon," everyone said at once.

"Yes," Ella nodded. "We do need a wagon. And a team."

Caroline spoke up. "I've got a hundred dollars," she said. "That's all my money. But I'll put it in." She glanced Jackson's way. "Jackson and I were going to make a little visit to the livery later today. I'll see what can be done about a wagon and a team—if that's all right with y'all?" She looked pointedly at Ella. "I . . . I know about horses. I was my daddy's stableboy."

"If the railroad will refund the part of my ticket I didn't use," Hettie said, "maybe I can put in something. I've only got two dollars to my name right now."

"You'll be tending folks and bringing in who knows what once word gets out that we've got the next best thing to a doctor on our place," Ella said. Then she looked around the table and asked, "It is settled, then? We are agreed?"

When everyone nodded, Mama said, "May the Lord bless it."

"M-maybe we should ask him, too," Hettie said.

And so they did.

*For I know that in me (that is, in my flesh,) dwelleth no good thing:*
*for to will is present with me;*
*but how to perform that which is good I find not.*

ROMANS 7:18

Mrs. Jamison!" Linney sang out from her place behind the mercantile counter. "You're staying! Will said you're *all* staying. We're so glad!" She glanced down at the yard goods stretched on the counter. "And *I'm* glad you agreed to help at the store for a while. It's getting harder and harder to keep up with things, what with new people coming in every day and Martha so busy at the dining hall and the Immigrant House. It's too much for her. Will says it's too much and he's right." She frowned. "Oh, blast," she said. "Now I can't remember if this is a yard or a yard and two-thirds." With a sigh, she pulled out a yardstick.

"If you'll hand me a sheet of paper, I'll cut it into small squares and pin notes on each piece so you know what you've cut."

"That'd be fine," Linney said. She remeasured the fabric. "A yard and *one*-third." She motioned to the bolts of calico sitting at the far end of the counter. "Those are all just end pieces. Martha wants it all measured and rolled up and put in one of the new washtubs by the front door. She's hoping for a big crowd for the wedding."

"Wedding?"

"I thought you would have heard. James McDonald proposed to

Mrs. Smith while you ladies were gone with Will looking at home-steads. And she said yes."

"I didn't know there was another Mrs. Smith in Dawson County."

"Well, there isn't. I mean, it's the same Mrs. Smith. The one that came with you ladies."

"But . . . they hardly know each other."

Linney shrugged. "I guess they know enough." She leaned forward as if about to share a secret. "If you want to know what I think, I think it was *Davey* McDonald that made Mrs. Smith say yes. He needs a ma worse than anything, and he is awful cute. Mrs. Smith said it was love at first sight with her and Davey. Mr. McDonald telegraphed over to Cayote to have the circuit rider come here after he does all the weddings over there."

"*All* the weddings?" Caroline said.

Linney nodded. "Uh-huh. Five so far. All on the Sabbath."

*I wonder if the sisters are getting hitched. I wonder if they'll wear plaid.* Stifling a soft laugh at the idea, Caroline rolled the length of cloth up, tied it with a string, attached the paper with the measure-ment, and tossed it in the washtub. "Did you say Martha's opening the store on Sunday?"

"I know. It's the Lord's Day. But Martha says the Lord will under-stand that folks need a store open when they come to town, and sometimes that's Sunday." Linney tilted her head. "Do you think she's right? Will God understand that?"

Caroline didn't feel qualified to speak for the Lord. She could just imagine Mother Jamison's reaction. But then, Mother Jamison wasn't someone Caroline had ever wanted to emulate. Martha, on the other hand, was exactly someone to admire. God had always seemed so far away, Caroline had never considered that he might have an opinion about things like running a store, much less "understand" a business-woman's decision about hours. She reached for another bolt of cloth.

"Not that one!" Linney snatched it away. She counted the folds along the end. "Martha would have my head. There's still enough here for a dress."

"But who would want to *wear* it?!" Caroline blurted it out before she thought, then forced a laugh as she pointed to the bright orange calico. "Can you imagine twenty-some yards of that sashaying down Main Street?" She shuddered.

Linney giggled. "Well, you do have a point." She considered the fabric. "I think maybe the mill included it by accident."

"Or to get rid of it, hoping no one would notice."

Linney began to unwind it. "It wouldn't be so awful . . . in little tiny pieces. Maybe in a patch quilt?"

"There's no way to make that blend," Caroline said. She pondered the rest of the cloth in the washtub. "But maybe . . . if a woman scattered it about . . . with some dark blue . . . then it might . . ." She searched for a word . . . "glow. Or glimmer?"

"Shimmer," Linney said, savoring the word.

"Yes." Caroline nodded. "That's it. It will make your quilts shimmer."

"We should make a sign. If Mrs. Bailey comes in and we can get her to use it and talk about it, the rest of the ladies who come to town will likely buy it all by day's end. Everyone admires Mrs. Bailey's quilts. And wouldn't Martha be pleased if we sold all of it?"

The bell rang, announcing a customer. Linney looked up from her work and, with a squeal of delight, launched herself at the man who'd just come in the door. The man who'd rescued Caroline's parasol . . . carried her into the Immigrant House when she twisted her ankle . . . and now stood with Linney on his arm . . . staring at Caroline with those blue eyes.

"It's Mrs. Jamison, Pa. You remember her. From the dance."

Caroline could feel herself blushing. "A-actually, Linney . . . I didn't see your . . . pa. . . . I left when—"

"Oh . . . right. You left after Mr. Cooper escorted Lowell Day—" She cleared her throat. "Well . . ." Linney looped her arm through her handsome father's. "This is my pa, Matthew Ransom." She gazed up at him adoringly. "This is Mrs. Jamison, Pa. She's one of the Emigration Society members who stayed here in Plum Grove. And they're really staying. They're getting homesteads!"

Beneath the gaze of those blue eyes, a self-conscious Caroline reverted to her upbringing and bent her knees in a little curtsey, even though it pained her ankle to do it. "How do, Mr. Ransom. Pleased to meet you." She was aware that she grimaced and apologized. "I really am pleased . . . it's just that my ankle still pains me some."

"Pa-a," Linney sang out, sounding embarrassed when he still didn't speak.

Ransom started, then walked to where Caroline was standing beside the mercantile counter and held out his hand. "Excuse me, Mrs. Jamison. I've been out of proper society for so long, I'm afraid I've forgotten my manners." When Caroline extended her own hand toward him, he bowed low and touched the back of her hand with his lips. Or his beard. Either way, it deepened Caroline's blush.

Her heart hadn't pounded this way since that day at Union Station. That had been fear. What was this? *You are losing your touch, Miss Caroline. The ladies of Mulberry Plantation*—well. Whatever it was they did in situations like this didn't apply anyway, because now it was Caroline's turn to stare as she realized all in a rush that the man who rescued parasols and such was the very same man about whom Martha and Will had despaired for so long. The one they said was doing better. The one who had abandoned a perfectly nice little homestead on account of his wife's death. All of that flew through Caroline's mind in such a rush, she had to ask Mr. Ransom to repeat whatever it was he had just said.

"I was wondering if you would mind watching over the store for a few minutes for Linney," he said. "I've something I need to discuss with her. Something I intended to talk over last Friday."

How she knew it Caroline could not say, but at that moment the thought flashed through her mind and then fixed there. Matthew Ransom had not yet told Linney he'd sold her birthplace. She looked away to keep from showing her disapproval. She could see the flash of dread in Linney's eyes. The girl knew her father well. Caroline spoke, not to Matthew Ransom but to Linney. "I'll be right here, honey. You take all the time you need."

Martha returned to the store before Linney came back. Caroline told her what had happened—without her personal opinions attached as to a man's being a coward to do something so monumental behind a child's back—and then asked, as coolly as possible, "What is it exactly that Mr. Ransom does? Linney seemed surprised to see him."

"Oh, Matthew traps. Trades. Hunts." Martha frowned. "I can't remember the last time he came into Plum Grove twice in one week. Did he say *why* he was in town?"

"Only that he needed to speak with Linney," Caroline said. She bit her lower lip to keep from saying more and concentrated on tying the knot around a small roll of calico.

"By the way, that 'shimmering' idea is a good one."

"It was as much Linney's idea as it was mine." The silence grew uncomfortable. Finally, Caroline spoke up. "This is none of my affair and I will say that for you. But the fact is, I like Linney." She swallowed. "He came to town to tell her he's sold her home, didn't he? Without discussing it with her. He just went and did it."

Martha gazed out the front store window. "I'm afraid so." She sighed.

"Well," Caroline said. "I can understand why he might not want to go on livin' there. And I can even see his sellin' it if he's wantin' to move forward. But not tellin' Linney until it's done? That is just downright cowardly."

Martha sighed again. "You're right. The thing is—Matthew would probably agree with you. That's not who he is . . . who he was—" She broke off. Shook her head. "If you could have seen him with Katie." Martha paused. "I am so sorry, Caroline. Now I'm the one who's being insensitive. You know how Matthew feels much better than I ever could. You've been widowed, too. Again, I apologize."

Caroline waved the apology away. "Marryin' Basil was a childish act of defiance. My daddy said it was a stupid thing to do, and he was right. I may be a widow, but I've no idea what it's like to have someone you deeply love die." She faltered. "Which, I suppose, means I've got no right to say unkind things about Mr. Ransom behind his back."

Martha didn't speak to that. Instead, she spoke of Linney. "She likes you, and she's getting to an age where a girl needs someone besides her mother—or the woman who raised her—to talk to." She covered Caroline's hand with her own and squeezed it, then went back to measuring calico, talking while she worked.

"Matthew and Katie had just set up camp on their claim when Will carried me across that threshold." She nodded toward the mercantile doorway. "My, but they were a beautiful pair. Purely crazy over one another. Matthew had just finished the soddy you saw yesterday when his team bolted. The wagon overturned and they were all three thrown out. It's a wonder they weren't all killed."

Caroline glanced up at Martha, who was standing still, gazing into the past as she murmured, "I'll never forget it as long as I live. I was standing right behind this counter and Matthew came into the store. He looked like he'd been in a terrible fight. And he moved like he was a hundred years old. He'd been hurt in the accident, too, but he didn't even seem to feel it. He had Linney by the hand and a little bundle tied up with her things in it. He picked her up and set her right here on this counter," Martha said. "And all he said was 'Katie's gone, Martha. I lost her. And our baby.' I didn't even know Katie was expecting again. They hadn't told anyone. He almost broke down when he said that, but he managed to ask me if I could keep Linney for him until he decided what to do." Martha sighed as she returned to the moment, her gaze meeting Caroline's. "That was nearly eight years ago."

Just hearing the story opened up something deep inside Caroline. She thought of Hettie and the way she trembled when the subject of husbands came up. Poor Hettie couldn't even talk about her husband without crying. Ruth made no secret of the fact that her General had been "the love of her life." And now all of this about Matthew Ransom's broken life. It shamed Caroline that all she felt about poor Basil's being gone was relief.

Martha sighed. "Linney's grown up with Will and me just as much as her pa. But Matthew loves that girl. Oh, how he loves her. You call him a coward and maybe you're right. Maybe there is cowardice in not telling her about selling the place. But it was no coward who brought me his little girl all those years ago. That was a man protecting his child from seeing what he might do or say while he grieved for Katie. He gave up everything when she died. Moved out of the house . . . just left it all the way it was. The last time I went with Linney to put flowers on her mother's grave, the house hadn't changed a bit. Katie's needlework was still hanging above the front door."

"*Hope On, Hope Ever*," Caroline murmured.

"That's it. That's the one."

"Linney will be devastated."

Martha nodded. "Yes. At first. But she's also uncommonly wise for a child her age. And after she gets past being angry with him for the *way* it was done, I think she'll see it as a sign he's letting go of the past—in a good way. She dreams of keeping house for him. She's even begged him to move to town. Maybe that's going to happen." Martha smiled. "Wouldn't that be something. After all this time."

Caroline finished tying up the last bundle of orange fabric. She carried the washtub full of remnants to the door and placed it right where a woman would see it the minute she set foot in the mercantile. She gestured to the tub. "I could make a sign."

"A sign would be grand."

As Caroline lettered a sign, Martha cleared the countertop of the empty cardboard around which the fabric pieces had been wrapped. She brought another box from the supply room and began to arrange cards of black jet buttons on a shelf inside one of her glass display cases. Every sound had her looking toward the door.

*Look! Remnants at the best prices! Make your quilts shimmer!* Caroline had just set her sign in place in the washtub when Linney bolted through the door, her face streaked with tears, her father at her heels, pleading for her to listen.

"I'm sorry. I was wrong. I'm so sorry, baby girl."

Linney whirled about. Swiping at her tears with the back of one hand, she said, "Don't call me your baby girl! Don't you ever say anything to me again!" She ran out of the room. Caroline could hear her stomp up the outside staircase leading to the living quarters over the store. The door slammed. Caroline couldn't think what to do. A trapdoor beneath her feet would have come in handy at that moment. When she finally managed to move, Matthew Ransom was still standing by the washtub. Caroline slipped by him and out the door.

Matthew sat up, his body drenched in sweat, his beard soaked with tears. Time was supposed to heal all wounds, wasn't it? Then why was he having *more* nightmares just when he was trying to break the bonds that kept dragging him into the past? Selling the homestead was the right thing to do. And yet these past couple of nights had been among the worst in recent memory. *Well, what do you expect? You're such a coward. Afraid to face your own daughter. Going behind her back. You should have told her and taken her out there. Packed Katie's things together. Made sure she met Jeb Cooper right away. She'd like Jeb and you know it. That would have helped. Coward. Fool.*

With a sigh Matthew swiped at his face with the back of his hand. Some nights he thought that if he had eyes to see the spirit world, he would see Katie or an angel or his mother or maybe even Jesus himself looking down on him with sad, disappointed eyes.

At times like this it didn't do any good to try and go back to sleep. He'd just lie there and debate the ghosts in the room, and he'd end up in the same place he always did.

Feeling lost and bitter and as if those things Jesus said about forgiving others just didn't apply in some cases. It had taken Matthew long enough to get to the point of forgiving Katie. But he'd done it.

He'd finally gathered enough pelts for Martha to order a proper tombstone, too. A metal one from Iowa with a border of oak leaves all around the lettering that no amount of weather would ever wear away. Katie had lamented the absence of oak trees out here. She would have them on her gravestone at least, and he would plant another one this year. Cooper would be glad to keep it watered, and Linney would like that, too.

*Linney.* What a mess he'd made of things earlier today. And right in front of Caroline Jamison. At least she had the decency to slip out the door and give him some privacy. He'd wanted to chase Linney up Martha's stairs, but Martha said no. *Give her some time, Matthew. You've handled this badly, but she'll come around. Just give her some time.* How much time was what Matthew wanted to know.

*Time.* It had taken him eight years of time to get to this point, but he had made progress, and with Jeb Cooper on the homestead, Matthew somehow felt that would free things up for both him and Linney. He wasn't ready to buy a place again, but he was at least thinking of spending more time in Plum Grove. In fact, he was almost ready to tell Vernon Lux he'd take that job building wagons and move into his back room. And didn't that show the progress he had made? As for the rest of it, the best he could do was to keep it buried where it could do no harm beyond his dreams. Some people did not deserve forgiveness, and no amount of dreaming or imagined whispers from the very mouth of God could change that.

With a sigh, Matthew threw back the tangle of furs he used for bedding. He rose and made coffee and fried an egg, savoring the rare treat. Martha had nestled a few eggs in straw in the pocket of his buckskin coat before he left town yesterday. "They won't make it back to the dugout," he'd protested.

"But even if only one does, won't it be a nice treat?" And it was. Especially with the yolk left runny to soak into the biscuit crumbs he sprinkled on top. Wide awake now, Matthew sat at his table and looked around the dugout. That stack of pelts collecting in the far corner might just be his last. With people pouring in to settle the area, the good days of trapping would be over soon.

Thoughts of newcomers in Dawson County made him think about Caroline—Mrs. Jamison—again. With a last swig of coffee, he stood up. After collecting a few tools, Matthew slid his rifle into its scabbard and stepped outside. As daylight washed the deep shadows off the hillside above his dugout, he pulled his door closed behind him. It was going to be a fine day. Sunshine. Warm air. Lifting his face toward the sky, Matthew said thank-you to whatever spirits might be listening. As he mounted his pinto pony, he saw a hawk soar across the sky in the distance.

Linney had a right to be upset with him. But she'd forgive him. She was better than he was in that. Linney had a forgiving heart.

*For my thoughts are not your thoughts,*
*neither are your ways my ways, saith the Lord.*

ISAIAH 55:8

One loud thwack, a few beats, another thwack, a few beats, another thwack. Whoever was working—and Matthew assumed it to be Jeb Cooper—was taking exactly one smack of a hammer to drive nails. That indicated both physical power and prowess. But what would Cooper be building? On a day like this a man should be plowing and planting. He'd never be a successful homesteader if he didn't. *It's not your homestead anymore. And it's definitely not your place to tell a man how to farm.*

Even after he topped the rise just behind the house and could see Cooper down below, Matthew wasn't sure what the man was building. The wagon stood near the back of the house. It didn't look like he'd unloaded anything, save for the pile of lumber they'd strapped atop all those boxes. A series of rectangular frames leaned against the back wall of the house to the right of the door. As he got closer, Matthew realized Cooper was hammering at yet another. Why would a man need that much shelving? Was he one of those hermits who laid in stores for a year so he wouldn't have to go to town? *Look who's talking.*

Cooper's oxen grazed off in the distance near a couple of cows, the latter staked out. They'd already grazed a semicircle clear. As Matthew watched, first one and then the other folded its legs and sank down into the grass, content to bask in the morning sunshine and chew their cud. A sow suckled her newborn farrow inside the small sod enclosure built for such. And then Matthew saw the spot on the prairie where his heart lay buried. *Inside an iron fence.*

Cooper looked up and called a greeting. He glanced over toward the grave, then back at Matthew. "I hope you don't mind." When Matthew still didn't respond, Cooper frowned. "If you don't want it, I'll—"

"No." Matthew swallowed. "It's not that. It's—" He dismounted and walked to the fence. "I've never seen ironwork like this. Where—how?"

"I made it," Cooper said, and drove another nail.

"You . . . made . . . this?" Matthew touched a cluster of leaves.

Cooper shrugged. He didn't look up. "I was a blacksmith before the war. Couldn't figure out how to do it with one hand. At least not as well as I used to, and I wasn't willing to settle." He drove a nail. "So now I'm a farmer. I'm a little worried about the plowing, but I believe I've about got it figured out."

He looked down at the forearm that ended in a stump. "I'm grateful for the elbow joint. It does make a difference. I can wrap the reins—" He broke off. Shrugged. "Anyway, I've about got it figured out." He pointed at the fence with his hammer. "I'm glad you don't mind about that."

"Mind? It's astonishing. But where was it when we took your freight off the train?"

"Already in the wagon I brought with me. Frankly, the fence is why I brought the wagon. It has a false bottom built exactly for the fence."

"But the boxes we loaded are still in the wagon."

Cooper shrugged. "Unloaded, reloaded—" He smiled. "After I met Linney, the fence took on a kind of urgency. I think it was meant to be, Matthew. I had exactly enough. Not one foot too much or too little. It's as if God was designing it long ago."

*Oak leaves.* The whole thing gave Matthew goose bumps. He scanned the back of the house. Cooper had cleared away the pile of old barrels and assorted debris from along one side. The rake that had been up on the roof was leaning against the wagon. Katie's overgrown garden was weeded. "It's obvious the right man bought the place," he said.

Cooper thanked him before pointing toward the shelves leaning against the house. "Lend a hand?"

"Happy to." As Matthew passed by the wagon he glanced into an open crate. *Browning. Longfellow. Defoe. Hawthorne. Euripides.* The idea of Jeb Cooper being a scholar didn't fit, either with blacksmithing or with plowing. Men who read books like that ended up teaching at universities. Didn't they?

"I am hatched from a long line of deep thinkers," Cooper said, as if he'd read Matthew's mind. "But I always preferred working with my hands. I am, therefore, a great disappointment to what little family I have left. My great-aunt expected my injury to finally show me the error of my ways." He shrugged. "This being polite company, I shall not repeat her last words to me as I drove away from the family home to begin a new life out here."

Matthew shouldered his part of the first empty shelf, and together the men took it inside. "You've sanded the floor," he said as they settled the shelf against a wall. "And whitewashed the walls."

"As to the floors, I couldn't risk a shelf toppling over. A man could get killed. Buried under books." Cooper smiled. "Not a bad way to die, I suppose. But I'm in no hurry. As to the rest, I had to get it done before moving the books in, or it never would happen. Don't be too impressed. The front room is still sadly in need of attention."

He laid a hand atop the sewing machine. "Help me take this out by the wagon, will you? I promised to deliver it to Mrs. Grant in return for her making a few shirts." He hesitated. "But maybe—" He scratched his beard. "I'm sorry, Ransom. I should have checked with you about it. Maybe you want it for Linney."

"If Mrs. Grant can use it, that's fine. Martha has one with all the newfangled gadgets. At least that's what Linney says." He paused. "I meant to bring her out here to see for herself that it's all for the best." He shook his head. "I've bungled things with Linney badly." He looked toward the front of the house, and suddenly everything seemed to be a treasure, from the framed motto above the door to the cradle to the cracked blue-and-white teapot.

Cooper's voice was gentle as he said, "There's a trunk by the front door that's full of things she should have."

*Katie's trunk. Her wedding dress. Her clothes. The baby's things . . .* The lump in Matthew's throat made it impossible to speak. He nodded.

"I've an idea," Cooper said. "You help me finish with the shelves and my books. Once the wagon's empty, we'll reload it with the things you want Linney to have. Take it all if you want. Obviously I can build anything I need—although I'd appreciate keeping the stove." He paused. "Tomorrow we'll take it all into town, and you can make your peace. I heard there's a circuit rider coming through. Thought I'd go to church. If things go well with you and Linney, I'll buy us all lunch at the dining hall. If not—well, we'll work that out, too."

Matthew had no interest in attending church, but seeing Linney was another matter. He hated the idea she was mad at him. And he missed her. Just looking at the cradle brought a fresh realization that his little girl was growing and he'd missed so much of it. It was time he talked to Vernon Lux.

Hettie and Ruth sat at the kitchen table in the Immigrant House, a dozen lists with headings like "Have" and "Need" and "Buy" and "Build" spread before them. Hettie ran her finger down the "Have" list, then shook her head. "No, it says right here that Ella and Zita brought two Dutch ovens, so we won't need to order one." She frowned. "Although I don't see that we have a frying pan."

Ruth turned to the appropriate page in the Wards catalogue. "What do you think?" she asked. "Twelve-inch or sixteen?"

"I . . . I don't know," Hettie said. "We'll be cooking for seven people three times a day. What do you think?"

"Sixteen," Ruth said, and wrote it down on the ever-growing list of things Martha Haywood would order for them.

"How are we going to afford all of it?" Hettie said, pointing at the list.

"A little bit at a time. After we get everyone's input, we'll have a meeting and prioritize."

"You're good at organizing things," Hettie said.

"I just thought of another list to make, though." Ruth stood up. "You can make this one by yourself. I need to get this catalogue back to Martha so she has it tomorrow. She's expecting a lot of business, what with the circuit rider and Helen's wedding."

"What kind of a list do you want me to make?"

"Medical supplies. So we have what you would need should anyone take sick or, God forbid, get injured."

Ruth left and Hettie began to write. *Carbolic*—when Sally burst in the back door with a man in tow.

"Here she is," Sally said, pointing to Hettie, "the closest thing to a doctor in town. I bet she can help." Sally stepped aside so the man and his petite wife could come in.

Hettie stood up, hurrying to collect the lists before they blew off the table.

"This here's Frank Darby," Sally said. "And his wife, Nancy. Nancy's feelin' poorly."

Indeed, before Sally was finished with the introductions, Mrs. Darby turned white as a sheet and plopped into a chair, her hand to her mouth.

The look of terror that came across Frank Darby's handsome face as he murmured "Darlin'," and put his hand on his wife's shoulder overcame Hettie's resistance. As she slipped into the chair nearest Mrs.

Darby, she reached for the woman's slim hand and leaned forward. "Tell me," she said, and looked up into the young wife's frightened eyes.

"I . . . I just can't keep a thing down," she said in a half whisper.

Hettie put her hand to the woman's forehead. Expecting to feel indication of a fever, she was pleasantly surprised.

"And I'm so tired all the time."

"That's not like my Nancy," the rancher said. "She's always been real pert."

Finally, as both the rancher and his wife listed the changes in her health in recent weeks, Hettie began to have trouble suppressing a smile. Finally, she adjusted her glasses and cleared her throat. "And your . . . personal . . . calendar . . . Mrs. Darby. Has it . . . changed?"

As the meaning behind Hettie's question dawned on the couple, Mrs. Darby's face turned scarlet. "Well," she said, so quietly Hettie had to lean close to hear it, "now that you mention it—"

"Mrs. Grant." Hettie looked up at Sally. "Would you be kind enough to go next door and see if Mrs. Haywood might send us a pinch of peppermint tea leaves?"

While Sally was gone, Hettie went about preparing to serve tea. "I believe it will settle your stomach," she said. Then she smiled up at Mr. Darby. "And if you'll give us a moment with the almanac"— she pointed to the little book she and Ruth had been using to plan a garden—"I believe we'll be able to predict just when Mrs. Darby will feel her old self again. Although, if I'm correct in my diagnosis, your lives are about to change in the most profound way possible."

When the rancher looked confused, his wife reached for his hand. "The doc thinks I'm . . . uh . . . in a family way, Bill."

The rancher's eyes showed amazement. "He—she—does?" He stared first at Hettie and then down at his wife. "Do *you?*"

"I suppose it was bound to happen sooner or later." She put her hand to her mouth. "I just didn't expect it to make me so *sick.* Mother was never sick a day. And I'm one of thirteen."

"Well," Hettie said as Sally returned, tea tin in hand, "every woman is different. But most find peppermint tea to be very helpful." She brewed the tea. The color returned to Mrs. Darby's face after only a few sips. With Hettie insisting that she didn't expect to be paid, the couple left.

Ruth returned a few minutes later with a message. "Martha said to tell you that you have five dollars on account at the mercantile." She smiled. "Mr. Darby was extremely grateful. Apparently he intends to tell everyone he knows that Plum Grove might not have a real doctor, but they've got the next best thing."

"Well, ain't that somethin'," Sally said, and patted Hettie on the shoulder.

Hettie forced a smile, but inside she trembled at the idea of Frank Darby's talking about the woman in Plum Grove who knew doctoring.

On Sunday morning while Zita, Ruth, and Ella worked on Helen Smith's wedding cake in the Immigrant House kitchen, Caroline and Sally headed over to the dining hall early to help rearrange things for the combination wedding/church service. As they moved tables to one side, Sally joked, "I suppose it's too much to hope for another dance tonight, it being the Sabbath and all."

"You never know." Caroline grinned. "The folks in Plum Grove don't seem to always observe the rules when it comes to the Sabbath. After all, Martha's going to open the mercantile after the service. I suppose if Bill Toady shows up with his fiddle, there'll be more than just you hoping for a dance. Although"—she smiled—"it might depend on whether or not the preacher stays in town. It wouldn't do for an up-and-coming town to offend a man of God."

As the two worked together arranging chairs, Will Haywood ⸱ked up three empty crates for a makeshift podium. Linney came in with a bunch of wildflowers she'd collected and tied with a bit of ribbon. "It's for Mrs. Smith," she said.

"What a sweet thing to do. Helen will be so touched."

"I saw her a little while ago and she looked nervous. I thought maybe some flowers would make her feel more like a real bride."

"Marriage is a big decision," Caroline said. "It's only natural to have second thoughts."

"Would you do it?" Linney asked abruptly. "Marry a stranger, I mean?"

Caroline smiled. "Well, in a way I did. As it turned out, I didn't really know my husband. But he looked so brave and so dashing in his uniform—"

"My pa was in uniform when he first saw my ma," Linney said. "He says he wasn't the most handsome one in the room, but I think he was."

Caroline turned away and began to straighten the row of chairs Sally had just arranged. "I'm sure he was very handsome," she said, in as noncommittal a tone as possible.

"You can't really tell," Linney said. "He's all scraggly right now." She sounded wistful. "But you should see him in their wedding picture. He's . . . beautiful. Oh, not like Ma was. But still—"

Sally broke in to suggest Linney seek out Mrs. Smith and deliver the bouquet personally. Then, as soon as the girl was gone, she made a show of fanning Caroline to help her "cool off."

Caroline waved her away. "All right. Enough of that. Point taken." She avoided Sally's eyes. "Maybe we should see what else we can do to help Martha." She glanced toward the kitchen.

Sally called her back. "I don't mean no harm when I tease you," she said. "I hope you know I just like joshin' with ya."

"I know," Caroline said.

Sally rubbed her arm. "I married a stranger, too, when it comes right down to it. And I won't make that mistake again, I can tell you that."

"Well, don't say that too loud," Caroline teased. "All those men who danced with you last Friday will be crushed."

"Aw, I was just havin' fun. I like to dance. Don't mean I want to get hitched. Don't mean I don't. But it ain't likely to happen anytime soon is all I'm sayin'." She shook her head. "How's a woman supposed to know what a man's really like, anyway?"

Caroline sighed. "I'm not sure."

"Well, I hope Helen don't regret what she's doin' today. Mr. McDonald seems nice enough, but—"

"I think we can believe the best for Helen. Little Davey McDonald loves his pa. If his child loves him, that's a very good recommendation for a man."

Sally grinned. "Linney sure loves her pa."

Caroline shook her finger like a schoolmarm scolding a naughty student.

"I'm just sayin'," Sally said, and sashayed toward the kitchen.

"You go on ahead," Matthew said, hopping down almost before Cooper's wagon came to a halt in front of the livery. "I'll see to the team. Then I'm going to take the small box of things on up to Martha's. We can unload the trunk and the sewing machine later. Depending." *Depending on how Linney reacts.*

"Linney might just be so happy to see you in church that she'll forget she's mad at you."

"She isn't likely to forgive quite that easily. Besides, I don't begrudge any man's personal religion, but God isn't doing me much good these days. I don't see the point in pretending I believe when I don't."

Cooper seemed to accept the answer, but then after only a few steps in the direction of the dining hall, he turned around and came back. "What you said about God not doing you much good. Does that mean there was a time when you thought he did—do some good in your life, I mean?"

Matthew shrugged. "You could say so. I was grateful for Katie. And for Linney. It felt like God was smiling down at times."

"But you don't feel that way anymore."

Matthew shoved his hands into his pockets. Looked toward the far horizon. Shook his head.

"I've had some of the same feelings. And for all the reading I've done—I have read most of those books you helped me unpack—I've yet to understand what philosophers call 'the problem of evil.' Some of the vilest men in my company sailed through the war with nothing worse than a powder burn. Some of the best died in horrible ways. None of it made much sense to me and most of it still doesn't." Cooper held up his stump. "And this? I don't understand why God would allow this at all."

"And yet you're still headed up the street to church."

Cooper thought about that for a minute, and then he smiled. "I'm not smart enough to have answers to all your questions, Matthew. I'd be lying if I said I did."

It was hard to believe a man who read Hawthorne didn't think of himself as being smart. "But you do have some kind of an answer."

Cooper sighed. "I'll tell you what. Someday when you've time for it, you stop by my place, and I'll let you read the book that helped me the most. Those questions you're struggling with—a man has to find his own way to the answers. Mine might not suit you at all. Besides, you already told me you've got no need to hear a sermon today. I respect that."

Cooper nodded toward the wagon. "Don't forget to ask Linney about the sewing machine, just to make sure. I'd like to settle with Mrs. Grant about it one way or the other before I leave town today." He smiled. "If things go really well and you want to bring her out to the homestead, maybe Ermisch would let us borrow a horse. We could hitch him to the wagon, drive home together, and then Linney and you could ride back to town in the morning."

"We'll see how things go."

Cooper took his leave and Matthew lounged beside the wagon, watching the considerable number of folks driving or riding into town. There was a flash of red hair up the street, and he caught a glimpse of Linney walking along with that boy whose mother was part of the "Desperation Society." Jackson. That was it. Jackson Dow. And his mother was Ruth. Katie had been married at seventeen. Linney would be seventeen in less than three years.

He looked down at the box in his hands, pained by how little remained on the earth to prove that Katie Ransom had lived. Oh, the trunk was full of clothing and quilts and such, but it was so very little to represent a life. A cracked teapot. A little quilt Katie'd been making for the new baby. A matching doll quilt she'd worked up for Linney, hoping to keep the little girl from being jealous. Her wedding veil. The set of silver spoons she'd brought from home. The elegant china cup and saucer—the only ones of the whole set that had survived the trip west. She'd cried over that. And then in the next month she'd created that framed needlework. *Hope On* ◆ *Hope Ever.*

*Hope.* He glanced up at the implement store sign. He might not have much in the way of hope, but he could give Linney some. He could tell Vernon Lux he'd give building wagons and living in town a try. And if things went well today, he would take Cooper up on his offer to take Linney out to the place. They could ride back to town together, just like Jeb suggested. Linney could help him set up the room at the back of the implement store. *Maybe she could help me pick out a lot in town. A place to build a house.* Maybe, just maybe if he did all those things, maybe Katie would forgive him from beyond the grave. Maybe the demons would die.

Now *that* was something to hope for.

*He that hath no rule over his own spirit*
*is like a city that is broken down, and without walls.*

PROVERBS 25:28

All right. He didn't plan it. He couldn't have planned it. After all, that one seat next to Mrs. Darby right at the end of the row in front of the row of Caroline and her friends was the only seat left. Well, almost the only seat left. And Frank Darby was a rancher, so that made sense, didn't it? A person liked to sit near their friends, even in church. After all, she was right here in the row with her friends. But *laws o'massey,* Caroline was having trouble paying attention to what was going on up front, and after all, Helen Smith was signing over her future to a near stranger. Never mind that he seemed nice enough, and never mind that little Davey McDonald had caused a chorus of *ooh*s and *aww*s when he slipped out of his seat and went to stand between the bride and groom and then slipped one hand into Helen's and one hand into his pa's.

Never mind all of that. This was a serious moment and Caroline could not pay attention. And why? All because of the varmint sitting right there a few feet away dangling a Stetson on his knee and making it a point, Caroline thought, *not* to look her way. And didn't Lucas Gray look fine today, with his hair all wavy and his beard trimmed close enough to accent that square jaw and— *Stop it, Caroline. Just stop it right now.*

She looked away. Stared straight forward. And she didn't even notice that Gray had a passably good singing voice. Nor did she pay any mind when he actually pulled a little New Testament out of his coat pocket and followed along when the preacher started his sermon. She barely noticed that Gray seemed somewhat familiar with the contents of that little testament, or that he could find the Scripture reading without an undue amount of flipping of pages. *You'd be lost trying to find Thessa—Thessa—whatever.*

Gray was just showing off. It was just a self-righteous kind of vanity, that's what it was. There weren't four men in the entire dining hall who had their own Bible. Caroline noted that Jeb Cooper was one of them, and that it wasn't a little testament, either. Cooper had a full-sized well-worn tome that settled across his knee like it belonged there, not some little sissy book a pretender could hide in his coat pocket.

She turned slightly in her chair, just enough to put Lucas Gray where he belonged, far in the periphery of her vision. And when the service concluded, Caroline slipped past Ella and Zita, Sally and Ruth, Jackson and Mavis, and escaped out the door and toward the mercantile without so much as a glance Mr. Gray's way. After all, she'd promised Martha Haywood to help out over at the mercantile. And she wanted to meet Alice Bailey and see to it that Alice decided to make her next quilt "shimmer" with bits of pumpkin-colored fabric.

Matthew slipped in the back door of the mercantile, his heart pounding. Even proposing hadn't made him this nervous. After all, there'd been no doubt that the woman he loved was going to say yes. Today was another matter. The results weren't guaranteed. Linney might not even listen long enough to hear the news about his moving to town. She might refuse to open this box of Katie's things, refuse to ride to the homestead and see the beautiful fence Jeb had erected around Katie's grave. In fact, it was quite possible Linney wouldn't let him say much more than one sentence before throwing a fit.

He hesitated in the storeroom, mentally rehearsing his speech one last time. At the sound of laughter, he set the box down atop a stack of crates. *Mrs. Jamison. Caroline.* Her voice was unmistakable, and she was just the one to discuss *shimmer.* Everything about that woman shimmered. Maybe he'd come back later. He could walk down to Lux's store and start clearing out that room in the back where he'd be living now. He'd leave Katie's things right here, and maybe catch up with Will Haywood somewhere in town and ask him to tell Linney—

"The older you get the more you look like your mother. Although the red hair is from your pa's side."

"It is?"

"Definitely. *His* ma had red hair. Didn't he ever tell you that?"

Matthew stepped into the doorway and took it all in. Luke, leaning on the counter across from where Linney stood with that hungry look in her eyes. The look she always got when there was any mention of Katie. *Luke.* Talking about things he had no right—*smiling* as he spoke Katie's name. And even as he smiled, he was aiming it all right past Linney toward Mrs. Jamison. Of course he would. That was how Luke did things. Use one to get to the other. Be nice to the toddler so you can lure the mother—

It all came back. In one instant the hurt and regret and doubt and guilt of the past few years all balled themselves up into Matthew's right fist. Emotion launched him across the mercantile toward Luke. Just as the tall cowboy turned toward the sound of fast-moving feet, Matthew planted his fist on that square jaw. Luke's eyes rolled back in his head and he fell backward into the washtub of fabric. Landing on his back, he lay sprawled out on the mercantile floor, his body peppered with rolls of varicolored calico.

Linney screamed "Pa!" and at the sound of her voice, Matthew's rage departed. His hand hurt. A lot. He spread his fingers and shook his hand out. In the silence he was only aware of the eyes. Linney's filling with tears. Caroline's, dark and troubled. Alice Bailey's communicating disapproval and, he supposed, already formulating a good story to spread about town. And then from behind them, Martha's voice sounding from the storeroom door. "Oh, Matthew." A world of sadness collected into two words.

Caroline moved first. She went to Luke, of course. The ladies always did, didn't they?

Matthew did what he always did. He ran.

Someone pounded on the door. Matthew didn't answer, but neither did he drink the whiskey he'd smuggled out the back door of the saloon on his way here. Instead, he stretched out on the bare cot in Vernon Lux's back room and tried to ignore whoever it was.

"It's Martha, and I'll stand out here and beat on this door all night if I have to. Or get Will to help me break it down if it comes to that. You *are* going to talk to me."

Matthew sat up. Raked his fingers through his tangled hair.

Martha rattled the door latch. "Open this door. I've got some things to say that I should have said years ago, and by gosh and by golly, they are going to be said. But not until I'm looking you in the eye."

He set an empty box over the whiskey bottle.

"I've raised your daughter for you, Matthew. You owe me this. And you owe it to Katie, too. For Linney's sake."

With a groan, Matthew scooted off the cot. He unlatched the door and, backing into the room, motioned for Martha to sit on the cot while he perched on a chair-high block of wood in the corner.

"I don't need to sit down. This won't take long. But we should close the door. So you light that lamp. I want to see you when I'm talking to you, and Lord knows *you've* been living in the dark for quite long enough."

Matthew lit the lamp. "All right," he said, and sat back down. "Let's get it over with."

"By all means, Matthew. Let's. It's time *someone* got over it, don't you think?" Martha took a wavering breath. Swallowed. When next she spoke, her voice was almost gentle. "There was a time when Katie Ransom thought she loved two men. Cousins she'd met at the same ball. Maybe she did love them both. I don't know. But, Matthew, Katie chose *you*. And she gave you a beautiful daughter."

"Did she?" He let the anguish sound in his voice. The question was almost a keening as he freed his pent-up emotions. "Did Katie give *me* a beautiful daughter? Or did Luke do that?" He stared at Martha, his heart pounding, his eyes filling with tears as he finally translated the anguish of years into words.

Martha just stared back. For a long while, she just stared. And then understanding dawned. "You think Linney isn't yours." She sat down on the cot and repeated the words, more slowly this time. "You think Linney isn't yours."

Instead of relieving the burden, the act of speaking it aloud only served to make it more real. An almost palpable weight settled across Matthew's shoulders, and he leaned forward and put his hands to his head. He took a deep, wavering breath and spoke without looking up. "The day of the accident . . . she'd left me. Taken Linney and gone . . . to *him*." He groaned the rest of it. "I went after her. We had a terrible fight. Linney screaming, Katie crying, and Luke . . . denying everything."

"What do you mean, 'denying everything'?"

Martha's voice was calm now. Matthew looked up at her and shrugged. "He said the girls were out picking chokecherries. Said Linney got stung or some nonsense, and he 'just happened' to come along. He said he took them over to the ranch so that Chinaman of his could treat the stings."

"That sounds very plausible."

"Well, there wasn't any sign of a sting on Linney's person."

"Wah Lo's remedies can be very effective, Matthew. You know that. Maybe you just couldn't see it all those hours later."

"She loved him, Martha. She *told* me she loved him." He waited for that to sink in before continuing. "But she said she wanted to make it work between her and me. And so she got in the wagon and we started for home. But—" He broke off. Shook his head.

"She chose *you*, Matthew. *She chose you*."

He got up and began to pace. "Did you know he built that house of his hoping she'd come to him? The house, the ranch—everything a woman could want . . . and she . . . she . . ." His voice broke. He let the tears come. "And still, she chose *me*. And the best I could do . . . the best I could do was . . . drive like a madman and risk our lives and . . ." He covered his face and began to sob. "I killed her, Martha. I killed her and I loved her and I hated her and . . . oh . . . God . . ." He leaned away from Martha, into the wall. He made a fist again, but this time he didn't use it. Instead, he stood weeping.

Martha came to his side. Leading him back to the cot, she sat down beside him and took his hand. "All right, Matthew. It's going to be all right." She held on.

"I don't even know if she's mine," he groaned.

"She's yours in every way that matters. You have to stop this. That girl thinks the sun rises and sets in you. The *only* thing she wants in this life is to keep house for her pa. She used to talk about it all the time. How she had to learn to cook really well so she could take good care of you. How she had to learn to sew so she could make your shirts." Martha paused. "She stopped talking like that two years ago, and do you know why? Because she stopped believing it's ever going to happen. She doesn't know why, but for some reason the one person she loves most in this world can't seem to stand being around her all that much. She sees the pain in you, Matthew, every time you look at her. And as all children do, Linney thinks it's her fault. Well, it's not. And you know what? It flat-out doesn't *matter* which of you sorry men made that child, because *you* are the one Katie chose to raise her."

She stood up. "It's time you forgave the past, Matthew. Katie and Lucas and yourself. And most of all it's time you forgave Linney for reminding you of the few moments in your life when you made a terrible choice and terrible things happened. *Yes,* your recklessness caused a wagon to overturn. But you didn't mean to hurt anyone. Are you going to let one bad decision ruin the rest of your life? Are you going to let it ruin Linney's life? And Luke's? Hasn't he done everything a man can do? Don't you think he grieved Katie, too? Don't you think he'd take back a few of *his* decisions if he could?"

"I'll never forgive him." Matthew was surprised by the lack of venom in the words. Still, he had to say them. Didn't he?

"You must. Because you will never have any kind of life as long as you are carrying this rottenness inside of you. Don't you see, Matthew? It's robbed you of the only thing that keeps us all going. It's robbed you of hope. Linney hopes for a normal life with her pa. You hope for happiness. And I'd stake a lot on the idea that Luke hopes you'll forgive him someday."

Matthew curled his lip and made a sound of disbelief.

"You two grew up together. As close as brothers. Don't you think he misses you? And if you're right, if he built the ranch house with Katie in mind, can you imagine what's it like facing that every single day?" She paused. "You abandoned the house that reminded you of Katie. Luke faces his every day unless he's chasing after cattle. In fact, it could just be that riding trails and chasing cattle is his way of doing penance." She waited a moment. "And perhaps, just perhaps, he isn't the only one guilty of what happened between you and Katie."

Matthew took a deep breath. Memories reeled in. Memories he'd avoided, except in the night when what he called his demons came to visit. Luke telling him to spend more time with Katie and less time out in the fields. Luke telling him Katie was lonely. Luke telling him how lucky he was to have a woman like her. And Katie. Crying. Her expression when he said no, he was too tired to go to the neighbors' for the dance tonight. No, he couldn't drive her to town for another piece of that pink calico. No, he didn't think it was a good idea for her to invite the ladies over for a quilting party. No . . . No . . . No.

Martha sighed. Her voice was weary when she next spoke. "Well, I've said what I came to say and then some. Plain and simple, you are breaking Linney's heart, and she's done nothing to deserve that. She's done nothing but love you. Please, Matthew. Find a way to let some light into those dark corners in your heart. Jesus said—" she held up her hand—"and I know you don't want to hear a sermon, and I'm not about to preach one. But Jesus did say that anyone who was weary could come to him, and he'd give them rest. Maybe you could start there. Ask Jesus to help you put the past to rest. Just *think* how good it would be to lay all that down, Matthew."

Matthew gave a wry smile. "I knew the name of Jesus would have to come up."

"You mean the Jesus who asked God to forgive the men pounding the nails into his hands? The Jesus who asked God to forgive the men gambling over his clothes while he dangled above them in agony?" She shrugged. "All right. I suppose I am giving a little bit of a sermon after all. But you know, Matthew, it just seems to me that what Jesus forgave was a bit harder than your possibly forgiving your own cousin for loving a beautiful, gentle, kind woman."

She stood up. "If you care to know, Luke rode north a while ago. He made a bad joke about you two always seeming to get tangled up and said to tell you he was sorry. That he didn't know you were in town. I take that to mean he's trying to be mindful of you, Matthew. I don't think he expected Linney to be at the store. She was helping serve wedding cake at the dining hall when I saw him leave. I think he was looking for Caroline. He never intended to talk to Linney, and that comment about Katie—well—she *does* look like her mother. And it probably just slipped out. He's not an evil man, Matthew. There's no plot to steal your daughter away from you. Surely you know that."

Matthew took a deep breath. Martha was likely right. About a lot of things.

*And I will restore to you*
*the years the locust hath eaten. . . .*

JOEL 2:25

Grateful for Will Haywood's presence in the store, Caroline busied herself wiping down the display case glass and dusting shelves as far away as possible from the raggedy men who'd come in on the heels of Matthew Ransom's attack on Lucas Gray. As the men settled near the storeroom door around the upended barrel supporting a checkerboard, Caroline wished for Martha's return even as she worried about Linney and wondered over what had happened earlier.

If Matthew Ransom was given to outbursts like the one Caroline had just witnessed, perhaps it was a good thing Linney wasn't keeping house for her father. And for all Caroline's negative thoughts about Lucas Gray, she'd been impressed by the way he handled the attack. Most men would have been raving mad when they finally came to. Not Mr. Gray. He rubbed his jaw and made a lame joke, and then took his leave without saying one unkind word about Mr. Ransom.

Caroline had gone to the front window and watched Lucas mount up and ride away. She half expected him to head for the saloon and apply whiskey to his wounded pride, but he hadn't done that, either. Instead, he'd urged his gelding into a lope and headed straight north. None of it seemed to fit with the cocky cowboy who'd flirted with her and Ruth on the train. And now, as the men around the barrel glanced her way, Caroline wished him back. With him in the room, she was fairly certain those men would mind the checkerboard instead of watching her every move.

At least there were a few customers in the store. Nancy Darby had just had Caroline cut two yards of a soft flannel. When she selected a card of tiny buttons, Caroline smiled to herself. Mrs. Darby must be in a family way. A woman who introduced herself as "Mrs. Homer Peterson of the Lazy J Ranch" bought every remaining roll of the orange fabric, commenting as she did so that Alice Bailey wasn't the only quilter in the county who knew how to use a challenging color to its best advantage. After the ladies left, Caroline picked up the feather duster again, working as far away from the checker game as possible. She scolded herself for judging by exteriors, but *laws o'massey,* how'd a man stand smellin' like that?

Only a few minutes after Mrs. Peterson left, Lowell Day wandered in. He looked around the store. Caroline followed his gaze, certain Will wouldn't allow the man who'd all but attacked her at the dance to stay. Much to her dismay, Will was standing with his back to them as he was telling one of his stories. Day made a show of inspecting the candy jars lined up along one edge and finally selected the peppermint. Five sticks. Caroline handed them over and moved away. He bit off a chunk of candy and munched it.

"Guess I owe you an apology. Got a bit . . . rowdy . . . the other night. I don't remember it too well, to tell you the truth. I was a little drunk. But the thing is, Hamilton Drake was in the saloon before he left for St. Louis to round you all up, and he said the Society was all about sparking and getting hitched. But then you and those friends of yours decided different, I guess. I didn't know. I just wanted what I paid for."

Her heart pounding, Caroline glanced toward the rear of the store, wishing Will Haywood would look this way and come to rescue her, but Will was oblivious.

Day took a disgusting swipe at the peppermint stick with his tongue. "Well, now, there's some that don't think you ladies can make a homestead work. I, on the other hand, realize that a woman can do a lot of things that would surprise the average man."

To keep from shuddering visibly, Caroline headed for the back of the store and Will Haywood, who was just saying, "So Martha tells me, she does, that all six of 'em have decided to be in control of their own destiny. Now, you take Mrs. Barton, for example. There's a woman who knows what she wants. Why, the minute she saw the cottonwood spring, she was ready to file. She's got a good plan, too. If any woman on earth can homestead and make it work, Mrs. Barton is likely that woman."

"You got that right," Day agreed, sauntering back to where Caroline stood right next to Will Haywood. Day didn't miss a beat. "Now, Will, I know what you're thinking. But I just apologized to this little lady a minute ago for being so drunk the other night and assuming things that just weren't true—why, we all got to realize you just can't assume anymore. Like this homesteading thing they've got in their heads. Just like Will says, if a woman could do it, Mrs. Barton surely can. I never saw such a woman. What is she? Six feet tall? Hands like a freighter. Why, she reminds me more of a lumberjack than—"

What Lowell Day said next made Caroline so angry that if she hadn't seen Jeb Cooper step in through the storeroom door in time to hear Day's remarks, she would have used one of the new kerosene lamps lined up on a nearby shelf to brain him herself. But by then Day's throat was enclosed in a beefy hand.

Jeb Cooper gave him a shake. "When are you going to learn your manners?"

The peppermint stick in Day's mouth broke off and fell to the floor. His hands flailed at Cooper's to no avail. His eyes had just begun to roll back in his head when Cooper let go.

"I was just havin' a bit of fun." Day coughed. "I didn't mean no harm."

"Have your fun somewhere else," Jeb said. Day stumbled out the door.

Martha came in the front as Mr. Cooper was leaving, then hurried to where Caroline sat at the cutting table adding a column of figures in the store ledger.

"What was Lowell Day doing in here? Please tell me my Will kicked him out."

"Actually," Caroline said, "he was apologizing for Friday night—after a fashion. And Will didn't have a chance to kick him out, because Mr. Cooper did it for him."

"Did you say Day *apologized*?"

"I think he did. At least as well as he knows how," Caroline said. "But then in his next breath he said somethin' unkind about Ella, so Mr. Cooper invited him to leave."

Martha scowled toward the back of the store and muttered, "I can appreciate Will's trying to keep them out of the saloon, but—" Raucous laughter drowned out the rest of the sentence.

Caroline decided to let the matter of Lowell Day lie. *HARDY women don't take every little thing personally. Lowell Day's just a crass wrangler looking for a little fun. If he thinks he's got my goat, it will just encourage him. Forget what lies behind. Press on with hope.* She reached into her apron pocket and withdrew Mr. Cooper's note.

"He left this for Linney's pa. I told him I'd do my best to see it got delivered. He said to tell you he unloaded the sewing machine and the trunk out back."

"Sewing machine? Trunk?"

"He said something about thinking Linney and Mr. Ransom were going to ride back to the homestead with him tonight, but that it didn't look like that was going to work out after all. So he unloaded Linney's things—that's what he called them—*Linney's* things—and headed out. There's a small box in the storeroom and a big trunk and a sewing machine just outside the back door."

Martha spoke to Will, who assured her he would "keep an eye on the boys," then closed the store, locking the front door and pulling down the blinds. Motioning for Caroline to follow her toward the back room, Martha glanced first into the box Matthew had left behind when he charged Lucas Gray. Peering out the back door at the large polished trunk, she murmured, "Finally. He's brought all of Katie's things into town." She glanced toward the upstairs. "I don't know whether to bring Linney down or wait for Matthew." She glanced at Caroline. "What do you think?"

"Me?" Caroline put her hand to her chest. "Why, I have no idea." She paused before blurting out the question that had been circling in her head all evening long. "Is Linney's father given to violence? Is that the reason you've kept her with you? To keep her safe?"

Martha's mouth dropped open. "Matthew? Violent? Oh, my—no." She shook her head. "Matthew's always been one of the sweetest, gentlest—" She broke off. "It was wrong, what he did today. But it's the culmination of years of tension between him and Lucas. They were rivals once for Katie's hand. Today was just an unfortunate coincidence, really. Lucas only came into the store because he wanted to see you. He expected Linney to be busy at the dining hall serving cake. But then—" Martha sighed. "I can't really explain any more than that. It's something the two of them need to face and fix."

"I just appreciate knowing—for Linney's sake—that outbursts like that aren't commonplace."

"The only person Matthew's ever struck out at before was himself. Over things from the past that should have been laid to rest long ago." Martha smiled softly. "But I think—oh, I think and hope and pray—that after today, things will be better." She paused. "I think he was planning on telling Linney that he's moving into town. But none of that needs to be your concern. I don't know how to thank you for all your help today. Obviously there will be a generous credit on a new ledger page for you."

Caroline followed Martha's lead, happy to close the conversation about Mr. Matthew Ransom and his problems with Lucas Gray. "The orange fabric is gone," she said, and told Martha what Mrs. Peterson had said about Alice Bailey's not being the only skilled quilt maker around.

Martha chuckled. "You know, men can jaw all they want about who rode the toughest bronco or who's the best shot. They can't hold a candle to the intensity with which Alice Bailey and Susan Peterson compete with needles and thread. It was pure genius bringing that horrible fabric to their attention. Mrs. Barton won't appreciate my saying this, but part of me wishes you were staying in town, Caroline. For the store . . . for myself . . . and for Linney, who likes you very much."

The last thing on earth Caroline wanted to do was get mixed up in whatever was going on with the Ransoms. Linney was very sweet, but her father? A man who would charge across a store and knock a man flat was not someone Caroline cared to get to know any better, no matter how fast her heart might beat when either of those two men came into view. Following her emotions had nearly ruined her life once. She wouldn't let it happen again.

"I'm fond of Linney, too. But we've got our plans all set, and it would be wrong for me to back out on my friends." She grinned. "Besides, I'm just ornery enough to want to make the folks laughin' behind our backs eat a little praline crow pie."

Wishing Martha a good night, Caroline crossed the expanse of prairie between the mercantile and the Immigrant House, enjoying the beautiful spring night. As she lingered on the back porch looking up at the starlit sky, the checker players exited the back door of the mercantile. It was only when he lit a match and it illuminated his face that Caroline realized Lowell Day had been waiting out back for just this moment. When she shrank back, hoping he hadn't seen her, a voice sounded through the dark. "Now, Johnny, you know how partial I am to candy. Especially southern candy."

Caroline would have thought it only a crude joke between two crude men. Except for one thing. As they walked away, Lowell Day wished her a good evening. In a poor imitation of a southern drawl.

It was real. As she stood outside the U.S. Land Office in Grand Island, Ella looked down at the document dated April 19, 1871. "Pursuant to the provisions of the Act of Congress, approved May 20, 1862, entitled An Act to Secure Homesteads to Actual Settlers on the Public Domain," Ella Maria Sophia Romano Barton was entitled to a patent for the NW 1/4 section 14 in Township 11 of Range 15 of Dawson County, Nebraska, comprising 160 acres.

"Somehow," Ruth said, "I think *this* document has a bit more promise than my membership certificate to the Ladies Emigration Society." She reached over to give Jackson a one-armed hug. "We'll have a home now. A home no one can tell us to leave."

Ella swallowed to keep back her own tears. Four pieces of paper and yet they represented so much more. Crops. Livestock. Calves. Hens and chicks and gardens and an everlasting amount of work. Perhaps she should feel overwhelmed, but at this moment all she felt was *joy*. Joy and hope and still more joy. She smiled until her face hurt.

"We should frame them all," Zita said. "One for each of the four corners of our home."

"Four Corners," Ella said. "That's it, Mama. That's what we'll call our place." She glanced around at the others to get their reactions. Their home had a name.

Sally waved her petition in the air even as she spoke toward the east. "Take *that*, Ray Gosset. Sally *did* amount to something after all." She linked arms with Caroline and Zita and sang out, "Swing your partner and do-si-do, we've got land now and here we go—"

Ruth and Ella held their hands high, forming an arbor for the others to dance through, and then everyone chanted as Jackson crouched down and did a ridiculous duck walk around them all. "Here comes the train, we're ready to go—folks think we're crazy, don't you know—"

"Yep, we're crazy, that's the truth—Sally, Zita, Caroline, and Ruth—"

"April nineteenth is the day—six ladies and Jackson came to stay—"

"Built Four Corners, saw things through—Nebraska's where their dreams came true."

Had it really been only two days since they'd all performed that joy-crazed dance outside the land office over at Grand Island? Perched next to Jackson as he drove their supply-laden wagon toward the homestead, Ella pondered how hard it had been to wait while Will Haywood finished up other business so he could help them today. Oh, they had kept busy planning and packing and loading supplies, but Ella was thankful the wait was over. Now, as they trundled along, she glanced over at the second wagon in the small procession and thanked God anew for Will Haywood. Today he would help them drive stakes to designate the homesite. They would lay out a barn and corrals and a henhouse and a garden, and by the time the sun set on today, the Four Corners would be more than just a dream.

As the wagon topped the last rise, the team threatened to bolt. Ella reached over and, putting her hands over Jackson's, pulled back and hollered, "Whoa!" Jackson flushed with embarrassment. "It's all right," Ella said. "You'll learn." She nodded toward the rented team. "They don't know your voice, and they can smell that cold spring water."

"They don't know yours, either," Jackson muttered. "But they slowed down."

"Well," Ella said with a shrug, "horses from a livery—even ones as fine as Mr. Ermisch's—can be more of a challenge. When we get our own team, they'll get used to you."Jackson looked doubtful. "They will," she insisted, and smiled. "After all, you'll be our main driver once we settle out here." She motioned around them at the broad expanse of prairie.

"Really?" Jackson sounded hopeful.

Ella nodded. "Of course. It's a man's job, after all." She didn't like the idea of assigning jobs that way, but Jackson obviously needed a boost, and she was more than willing to give it. He was a good boy.

Finally, they arrived at the new homesite. As Ella tied off the reins and climbed down, the other ladies—who'd followed the loaded wagon in a buggy—followed suit.

Ruth spoke up. "Let's pitch the tents first," she said, and pointed toward the cottonwood tree. "Over there. Where we'll have some shade in the afternoon." She reached for one of the long rolls of canvas atop the loaded wagon. Sally stepped up to help.

"You know how to pitch a tent?" Jackson sounded surprised.

"Your father and I pitched many a tent in our day," Ruth replied. She reached into the wagon and handed him a bundle of stakes and a sledgehammer. "Off we go." She grinned. "Let's see if we can get the first one pitched before Mr. Haywood and Ella get the parlor staked out."

While Ruth and Sally and Jackson worked to pitch what Ruth called a "Sibley tent," Will Haywood and Ella paced off the rooms for the soddy. Will said that fourteen by sixteen was large for a central living area. Ella stood in the center of the future room and held her arms out, pointing first to the left and then to the right. "Front and back doors," she said, "with a window on either side of each door. So we have plenty of light."

Once the stakes were driven at the corners and string attached to the stakes, Ella motioned for Caroline and Mama to "think about how things will be arranged in here," while she and Will staked out the two bedroom wings. Each wing would measure ten by fourteen, giving just enough room to tuck a narrow bed into each corner with a trunk at the foot of each bed and a window in the wall between the headboards.

"You might want more windows," Will suggested. "Crosswinds are a good thing on a hot summer night. You can always hang a quilt up to keep the winter winds from blowing through."

Ella considered. That would mean four more windows, and windows weren't cheap. She called a meeting of the minds, and the ladies decided that more windows would be worth the extra expense. And so it went all that day. Ella was clearly in charge, and yet she was careful to ask for advice and opinions. The only real disagreement came when Hettie insisted that she didn't need a "high-hipped roof" above her loft.

"Th-that's going to cost way more in labor and shingles and all," she said. "I don't mind ducking down a little. Goodness, it's only a sleeping loft. I don't plan to *live* up there."

Ella glanced around at the others. Words weren't necessary. Only nods. She looked at Will. "A hipped roof. A high one." She glanced at Hettie. "It's not just for you. It's for all of us. We've come to stay. We build to give that message. To others, and to ourselves."

By day's end, Four Corners boasted three Sibley tents—one for eating, one for sleeping, should the ladies decide to camp over at the homesite, and one for storage. Stakes and twine suggested a good-sized sod house, a small barn, and, much to Sally's delight, a large henhouse. As the afternoon sun lengthened the shadows from the one tree within sight, Ella looked over the place, and for the first time, the enormity of what she had proposed threatened to override her enthusiasm. Could they do it? Could they really do it? Create a home and raise enough food to survive a winter out here?

As the wagons and buggy made their way back toward town and the white of the three tents receded into the distance, Ella almost lost courage. Almost. But then Zita said something about how God was going to restore the years the locusts had eaten.

"I hope you're right, Mama," Ella murmured.

"Hope on. Hope ever," Ruth said, from the buggy next to them.

"Hope springs eternal," Caroline offered.

"Hope does not disappoint," Hettie chimed in.

"I hope Red and the hens like it out here," Sally said. And everyone laughed.

*Faithful are the wounds of a friend;*
*but the kisses of an enemy are deceitful.*

PROVERBS 27:6

Jackson Dow, you're cheating!" Linney jumped up, upsetting the checkerboard and sending checkers skittering across the general store floor. "I'm *glad* you're moving onto that stupid homestead on Monday! *Caroline* won't let you get away with cheating. Neither will Zita or Hettie or anyone else. It'll be like having a dozen mothers, and you need every one of 'em to teach you right from wrong!"

"I am *not* cheating!" Jackson shouted back.

"Well, how else can you explain beating me four times in a row? My pa says I'm the best checker player he's ever seen—besides Mr. McDonald, and no one *ever* beats Mr. McDonald."

Jackson glowered. "Well, maybe your pa was just being nice and letting you win! Or maybe I'm just better than you. Did you ever stop to think somebody might actually be better than you at something?!"

"Are you calling my pa a liar?"

Caroline, who'd been helping Martha check things off the list of provisions the women were planning to take to the homestead on Monday, decided it was time to intervene. "Hey, you two." She laid her pencil down and walked to the back of the store. "First of all, Jackson, a gentleman doesn't *gloat* when he wins a game. He is gracious whether he wins or loses." Then she turned to Linney. "And,

Linney. Your pa isn't a liar, and Jackson didn't say he was. On the other hand, he does dote on you, so perhaps he doesn't try as hard to win as he might."

"He doesn't *dote* on me." Linney swiped at a tear. Grabbing a feather duster, she marched to the far corner of the store and began a furious scattering of dust.

Caroline exchanged glances with Martha, who nodded toward Linney. *Talk to her* was the unspoken message. In turn, Caroline nodded toward Jackson. *Distract him.* Clearing her throat, Martha said, "Jackson. I've a couple of crates of things in the storeroom I haven't been able to get to. Could you help me unpack them?" She laid an arm across the boy's shoulders and together they headed out back. As soon as they were gone, Caroline crossed the store to where Linney was dusting—and sniffing.

"You know Jackson didn't mean to yell. Not really."

"I know. It's just—everyone talks about how much my father *adores* me. And I know he loves me, but—" Tears began to slide down her cheeks in earnest. She moved to the front window and stared out at the sodden landscape. "Never mind. I'll be fine. I get moody when it rains. You don't have to worry about me. Really." She looked over at the checkerboard and forced a smile. "I was just being . . . sulky."

"We all get sulky now and then."

Linney's dusting slowed. "I know he couldn't have managed when I was little," she said. "But he keeps promising we'll have a home again." Her voice quavered. "And then he just goes and sells it and doesn't even tell me." She sniffed. "Mr. Gray said I remind him of my mother. Pa still has nightmares about her. He talks about her in his sleep. He talks *to* her." She paused. "I know he loves me, but Pa can only take so much of me, and now I know why. It's because I remind him of her. I just wish he'd quit lying about our having a home."

She touched the feather duster again, tracing its handle as she murmured, "I'm not really angry with Jackson." She sniffed. "I'm glad he's going to get a home, even if I'm not. At least not until I grow up and get one of my own." She gazed toward the storeroom. "I've been asking God for a special friend for a long time. I didn't think it would be a boy. From the city."

Caroline chuckled. "You know what Mrs. Romano would say about that?"

Linney shook her head.

"She'd say that God answers our prayers with what we need, not necessarily what we ask for."

Linney pondered that. Finally, she smiled. "Well, I don't quite understand why God would think I need a friend who can play checkers better than me . . . but I'm glad he finally sent me a friend."

"Jackson is thankful for you, too. He may not say it in so many words, but—"

"Oh, he'll never say it 'in so many words.'" Linney rolled her eyes. "That's okay. Martha says a woman has to let a man keep his pride. She says they don't usually talk about their feelings, but we can see how they feel about us if we pay attention. She says Pa shows how much he loves me when he takes the time away from hunting and trapping to spend time with me."

"Martha's a wise woman," Caroline said.

Linney nodded. "I know. I just wish—" She broke off. Forced a smile. Shrugged. "He's not like that, you know. He doesn't hit. I've never seen him hit anyone before. Ever." She frowned. "I don't know what made him do that. Mr. Gray was being nice. Why would that make Pa angry?"

Caroline's heart raced as she tried to come up with an explanation. "Well, what you said about men and pride and all? Maybe your pa was a little jealous. I mean, you're growing up and maybe—"

"Mr. Gray is old enough to be my pa!" Linney shuddered.

"I didn't mean it that way," Caroline said quickly. "I mean that maybe he realizes that you're growin' up and he's gonna lose you—and maybe he regrets not spending more time with you."

Linney thought about that for a moment. "I still wish he could just see *Linney* when he looks at me. And I wish he didn't get so sad when he thinks about my mother. And I wish we could have a real home."

Not knowing what else to say, Caroline opted for a hug. It seemed to have a good effect, for a few minutes later Linney hollered into the storeroom, "All right, Jackson Dow, get back out here and give me a chance to beat you!"

"So," Caroline said, settling next to Jackson on the front stoop of the Immigrant House Saturday afternoon, "did you let her win at least once?"

Jackson grinned. "Of course. I'm not *completely* stupid." He sighed. "Besides, that wasn't really about checkers anyway. For either of us. Linney's upset about her pa. And I—" He shrugged. Shook his head. "I don't know how to do any of the things people out here need to know. I don't know how to drive a team or harness them or saddle a horse or anything. I don't even know how to dig a *hole*. And we're going to need at least a thousand holes to put up the fence Ella says we're going to need to keep Mr. Gray's cattle out of our fields." He stood up and kicked at an imaginary rock. "I'm a dud."

"Jackson Dow . . ." Caroline rose and grasped him by the shoulders. "That is the most ridiculous thing I have ever heard. I don't know the first thing about gardenin' or cookin', and to tell you the truth I've always been a little afraid of cows, but I don't consider myself any kind of dud. I'm gonna earn my keep. But I'm just plain scairt sometimes. Some of the stories I've heard this week about how snakes and mice like to live in the walls of soddies . . ." She shuddered.

"Aw, snakes and mice won't hurt you. Unless they have rattles." Jackson grinned.

"Well, you just keep that attitude handy, because I'll be callin' on *you* if any kind of critter decides to come to my side of the house for a visit."

Stuffing his hands into his pockets, Jackson gazed up the street toward the livery.

"We never did go see if Mr. Ermisch has any horses I could learn to ride."

"You're right. I turned my ankle and then we got all caught up in other things." She looped her arm through Jackson's, and together they headed toward the livery at the opposite end of the street. "While we're up there, we can see if that horse trader brought in anything new. Ella's impatient about gettin' our own team, and I can't say that I blame her."

"Howdy."

Caroline looked up to where Otto Ermisch stood peering down at them, pitchfork in hand. At the sight of Caroline, he tipped his cap. "I'll be right down." And with that, Ermisch virtually dropped through the hole in the haymow floor to the earth nearby. "Sorry to say the horse trader hasn't been through yet. Maybe he'll show on Monday." He frowned. "Although I guess that'll be a mite late, won't it?" He scratched his beard. "Wish I knew what to tell you."

"Well, there's more to this visit than the search for a good team. Jackson needs to learn to ride." Caroline summoned her most charming smile. "Now, I realize a businessman can't just turn his horseflesh over to anyone. Horses are valuable commodities, and you can't have just anyone taking them out. I remember a time when my daddy let some fool ride his Pacer—" She shook her head. "Of course I never rode such a monstrous creature as that. My little mare was a Morgan. Shiloh had the sweetest canter a lady could wish for. Of course, with a Morgan a person doesn't exactly try to clear fences, but Shiloh had the heart of a steeplechaser. Whatever I asked, that li'l mare tried to give."

Having let Mr. Ermisch know that while Jackson might be a novice around saddle horses, she was not, Caroline continued, "Now, I told Jackson we'd have to ask permission to see what the livery has to offer. You don't just stroll into a barn and make yourself t'home. Not if you know what's good for you." She shrugged. "I guess it was mighty clear I don't know much about work horses the other day. Saddle horses, on the other hand—"

Ermisch grinned. "Tell you what, Jackson. As long as you're with this little lady you are welcome in my livery anytime." He gave Jackson a friendly slap on the shoulder even as he spoke to Caroline. "Watch the big bay with the white here." He tapped his forehead. "He bites. And of course watch where you're stepping. I've been running behind all day and haven't mucked the place out as well as I should."

Together, Caroline and Jackson headed toward the double row of stalls stretching between them and the back doors. As they walked, Ermisch opened those doors and the aroma of warm horseflesh and hay wafted their way. Caroline inhaled. "I *love* that smell." The next aroma wasn't quite as pleasant, and she chuckled. "I don't even mind that one so much." They paused at the first stall when a sorrel mare whickered and thrust her head over the door.

"That's Maude," Mr. Ermisch called from the back. "She's mine and she's an unrepentant beggar. She'll nibble on your pockets, but she doesn't bite. She's just hoping for a treat. And she doesn't really care what it is, as long as it's people food."

Jackson shied away as the horse thrust her head against his chest, but presently he was laughing as she snuffled his pockets. "Hey," he said when she lipped his jacket. "It only smells like horehound. I ate it." The horse sighed as if she understood him. "Well, I'm *sorry*," he said. "I'll bring you some directly." He called out to Mr. Ermisch. "Is it all right if I bring Maude a treat?"

"Sure. But be warned. She never forgets a treat-bearer. She'll hound you for the rest of your born days every time she sees you."

"Go ahead," Caroline said, nodding toward the mercantile.

"Bribery isn't a bad way to get to know a horse." She smiled. "I'll wait here." She meandered down the stalls alone after Jackson left, looking over the individual horses. One was swaybacked, another shied away from the human hand, one ignored her, and another nibbled at her coat playfully. True to form, the bay Ermisch had warned her about bared his teeth the minute she got near his stall. Sadly, there didn't seem to be a good prospect for a greenhorn boy wanting to learn to ride.

The cadence of an approaching horse sounded from the direction of the street. Caroline turned around just in time to see Matthew Ransom astride a paint pony, a big-boned pack mule in tow. Jackson came trotting into the livery just as Mr. Ransom dismounted. Stammering a hello, Jackson unwrapped a peppermint and shared it with the mare.

Matthew fumbled with both his hat and his words. "I . . . uh . . . thank you for being a good friend to Linney. Martha said you've been a good listener since—" He broke off. "Since her pa behaved like a raving idiot."

*Well. At least he has that right.* "Linney's a wonderful girl," Caroline said. *Thanks to Martha.*

Matthew nodded. "All the credit for that goes to Will and Martha." He looked down at the hat in his hands. "And her ma. She's a lot like her ma."

"So I've heard," Caroline said. And then for some reason she waded right into a situation that was really none of her business. "Linney thinks that's why you can't stand to be around her."

Mr. Ransom frowned. "Can't . . . stand . . . ?"

"Yes. After you laid Lucas Gray out cold on the mercantile floor, Linney told me you don't like being around her too much because of how much she reminds you of your wife. Of course, I told her she must have misunderstood the real reason behind your bein' gone for—what is it now—nearly a week? I told her a daddy would never punish a child like that. That havin' a living, breathing reminder of someone you deeply loved would be a wonderful thing. Like a gift from God."

"A gift." Ransom murmured the words, as though he'd never thought of them before.

"Well, hello there, Matthew." Otto Ermisch strode up and offered his hand. "Glad to see you back in town." He nodded at the pack mule. "Looks like you brought just about everything."

Ransom nodded and handed Ermisch the paint's reins before untying the pack mule's lead. "I'll walk Barney around back. I can unload things right in the door that way."

Ermisch smiled. He glanced at Caroline. "This man is the best carpenter I've ever seen. You ladies need anything done for that new place of yours, Matthew here is the one to hire. Wagon building, shingle cutting—anything that involves wood, he's a master."

He turned back to Ransom. "I'll put this guy in that back stall for the night and give him a real good rubdown. You can just turn Barney into the corral out back. There's fresh water and I'll get some feed before too much longer."

Mr. Ransom nodded. "I was ... uh ... hoping I could hire a buggy tomorrow." He glanced Caroline's way even as he spoke to Ermisch. "I've been gone without an explanation for nearly a week, and I may have to hog-tie her to get her to do it, but I want to take Linney to see what Jeb Cooper has done with the homestead. And with her ma's grave." He paused, then directed his next comment to Caroline. "It seemed like a good idea to do something about all the promises I've made over the years." He pointed to the pack mule's load. "My things from the dugout. Vernon Lux next door offered to let me stay in the back room of his store. It's not what I promised—yet—but it's a beginning."

Something in the man's blue eyes as he looked down at her made Caroline forget for the moment that Matthew Ransom represented one long list of problems she wanted nothing to do with. She almost reached over to touch his arm, but instead she clasped her hands behind her and said simply, "Linney will be thrilled."

"Will Haywood told me about Cooper's fence around Katie's grave," Ermisch said. "The man who would do something like that— well. Some say Cooper's a little odd. But I say he's all right. More than all right." Ermisch rubbed his jaw with the back of his hand as he said, "Now, about the buggy tomorrow . . . Mrs. Jamison and the other ladies spoke for it most every day—"

"—we'll be fine," Caroline interrupted. "We can manage with a wagon or two. No one will mind. We're . . . partial to Linney."

"Well, then." Ermisch nodded. "That's settled." He called back to Jackson, who was still rubbing behind the mare's ears while she stood, eyes half closed. "Here ya go, son," he said, and handed Jackson the reins to Ransom's paint.

Jackson's eyes grew round as he stared up at the horse.

"He won't bite," Ermisch said, and motioned toward the back of the barn. "Just lead him back there to that last stall on the left. I'll be there directly, and you can help me rub him down."

Jackson looked embarrassed. "I don't know how to do that."

"Well, that's all right. Patch is a good old boy. Just the kind of horse to learn on. You walk that way and he'll follow."

When Jackson hesitated, Caroline spoke up. "If you're going to own a horse, you're going to have to be taking care of it. There's no time like the present to learn."

"That's right," Ermisch said. "Can't be afraid of hard work if you expect to be around horses."

"I'm not afraid!" Jackson said, his tone defensive, and he headed toward the stall with Matthew's horse in tow.

Movement across the street caught Caroline's eye. Lowell Day was leaning against the front wall of the saloon, his arms folded, his head bowed. He likely wasn't even looking this way, but the idea of walking back to the Immigrant House alone had lost its appeal. It was probably just her imagination, but just as Matthew headed through the barn and out the back, Caroline could have sworn she heard someone whistling "Dixie." She decided to walk back through the livery and watch Jackson work with Patch. At least for a while. She'd take the back way to the Immigrant House when the time came.

*Let them be confounded and put to shame that seek after my soul:*
*let them be turned back and brought to confusion that devise my hurt.*

PSALM 35:4

Caroline had made her way back to the Immigrant House when clouds moved in and obscured the sunset she'd been watching from the front stoop. When a steady drizzle began to fall and Jackson still hadn't returned from the livery, she headed inside to the kitchen, where Ruth was busy serving up hot tea while Hettie spread out the various lists again. As the sky grew dark Zita lit more lamps and set them in a row down the center of the table. Presently all six ladies gathered for the last meeting before Monday's move out to the Four Corners.

Caroline spoke first. "The horse trader hasn't come through yet, so I don't have any good news to report about a team. Mr. Ermisch is hoping maybe Monday—of course, with us leaving early that mornin' I guess we'd better hope plenty of neighbors show up to help us out, or we'll be in a fix." She sat back with a little frown. "Do y'all think we should delay leavin' town until we have our own team?"

"Will says we can count on plenty of help," Ella said.

The back door opened, and Mavis Morris trundled in. "What you can count on," she said abruptly, "is getting work and husbands right here in Plum Grove. Mrs. Haywood needs help and so will the other business owners the minute those places across the street open up.

There's just no need for y'all to pick up and move out to the middle of nowhere."

"Well, now, Mavis," Sally said. "You're just missin' one little thing, and that's the fact that we don't want 'jobs and husbands right here in Plum Grove.'"

"That's what you all keep saying." Mavis shook her head. "I guess you're gonna prove it or die trying." She changed the subject. "You might as well know Martha's appointed me manager of the Immigrant House." She glanced around the table. "And I'll need a cook or two to keep things running, so if any of you has a moment of sanity and decides to stay put, just let me know." She walked toward the doorway on the north wall leading into a small storeroom. "I'm turning the back room into my private quarters. So I'll be working at that while you all have your meeting." She headed for the storeroom, talking as she moved. "Don't mind me. I don't need any help at all. I can handle things just fine by myself. All I have to do is move one of the cots in here. And my trunk. It won't take long—"

With a roll of her eyes, Sally stood up. "I'll lend a hand, Mavis. You don't have to do it by yourself."

"Now, now, don't feel obligated," Mavis said, even as she turned about and handed Sally the bag she'd carried in with her. She glanced toward the others. "As to your needing a team, the horse trader came in for a late supper. Said something about a whole string of horses up at the livery." She paused. "Real nice fellow. Kind eyes." She glanced at Caroline. "So I expect if a body really wanted to go ahead with homesteading and really wanted a good team, they'd hightail it back to the livery, even if it is raining to beat the band."

Thanking her, Caroline stood up and excused herself. Retrieving a shawl she headed out the front door. The rain had let up, leaving a swirling mist in its wake that threatened to thicken into an honest-to-goodness fog. But she was *hardy*. A little mud, a little fog . . . no problem. In spite of her best efforts at holding her skirts up and skipping over the worst of the puddles, the hem of her dress was much the worse for the journey from one end of Main to the other.

Mr. Ermisch had pulled the double doors closed as a guard against the rain. Caroline went in the side door and made her way through the gloom and to the back, where after opening another single door, she peered out at the corral. Mavis was right. At least a dozen horses had joined Matthew's mule in the corral. For the next few minutes Caroline watched them, finally deciding to look more closely at two bay geldings and, if they didn't prove sound, then the gray mares—by daylight.

Piano music sounded behind her from the direction of the saloon. The noise emphasized the quiet in the barn. Jackson was likely back at the Immigrant House by now. As for Mr. Ermisch, Caroline didn't know where he spent his hours away from the livery. It didn't really matter, she supposed. Contented snuffles and soft grunts and the sounds of chewing filled the air now. Time to get back to the meeting with the good news.

As she turned to go, a shrill screech sounded from a stall. Then a kick to a board. Another kick. Another snort. "Hey, boys," Caroline said. "What's wrong back here?" She made her way toward the stall where Matthew's Patch was causing a ruckus, snorting and tossing his head. As Caroline approached, the horse whinnied and whirled about.

"Hey, now. Whoa, there." Apparently Patch wasn't accustomed to stalls and stables. Hopefully Mr. Ermisch had realized the horse wasn't really all that gentle *before* Jackson got kicked. The horse stomped its feet and, stretching its neck out, bared its teeth. "Oh, now, stop that. You don't want to be that way. Just settle dow—" A gloved hand covered her mouth. An arm encircled her waist and she was lifted from the earth and carried backward. Patch whinnied again. Caroline kicked and squirmed, but whoever it was only held her tighter as he dragged her toward the back corner of the stable. The harder she thrashed, the harder he held on until it felt like he might break every rib and her jaw at the same time.

He smelled of whiskey. Sweat. And . . . as he whispered into her ear, his hot breath carried a hint of . . . *peppermint.* "I been thinkin' about you since I first saw you. I like a woman with a little spunk. You gave old Lucas Gray a run for his money on the train, didn't ya?" He nuzzled her ear. "You coulda been a little more sociable at the dance, you know. But you southern gals, you always got to put that little nose of yours in the air. Like you smell something bad when regular folks come around. That's how you made me feel at the mercantile the other day." A guttural chuckle. "Don't mind telling you I couldn't believe my good luck when I come out of the saloon and saw you comin' in here all by yourself."

The man's hand left her waist and groped higher, but he still managed to keep her arms clamped to her sides. "Now, you and I are gonna get to know one another real well this evenin'. And when I'm done—"

A faint click. And then the sound of Sally Grant's voice. "You *are* done, you low-down—" She strung an impressive series of descriptive words together before continuing. "Now, here is what you are going to do so that I don't have to pull this trigger. In just a minute, you are going to let my friend go. And you are gonna move real slow when you do it because this here gun of yours has a hair trigger and it would be a shame if it went off. Now, Caroline, the minute he lets go, I want you to jump clear. But don't run off. Just wait for me to tell you what to do next. All right?"

Caroline managed muffled agreement.

"All right, then," Sally said. "You turn Mrs. Jamison loose, now— and be sure your hands go up in the air the minute you do."

Day loosened his grip and Caroline leaped away. When she spun around she saw his hands in the air, his eyes glittering with rage.

Sally never took her eyes off him as she said, "Now, Caroline. Real slow-like, you take that other gun out of his holster and then back yourself as far into the corner there as you can get. Of course, if you feel inclined to point the gun at him once you're over there, that'd be just fine, too—as long as you can keep from shooting me."

Caroline stared at Day's empty holster. How had Sally done that? How had she managed to take the gun without him reacting . . . without him slapping her away? She hesitated.

"It's all right. This here gun is a military issue Remington—.44 caliber if I'm not mistaken. It's a marvel. And this here varmint likely knows that if he moves at all, nervous woman that I am, the darned thing just might go off. And since the barrel is pressed to the back of his head, that wouldn't be too good for him."

Caroline looked past Day and into Sally's eyes. She didn't look nervous. She looked deadly. Sally nodded. "You can trust me. Just get the other gun." Caroline snatched the pistol out of its holster and backed away. She had no stomach for pointing it at anyone.

"Now," Sally said to Day, "I'm gonna take a step back. Please do not do anything foolish like trying to run off, because as sure as I know what kind of gun this is in my hand, I know how to use it. And as sure as I don't *want* to use it, I will if I have to. So we're gonna walk out that back door and around to the saloon, and you're gonna mount up and ride away. And you will keep riding, because if you don't, it will be bad for you. That boss of yours has taken a shine to my friend here, and I don't think he'd like knowing what you tried just now. So let's go. Caroline, you might want to follow. It's up to you."

Her knees quaking, Caroline followed. Day did exactly what he'd been told. He didn't say a word, he didn't try anything, and he didn't look back as he rode west into the swirling mists. Sally looked down at the gun. "I always wanted me one of these."

"Here," Caroline said, and held out its mate. "Now you have two." She shuddered. "Do you think he's really gone?"

"Well, I don't imagine he wants to face a Lucas Gray who knows what he almost done here tonight."

Caroline wobbled to the watering trough by the corral and perched on the edge, her head in her hands.

"Hey—" Sally sat down beside her, laid the guns down, and put a hand on her shoulder. "You ain't gonna faint on me, are ya?" She patted Caroline on the back. "Breathe. Come on, girl. Just take in some fresh air."

Caroline tried, but she couldn't keep her voice from trembling as she asked, "H-how did you do that? H-how did you get that gun without him even knowing you were there?"

Sally cleared her throat. "Well, I . . . uh . . . I got some talents I don't use no more. Now that I'm starting fresh."

"As what—a gunslinger?"

Sally nudged her with an elbow. " 'Course not." She scratched her nose. "It weren't all that different from gettin' a money clip out of a pocket." She was quiet for a moment, then murmured, "You won't tell nobody—will ya?"

Caroline shook her head. She shivered and drew her shawl around her. "It was stupid of me to walk down here alone in the dark like that. I never would have done something like that in St. Louis. I just thought—I guess I've thought of Plum Grove as a sleepy little town where nothing bad would happen."

"Yeah, well . . . I shoulda known better than to let you do it. But I figured it was only a little ways and Jackson would walk you back." Sally sighed. "But then Jackson popped in the back door after you left, chattering about Linney's pa and how he's moved into town and—" She broke off. Shrugged. "It dawned on me just how close the livery is to the saloon and—I don't know, I just run with my instincts, I guess."

"Thank God for your instincts," Caroline said. "I don't know how I'll ever thank *you*."

Sally chuckled. "You did say I could keep the guns, right?"

"Checkmate," Ermisch said, slapping his knee and laughing.

Matthew leaned back and stared at the board. It was just him and

Otto tonight, playing chess in the back corner of the mercantile, and Matthew was glad. He didn't need witnesses to the wholesale defeat Otto had handed him three times now. He shook his head.

"You're just rusty," Ermisch said, chuckling. "Give yourself a week or so, and it'll be you hollering checkmate and me wondering how it happened." He stretched, then pointed to the board. "Go again?"

Matthew nodded. "Set it up. I'll be right back." He headed out back, pausing in the clear night air, inhaling the scent of clean grass, wishing for the silence of the landscape outside the dugout. Tilting his head, he listened. He could hear Patch all the way at this end of Main.

Otto had followed him outside. He lit a cigar. "Old Patch hasn't been in a barn in a long time. There's bound to be some noise while he finds his place in the pecking order. He'll settle in before long. I'll check in on him before I turn in tonight."

"It's all right," Matthew said. "You set up the board. I'll go see if I can't calm him down. Be right back."

"Take a gander at the corral, too. They're probably milling around— could be what's got Patch all riled up."

Matthew was halfway to the livery and behind Lux's implement shop when he thought he heard a woman's voice from the direction of the street. Plum Grove might be mostly good people, but a woman shouldn't be out alone. A little yelp sounded just as he stepped out of the shadows and onto the boardwalk in front of the implement store. As he turned toward the yelp something flashed, and without thinking he crouched down and snatched the bowie knife from where he kept it tucked into the top of one boot.

"Mr. Ransom? Is that you?"

The voice and the gun didn't match. Matthew blinked. It made no sense, but there was Sally Grant. Lowering a gun. And Caroline beside her.

"I heard . . . something," he said as he stood up and put the knife away. They were coming from the direction of the livery. "Is everything all right?"

"Everything is just dandy," Sally replied. She ignored the gun, and for some reason Matthew felt compelled to follow her example.

"Can I . . . walk you somewhere?"

"Well, now, that'd be just dandy. Wouldn't it, Caroline? We're headed back to the Immigrant House." Without waiting for an answer, Sally took his arm. Caroline took the other. She said nothing.

Matthew could feel Caroline trembling as they walked along. He had the ridiculous idea that the hand hidden in the folds of her dress held another gun.

"I like me a clear night after it's been rainin'," Sally said, inhaling deeply. "This is just dandy."

Matthew could almost sense the demons gathering to laugh. This wasn't going to work. Martha had put the note saying he was waiting downstairs just outside Linney's bedroom door and then let him in the back door of the mercantile just before dawn. It felt as if he'd been sitting here in the dark for half the night. In fact, the sun was up now.

He probably wouldn't get three words into his apology. He'd hunkered in that dugout too long. He'd lost her. One well-planted right fist into Luke's jaw and everything imploded. He'd never forget the horror in Linney's eyes at the sight of it. She'd want an explanation, too. And he couldn't give it.

If only Luke had stayed away. Leave it to him to follow the prettiest girl in town like some tail-wagging pup. Not that Matthew could blame him for that. Caroline Jamison was a beautiful woman. Hers was a more exotic beauty than Katie's had ever been, but still . . . a beautiful woman. No, Matthew didn't suppose he could blame Luke for being attracted to Caroline. He couldn't even blame Luke for talking to Linney. After all, what did Matthew expect him to do? Pretend she didn't exist? She did, and she was a living, breathing monument to the best thing that had ever happened to either one of them.

*She chose you.* That's what Martha had said. More than once. And it was finally sinking in. A little glimmer of hope had begun to shine through the shadows of the past few years. Now, if he could just get Linney to listen. *Please, God. Make her listen.*

He had so much to make up for. So much darkness to conquer. He still wasn't sure he could do it. But if he didn't, he was going to lose the best part of life once and for all. He had to get past the mile-high stack of regrets and do something right for a change.

He heard footsteps above. Looking up, he followed them across the ceiling to the second-story door. Down the outside steps. He stood to face the door. And there she was, her blue eyes looking so sorrowful Matthew thought his heart just might shatter and fall into pieces on the floor between them.

"Will you . . . will you hear me out, sweetheart?" His voice cracked.

She put her hands behind her. "I'm here, aren't I?"

Matthew nodded. Suddenly the speech just vanished from his mind. He looked at his daughter and the pain in her eyes, and knowing he was the reason it was there brought tears and he couldn't hold them back. He didn't even want to. He took a deep, wavering breath. "Those nightmares," he began. "They aren't about the war. They're about the day your ma died." He paused. Could he really do this? *I have to.*

"Lucas Gray is my cousin. He was the cadet your ma was dancing with when I first saw her. And even though she chose me and married me, I was always jealous of Luke. There wasn't any reason for it. But I chose to see it another way. I picked a fight with your ma that day and then I lost control of myself and the team. And your ma died. That's why I don't drive wagons anymore. It's why I have nightmares. It's why . . . everything." He swallowed. "I've been running from the truth for so long that I don't really know how to stop. Except I know that if I don't, I'm going to miss out on my last chance to be a real father. So I decided I'd sell the homestead and maybe that would help. It didn't stop the nightmares, but it did get me moved to town. And then, in the middle of all of it, I saw Luke smiling at you and—"

Linney held up her hand. "Wait."

Matthew stopped midsentence.

"You said . . . just now you said . . . moving . . . to town."

Matthew nodded. "Barney's in the corral over at the livery. He packed in everything I need from the dugout just last night. I'm all set up in that back room at Lux's. He's already got me promised to build three wagons and cut shingles for the ladies out at the cottonwood spring. Will seems to think a good carpenter—"

"—you . . . moved. Already. Into town."

Matthew nodded again. "Just last evening. And I want to take you out to the homestead tomorrow. I want you to get to know Jeb Cooper and see what he's done. He's a good man, Linney. You should see the fence—"

He never finished the sentence. He couldn't because his arms were full of a redheaded little gal clutching his neck and crying. "Oh, Pa," she said, her words muffled against his shoulder. "I love you, Pa. I love you *so much*."

CHAPTER
SIXTEEN

*But thou, O Lord, art a God full of compassion, and gracious,*
*longsuffering, and plenteous in mercy and truth.*

PSALM 86:15

It was nearly over for Hettie. She'd stood here four times a day for the last three weeks watching people get off that train, but tomorrow that would end. The others might decide to come back into Plum Grove to stay until the house was finished, but Hettie would not. She'd camp on the land and be happy to never hear another train whistle. At least until she had things figured out. For now, she needed distance from the past. A blank canvas for a future. And time. Four Corners would give her all those things, and the only cost was a narrow cot, perhaps in a tent for a week or so, and then in the loft of a soddy. To Hettie's mind, that wasn't a trial. It was a blessing. The word came without warning and when she pondered it, it made her smile a bit. *Blessing.*

She'd used religious words so easily for years and years. But they'd slipped away, one by one, until here she stood beside the front door of a hastily constructed building in a fledgling town she'd never heard of only weeks ago. The religious words had started filtering back lately, mostly, Hettie knew, because of Zita Romano. The way she slipped in little phrases just as naturally as can be. The way she prayed over every meal. And, oddly enough, the way the older woman could laugh at things—as if she and the Creator of the universe had a special relationship that allowed Zita to observe human frailty from a place of knowledge and hope that Hettie had lost. If she ever had it.

God was a thorny topic these days—for each of the six women in different ways. Perhaps, Hettie thought, God was a thorny topic for everyone when life didn't give what they'd come to expect from love. The other day Caroline had said something about people in the West having different meanings for some words. Maybe that was it, Hettie thought. Maybe God had different meanings for words.

At least for now, Hettie liked the idea of God staying where he was, which seemed to be along the fringes of things that pertained to her. She hoped he refrained from stepping into her personal life, at least until she was safe at Four Corners. *Safe.* Now, there was a word. Would she ever feel safe again? She'd ponder that another time.

For the moment, the last passenger on this evening's westbound train was limping his way to the new hotel that had just opened a couple of days ago. The limp had caused a few heart palpitations for Hettie until she realized the owner of the limp was a stranger. She could breathe again. But now—what?

Two riders came tearing across the prairie from the north. Hettie went to the door and stepped outside just as they parted north of the railroad tracks. One continued to the east while the other charged toward the Immigrant House and, bringing his horse to a skidding stop when he saw Hettie, hollered, "Need the doc! The lady doc. Fast!"

Hettie pressed her open palm to her chest. "I . . . I . . . there's no . . ." She swallowed. "I keep telling people I am *not* a doctor!"

"You're the closest thing we got and we need you." The cowboy pointed east toward the other rider, who had already nearly disappeared into the distance. "Johnny's headed to the fort to bring their doc if we can get him, but that'll take hours longer. You've got to come, ma'am. The boss is hurt. Real bad."

Ruth Dow came out to join her. "What is it? What's happened?"

The rider repeated his desperate plea.

"Who's your boss?"

"Lucas Gray," the man said, gasping for breath and motioning at Hettie. "He said to bring you." He gulped. "That new stallion tore loose and nearly killed him. Don't know what all is wrong, but he's busted up bad. Please, ma'am."

Hettie took a step back as she shook her head. "I told you I'm not—"

"You knew what to do for Frank Darby's wife. She said you treated some gal's ankle, too. Anyway, the boss heard about it. He said to bring you. I can't go back there without you, ma'am. Please. Anything you can do is gonna be better than what the rest of us know." He glanced at Ruth and back to Hettie. "Your friend can come, too, if you're worried about—if you think it won't look right. Just please, could we not wait any longer. It'll take us till nearly dawn as it is."

Hettie pushed her spectacles up on her nose with a trembling hand.

"You know more than any of the rest of us," the man repeated.

"A-all right," she said. "Tell me what happened."

"His horse—"

"I heard that. What exactly did the horse *do*?"

"Reared up and fell back on him. And then pounded on him while he was down."

Hettie's stomach began to churn. "Is he conscious?"

"In and out."

"Is he bleeding?"

"Not really. Except his leg. Some. Not bad, though. The boys were wrapping it when Johnny and I left."

"Bleeding how? From where?"

The wrangler shrugged. "It's broke, I think. Maybe some bone poking through? There wasn't really all that much blood—"

*Dear God in heaven. A compound fracture?* Hettie ran her hand over her hair. She glanced at Ruth. "W-will you come?"

"Of course. Just let me see to Jackson."

The wrangler nodded. "I'll get the livery to hitch up a light rig." He hesitated. "You can drive?"

"I can," Ruth said briskly.

Hettie closed her eyes, trying to think. "We'll need carbolic acid, soap, bandages, alcohol—whiskey if we can't get alcohol." She looked at the wrangler. "Did they splint the leg before they moved him?"

He frowned. "I don't know, ma'am. Johnny and me were in the saddle on our way to get you before they had it so much as wrapped up."

"All right. Ruth and I will meet you at the livery in a few minutes." Summoned by the commotion, Ella and Zita, and Caroline and Sally had all come outside. Now they waited by the door, ready to help.

"You need anything else you can think of?" Ruth asked, ticking off the list Hettie had already given her.

"Camphor. And mustard for a poultice in case there's—" she gestured toward her lungs—"in case there's complications. If his leg's broken, he's going to have to be in bed for a while. Pneumonia will be a threat."

Zita spoke up. "I'll get you some of my remedy."

"Put my cough right to bed the other night," Sally said, nodding. "What's in it?"

Zita shrugged. "Old Italian secrets."

"I had pneumonia when I was little," Ella explained. "Mama got this remedy from someone in the village. She's always believed it saved my life."

Hettie glanced Zita's way. "Th-thank you." As Zita went after her remedy, Hettie gave orders, calming a bit as the ladies scattered to do her bidding. At least Forrest had been good for that. He'd taught her well. She shivered momentarily. He may have taught her too well. She'd helped him do amputations, and if Lucas Gray had a compound fracture, it was going to take a miracle to keep him from needing one.

"Young man," Ruth said to Gray's wrangler as Hettie settled the last box of provisions into the carriage, "my husband was General George Washington Jackson Dow. We posted in some fairly remote areas, and I once drove a carriage back to the fort with a war party of Apache a few minutes behind me, so stop worrying and mount up." As the wrangler obeyed, she hugged Jackson and told him to mind the ladies, then for some reason felt compelled to reach out to Zita. "I'll be trusting you to pray for us."

Zita's eyes sparkled with love as she grasped Ruth's hands in hers, lifted her face to the sky, and said aloud, "Courage. Safety. Healed bodies. Healed hearts. Mighty faith. Please, Father. Amen."

The minute Ruth and Hettie scrambled into the carriage seat, the wrangler took off at a brisk canter. Ruth chirruped to the little roan mare Ermisch said was his best carriage horse. Settling the mare into a lope, Ruth sat back, alert but relaxed. She glanced at Hettie, who was telegraphing tension both in the way she leaned forward in the seat and in the tightness of her grip on the lap robe they shared. "Try to relax," she said. "According to that wrangler we have a long night ahead of us. It won't do to have your back cramping up halfway to the ranch."

"Y-you really do know what you're doing," Hettie finally said.

Ruth only nodded, although the surprise in Hettie's voice made her smile.

"I . . . I didn't mean to sound so s-surprised."

"It's all right." Ruth took a deep breath. "Thank you for asking me to come. For trusting that I could be useful." And she could be useful. Somehow, she was finding herself again. Finding the capable woman who'd been lost all those years ago when the General's sudden death swept everything away. For several months it had taken all her energy merely to climb out of bed every morning and feed Jackson. She'd moved through the days like a woman clawing her way through a thick fog. And she'd been so grateful for Margaret's willingness to make decisions for her. So grateful for the invitation to move in with

Margaret and Theo. *A lifesaver,* Ruth had called it. And for a time it was. *Until Cecil Grissom.*

Perhaps that was the beginning of her awakening. Certainly Margaret's insistence had been a jolt. How had that happened, anyway? How could she have allowed Margaret to think she could not only tell Ruth to marry, but also select the groom? Thinking back on it now, Ruth realized that for most of Jackson's childhood, she'd been disconnected. Margaret's willingness to help had only enabled Ruth to lose even more of herself. It was as if she had folded the part of herself George loved away. He never would have wanted that to happen. He would *not* have been pleased with a weak woman longing so much for the past that she simply allowed things to happen instead of taking the reins and—

Ruth looked down at the reins in her hands. *Taking the reins.* That's what she was doing, wasn't it? She was driving a carriage across the prairie toward the unknown. And she wasn't afraid. *She wasn't afraid.* George would be so much more pleased with this Ruth Dow. He would be proud of her. Proud of the way she'd said yes to Hettie without hesitation. Proud of the way she'd taken the reins in hand and told that cowboy not to worry. And proud of the way she was driving. Carefully, lest a carriage wheel begin a slide down one of these sand ridges, but with a strong hand that told the little mare there would be no nonsense tonight.

The wrangler they were following slowed his mount. Ruth drove alongside. "There's a watering hole ahead," he said. "We can give the horses a breather. You ladies can just stay seated—" he hesitated—"if you can keep the horse from overdoing it with the water. Otherwise—"

"I can handle the horse," Ruth said, and grabbed the buggy whip from its stanchion. "Lead on." Yes. Ruth Dow was definitely finding her way back.

Late Sunday night, Caroline stood alone in the pool of pale moonlight shining into the Immigrant House through the tall double windows on either side of the front doors. How long, she wondered, would the bad dreams last? How long would it be before she could sleep without smelling Lowell Day's peppermint-laced breath, without hearing his voice? She shivered and turned her thoughts toward the northwest and Lucas Gray's ranch, wishing she'd been nicer to him. Hoping the messenger was somehow wrong about the seriousness of Gray's injury. Images of the men in Basil's hospital rose up even as wolves—or maybe it was just coyotes—howled in the distance. The lonely sound sent another wave of sadness through her. Jackson slipped up beside her.

"You're supposed to be asleep," Caroline chided. "We promised your mother we'd watch over you. She wouldn't want you up half the night."

"I don't need watching over," Jackson groused. "And anyway, I can't sleep, either." He was quiet for a few minutes. "At least it's a clear night. The moonlight will help Mother drive safely—won't it?"

"I'm sure it will. She seemed confident about her driving."

"I didn't know she'd done that. Driven a carriage ahead of a war party. She doesn't talk very much about her times with my father. Oh, she talks about *him* all the time, but—I never thought about the adventures she might have had *with* him before I was born. I mean, I knew she was always with him and that some of the posts weren't very . . . luxurious, as Mother put it, but I never pictured her as . . . *tough*. She's probably done some of the things I read about in *Texan Joe*. Or at least seen them. But she never let on. Not once." He murmured, "I hope they can help Mr. Gray. I hope he'll be all right."

"So do I," Caroline agreed.

"Back in St. Louis we had a doctor—three of them, in fact— just around the corner. And when it snowed the wind didn't whistle through the walls. Aunt Margaret's house had gas lighting." Jackson paused. The quiet made the coyotes sound closer. *Or maybe they* are *closer.* Jackson nodded toward the north. "It would be really dark out there if the moon weren't shining tonight."

*He's trying to be brave, but the adventure is wearing thin.* Caroline forced a confidence she wasn't sure she felt into her tone. "Martha says people tend to keep a lamp lit in the window. And she said soddies are warm and cozy."

"But we'll be a long way from . . . anyone else. Just like Mr. Gray."

"Probably not for long. There's Mr. Cooper. And Mr. Haywood seems to think people are going to be flooding into this area. Things are going to change fast. The town board is already trying to recruit a doctor and a blacksmith and a schoolteacher and more builders, and Linney's pa is a carpenter and—"

"Linney says her pa is the best carpenter ever." Jackson gave a little snort. "She thinks he's the best *everything*."

Caroline felt she should choose her words carefully when it came to Matthew Ransom. How grateful she'd been for the strength of the arm Matthew had offered last night after—after Lowell Day. He didn't know how close she'd come to weeping in his arms. Thankfully Sally didn't either, although Sally had teased Caroline a few times about how Matthew Ransom just seemed to appear whenever she—or her parasol—needed rescuing. Of course that was ridiculous. Sally had done the rescuing that night. And yet . . . *You think about Matthew Ransom far too much.*

"He can't be the best *everything,*" Jackson muttered.

"It is wonderful the way they're getting along now, though, don't you think? And wonderful that he's moved to town."

"Sure. Linney's hard to understand, though. I mean, she was so *mad* at him. And then they drove off together in a carriage and when they came back everything was fine. Just like that." Jackson sighed. "I guess that's good, though. At least she *has* a father."

"And you have a mother who loves you very much."

"I know. But Linney has Martha. And lots of other ladies who care about her and teach her all the girl stuff."

*And you don't have anyone stepping into your pa's shoes.* Jackson was more than lonely. He was missing having a father. Matthew Ransom's moving into town must have opened an old wound. Now that Caroline thought about it, it was no wonder Jackson had been so thrilled with Mr. Gray's invitation to the ranch. After all, how often had he been around someone who exuded such masculine...masculinity? Caroline frowned. Handsome face, psalm singing, and testament toting aside, she didn't think Lucas Gray was a good candidate to be a father figure for Jackson. Matthew Ransom, on the other hand ...

"I'm glad Hettie's going to live with us," Jackson said abruptly. "What I mean is, it's especially nice to have someone like her with us. In case anyone gets sick. Or hurt." He paused. "I never thought about all the things that could happen out here. I guess it's kind of ... dangerous in a way."

He turned to face Caroline. "I have to learn to ride, Caroline. I need to be able to do my part. I can't be a little kid out here. If I could ride, then I could be like that wrangler who came for Hettie tonight. I could be the one going for help if something happened she couldn't handle."

Caroline wanted to hug him. She wanted to comfort him and tell him that everyone was going to be fine. To reassure him that nothing bad would happen to them ... and that she would teach him to ride, not because he would need to rescue anyone, but because horses were wonderful animals and a boy should have a horse. But she couldn't promise that nothing bad would happen. Look what had almost happened to her. And she'd heard her share of stories these past two weeks. Stories of violent storms and cattle stampedes, of prairie fires and blizzards. Jackson had likely heard his share of similar stories. People out here either liked to exaggerate, or they liked to celebrate survival. Part of her hoped it wouldn't be as hard as it sounded to succeed on a homestead. Part of her knew it likely would.

Abruptly, she tore herself away from the idea of blizzards and prairie fires. Jackson was right about one thing. They all needed to be willing to learn and grow, and she could help him with one part of the process. She put her hand on his shoulder and forced a lighthearted tone. "I'll tell you what. Before we leave for the homestead in the morning, I'll ask Mr. Ransom if he meant it when he offered Patch for ridin' lessons. Ella's already hired him to do some of the carpentry out at the Four Corners, and while he'll likely drive out with a wagonload of tools and such, maybe if we ask him, he'll bring Patch along. Maybe you and I can manage us some ridin' lessons. Why, if things go well, you just might be a regular cowboy before your mama and Hettie get back."

From what Ruth could see in the predawn moonlight, Lucas Gray's ranch was a random collection of small buildings nestled into a valley surrounded by sandhills. It was too dark to see details, and the instant she pulled the carriage up to the house, a figure appeared out of the shadows to take the little mare in hand. Two more wranglers appeared at either side of the carriage to help Ruth and Hettie down. Yet another one led the hard-riding messenger's worn-out mount away. Ruth realized she didn't even know the man's name.

"I've got it, ma'am," the wrangler on her side of the buggy said when she reached for her valise. He smelled of tobacco and sweat, but Ruth didn't mind. In a way, it was one more detail calling her back to her old self as an organized, capable military wife. Woolen uniforms and desert sun created pungent cologne. As Ruth stepped back to let the man get her valise, she thanked him. "Oh no, ma'am," he said. "Thank *you*. For coming all this way. Pete was mighty impressed with your drivin'."

Ruth smiled to herself. A young cadet named George Dow had been impressed more than a time or two, as well. It was one of the things she'd used to get his attention in the long-ago days when she was a somewhat attractive young woman among a bevy of beauties.

The ranch house cast a much longer shadow than Ruth would have expected. Lamps glowed in four sets of double-hung windows set beneath the overhang of a long, low porch. Pale lines of chinking glimmered in the moonlight. Lucas Gray lived in a log house, not a soddy.

A slight figure waited just on the other side of a screen door. *He has screens.* At the ladies' approach, the little man stepped outside and bowed. "My name is Wah Lo. Mr. Gray hurts very much. Thank you for coming." He bowed again and looked at Ruth. "You doctor?"

"No," Ruth said. "I am Mrs. Dow." She turned toward Hettie. "Mrs. Raines is—"

"—*not* a doctor," Hettie said. "My husband was. I assisted him. I'm only here to help until the *real* doctor gets here from the fort."

Wah Lo nodded. "Very good. You help now. That's very good." A bellow erupted from a room toward the back of the house and Wah Lo waved them inside. "He hurts very bad. Hurry, please."

Either Lucas Gray had landed in Nebraska with money, or he was a great deal more successful than Ruth had imagined. The house was large and the furnishings very near luxurious. Even a brief glance to the right as Ruth and Hettie hurried after Wah Lo revealed surprising details about Lucas Gray's life as a rancher. A large rolltop desk opposite the front door was cluttered with papers and an open book. Beyond the desk in the corner of the room, a fainting couch and two overstuffed chairs encircled a heavily carved low wood table. The room seemed more suited to ladies' sewing circle meetings than card playing and smoking. The hallway was a long one. It opened onto another large room, which was, again, a surprise because of the number and quality of the furnishings. Ruth couldn't help but think that perhaps Lucas Gray had earned the right to a certain amount of strutting.

Once in the back bedroom, Ruth held back while Hettie went

to where Mr. Gray lay atop crisp white sheets in a massive bed made from tree limbs someone had knocked together. He seemed to be unconscious, but he'd tossed back a considerable pile of blankets and quilts. Again, the obvious elegance was surprising. From where she stood just inside the doorway, Ruth noted wide lace trim on the pillows and heavy damask drapes at the windows across the room. The details were lost in shadows, but it appeared that Lucas Gray's bedroom included another sitting area.

When Hettie demanded more light, Wah Lo retreated with a promise to bring more lamps. The instant she laid her hand on the seemingly unconscious man's forehead, he grasped her wrist. With a little gasp, Hettie said, "It's Mrs. Raines. You sent for me, remember? I've asked your man to get us more light."

"I know who you are," Gray said through clenched teeth. He pulled her close. "I'm keeping my leg."

Ruth stepped up to the bedside. And that's when she saw the gun.

CHAPTER
SEVENTEEN

*As we have therefore opportunity, let us do good unto all men,*
*especially unto them who are of the household of faith.*

GALATIANS 6:10

Will Haywood had reassured the ladies of Four Corners that at least half a dozen homesteaders would turn up to help build their soddy. "That's just how things work out here," he said. "The ladies have quilting bees, and the menfolk have building bees. You'll see. You'll be moved out of those tents and into a snug soddy before you know it."

Early Monday morning, Caroline and Ella hurried down to the livery to take a look at the two teams Caroline had singled out. It wasn't a difficult choice. When one of the gray mares nudged Ella in the back and nibbled her shoulder, that was that. Laughing, Ella said, "Well, it seems this one has chosen me." She nodded at a wagon that had been sitting in the same spot for the past two weeks and asked Mr. Ermisch about buying it.

He shook his head. "I can't take money for that. It's got rotten floorboards, and the running gear needs greasing. It's not good for much more than parts for my new wagon builder." He hesitated. "Of course Matthew can repair it—but he'll be busy cutting shingles for a while. I suppose I could grease it up for you and you could use it today." He shrugged. "But mind, it needs an overhaul."

"You must name a price," Ella said, but when she reached for the community purse, Ermisch waved it away. "We'll work somethin' out later. You can catch up with the trader at the dining hall about the mares. I'll get the team harnessed and hitched up while you settle." He tugged on his beard. "Now, you don't need to say I told you this, but he's overpriced those teams. You should be able to talk him down at least ten dollars."

"Not for the grays," Caroline said. "I think the one mare's in foal." She blushed. "At least there's a good chance." She wasn't about to expound on how she knew that. Surely Otto Ermisch realized that old stallion he'd put "out to pasture" in the corral wasn't completely . . . old.

It took a moment for Ermisch to realize how Caroline could possibly know—but then he grinned and glanced toward the corral. "You old devil, you," he chuckled.

Whatever Will Haywood might have said about "the way things work out here," none of the Four Corners ladies—least of all Caroline—had anticipated the sight they beheld as they brought the grays to a stop and looked down on their building site. Half a dozen wagons and two more coming from the opposite direction. A gathering of sun-bonneted women near the supply tents, and a dozen or more men scattered all across the place, inspecting the stakes by the house, yoking oxen, and watering teams.

Caroline joined the ladies in a collective gasp.

"Well, ain't that somethin'?" Sally said.

"Linney came!" Jackson pointed toward the spot where she and her father stood waiting. "And Patch is already saddled! Can we do a lesson right away, Caroline? Can we?"

"We'll have to see," Caroline said. And oh, did she see. Folks heading over to greet the ladies. Zita nearly skipping with anticipation as she made her way to the supply tent. Ella greeting and thanking people for coming. Sally clucking to the hens as if they needed reassurance as Mr. Cooper lifted their crate down from the wagon. Linney, grabbing Jackson's hand and hauling him over to where Patch waited. And Matthew, all six feet of him, walking this way with a smile God must have designed to melt a woman's heart.

The farthest thing from Ella's mind was to create a sensation. She didn't even think about the ramifications, really. She just did what she naturally wanted to do and what she was gifted to do, which was *not* lingering near the supply tent pouring lemonade and coffee or sharing community gossip while the ladies sliced bread or opened jars of pickles or served up pie. Those things were part of Mama's world, but not Ella's. And so, after Mr. Cooper plowed the first furrow, and Will Haywood cut the curls of sod into three-foot lengths, and after Frank Darby drove his flatbed wagon up so the sod strips could be loaded and hauled to the building site, it was the most natural thing in the world for Ella to begin loading sod. The thing was, that didn't seem natural to anyone else.

"Now, Miz Barton," Mr. Darby protested, "there's no call for you to do that. You just let the boys handle it." He took a blue kerchief out of his rear pocket and swiped the back of his neck. "You ladies got much better things to do—"

"There's nothing better for *me*," Ella said, "than this." She bent to lift another strip of sod and hoisted it onto the flatbed wagon.

"Please, ma'am," Darby pleaded. "It ain't right."

"For who?" Ella said. She lifted a third strip of sod.

"The men won't like it, ma'am."

Ella put her hands on her hips. "Let's ask them," she said, and with that she strode toward where Jeb Cooper was plowing.

"Mr. Cooper. Mr. Darby here thinks the men will object to my helping build my own house. Do *you* object, Mr. Cooper?"

Cooper looked at Ella . . . the rancher . . . the homesite . . . and back to Ella.

"Well, Mr. Cooper. Do you object?"

"It is . . . unusual."

"*I'm* unusual," Ella snapped. She thought she saw a sudden flash of amusement in the man's blue eyes. "Well, Mr. Cooper, are you going to refuse to plow for a woman who dares to venture into a man's world of work?"

"No, ma'am."

At least he said *that* with conviction. "And what do you say to Mr. Darby's objections?"

Cooper took his hat off and swiped at his forehead. Finally, he spoke. "Well, Frank, to my mind, what a woman does or doesn't do should be up to the woman. She should be who she is, not what others expect her to be." He shrugged. "It's her land. As far as I'm concerned, she's the boss."

It took a minute for Ella to believe what she'd just heard. For a moment she thought perhaps Jeb Cooper was mocking her. But he met her gaze honestly, and so she merely thanked him and then bent to pick up another slab of sod.

Frank Darby didn't say another word about "women's work."

And as the afternoon wore on, Ella decided that Jeb Cooper was not only strong and clever in the way he'd overcome losing a hand. He was also a singularly wise man.

"I'm keeping my leg," Gray repeated through clenched teeth, "and I'll shoot the first person who tries to do anything against the idea."

Hettie tried to pull away from his grip on her wrist. "Th-there's n-no need t-t—"

"Yes. There is." He raised the gun a little higher off the bed with his free hand. "I heard what the boys said when they were wrapping it up.

They thought I was out cold, but I wasn't. I know what they do when there's bone stickin' out of a man's leg." He released Hettie's arm.

His gaze moved from Hettie to Ruth. Recognition flickered in his eyes. He swallowed. "You know what I did in the war?" When Ruth and Hettie both shook their heads, he said, "Well, while the officers pored over their battle maps and stood back and watched the rest of us die, I was burying legs. And arms. And hands and feet. Mountains of limbs piled high outside the surgeon's tent." He swallowed. "So believe me when I say that the only way my leg gets buried is if I'm attached to it." He waved the gun in the air for emphasis.

It was a monstrous thing. The barrel looked a foot long. Did he really think he could bully them into— Poor Hettie. Ruth saw her hands tremble as she swept them over her frizzy hair. Saw her stance waver slightly. Was she going to faint? Ruth stepped forward and put a hand on Hettie's shoulder. She could feel the poor woman trembling through her cloak. "Mr. Gray," she said, her tone severe, her expression even more so. "Stop talking nonsense. No one is talking about cutting off anything. We haven't even *seen* your leg." She patted Hettie's shoulder. "You are frightening the only doctor you've got for the next few hours, and that's very unwise." She held out her hand. "Now, hand me that gun and hush."

Wah Lo came into the room, a lighted lamp in each hand. Without taking her eyes from Gray's face, Ruth gave instructions. "We'll need hot water, Mr. Loh. And clean bandages. And soap." Still, she held Gray's gaze. "I have dealt with tougher men than you, Lucas Gray. Hettie and I will help you, but I won't countenance any more nonsense with guns." She continued to hold out her hand. "Now, give me that thing." Gray hesitated. Ruth had the feeling she was being measured. She kept her gaze locked on his. Arched one eyebrow. Lifted her chin.

Gray looked from Ruth to Hettie and back again.

He handed Ruth the gun.

Gray had a daunting list of injuries. Under Ruth's relentless questioning, he finally admitted he had lost consciousness for a while. He had a goose egg on the back of his head, but his pupils seemed to react normally to the light when Hettie moved a lamp close and then pulled it away. He had two nasty bruises on his right side that looked suspiciously like the outline of a very large horse's hoof. "But," Hettie whispered, "I don't think he has any more than two ribs broken." Amazingly, he seemed able to flex or move every joint in his body except the knee above and the ankle below the fractured bone in his left leg. Hettie didn't want him to try moving those until she'd examined his leg in the full light of day.

The man's dogged ability to endure pain was nearly miraculous. From what the wranglers said the stallion did to its owner, every fiber of Gray's body had to be crying out in one way or the other. But other than a couple of bellows when Hettie wrapped his ribs, Gray hadn't complained. When Wah Lo offered him whiskey, he waved it away with a mild curse—and an instant apology "to the ladies." He even glanced Ruth's way and joked, "I've been told they won't tolerate any nonsense."

Ruth spoke as soon as Wah Lo set their traveling cases on the low dresser across from the carved oak bed and slipped out, closing the door behind him. He'd insisted the two women retire and get some rest until daylight. "You do no good you too tired to think," he said. "I'll see to Mr. Gray now. Call you at dawn—or if he gets worse."

Dressed only in her chemise and petticoat, Ruth pulled back the finely wrought red-and-green quilt serving as a spread and lay down. "Tell me," she said as Hettie freshened up at the washstand. "Tell me everything."

While she rinsed off, Hettie repeated Gray's list of injuries.

"And now," Ruth said, reaching for an extra pillow and clutching it to her midsection, "what about the leg?"

"Well." Hettie sighed. "If what that one wrangler said is right and there is exposed bone, then—" She dried her hands and draped the towel across the bar above the washstand. "Then it's called a compound fracture."

"And how will you treat that?"

Hettie looked away. Shook her head.

Ruth sighed. "I thought so." She waited until Hettie had stretched out next to her before speaking again. "If it comes to that kind of procedure—I mean, how would you do that without the proper . . . tools." She shuddered envisioning the surgeon's case she'd once seen. Surgical saws. Pliers. Retractors. Clamps.

"It won't come to that," Hettie said quickly. "At least not for you and me. The doctor from the fort will be here by then."

Ruth had seen her share of wounded soldiers and even been called on a time or two to assist a military physician with minor things like sewing up cuts or applying compresses to keep a fever down, but she'd never been involved in anything like this before. As morning light streamed in their bedroom window, Hettie explained what Ruth should expect.

"The most important thing we can do for Mr. Gray," she said, "is to remain calm. No matter what you see, no matter what he does, we must remain calm." She peered at Ruth over her spectacles. "A man who would wave a gun in a doctor's face is a desperate man. Forrest always said that such emotions can impede healing. He believed it was very important for a doctor to mask whatever they *feel* about what they see behind a smile. And if you can't smile, then at the very least *do not frown.*" She paused. "If you feel queasy, just slip out of the room. That's much better than fainting in the patient's presence."

"Understood," Ruth said, barely able to hide her amazement at Hettie's newfound calm. Where was the woman who trembled at the sound of a train whistle, who skittered about like a little bird and jumped at the slightest noise? The woman Ruth followed into Lucas Gray's bedroom was a different person. First, she asked Wah Lo to open the drapes. With sunshine spilling into the room, Hettie unbuttoned her cuffs and rolled up her sleeves. She washed her hands and directed Ruth to do the same. Together, they went to work.

Hettie seemed to grow calmer with every passing moment. She talked—without stuttering—while she worked. "All right, Mr. Gray. I'm going to cut away this last strip now. I don't want you to move at all. I'll tell you when—and if—I think that's a good idea. Until then, you just lay still." She had him take a swallow of whiskey and then, when the length of cloth fell away and she saw the wound, she calmly told Wah Lo that he should get two of Mr. Gray's "most trusted employees" and have them roll up their sleeves and wash. She explained how she wanted them to wash—with the hottest water they could stand and lye soap. "I want them so clean there's not a speck of dirt beneath their fingernails," she said quietly, and then she explained that her husband had been reading new research and it seemed to indicate a connection between cleanliness and infection.

"I don't know if any of it's true, but Forrest is—*w-was* a good doctor." She stood back at that point. "So now Mrs. Dow and I are going to go and do a similar cleanup, and when we come back we'll see to this." She waved at the leg as if it were nothing to be worried about. When Gray tried to speak between clenched teeth, Hettie put a hand on his shoulder. "I remember what you said in the night, Mr. Gray. You have my word. There will be no attempt to amputate while I am here. So please. Try to relax."

She turned back at the doorway. "And when I tell you to drink more whiskey, trust me. I'm not trying to get you drunk so I can have my way with you." She smiled. "We'll save that until you're feeling much better."

Gray barked a laugh.

When Hettie paused halfway up the hall and closed her eyes, Ruth reached out. The frightened Hettie had made an appearance. "If . . . if you pray," she said, "n-now would be a good time." She sucked in a breath.

Wah Lo had heated up water and produced lye soap. The cowboys arrived, and Hettie demonstrated just how thoroughly they must wash. Ruth thought she recognized the man who'd come for them in Plum Grove, and when she asked, he nodded.

"Yes, ma'am. I'm Pete. Mr. Gray's foreman." He nodded at the man next to him. "This here's Del. Del and I have been riding trails with Mr. Gray since right after the trouble with Ransom—" He paused. "Since the start. Anyway, I figured Mr. Gray wouldn't want a lot of the boys to know how bad it is. Word gets out he's not in the saddle, could be some of the other less honorable men in the county might take it upon themselves to take advantage. The late storm was bad enough on the calves. We don't need rustlers taking an extra toll."

Ruth couldn't help but wonder why Lucas Gray traveled with the likes of Lowell Day when he had men like these two working for him. She stepped back from the hot water and, wiping her hands dry, followed Hettie up the hall. Pete and Del followed.

Once again, Hettie spoke calmly as she worked. "Now, I'm going to do some things that may not seem right to anyone who's seen things like this treated before. My husband's uncle sent him a paper this past year from a conference he'd attended in Karlsbad. Karlsbad, Germany."

Hettie spoke directly to Gray. "I'll explain everything I'm doing. Try to listen to my voice and forget about your leg. If you can, just concentrate on my voice." She talked, even as Gray sweated and moaned with every one of her movements. "The paper seemed to indicate that sepsis and some of the other complications might be avoidable. First we need to keep it clean. So I'm going to douse it with water . . . and carbolic acid. . . ."

Ruth saw Pete's face go pale. She leaned close. "Don't look at what she's doing," she said and nodded toward the windows. "Look out there. Find something and focus on it." As she glanced outside she saw the gray stallion in the corral. Pete's gaze narrowed. He set his jaw and held on.

Hettie continued to work. When she switched positions with Del and set the bone, Gray fainted. Instead of stitching up the wound after the bone was set, she packed it with bandages she'd had Wah Lo boil. Then she rewrapped the leg, leaving the wound to heal, she said, from the inside out. "At least that's the theory behind the paper," she said with a little shrug. "Forrest said the statistics proved it a promising development."

Back out in the hall, Hettie's voice wavered when she said, "I h-hope I remembered everything." She sighed. "And I hope the doctor from the fort comes soon."

Ruth squeezed her hand. "He will. Wah Lo said he should be here by sundown. And then we can get home." *Home.* Had she really just said that? "In the meantime," she said, "I don't know about you, but I'm exhausted." Once they had washed up, Ruth led the way back to their room.

A soft knock at the door woke Ruth first. She sat up and blinked in surprise. The sun had gone down. Wah Lo was at the door. Gray was still asleep, but Wah Lo had a supper cooked, and Pete was waiting to speak with them. Wah Lo said it was urgent.

"We'll be right out," Ruth said, and roused Hettie. Together they walked down the hallway to where Pete waited just inside the front door, his hat in his hands.

"I don't know any other way to say it than right out. There's no doctor coming. 'Relieved of his duties' is all the commanding officer would tell Johnny. They don't know when they'll get a replacement. I sent Johnny to telegraph up the line to the next few stations to see about getting a doctor to come this way. That's the best I could do." Pete shifted his weight from one foot to the other. "But I've got to tell you, I don't hold out much hope for that happening." He fidgeted with the hat in his hands. Cleared his throat. "I guess it's plain that we need you to stay."

Hettie ran her palms across her hair and touched the place at the bridge of her nose where her spectacles should be. "I . . . I've done everything I know to do. Mr. Gray needs a trained physician."

Pete nodded. "Yes, ma'am. But all he's got is you and Mrs. Dow. We need you to stay. Both of you. Please."

Ruth glanced at Hettie, who looked pale and panicky. Exactly the way Ruth felt, but somehow she managed not to sound that way. "Can you keep the ranch going? I ask because Hettie says the patient's . . . sense of things . . . is important in healing. So . . . will Mr. Gray be worried about the ranch or will he be able to concentrate on healing?"

Pete looked off toward one corner of the room, thinking aloud. "We've got calves coming by the dozen. And with all the homesteaders pouring in we're going to have to start running fence. Lowell Day's disappeared. Luke had him in charge of collecting fence posts and such. Who's to replace him would of course be Luke's call."

"But you *can* handle things," Ruth said. "I can sense you're already figuring out how."

Pete drew in a deep breath and nodded. "Yes, ma'am. I can."

"Well, then. It would appear we are all in the same position. We are all Mr. Gray has. And that will have to do." As Pete nodded and turned to go, Ruth asked, "Could you send word that we're going to be staying on for a while? Our friends were headed to our homestead today—this morning. It's—"

"Yes, ma'am," Pete interrupted. "We know where it is. You ladies claimed the cottonwood spring." He smiled. "Smart choice."

"Well. Thank you. I hate to bring this up, but I expect Mr. Ermisch in Plum Grove would appreciate knowing we haven't stolen his best carriage horse." Ruth frowned. "Do you think we should return it so he has use of it during our stay?"

"I'll see that someone checks in at the livery. If Mr. Ermisch is worried about the rig, we'll just tell him to consider it sold to Lucas Gray."

Ruth thought that a rather extravagant way to handle things, but she liked the idea of having the rig handy. Somehow she'd feel less stranded with it here. If Mr. Gray fared well, maybe she could even drive to the homestead in a few days and check on Jackson. Of course Jackson was just fine, but she wouldn't mind being really certain. This was, after all, the first time they'd been apart in all of Jackson's young life.

*Except the Lord build the house,
they labour in vain that build it....*

PSALM 127:1

The homebuilders began in one corner—by chance it was the corner that would be Ella's side of the west bedroom wing—and laid two adjacent rows of sod strips grass-side-down and end-to-end along the guide string until finally the long rectangular outline of the forty-two-by-twelve-foot house appeared atop the prairie. Sally and Caroline helped pack the seams between each strip with loose earth before the next row of strips was stacked atop the first. And so it went, with lengthwise strips staggered so seams didn't line up with the row below, and every third row laid crosswise to the two below.

As the walls rose, two men wielded spades to shave the inside surface as clean as possible in preparation for plaster. They would shave the outer walls, too, Will explained, because "a smooth surface weathers better."

While the house walls rose, Matthew Ransom worked on the door-frames, his daughter alongside holding, fetching, sanding, laughing. It was obvious the girl was thrilled to be with her pa, and Ella noticed it wasn't long before Jackson was helping with the carpentry, as well. When she took a short break to get a drink of water, Ella paused at the "carpentry shop" long enough to listen to Ransom tell Linney and Jackson why he was having them drill holes in each of the doorframes.

"When I hammer a dowel through into the sod," he said, pointing to a hole, "that will hold the frame in place."

By the time the third row of sod was laid, Ransom and his two assistants had the doorframes built. Jackson helped him set them in place, obviously pleased with his contribution to the effort. When Ransom began constructing window frames, Ella noted that he had Linney drill all the holes while Jackson built his own window frame. Knowing the future Ruth had mapped out for Jackson, Ella wondered if she would mind her son's apparent interest in carpentry.

They lunched standing at long planks laden with sandwiches and boiled eggs, pickled beets, and dried-apple pies. Caroline didn't think she'd ever seen so much food consumed in one sitting. It made her smile to think how shocked the proper Mother Jamison would be to see mugs of soup drunk down like so much coffee by men with dust-streaked faces and muddy work boots.

By afternoon Will had to park a flatbed wagon alongside the soddy walls so the builders could reach the tops of the ever-growing walls. Matthew had Jackson and Linney begin filling buckets with loose earth and handing them up to Caroline and Sally so the two ladies could stay put atop the flatbed. When the walls were chest-high, Matthew stepped inside, plumb line in hand.

"If they aren't straight now," he explained as Caroline and Sally looked on, "they could start to lean when the house settles, and with all that weight . . ." He held one forearm up and mimicked a collapse.

The thought made Caroline shudder. Late in the day, Matthew brought a bucket of loose earth, and when he handed it up, two pair of work gloves lay atop the earth. When Caroline looked surprised, he smiled. "Sturdier gloves." He winked at Sally. "A lady's hands deserve protecting, right?"

"What about your hands?" Caroline asked as she pulled on a glove and wiggled a wave at Matthew.

"Won't need them for a while. Since you're . . . occupied and I've finished the door and window frames, I told Jackson I'd show him a thing or two about riding." He reached up and tugged on one of the half-empty glove fingers. "But I'll be needing these back tomorrow. Will's going to bring out some small sizes." He shook his head. "No one really expected the ladies of Four Corners to build their own house, you know."

"Folks should get used to the ladies of Four Corners doin' unexpected things, then," Sally said.

Matthew nodded. "So we're learning."

Ruth had just dozed off—she and Hettie were taking turns staying at Gray's bedside—when he moaned in his sleep. "Darlin'. Don't go, darlin'. Look what I did. All for you. All for you. Don't go—don't leave me alone—please. . . ." Ruth studied the handsome face as Gray continued to mutter, lost inside the nightmare . . . or was it a memory? Tears slipped out of his closed eyes.

Ruth's heart softened toward the man who, when healthy, seemed so arrogant. As he continued to beg whoever it was not to leave him, Ruth rinsed a cloth in cool water and laid it on his feverish brow. She murmured, soothing him with the same sounds she'd used when Jackson was a babe in arms. "Shh . . . shh . . . it's all right . . . there now . . . shh."

It calmed him somewhat, but not enough. Finally, Ruth moved her chair close. She reached out and put a hand on his arm. "It's Mrs. Dow, Mr. Gray. You're right here at home. Safe in your bed. In your very own room. You've got a bit of a fever, but you're going to be fine. No one's deserting you. No one's leaving you alone. Just relax now . . .

there's no reason to be upset . . . it's just a bad dream. That's all. Shh . . . shh . . ."

Slowly, Gray relaxed. The lines across his brow disappeared. He stopped muttering. His breath evened out as he sank deeper into what Ruth hoped was a restful sleep. Hettie had said to just bathe his face and try to keep him comfortable. There was nothing else to be done. They wouldn't bother the dressing for at least two weeks. "I cleaned it as best I could. If we mess with it now, we're just inviting infection."

"But how will we know if the wound is healing?"

"We'll know," Hettie said.

"But—"

She touched her nose. "You never forget the smell of gangrene."

Gray's eyes flew open. With a vacant stare he grasped Ruth's forearm. "My leg," he croaked. "Don't let them take my leg."

"Your leg is fine. You have a little fever is all. Nothing serious." She hoped it wasn't a lie. After all, they hadn't seen the wound since Hettie reduced the fracture and tended it. Only a little blood had seeped through the first bandage. Hettie said that when it dried, it would help seal out infection. They would leave it be and wrap over the seepage with clean bandages.

"You keep that sawbones from the fort away from me," Gray said, his voice desperate. "You were talking about—someone was talking about him—"

"That was yesterday," Ruth said. "He's not coming."

"Well, that surgeon's a drunk. If he comes near me, I'll shoot—"

"All right," Ruth said. The man's grip was going to leave bruises on her arm. She put her free hand on his shoulder and forced amusement and a gentle scolding into her tone. "You won't need to shoot anyone, Mr. Gray. You have my word on that."

He relaxed a little and closed his eyes, but he still held on to her arm. "Lucas," he murmured. "Call me Lucas."

"And I'm Ruth, and the one who's really directing your care is

Mrs. Raines. Hettie. Now try to sleep. You need to rest and let your leg heal."

"It hurts," he muttered.

"And will for some time to come, I'm afraid," Ruth said.

He opened his eyes again and frowned a little. "I thought nurses were supposed to . . . comfort."

Ruth smiled. "It seems to me you'll be most comforted knowing I'm telling you the truth." With a little nod, he sighed and settled back. Ruth pressed a freshly rinsed cloth to his forehead, then leaned her head back and closed her eyes.

The rancher seemed to be resting peacefully when he suddenly whispered, "Darlin'. . . I did this for you . . . can't you see . . . for you . . . don't go . . . please . . . stay, sweet Katie . . . *stay*. . . ."

By the end of the week a long, roofless sod structure stood exactly over the corner of land where four surveyed homesteads met. It had taken a couple of days, but even Bill Darby finally agreed that he supposed a woman had a right to do whatever God gave her the strength to do—although he personally didn't think building a sod house was the best use of her strength. Ella supposed the rest of the men and most of the women probably agreed with him, but they weren't rude about it. In fact, the building bee had gone a long way toward making the five ladies feel like a part of the community. Mama had promised to show some of the women how to make real Italian tomato sauce when their gardens came in later in the year. Sally Grant reported that she had gotten some good advice about tending poultry, and Caroline had a sketch of a new quilt pattern she wanted to piece.

As for Ella, while she felt weary at day's end, she woke each morning feeling joyful about the promise of her new life and grateful for the fine spring weather. She'd heard the men joshing about "gully-washers" and cyclones as they worked, and while she was suspicious they might be exaggerating about the ferocity of storms and the speed with which they could move in, the April snow gave her cause to wonder. One night when she worried aloud to Mama about rain, Mama just shook her head. "You know how my old bones ache when the weather's going to change. I haven't felt so much as a twinge."

Ella stopped worrying quite so much. But then on Saturday Mama wasn't quite as spry as usual. Right around lunchtime, a few gray-tinted clouds started to gather along the western horizon.

It was time for folks to return home anyway. A couple of the men had ridden from place to place each day tending each other's livestock, but with the soddy walls finished and only the roof remaining, fewer hands would be needed. Still, as neighbor after neighbor loaded up and moved out, as the clouds darkened, "getting home" seemed to take on a new urgency.

When the few clouds became a dark wall, Will said it might be a good idea if the ladies changed their minds about camping out and came back to town. "Could be nothing," he said, nodding toward the horizon. "But then again—" They could pull canvas tarps over the walls to protect them from a gully-washer.

"What if the tarps blow off?" Ella asked.

"I'll see to it."

It was Jeb Cooper, offering to hunker down and make sure things stayed put. When Ella hesitated, Cooper smiled. "A man ought to be allowed to be and do what he thinks is right. Don't you think so, Mrs. Barton?"

What could a woman say to that? And besides, those clouds did look angry. If it were only her, Ella realized, she would stay, but it wasn't only her. It had become increasingly clear as those clouds rolled toward them that Mama's bones were aching. She'd be much better off at the Immigrant House tonight. There was Jackson's safety to consider, too. What if it did storm? What if a cyclone blew through?

And so it was that the Four Corners ladies—plus Jackson—left the tending of their roofless sod walls to Mr. Jed Cooper while they headed for Plum Grove ahead of what looked increasingly like storm clouds.

Mr. Cooper was the topic of conversation among the ladies as Ella drove the wagon. He was going to be a good neighbor. Anyone could see that. He was so kind. The fence he'd put up around Mrs. Ransom's grave had been quite the topic of conversation these past few days. Apparently several of the folks in the county had driven over just to look at it. It was, everyone said, a marvel. And wasn't it a shame that Mr. Cooper couldn't blacksmith anymore, what with Plum Grove needing one. But wasn't it a wonder the way he'd learned to plow without a hand. And had you heard that he had a whole room in that soddy filled with books. Who had ever heard of such a thing. A bookish man out here homesteading. He certainly didn't look like a bookish man, now did he.

As far as Ella was concerned, whether Mr. Jeb Cooper liked books or not was no one's business. As he said, a man should be allowed to do what a man wanted to do. As she drove the team along, she smiled, remembering the way he kept calling her Boss. She had to admit she liked the way his eyes crinkled up at the corners when he said it. Like they shared a joke. A special friendship. Which was all Ella was interested in. Just friendship. Nothing more.

Hettie staggered into the ranch house kitchen and sank into a chair at the table. What was wrong with her? She'd slept soundly for the last two nights, and still she felt exhausted.

Wah Lo wished her a good morning as he set a cup of tea before her. "Eggs come soon," he said. "How you like?"

"Anything is fine," Hettie said. She didn't feel like having breakfast, but she knew better than to refuse Wah Lo's offering. He might not be a large man physically, but he had the will of a giant. If he offered tea, it was best to drink some. As for breakfast, he'd minded the ways of a busy rancher far too long to believe that anyone anywhere could live without breakfast.

The aroma of the tea Wah Lo offered this morning was different. More pungent . . . almost sweet. "This is delicious," Hettie said, and sipped it gratefully.

"Glad you like," Wah Lo said from where he stood cracking eggs into the iron skillet on the stove. "Mrs. Dow, she like, too. I make last night. After you sleep."

Hettie took another sip of tea and then stood up. "I'm going to check in on Ruth and the patient," she said. "I'll be back in a moment."

"Eggs be ready," Wah Lo said without turning around.

Hettie yawned as she slogged down the hallway. At least her stomach had settled. Ruth was sitting in the wing-back chair beside Mr. Gray's bed, her eyes closed, her hand resting atop the mattress. Gray stirred in his sleep. When he coughed, Ruth woke with a start and was on her feet bending over him before she even realized Hettie was in the room.

"Shh, Lucas," Ruth murmured, and put her hand to his forehead.

"I'm all right," he said. "Could use a drink of water, though."

"How about some hot tea?" Hettie asked from the doorway.

Gray opened his eyes. "Tea sounds good. Just tell Wah Lo not to send in any of that sweet-tasting garbage. He'll know which stuff I mean."

"I believe I just drank a cup of it."

Gray turned his head to look at her, and a ghost of a smile flitted across his face before he grimaced. "Figures. He always makes that for the ladies." He grunted.

Hettie went to the bedside. "How's the pain?"

"Dancing up and down my leg." A fine sheen of sweat shone on his forehead.

"Let me have a look," Hettie said, and carefully rolled the blankets away as she spoke. "Tell me if you can feel this."

Gray's brow furrowed. "Feel what?"

"Good." He wasn't trying to fool her into thinking he was doing better than he was. He hadn't felt anything because she hadn't touched him. Now she did, pressing into the ball of his foot with her index finger.

"Pressure," he said. "Near my toes."

"That's right." Hettie nodded as she laid her fingers over the pulse point at his ankle. "Your pulse is strong, and both the color and temperature of the skin below the break are normal. That likely means that even though that bone penetrated muscle and soft tissue, it didn't do damage to the veins or the nerves that feed your lower leg and foot."

"Sounds like good news," Gray said.

"It's very good news." Hettie took a deep breath, trying not to be too obvious about it, relieved when the only thing she smelled was the expected stale air typical of a sickroom. *No gangrene.* At least not yet. "Mr. Gray," she began—

"You've seen my naked feet, ma'am. I believe you can call me Lucas."

Hettie smiled. "All right, then, Lucas. I'd like to give you something to help with the pain. So you can rest better. Rest will help you heal."

Ruth spoke up. "Hettie's brought some of Zita Romano's magic remedy with her. To be quite honest, we have no idea what's in it. But whatever it is, it's been tested and found to be effective." She smiled. "And I give you my word. If anyone tries to take off your leg while you are resting, I will personally shoot them."

Lucas burst out laughing. "All right. But first—tell Wah Lo I'd appreciate his help with some kind of bath." He made a face. "It smells like I've been keeping a goat in this room."

After Lucas washed up he finally agreed to take a dose of Zita's remedy and fell into a deep sleep. Hettie and Ruth took some of Wah Lo's tea outside and sat down beneath the ranch house overhang.

"Do you think he's out of the woods yet?" Ruth asked. "He slept well. No nightmares or mutterings."

"That's a hopeful sign. But it's just too soon to know for certain."

Ruth lifted her teacup to her lips. "I don't understand his objection to this. It's delicious."

"I thought so, too, at first," Hettie said. "But now I'm not sure it agrees with me." Her hand went to her stomach and she set the cup down.

"I hope you aren't coming down with something."

"I'm fine," Hettie insisted. "I've always had a nervous stomach. And this . . . case . . ." She sighed.

"You've done a wonderful job of doctoring. You should—"

"I am *not* a doctor!" Hettie protested. "I wish people would *listen* to me and stop insisting . . ." Her voice wavered. She took a deep breath.

"I meant it as a compliment," Ruth apologized.

"I know." Hettie softened her tone. "I know you did, but—" She pushed her spectacles up. How could she explain herself without actually . . . explaining? Taking a deep breath, she said, "If you left something behind—something painful—how would you feel if it followed you—if circumstances kept you from being free of it?"

"What could possibly be painful about what you've done here? You've likely saved a man's life."

Hettie closed her eyes. She leaned her head back against the high-backed rocker. "Sometimes you *can't* help. Sometimes every single thing you know is completely useless. And then—" She broke off. Shook her head.

"I am so sorry, Hettie. For whatever it was."

"It's all right. I know you mean well." Everyone meant well and no one understood. And they never would if she had anything to say about it. She changed the subject, pointing toward the maze of corrals over by the bunkhouse, where a handful of wranglers were saddling horses. "Lucas seems to have a successful operation going."

"Yes. It's all very impressive."

"I certainly didn't expect to find a house like this anywhere near Plum Grove. It's lovely. And the furnishings ... they seem better suited for a married couple than a bachelor rancher. I can't imagine Lucas chose those pillowcases with the lace trim."

Ruth agreed. "Everything about the house seems very genteel. And that just doesn't describe the man we met on the train, does it?" A gust of wind blew in from the direction of the corral. Ruth sniffed and made a face. "However, I will say he might have put the barns and the corrals a bit farther from the house." The women laughed.

CHAPTER
NINETEEN

*A friend loveth at all times,*
*and a brother is born for adversity.*

PROVERBS 17:17

More dark clouds rolled in from the west when the caravan of wagons was less than a mile from Plum Grove. Matthew nudged his horse alongside the ladies and asked Ella if Linney could ride in the back of their wagon. As soon as Ella pulled the team up, Ransom reached around and lifted Linney from her perch behind him directly into the wagon bed. They'd only gone a few more rods when great bolts of lightning began to dance between sky and earth in the distance. Thunder rolled in. The team quickened its pace. The wind picked up. Ella wasn't sure what to do. Matthew galloped up to them and shouted for Ella to "hightail it for town. I think we can beat it."

Terrified, Ella told Mama to get in the wagon bed with the others. They hunkered together, pelted by huge raindrops and clinging to the edge of the wagon, their faces white with fear. Matthew's horse whinnied. The team snorted. Lightning and thunder were all around them now. The light was odd—everything had a greenish cast to it. The wind roared.

Ella urged the team to go faster and faster. Matthew kept even with the team, and Ella finally realized he was doing his best to prevent a runaway. She took heart.

Finally, a pathetic little row of wooden buildings strung along a piece of prairie someone had had the audacity to call Main Street came into view. Ella had never seen such a beautiful town in all her life.

Ruth slid her hand along the edge of one of the heavy damask drapes in Lucas's bedroom and opened a slit so she could peer outside. Every few minutes lightning illuminated the sodden landscape, and every few minutes a clap of thunder made her cringe. Were storms always this savage out here? Just now she'd watched one of the wranglers charge through the rain to force a barn door closed. When he couldn't manage it one-handed, he'd had to sacrifice his hat to the gusting winds. The barn door finally shut, he slipped between the poles of the corral, and with the next flash of light Ruth caught a glimpse of him scrabbling about between the milling horses, then snatching up the hat. She could only imagine what that hat must look like after being trampled into the mud and manure.

What she could not imagine—and didn't particularly want to—was what this meant for the sod house at Four Corners. From what Lucas had said about the process, the house probably didn't have a roof yet. Was the entire week's work washing away even as she stood here at this window? Were her friends camped out in this storm? Was Jackson? Another clap of thunder made her jump. She let go of the drape.

"How bad is it out there?"

Ruth turned around just as Lucas struggled to raise himself to a sitting position in his bed. She went to the bedside and tucked one of the lace-edged pillows behind him. "Are you awake because of the storm or because you're in pain?"

"A little of both," he said. "Mostly the storm, though—and hoping my stallion isn't out in this."

"If you can worry about that horse, I'm thinking it's a good sign you're getting better." She smiled. "And as a matter of fact I saw one of your men lead him inside just a minute ago."

When lightning flashed again and she jumped, he asked, "Are you afraid of storms, Mrs. General?"

"Of course not," she said firmly, even as her hand went to the frill of lace at her neckline. "Maybe a little." She rubbed her arms briskly. "It's the lightning, mostly. One of my husband's men was killed by lightning at our first posting. I've been shy of it ever since." She paused.

"We pitched three Sibley tents out at Four Corners. The plan was to camp out all week while they laid up the sod walls. But there won't be a roof yet—will there?"

"Likely not. And after a week helping someone else, the home-steaders would need to call it quits and head home to tend their own places. Some of the old-timers probably had a sense a storm was coming. They would take one look at a tent—" he grinned—"even a Sibley pitched by a general's wife—and send your friends and Jackson back to Plum Grove to wait until the storm blows over and things dry out. Your boy's probably playing checkers over in the dining hall complaining of being bored."

When Ruth didn't say anything, he continued, "You can trust me on this. A man learns to keep one eye on the horizon out here. Weather and prairie fires both move in fast, and we've all learned not to take either lightly."

"That's not very reassuring."

"Ah . . . you want to be *reassured*." Gray wrinkled his brow. "Surely you already knew this isn't a very forgiving land. If Hamilton Drake painted it any other way when he was holding those meetings in St. Louis, then he was just . . . trying to fit you all with rose-tinted glasses, as they say."

Ruth crossed the room to peer out at the rain again. "Well, the most important thing he said was true. There's free land and promise for those willing to work hard."

"You're being kinder than he deserves. The first time I laid eyes on your group in St. Louis, I knew Drake must have spun quite a tale."

He snorted. "The Ladies Emigration Society. If he'd told you the truth about what he really had planned—"

Ruth turned back around. "It wouldn't have mattered. At least not to me." Gray looked doubtful. "Oh, I would still have objected to the dance card and the lineup waiting for us, but coming west was the least objectionable of a very short list of unattractive options for me. I'd be a terrible teacher, and dressmaking as a profession would drive me batty. As inept as I may be at homesteading, it's still the best option for Jackson and me. If I can hang on for those five years and prove up, I can sell for enough to get Jackson through St. Louis University. Thanks to Ella and the others, it's looking like it will work out."

"What about marriage? You might not approve of the way Drake handled things, but you're a handsome woman, Ruth. Didn't you even consider marrying again?"

*A handsome woman.* Did he honestly think that was flattering? And why did that particular choice of words sting? She was old enough to be Lucas Gray's . . . older sister, at the very least. Folding her arms across her body, Ruth cut the conversation short.

"You should be resting. And I shouldn't be boring you with personal drivel. I'm going to make myself some tea. I'll check back in a few minutes to see if you need anything." She moved toward the door.

"I've offended you. I didn't mean to."

"Nonsense. I'm not offended. You wanted to know about marriage and I've told you. Not every woman on this earth is waiting with bated breath to be proposed to, Mr. Gray. Some of us have other goals in life. I'm very hopeful that my friends and I will one day be able to surprise even a self-made man like yourself with a certain level of success in something besides landing a husband. Of course, Four Corners won't be anything like the vast property you own, but that doesn't mean—"

"Ruth." Lucas raised his voice. "Please. Whatever I said . . . I'm sorry." He swiped his hand across his forehead. "Listen. I know I strut and swagger. But in here—" he pointed to his chest—"in here I know the truth. Any man who thinks he's self-made is a fool. I came to Dawson County early enough to get a good piece of land. My cattle have stayed healthy and I've had the good fortune to hire on good men—with one or two exceptions. God's sent abundant rain and excellent grazing my way. And on top of that, I've been able to negotiate a good deal with the railroad to ship my beef to market. *All* those things have to remain in near perfect balance for any of this to work." He snorted. "I'm no *self-made* man. I'm *lucky*. Or *blessed*, if you prefer the religious view of things."

He paused. "And I'll tell you something else. I'd give every single steer and this fancy house and all I've worked for to have another chance at—" He broke off. Cleared his throat. "You may not have a house yet or a herd of cattle, but you've got a terrific son and the memory of a happy marriage. It's no small accomplishment to put up with the nonsense men expect of a woman sometimes." He gestured around. "This? This is just . . . window dressing."

Ruth returned to her chair and sat down.

Lucas smiled. "Not so angry now that I've let you look into the chink in my armor?"

"You asked why I didn't marry again. Well, the fact is that my sister had a husband all picked out for me. He seemed willing." Ruth arched one eyebrow. "He once called me a *handsome* woman, too." She shook her head. "I'd forgotten how annoying it was when he said that. Until just now."

"*I* meant it as a compliment."

"I know. I didn't hear it that way." She sighed. "I could have stayed in St. Louis and married Mr. Grissom and my future would have been . . . assured. And very conventional."

"But you didn't."

Ruth shook her head. "No. I may be middle-aged, but—"

Lucas snorted again. "That's ridiculous. Stop referring to yourself as if you're in need of a cane. You're no more middle-aged than me."

"As I was saying before I was so rudely interrupted," Ruth said. "I may be . . . mature . . . but I have this odd belief that a woman should actually love a man she marries. My sister Margaret, on the other hand, thought that since I had already married for love once, I should be willing to marry for . . . convenience . . . this time. Both hers and mine, as it turned out. What she didn't realize was that I wasn't so concerned for myself as I was for Jackson. Mr. Grissom didn't love *Jackson*. I won't ever put him under the authority of a man who doesn't love him. Ever."

"So you came west in the company of a group of strangers. Even though you don't know the first thing about homesteading or Nebraska. Even though you hated the idea of maybe having to take in sewing to make ends meet. Even though you didn't know anyone out here."

"Yes."

As Lucas looked her over, Ruth couldn't help but think of that phrase in the Bible about a person being weighed in the scales and found wanting. He had to think she was insane. The silence in the room grew large. Ruth realized the storm outside had abated. She rose from her chair and went back to the window. "The clouds are clearing out of the sky," she said. "I can see a cluster of stars right above the barn."

"Ruth," Lucas said, his voice low.

She turned around to face him. "Yes?"

"I'm proud of what I've done here. Maybe a little too proud, sometimes. I'm not very vocal about giving God his due, and I'm fairly conscious of my own hand in things. But as I said, I've been blessed. No one dared to tell me I couldn't do this or that I was crazy to try. No one was waiting to say, 'See, I told you so,' or second-guessing my decisions and waiting for me to fail to prove how smart they were. I didn't come out here alone. I came with my cousin, who, at the time, was my best friend. And had I failed, no one but me would have paid the price for that failure."

Ruth frowned. "I'm not sure I understand why you're telling me all this."

"Because I want you to know I mean it when I say I think you're one of the bravest people I've ever known. And I'd be honored if you'd consider me a friend. And I'm sorry I called you *handsome*. I'll never do it again." He grinned.

Heaven help her but he was a charming rogue. Ruth grinned back. "See to it that you keep that promise."

"Yes, ma'am."

"And now get some sleep. You're supposed to be healing. I can't play nursemaid forever. I have a homestead to . . . plant or farm or develop or whatever it is one says out here."

Ruth woke with a start.

"Pssst. Mrs. Dow. Psst."

She recognized Wah Lo's voice, although the bedroom door was only partway cracked and no part of the man was visible. "What is it? Is Lucas—"

"Not Mr. Gray," Wah Lo said. "He sleep. You come. Mrs. Raines very sick."

Grabbing her wrapper, Ruth hurried to the door and followed Wah Lo toward the front of the house. Hettie hadn't been herself for days now. She had no appetite, and at night she fell into bed so exhausted she barely stirred until the next morning when she woke to splash water on her face and smooth her wiry hair before padding down the hall to check on Lucas. He was doing well, but Hettie . . . Ruth was worried about Hettie. And now here she was out on the front porch where she'd fallen to her hands and knees, moaning as dry heaves overtook her.

Ruth knelt beside her and put a hand on her shoulder. "You must let me care for Lucas today and take yourself to bed. If you can tell me what you think it is—if there's anything—medicine we can send for—anything. Tell me what to do for you."

Hettie gagged again, then wiped her mouth with the handkerchief she'd taken from the pocket of her duster. She sat back on her heels. Her head bowed, her eyes closed, she breathed in and out, obviously concentrating on keeping her breathing even and steady. Presently she opened her eyes. "It's nothing to worry about."

"Nothing to worry about?! You listen to me, Hettie Raines! I can't have you getting sick. Not now. I don't know the first thing about tending a broken leg. We're going to have to change that bandage in a couple of days, and not only do I not know how to do it properly, I won't know what I'm looking at. You have to take care of yourself."

"I am. I've gotten a lot more rest the last few days while you and Lucas have been sparring. I'll be fine."

"That's just not an acceptable response. You have to—"

"Ruth!" Hettie almost barked the name. "I'm not sick." She took a deep breath and looked away, toward the eastern horizon, where dawn was beginning to tinge the sky with pink and crimson. "I'm not sick," she repeated. "I'm pregnant."

*Pregnant.* A thousand questions rose in her mind, but Ruth forced them into the background in order to take charge in the moment. After helping Hettie into one of the chairs just outside the front door, she headed inside. "I'm going to tell Wah Lo you're fine, and ask him to make us some tea. And then I'll be back." She did her best to sound convincing when she patted Hettie's hand and said, "It's going to be all right. I promise."

Back inside, Ruth did her best to reassure Wah Lo about Hettie without betraying her confidence. She made her way down the hall to Lucas's room, happy to see he was still asleep. And then she went into the kitchen and prepared a tray of biscuits while Wah Lo made tea. Back outside she helped arrange the light breakfast on a low table. Wah Lo went back in, and Ruth sat quietly watching the sunrise and sipping tea. Finally, she said, "I didn't realize widowhood was so fresh for you. I'm afraid I haven't always been very . . . sensitive."

Hettie bowed her head. She swept her hand over her hair and shoved her spectacles up on her nose. "You don't owe me an apology. I . . . I haven't wanted to talk about it. And I still can't—not the way you'd like."

"It's all right. Sometimes words aren't adequate." The idea of Hettie's being a young widow about to have a baby was heartbreaking. At least the General had had a chance to see his son. Everything would have been so much worse if he hadn't even seen Jackson. Just thinking about it brought tears to Ruth's eyes. "You don't have to do this alone. You have friends now. You know we'll help you in every way possible."

Hettie sighed. "I have an aunt in Denver. I was actually thinking maybe I'd go to her before I met all of you." She closed her eyes and laid her head back. "I suppose I should confess something else. I never really *joined* Mr. Drake's Emigration Society. In fact, I . . . I'd never heard of it until I got on that train and stumbled into you. But then you all just assumed . . . and I was confused and nervous and not really sure what I was doing and . . . I just let it happen. All of it." She glanced at Ruth. "I stowed away with you." She took a deep breath. "I like the quiet. I like being away from people. And I *cannot* be the 'lady doc.' Not because I don't know how, but because it hurts too much."

Ruth nodded. "When George died, it was two *years* before I stopped thinking I heard his footsteps in the hall. When my sister invited me to bring Jackson and come and live with her, I was so relieved. She was willing to make all the decisions, and I let her. I just didn't have the energy. I was grateful to have someone to think for me." She shook her head. "I know what it is to feel like you're just sleepwalking through life. You need time. I hope you'll stay with us. But if you can't—if you need your family and you want to go on to your aunt—then of course that's what you should do."

Hettie shook her head. "My aunt has very strong opinions of how things should be. She wouldn't be at all happy with me for refusing to—for refusing the role she thinks I should accept." She swiped at a tear. "If you'll still have me, I want to stay here. But no one expected a baby to come into the middle of this. It complicates things for everyone."

"I think having a baby at Four Corners would be wonderful." Ruth smiled. "Of course, he or she will be spoiled rotten with five aunts and one uncle hovering."

"Y-you really think the others won't mind?"

"I think . . . that you should ask them. And I will keep your confidence until you feel it's the right time to do so."

*Finally.* Main Street might still be something of a bog, but after nearly a week of intermittent storms, sunshine and a warm breeze began drying things out. Ella wanted to leave the Immigrant House and head to the homestead immediately, but Will advised them to wait at least a couple of days until the ground had a chance to dry.

"But we could take the tarps off the wall," Ella said. "Wouldn't everything dry more quickly that way?"

Will agreed with that, but also said, "You don't want to be building a roof with wet wood and soaked shingles. And to get a good hard dirt floor, you're going to want to let that dry, too—preferably without folks mucking around inside filling cracks and setting up rafters. You need to be patient."

Patience, Ella realized, was one of the virtues in short supply not only with her, but also with the others. That fact was made clear on Thursday of the "waiting for things to dry out week," when Sally and Mavis Morris nearly came to blows over Sally's use of the Immigrant House oven.

Mama saved the day when she brought up the idea of a side trip.

"Jackson has to be missing Ruth. And wouldn't we all like to see how they're doing up at the ranch—and have a change from this place? It's so crowded here now with all the newcomers staying in town. There's no place to settle in for an evening of knitting these days."

And so it was that right after dawn the next morning, Caroline, Sally, Jackson, and Mama piled into the back of Otto Ermisch's only available carriage. Ella took the reins and headed the team north on the trail toward the Graystone Ranch.

Ruth clasped her hands together and tried to look calm as she watched Hettie snip away the bandages that had sealed the wound on Lucas Gray's leg for the last two weeks. The tension in the room was palpable. Lucas winced as Hettie worked at the site of the injury. Sweat broke out on his brow. Ruth longed to reach for his hand and hold it, but she knew him well enough to know that he wouldn't succumb to a sign of weakness. At least not in broad daylight.

"Now," Hettie said calmly, even though Ruth could see her hands shaking. "Now, Mr. Gray—"

"—Lucas," he corrected her.

"All right. Lucas. There is going to be bleeding. I've let the bandages harden in place. As you will recall, I did that intentionally, knowing it would help to seal the wound and keep out infection. I've softened those bandages with water, but it's still going to bleed when I finally get this last bandage off, and it may bleed quite a lot, depending on how well it has healed. It's only been two weeks. Everyone is different, and I don't want you to worry no matter what you see or what you think—or, for that matter, what you smell. A putrid smell doesn't automatically mean gangrene. So please. Don't panic."

Lucas nodded. "Just so we're clear, though, I haven't changed my mind about how this will go if you think a doctor would recommend amputation."

"We're both aware of how you feel about that," Hettie said. "Let's not make any rash statements right now, all right?"

"It isn't a rash statement."

With a nod, Hettie went to work on the last bandage, moistening it and working to pull it free. When finally she could see the leg, she closed her eyes briefly. She bowed her head. *Putrid* wasn't quite a strong enough term for what assaulted their nostrils.

"Bad, huh?" Lucas said. His jaw clenched and his lips formed a firm line. He took a deep breath. "It's not your fault. You did everything you could."

"Lucas." Ruth took a quick breath.

He held up his hand. "No—no. It's all right. I'm in your debt. Both of you."

Ruth grabbed his hand. "It's *healing*, Lucas. It's healing well. There's no sign of infection." He stared at her, uncomprehending. "Look for yourself. It's *healing*. You're going to be fine." She dropped his hand and pointed at the wound.

With a grimace, he pushed himself forward until he could see his own leg. For a long moment he said nothing. Then he took a deep, wavering breath. "I . . . uh . . ." His voice broke. He cleared his throat. Sniffed. "I . . . uh . . ." He swiped at his nose. Nodded.

Ruth wanted to hug him. Instead, she reached up and pushed a lock of hair off his forehead. "It doesn't appear you're going to have to shoot anyone after all, Lucas. I hope you aren't terribly disappointed."

*. . . Jealousy is cruel as the grave: the coals thereof are coals of fire,
which hath a most vehement flame.*

SONG OF SOLOMON 8:6

Lucas Gray!" Ruth scolded from the doorway. "What do you think you're doing?!"

Lucas planted his foot on the floor and began to stand up.

"You stop that this instant. And get your sorry carcass back in that bed. You heard what Hettie said. *No movement* for another week. You have to give the bones a chance to knit and that wound a chance to close up. And this"—Ruth gestured at the man who was attempting to stand up beside the bed—"is *not* what she had in mind." She went to Gray and took his arm. "Now, get back in bed before I go get her to help me tie you down."

"I'm going to go crazy sitting here with nothing to do," he protested. "The boys need to know the boss is in charge."

"Well, if you weren't so prideful, you could tell them yourself. There's no reason Pete and Del shouldn't be in here giving you reports and getting orders every day."

With a sigh and a little cry of pain, Gray boosted himself back into the bed. "I don't want them to see me this way," he said. He glowered at Ruth as she smoothed the bedcovers back in place.

"Is it the lace on the pillows or the 'how the mighty have fallen' aspect of this situation that makes you reluctant? Because personally I think the lace on the pillows is attractive, you aren't that 'mighty,' and you haven't really fallen. You've just been waylaid."

Lucas narrowed his gaze. "You aren't much for coddling a wounded man, are you?"

"I can be as sweet as sweet can be when the situation requires it."

"I've got a broken leg, woman. I can't do my job. What more of a situation do you require?"

"You have a *fractured* leg, and you could do your job just fine if you'd stop tripping over that boulder of pride you're letting block the doorway to this room."

Lucas frowned. He stared at her. She met his gaze. He sighed. She folded her arms and waited. Finally, he relented. "Fine. Would you please tell Wah Lo to find Pete and have him come up to the house. And while Wah Lo is gone, could you and the doc get rid of the lacy pillows?"

"I'll ask Hettie to fetch the pillows," Ruth said. "And I'll find Pete myself, if he's to be found. I could use some fresh air. A woman could choke on the smell of self-pity in here."

Knowing that Pete was likely not too far from Lucas's infernal stallion, Ruth took her time strolling in the direction of the far corral, where they'd moved the animal after the storms blew through. She'd heard Pete and Del talking about that creature. Phrases like "kick the place apart," and "what a devil." They'd taken to referring to Hannibal as "the Prince of Darkness." It made her shudder. She worried that once healed, Lucas would feel it necessary to prove his manhood by trying to ride the creature again. And she worried that she was beginning to be far too concerned about Lucas Gray. After all, he'd set his cap for Caroline.

Try as she would, Ruth couldn't seem to rein herself in. From that curl that insisted on falling forward when he slept, to his penchant for teasing her, to his grin . . . *enough*. Taking herself in hand, Ruth made her way between the corrals filled with cows and bawling calves, past the smaller of the two barns erected on the place, and toward the bunkhouse and the isolated corral where, true to form, Pete stood watching the gray stallion while he talked to another wrangler.

"Ma'am?" Pete tipped his hat. "Everything all right?"

"Getting better," Ruth said. "He wants to see you." When Pete's expression showed concern she smiled. "No, it's not the leg. He just wants to talk business."

"Well, that's mighty good news." Pete took his hat off. "Excuse me, ma'am, I'm forgettin' my manners. This here is Clyde Day, Lowell's brother. Clyde has a reputation for being a first-rate horse breaker."

"Breaker?" Ruth tilted her head. "I'm not familiar with the term."

"Well, Mr. Gray doesn't like to take that approach most of the time, but every once in a while we come up against an animal that just won't listen to reason. And then we call in Clyde."

Ruth glanced at the gray stallion, which was, at the moment, standing quietly watching them, its head lowered, front legs braced. "He doesn't appear to be unwilling to listen to reason at the moment."

"First time he's stood still all day," Pete said. "He just doesn't seem to like people. Not one bit." He nodded at Day. "See what you think. I'll talk to the boss." And with that, Pete and Ruth set off toward the main house. They weren't far away when the stallion screamed. Ruth glanced behind her just in time to see the animal charge the fence where Day was standing. Day moved back. The stallion pawed the earth and tossed its head. Ruth shivered.

Pete had gone into the house, and Ruth was sitting beneath the overhang when Hettie joined her. They hadn't been there long when a cloud of dust on the southern horizon caught their attention. Ruth stood up. "Looks like Lucas has some company."

"Wouldn't it be something if we were finally getting a doctor?" Hettie rose to stand beside her.

The bright red hair gave it away. Ruth's hand went to her collar.

"I think it's—oh—look, Hettie—look! It *is*." She was embarrassed by how thrilled she was to see them . . . by the tears that came to her eyes as Jackson came into view. But embarrassment melted when Jackson leaped out of the still-rolling carriage and flew into her arms and literally lifted her off the ground and spun her around.

Breathless, Ruth laughed. "My goodness . . . you've grown a mile!" She called out to the others. "What have you been feeding this boy?"

"What *haven't* we been feeding him?" Zita said. "Beefsteak and eggs and bread and pie and pickles and . . . anything else anyone offers! We think he has a hollow leg. We really do."

"How's Mr. Gray?" Jackson asked.

"Thanks to Hettie and the good Lord, he's going to be fine. Although there has been some talk of possibly chaining him to the bed so he'll wait to recover before trying to rope any cattle." She glanced Caroline's way, instantly aware of the way Caroline took in the details of the house.

"It's . . . not what we expected," she said.

"Indeed not," Ruth agreed.

Wah Lo came outside. Hettie introduced him to the ladies, who kept interrupting each other with their reports of the progress at Four Corners and how the rain had kept them in town. The little man bowed to each woman and welcomed them as honored guests. He asked that they please sit on the porch and he would bring them tea, and said they would of course be staying over and that Mr. Gray would be insulted if they refused his hospitality. While he was carrying chairs out, Pete came to the door and motioned to Ruth. Lucas had summoned her, but before she headed back to his room, she introduced Pete to everyone.

Pete was about to step off the porch when he caught sight of Jackson. "You want to have tea with the ladies or help on the ranch?"

Jackson shot out of his chair, then glanced Ruth's way.

"You've never liked tea," she said. The look of joy on Jackson's face was worth whatever amount of worrying she would do for the rest of the day.

Lucas had donned a fresh white shirt and was sitting up in bed. "I'm sorry for all the noise," Ruth said. "You were right about things, by the way. Will Haywood insisted the Four Corners ladies follow him back into Plum Grove the day of the storm. They've been in town ever since waiting for things to dry out. And since your condition was a topic of concern and Will said the place wasn't hard to find . . ."

"Hold on. Did you just say I was *right* about something, Mrs. Dow? Call Wah Lo. I want a witness to this moment." He grinned. "So what you're really saying is Jackson missed his mama, and since the rain has interrupted work on the soddy, coming this way was a welcome diversion."

"No, I said people are concerned—"

"My health isn't something anyone in Plum Grove would be concerned about, Ruth. Unless, of course, there was news of my demise. There are those who would delight in that."

"What a thing to joke about," Ruth scolded.

"I asked for you because the ladies shouldn't try to make the drive back tonight. I'm sure Wah Lo invited them to stay. Just wanted you to know that's in keeping with Graystone hospitality. *You* might be able to handle a midnight run in a carriage, but I doubt many could, and I don't want a southern belle's demise—or anyone else's for that matter—charged to my account. So. Please extend my welcome. Wah Lo will make up the extra bedroom—including a pallet for the floor—and with your permission, Jackson can bunk with the boys."

"He'll be thrilled," Ruth said. "As to the rest . . . I'm sure they'll appreciate your hospitality, too."

"And since you seem all for my removing the boulder of pride from the doorway, I'd appreciate a chance to say a few words to Mrs. Jamison. If she's agreeable."

Ruth nodded even as her heart fell. "Of course," she said. "I'll send her right in."

Lucas nodded. "Thank you. And Ruth?"

She turned back.

"I'd like it to be a private viewing if you don't mind."

"I'm not your mother, Lucas. You can do whatever pleases you." She hurried away.

"Everything all right?" Caroline wanted to know.

"Wonderful." Ruth forced a smile. "He'd like to speak with you." Ruth held the door open. "Wah Lo will take you back."

As she watched Caroline glance around at the front room and kitchen, and then the bedrooms as she followed Wah Lo toward the back of the house, Ruth thought back to her own amazement at Lucas's home that first night. Even a southern belle who grew up on a plantation could be very comfortable on the Graystone Ranch. With effort, Ruth faced her friends with a smile, grateful when Sally said something about Pete Mills.

"Now, there's a fine bit of manhood. I didn't know whether to straighten my collar or unbutton a couple of buttons."

"You've been out in the sun too long," Zita quipped. "The *buttons*, of course!"

"Oh, Mama." Ella just shook her head as she took hold of one of the mares by the bridle and led them toward the barn.

Hettie said that she would linger behind to tend Lucas and send Caroline their way as soon as she was free. Ruth, along with Sally and Zita, followed Ella into the big barn, where they found two wranglers unhitching the team while Ella stood nearby eyeing the interior with a look that clearly said, "I want one of these someday."

"My Ella," Zita said, shaking her head. "Always looking up at the clouds for the next thing. Did you know she's already planning the *frame* farmhouse that will replace the soddy?"

"Well, if anyone can make that happen—" Ruth began the sentence, but everyone finished it together. "—Ella can."

Caroline joined them as they came out of the barn, and when they rounded the corner, there sat Jackson astride a buckskin gelding. Pete let go of the horse's bridle and crossed the corral to where Ruth stood. "Sam's not very flashy, but he's a good old boy. I hope you don't mind."

"Not a bit," Ruth said. Jackson was beaming with joy.

Pete called out. "About all you have to do is sit up there and get the feel of how he moves. And don't fall off. You grip with your knees. Only a greenhorn hangs on to that saddle horn." The instant Pete said it, Jackson let go of the saddle horn as if it were a hot poker.

"All right," Pete said. "Give him a little nudge. Tell him to move out."

Jackson nudged. The only thing the horse moved was an ear.

"You got to tell him so he knows you mean it," Pete said. "Nudge him harder and do this." Pete made a clicking sound with his jaw and Sam looked his way. When Jackson did it, the horse took one step, then stopped.

"Well, I won't have to worry about him losing control of a wild animal," Ruth chuckled.

"Mind if I take him for a little ride outside the corral?" Pete asked. "We'd be back by sundown."

"He'll be thrilled," Ruth said. When Pete took Sam's reins and told Jackson what they were going to do, he let out a whoop. Sam lifted his head and looked almost awake.

Matthew lay on his back staring up at the bare rafters of the lean-to in the predawn light. Dare he believe the nightmares were gone? He hadn't had even one since leaving the dugout. In fact, he'd been dreaming good things. Seeing Katie happy and whole. Watching Linney toddle off up a hill through blooming spring flowers. It was so strange to sleep soundly that it was its own kind of frightening. He didn't quite know how to think about feeling . . . good.

He also didn't know quite how to think about the way he felt when he was around Caroline Jamison. The fact that he liked that lilting voice of hers didn't make him feel guilty. The demon who'd always reminded him that he didn't deserve to be happy seemed to have up and left. Could that be true?

He liked the way Caroline laughed, too. The way she joked with Sally Grant—a rough woman most would think a southern belle wouldn't have anything to do with. But Caroline truly liked Sally, and that was another reason Matthew was drawn to her. A woman who could look past rough exteriors was an attractive woman. Caroline's exterior beauty was just a nice bit of coincidence. A very nice bit of coincidence.

He stretched and yawned and got up and opened the door. Blue skies. Beautiful blue skies. A day or two more of sunshine and he could get started on the roof at the Four Corners. He was looking forward to it. Another new feeling . . . looking forward to more than just seeing Linney.

He stepped outside and pulled his suspenders up over his bare shoulders. Opening the lid to the toolbox he'd made, he ran a calloused hand over the smooth handle of a mallet. It might still be too wet for the ladies to get much done, but there wasn't any reason he shouldn't hitch up the wagon and go on ahead. He could pull the tarps off the sod walls so they'd dry out faster. He could drive by way of Cooper's and see if Jeb wanted to join him. If things dried out fast enough, the two of them might even get the chord rafters in place as a surprise.

The idea of working with Jeb Cooper made Matthew smile, too. Cooper was easy to be around. Matthew didn't mind admitting—at least to himself—that he even liked the singing. There was comfort in those old hymns.

He looked over toward the wagon. He was going to do it. Head to Four Corners. See if Jeb wanted to help. Maybe Martha would let Linney come, too. She could open up those tents and air out the contents. *And pick some wildflowers.* That girl did like picking flowers. A flash of sweet memory brought back the mental image of Katie lying back on the spring prairie, her head encircled with flowers he'd strung together on a long-ago May Day.

Was this how it worked? A man carried the burden of grief, and for a while it obscured everything else around him, until slowly, the burden started to shrink until it could fit inside his heart instead of blocking out everything else in the world. And finally, it folded in on itself. And while it still remained a part of you, and you knew it always would, it made room in your heart for hope. You woke up one morning and there was no pain behind the enjoyment of the sunshine. Memories stopped slashing their way into your consciousness. Instead, they floated in, welcome and comforting.

*Linney.* It was going to take a long while for him to make things up to her. She'd nearly broken his heart the way she forgave him everything and threw herself into his arms. And all he did was tell her he was sorry. How could she forgive so easily? And why was it so hard for him to forgive others in return? Martha said he must. He was beginning to think she was right, but he still didn't think he could do it. He didn't even want to think about it all that much. Right now part of a new fear was that if he thought about things too much, the fragile new beginnings would prove to be little more than a celestial joke the demons were playing on him.

Still, something was changing. Something indefinable that shone in the way he felt when he visited the old homestead, in the way he felt when he stood at Katie's grave, and in the fact that for the first time in years, he'd been attracted to a woman and felt something besides guilt and the temptation to run away.

Back inside he washed up, then stood peering at the wild man staring out of the mirror nailed above the washstand. No wonder people in town looked at him the way they did. It was even more miraculous the ladies over at Four Corners had accepted him without question. He probably had Linney to thank for that. A man who was loved by his child couldn't be all bad, now, could he?

He dug scissors and a razor from the bottom of a parfleche he'd traded for years ago. A few minutes later an unfamiliar face emerged from beneath the beard. He kept the mustache but still wondered if Linney would even recognize him. He barely recognized himself. He turned his face from side to side, wondering if the resemblance was still as strong as it used to be. They were only cousins, but people used to think he and Luke looked like brothers.

Dressed, shaved, and feeling really . . . great, if he dared think it, Matthew made his way up the street toward the dining hall, where he found Linney at work setting tables for breakfast. There was a momentary hesitation when she first saw him.

"It's me," he said. "Do I really look that different?"

Linney nodded.

Matthew grimaced. "Bad, huh?"

She shook her head.

"Old?"

She shook her head again.

"Well?" He put a palm to his smooth cheek. "I can grow it back if you want."

"No!" she said quickly. "It's just—I never saw you before." She smiled then. "You're even more handsome than I thought."

To the aromas of frying bacon and fresh coffee, Matthew went over his plans for the next few days, suggesting that Linney might want to go with him to Four Corners. And of course she did, and of course Martha would let her, but she couldn't just walk out on Martha, now, could she? So Matthew found himself setting tables and helping in the kitchen all the way through the breakfast rush and taking joy in

Linney's laughter at the sight of her pa in an apron. He was up to his elbows in dishwashing when Linney said something about the crowded Immigrant House and how Jackson and the Four Corners ladies had headed out at dawn to go up to the ranch to check in on Mrs. Dow and Mrs. Gaines and to see how Mr. Gray was doing.

*Luke.* Maybe the demons weren't dancing in Matthew's dreams anymore, but he could have sworn he sensed one or two grinning as the bile rose in his throat at the thought of Caroline going to see about Luke.

*. . . there shall be showers of blessing.*

EZEKIEL 34:26

Caroline and her friends spent only one night in Plum Grove after their visit to Lucas Gray's ranch. They'd learned that Matthew Ransom was back to work at Four Corners, and if things were dry enough for him to make progress, they decided it was time for them to head back, too.

When Caroline caught her first glimpse of home, Ella pulled the team up. And there were Linney, Matthew, and Jeb Cooper, standing in a row, grinning a welcome.

"Where's Jackson?" Linney asked.

Caroline forced herself to look away from the nearly unrecognizable, undeniably handsome, newly shaven Matthew Ransom as she bumbled a response. "He . . . uh . . . he stayed at the ranch." *Laws o'massey*, she sounded like a tongue-tied ingenue.

Sally spoke up. "Seems to think he wants cowboy lessons or some such. Mr. Gray and his good-lookin' foreman cooked up a plan to keep that promise Mr. Gray made on the train. So Jackson's gonna ride with Pete for a while . . . the lucky little devil."

Linney nodded, then smiled up at Caroline, even as she put her arms around her pa's waist and gave him a hug. "It's him. Isn't he handsome?"

Still Caroline could not speak. Sally saved the day again. "Handsome is as handsome does." She waved Matthew over to help her down off the wagon. As soon as her feet alighted, she curtseyed. "Thank you, kind sir."

Matthew bowed. "My pleasure, madame." He reached up for Caroline next. Was it her imagination, or did his hand linger at her waist when he set her down. Imagination or wishful thinking . . . either way . . . she liked his hands at her waist.

"Is that what I think it is?"

Caroline started at the sound of Sally's voice at the tent flap. "Probably." She nodded as she fished a black silk cord out from beneath her blue-striped chemise and bent down to unlock the case.

Whistling her appreciation, Sally came to stand behind her. "That's a beauty."

"Thank you." Caroline lifted the shotgun from its padded case and ran her palm over the engraved silver plate on the gunstock. "I didn't really envision needing it out here. Until—"

"Yeah." Sally put a hand on her shoulder. "Me neither. I thought you were doing okay about all of that."

"I am. But one of the things Lucas wanted to talk to me about was a sort of . . . warning about Lowell Day."

"That so? Now, ain't that somethin'."

Caroline forced a smile. "The man who's working with that stallion is Day's brother. Apparently there was something said not long after we all arrived in Plum Grove. Something about me. Anyway, whatever it was—and Lucas wouldn't tell me—it traveled from Lowell to his brother Clyde to the foreman and finally to Lucas. By the time it got to Lucas, it was probably all twisted up. But he said I might want to be more 'vigilant' than usual for a while, at least until they can figure out what happened to Lowell Day, who, it seems, has disappeared."

"You don't say."

"Lucas didn't want to bring it up around any of the other ladies because Day has disappeared for a week or two before, and it probably doesn't mean anything. He didn't want to frighten everyone for no reason, but he also didn't want to keep it to himself, since Day doesn't have a reputation for being a particularly . . . virtuous person."

Sally grunted. "Do tell."

"So . . ." Caroline ran her hand along the shotgun barrel. "While I suppose we'll be expected to hang a fancy bit of needlework above the door, I believe I'll be putting a Winchester up there instead."

"Where'd you come by such a pretty thing, anyway?"

"I won it."

"Won it?"

"When I was fifteen." Caroline chuckled at the memory. "You should have seen the look on some of those boys' faces when they got beat by a girl in a shooting contest."

"How'd you even get *in* a contest? They let girls do things like that in Tennessee?"

"Well . . ." Caroline smiled. "They do if your daddy is General Harlan Sanford." She paused. "Daddy was something of a legend in the county. There weren't many who'd stand up to him. And if his li'l darlin' wanted to shoot with the boys, folks let her. Until she won. They weren't so agreeable to the idea after that."

"So . . . you already know how to use that thing."

"Of course, knowin' how to shoot doesn't always mean I'd react well in an emergency." She cleared her throat. "But I think I'd do all right."

Sally patted her shoulder. "Of course you would. Maybe you can shoot dinner from time to time."

Caroline nodded. "Maybe I will."

The morning sun of May 17, 1871, cast its rays against the walls of a completed sod house raised at the intersection of four homesteads near the well-known cottonwood spring in Dawson County, Nebraska. As she stood outside her new front door, Ella's heart was so full she thought it might burst with joy.

"Seems like we shoulda dressed up for the occasion," Sally murmured, then wished aloud that Ruth and Hettie and Jackson were there, too. "On the other hand," she said with a chuckle, "they don't have to help move in."

Mama led the way into the parlor, and while they all stood in a small circle and joined hands, she asked God to bless the house. She thanked him specifically for the good roof and the whitewashed walls, the double-hung windows, and the new stove. Then they all got to work spreading hay over the parlor floor and tacking down the rag rug presented as a housewarming by Nancy Darby and several others.

"Can we put my sewing machine right there?" Sally pointed to the window just to the right of the front door.

"And my cot here," Mama said, indicating the wall nearest the stove.

"The table here," Caroline said, standing in the middle of the room.

"And Caroline's shotgun there." Sally pointed above the front door. When Ella and Mama looked surprised, she shrugged. "I want to be prepared to defend my hens."

"Well, ladies," Ella said. "For better or for worse, we have married ourselves a homestead. Let's move in."

As another week began, life took on a new rhythm for Caroline and her friends. They rose at dawn. Zita served flapjacks on the stoneware plates with the brown tea leaf pattern Ella had purchased in St. Louis. They planted pumpkins, squash, and melons, all of it without plowing.

Ella slit the soil, and Caroline walked behind her, a bag of seed at her waist as she bent and tucked seeds into the slots. They planted corn that way, too. Five acres to start with, although Ella had plans for at least twenty. Caroline didn't know if her back would hold out through that many. She didn't complain, but she sincerely hoped Ruth and Hettie and Jackson would be back to help soon.

They'd missed their chance to put in potatoes, but one day when they drove into Plum Grove, they ran into Nancy Darby, who said she'd be happy to share some of the crop that would result from Bill's having bought ten bushels of that new variety of rose potatoes everyone was raving about. It was the least she could do after the way the lady doc had helped her out. Nancy wanted Hettie at her bedside when it came time for her confinement.

Caroline promised to relay the message, even as she tried not to show surprise at the idea of a pregnant woman planting ten *bushels* of seed potatoes. As her understanding grew of all that homesteading involved, Caroline wavered between thankfulness that they were a team working together and doubting that they would be able to succeed. At least she was too busy, and usually too tired, to worry over the likes of Lowell Day.

Two days after the other ladies of Four Corners had taken their leave, Ruth and Hettie had just sat down to lunch when a knock sounded at the door. Wah Lo scurried to answer. At the first sight of Pete, Ruth's hand went to the frill of lace at her throat and her heart skipped a beat. She stood up. "What's happened?"

"Nothing, ma'am." Pete shoved his hat back on his head and pursed his lips. "That's just the trouble."

"If Jackson has done something wrong, I need to know so that I can deal with it."

"Why, no, ma'am, that's not it. I don't know quite how to say it, but—that's why I thought I'd ride in and talk to you—and leave Jackson with the boys. He's . . . well, ma'am. He's not cut out for wrangling or riding. He just isn't."

"Are you saying he's miserable?"

"No, ma'am. Not exactly. But he isn't *happy*, either." Pete took a deep breath. He put one palm on the butt of the gun at his waist. "He's afraid."

"Afraid of what?" Ruth frowned.

"Just about everything. Horses—at least the ones with spirit. Cows. Coyotes. Falling off Sam. He's afraid of some of the boys, too. Of course we've a few rough ones, but they mostly don't mind him. The thing is, he doesn't know how to joke with them. He gets embarrassed and stammers around, and then it seems like he's afraid of whoever was joshing him."

Ruth had been at the ranch long enough to know that Pete Mills was a good man. Lucas trusted him. And she trusted Lucas. "Would you . . . would you let me think about what you've said? Would you put up with him for another night and just let me . . . ponder?"

"Of course, ma'am."

"I'll find you in the morning and we'll decide what's to be done."

"Thank you, ma'am." And with that Pete was gone.

Ruth headed down the hall to talk to Lucas. "I'm telling you this because I don't want you to misinterpret things when I tell Pete he won't have to put up with Jackson anymore. I don't want you to think I'm not grateful, but we'll be taking Jackson with us when we leave in a couple of days. I know we'd talked about his staying, but—"

Lucas frowned. "Why would you change your mind about that?"

"Well, Pete thinks Jackson isn't cut out for ranch life. He's miserable. And it isn't fair to expect Pete to put up with a child who—"

"I think what Pete was probably trying to tell you is that Jackson's been raised by a woman who has protected him too much. And it shows." Lucas held up his hand. "Now, before you start blustering about how I haven't raised a child, I'll agree with you. I don't know anything about raising children. But I do know what it takes for a man to survive out here. He has to be able to handle himself. There's no reason for Jackson to be afraid of horses or cattle. He should respect their strength, certainly, but when a man falls off, he just gets back on—"

"If he can," Ruth said, staring at Lucas's leg.

"Now, I'm not the subject here, but since you brought it up, I should have known better than to try to ride Hannibal that day. He was still riled up from the trip here, and he didn't know where he was or who was handling him. But I got a burr under my saddle about showing off. And I nearly got killed for it. That's not what I'm talking about with Jackson.

"Sam doesn't have a mean bone in his body. Jackson could lay down on the ground underneath that pony, and he wouldn't move for fear of stepping on him. As to working cattle, Pete's the best there is, and if Jackson will pay attention, *he* can be the best there is someday. If that's what he wants. Even if he doesn't want that, he's going to be plain miserable if he doesn't learn how to get along with the critters around him."

Lucas paused. "Life out here isn't a dime novel, and real cowboys aren't anything like Texan Joe. Jackson's learning that. Leave him here, Ruth. Let Pete and the boys—and me, when I can finally get out of this cursed bed—let us all grow him up a little."

"I hate the thought that he's afraid."

"Then tell him what I've just said about learning to respect what you fear and overcoming it—in that nice, tender way you have—" He smirked. "Give him a chance to face it and get over it."

Ruth sat down. "If I do that—if I leave him with you—what will that mean for Jackson? Exactly?"

"Well, Pete will keep him in the saddle until he knows what he's doing. He'll get so sore he can hardly walk before that's done. The boys will continue to tease him and make fun of him until he cries into his bedroll at night and wishes for his mama. Then he'll either buck up or he'll tuck his tail between his legs and come running home. But my guess is he'll buck up and you'll have yourself the beginnings of a man."

Later that evening, as she and Hettie were getting ready to turn in, Ruth asked Hettie, "What do you think I should do?"

Hettie shook her head. "I am the last person on earth you should be asking that question."

"Just because you haven't raised a son doesn't mean you don't have an opinion," Ruth said. "You know Jackson. And, frankly, you know me better than anyone else right now."

Hettie pulled her nightgown over her head and stepped out of her skirt. She draped the skirt over a chair and began to let her hair down. Ruth followed suit, and presently the women were standing side by side looking into the dressing table mirror.

"Do you trust Lucas and Pete Mills?" Hettie asked.

"As much as I trust any man. Underneath the strutting veneer, Lucas is kind and generous. I suppose my opinion of Mr. Mills is based on the fact that Lucas trusts him, so I can't see a reason not to."

Hettie nodded. "I feel the same way."

"But how can I knowingly give them permission to make Jackson miserable?" Ruth laid a handful of hairpins on the dresser and reached up to massage her scalp.

"Well," Hettie said, "maybe you should think of it as a kind of military school. I imagine the General had occasion to make cadets miserable in the interest of making them better soldiers and, ultimately, keeping more of them alive."

"So," Ruth murmured, "for Jackson to learn the things he says he wants, a short time of being miserable should be worth it—if he truly wants it."

"Exactly. And even if he doesn't want to live out here the rest of his life, I'd think learning he can do things even when they frighten him is a lesson that will do him good no matter what he faces in life." Hettie paused. "That being said, I don't know if I could make a child of mine go through it."

"I suppose this is my fault. I've been so afraid of what might happen for so long—"

"Things were hard. You did what you thought best."

"I did what was best for *me* because I was too afraid to do anything else." Ruth looked at herself in the mirror. "But I'm my true self again. I'm that woman who can drive a buggy across the prairie at night."

"The woman who threatened to handcuff Lucas Gray to his bed and got away with it." Hettie smiled.

Ruth nodded. "Yes. That's the Ruth Dow my General knew and loved." Her eyes filled with tears. She took a deep breath. "And that's the Ruth Dow who is going to find Pete Mills in the morning and tell him to give her son what he needs to become a man."

"Now, you know you have to keep off that leg for another week yet," Hettie said as she and Ruth prepared to leave on Saturday.

"Yes, ma'am, I do. And I will." Lucas was sitting in one of the overstuffed chairs in front of the window in his bedroom with his leg supported on a row of pillows. They all had a view of one corral, and just now Jackson was out there trying in vain to wrestle a calf to the earth for branding. Trying and losing the battle. Ruth's hand went to her collar.

"It'll be all right, Mama," Lucas said. "Pete thinks he's ready."

Ruth sighed. "I know. I just hope when he heads out on the spring roundup—"

"Pete could fix you up with a pony and a pair of boots and a hat all your own, and you could trail right behind the boy and make sure things go all right. If that'd make you feel better."

"Are you making fun of me, Mr. Gray?"

"Wouldn't think of it, Mrs. Dow." He winked, then grew more serious. "You've made the right choice. He will thank you. As soon as his sore muscles harden a bit and the blisters on his hands heal."

"He barely spoke to me when I went to say good-bye this morning," Ruth said. "I found him mucking out stalls. The charm of being a cowboy has completely worn off. He's exhausted. Pete's been working him hard. But I suppose it's good for him. Even if we only stay out here for five years, he needs to know how to ride."

Lucas nodded. "He'll be a better man for staying behind. I guarantee it."

"I'm trusting you to be right about that." Ruth turned to Hettie. "Any last-minute instructions for the patient?"

"Just don't be stupid. Leave the bandage in place. We'll be back in a week, and if everything still looks good, you'll be able to start walking—with a cane. Weight-bearing starts *gradually*, Mr. Gray."

"Do you need a dictionary so you can look up the word "gradual," Lucas?" Ruth added.

"For your information, Mrs. Dow, I know the meaning of the word. And it won't be a problem, as most ranchers *ride* through their workday."

Hettie spoke up. "Can you ride without standing in the stirrups?"

Lucas rolled his eyes. "Yes, ma'am. I believe I can."

"Then it'll probably be all right. But I have to warn you, another injury to that same leg, and you won't likely be so lucky as to keep it."

"I'll be good." When Ruth snorted in disbelief, Gray scowled. "It *is* possible for me to be good. And I resent the implication of that snort. I have future plans that do not include an early grave." Suddenly serious, he cleared his throat and said, "There is no way for me to thank you both for what you've done. But I will continue to look for ways." He motioned toward the door. "Wah Lo will escort you ladies outside to my first thank-you. There will be more."

Ruth bent down and kissed him on the cheek. "Behave," she said, and was then caught by surprise when he took both her hands in his and, pulling her close, kissed her back. He released her quickly and winked at Hettie. "I promise to be your star patient, ladies."

The buggy they'd driven from Ermisch's livery was waiting outside, and two wranglers were on their mounts alongside it. "Ma'am." Each one touched the brim of his hat with a finger by way of salute. "We'll be followin' you home."

Wah Lo interrupted. "Mr. Gray has paid Mr. Ermisch. The buggy and horse are yours now. Johnny and Del will see you home safe." He pressed a small packet wrapped in brown paper into Hettie's hand. "Make this tea every morning. Good for baby. Johnny and Del will come get you in one week. Don't try to come alone. That would upset Mr. Gray, and he must heal, not worry. Right?"

Ella might have worked a farm before, but she'd never marched out on a piece of virgin prairie and claimed it. It was at times overwhelming. There was just so much to do.

By the end of the first week with Ruth and Hettie back, they'd set out over a hundred cabbages. They planted onions and carrots, parsnips, beets, and peas. Nancy Darby brought them tomato seedlings, and they planted those close to the house inside wire cages lest a jackrabbit nibble the tender plants off. They planted lettuce and radishes, turnips and cucumbers.

Amazingly enough, Caroline Jamison knew how to clean the rabbits she occasionally shot, and joked that maybe she'd bring home a deer carcass one day and impress them all.

"What would you do with a deer?" Sally teased.

"Hang it from the corner of the barn. Gut it and skin it and carve it up." Caroline grinned. "Y'all would have to cook it, though. I've got no notion of how to do that."

"We could have us a deer roast. And a dance. And invite all the neighbors. Let 'em see the place all finished."

"First," Ella said, "we finish planting."

Everyone groaned in mock protest, but still they planted. A row of Osage orange trees and Russian olives to the north and west, tiny seedlings not even visible above the prairie grass. Caroline ripped a yellow apron to shreds so they could tie little flags on the twigs lest they forget they were there and trample them down. They dug up seedlings from the cottonwood and transplanted them along the front of the house all the way to the corners of each bedroom. They planted until every seed was gone, every seedling marked . . . and then they began to haul water to keep it all alive.

The prairie had awakened further and wrapped Four Corners in color. Wildflowers bloomed yellow and white, lavender and pink, dancing in the wind and bobbing up and down. If Ella hadn't known better, she would have thought God had sent his angels robed in a rainbow of petals to rejoice with the ladies who'd formed an unlikely alliance to create an unlikely life in an unlikely place.

The evenings had become warm enough for the ladies to move their chairs outside, where the breeze wafted the scents of the spring past, and the yapping of coyotes and the chirping of crickets melded together in a song Ella was learning to love. One evening when the stars came out and they were all still sitting outside, Mama murmured, " 'When I consider thy heavens . . . the work of thy fingers . . . what is man that thou art mindful of him?' " And then she added, "A person looking for God comes face-to-face with him out here. With such a sky and so much space . . . it all speaks of the smallness of man and the largeness of . . . something else. Some*one* else."

As Ella lay in her bed that night and her mind raced from one thing that needed doing to another, she reminded God that he had promised to be mindful of them. "There is so much I can't control," she whispered. "The wind. The rain. The temperature. So many things can go wrong." Insects could decimate the garden. Any number of illnesses or diseases could attack cattle and horses. The grip of fear clutched at Ella's midsection. *Don't let me fail them, God. Please. Don't let us fail.*

*Trust in the Lord with all thine heart;*
*and lean not unto thine own understanding.*

PROVERBS 3:5

Ruth knew from past experience that the way to overcome emotional turmoil was through hard work, and during the days after Lucas summoned Caroline to his bedside, Ruth did everything she could to work things through by working. She was up before anyone else every single morning, and she made certain to never linger in Caroline's vicinity. As a result, even if Caroline had been inclined to take Ruth aside and confide whatever it was Lucas had said during their private time together, there was no opportunity. Ruth made sure she was too busy for such things.

Ruth's attempts to talk herself out of her own attraction to Lucas didn't stop with busyness. All the while she was working long hours, Ruth maintained an internal dialogue about the matter. She reminded herself regularly that Lucas's wanting a *private* conversation with Caroline clearly meant there was *something* between those two. She replayed the way Lucas Gray had shown an interest in Caroline on the train, and dismissed his compliments to herself as little more than mild and meaningless flirtation. She took to reading Scripture late at night when her mind simply would not stay occupied with topics apart from a certain charming rancher. And she worried about Jackson's safety and how his latest adventure might distract him from the dream of an education—if that was even his dream. At times she thought it might just be hers.

Thanks to her working so she wouldn't worry, and then worrying her way through the work, Ruth was exhausted when the promised wranglers arrived at Four Corners to escort "the doc and Mrs. Dow" back to the ranch to check on Lucas and Jackson. And, she realized, all of her efforts to talk herself out of her attraction to Lucas had failed to bear fruit, for when Caroline declined to ride with them, Ruth was ashamed by her own response. No amount of inner scolding could change it, either. She was *glad*.

The drive to the ranch felt like it took forever. When the ranch house, and then Lucas himself, lounging on the front porch, his leg propped up on pillows, finally came into view, Ruth renewed her efforts to take herself in hand. *You must stop this girlish nonsense. There is absolutely no reason for you to feel this way just because a man smiles in your general direction. He's smiling at Hettie, too.* She forced herself to make certain that the first words out of her mouth were about Caroline. Caroline sent her best and regretted that she hadn't been able to come along, Ruth assured Lucas, even as she concocted an excuse on Caroline's behalf.

Lucas only nodded. "Jackson's lunging one of my horses in the corral next to Hannibal's. Ignore the stallion, and don't worry about the gelding your boy is working. Dakota's spirited, but he's absent the killer instinct Hannibal seems to have acquired. I believe you'll be pleased to see just how well Jackson's survived this past week without his mama." He nodded Hettie's way. "If she-who-is-not-a-doctor gives me clearance, I just might hobble out and join you in a minute."

When Ruth first caught sight of Jackson, the boy did little more than nod her way. The chestnut gelding at the end of the lunge line responded to his every "chirrup" and "hup" with fluid grace. When he finally said "whoa," the horse pulled up instantly. As Jackson walked toward the animal, he looped the rope through his gloved left hand. The horse pivoted and faced him. Jackson kept up a running commentary about how he was a good boy and had worked hard and deserved a treat. Which the horse obviously expected, because when Jackson got close, the animal lipped his shirt pocket.

"Now, you just mind your manners," Jackson said, and tapped the horse on its muzzle. The animal pulled back and shook its head, whickering and stomping the earth in an equine version of a two-year-old demanding candy at the general store. "All right," Jackson said, "since you insist." He reached in his pocket and pulled out a peppermint. The animal took it, bobbing its head up and down with pleasure as it crunched the candy. Jackson laughed.

"I'd say you've learned quite a bit about horses in only a week," Ruth said.

Jackson shrugged as he stroked the horse's neck. "I still don't ride very well." He walked toward her then and, after kissing her on the cheek, said, "And that's why I want to stay. Please, Mother. Pete says it's all right with him, and Mr. Gray—Lucas—said it was up to you. So . . . may I please stay awhile longer? I know you need me to work back at Four Corners, but I'll be of more use if I learn how to do these . . . western things."

When Ruth said nothing—mostly because she was distracted by the sight of Lucas hobbling their way with the help of a cane and Hettie's arm—Jackson kept going. "Pete says we'll be checking in the canyons for stragglers. And then there'll be roping and branding and . . . everything."

When Ruth still didn't respond, he tried another tactic. "Sam's a good pony, Mother. He's sure-footed and as tame as they come. And cattle aren't really dangerous. You just have to know them. Know the signs when they're getting ready to bolt and things like that. I don't really know the signs yet, but Sam seems to." Jackson smiled. "Actually,

Sam's a lot better with cattle than I am. Pete says I can learn a lot from Sam." He ducked his head and made her look at him. "Mother? Are you listening?"

She was. "It would appear you've gotten over being so angry with me for leaving you here."

"You were trying to help. I was just . . . afraid."

"How about now? Are you still afraid?"

He shook his head, then seemed to think better of it. "Sometimes. But mostly . . . no." He frowned a little. "I think I'd still be afraid if I heard a rattler hiss. Or a mountain lion scream. Or if I met up with some cattle rustlers. But I'm not afraid of the horses or the cattle. Or the wranglers, either. They joke a lot, but they don't mean anything by it."

The gelding snuffled at his pocket and Jackson shoved him away. "Dakota's one of Lucas's favorite trail horses. Dakota and Soda—the gray one you've seen. I was afraid of them for a while. But sometimes horses just like to show off. Underneath it all, they're both as kind as can be."

*Just like their owner,* Ruth thought.

As Lucas came near, Dakota whickered and stretched out his neck. Jackson unfurled the lead rope, and the horse walked to Lucas and thrust his head against Lucas's chest. "Hey," Lucas murmured, and touched foreheads with the horse.

"I think he's ready to have you back," Jackson said.

Lucas tugged on the chestnut's pale forelock. "Tomorrow, old boy," he said, glancing at Hettie. "Right?"

"As long as you keep your word about mounting up without jumping off that leg."

"I'll climb up on a box." Lucas grinned at Jackson. "And *you* are not allowed to laugh when I mount up like a girl."

Jackson held up his hand. "You have my word. But I can't speak for Pete and the rest of the boys."

Hettie cleared her throat and interrupted in an uncharacteristically stern voice. "Just remember, it's only *some* weight-bearing at first, and still a *great deal* of resting on the porch."

"You did hear that, patient-who-doesn't-want-to-behave?" Ruth asked.

"Yes, ma'am." Gray thanked Jackson for keeping Dakota and Soda in shape for him, then nodded Ruth's way. "Have you convinced her to let you stay on for the roundup?"

Ruth spoke for him. "I can't think of a reason to say no."

Lucas nodded. "Then how about we consider Sam as part of my payment for keeping my leg?"

Jackson gave a little whoop of delight that startled Dakota just enough to make the boy apologize—to the horse.

Ruth looked into Lucas's gray eyes. "You don't have to do that."

He winked. "Which makes it all the more charming that I want to. You know what I said last week about finding ways to thank you and Mrs. Raines? I'm just getting started. Don't spoil my fun. Jackson needed a horse. Now he has one. It will make him more useful once he does get back home. You can make him your errand boy. And just think—he'll be able to ride to *school*."

Jackson made a face. "That wouldn't have been one of my reasons for wanting a horse, sir."

Lucas laughed. "Spoken like a true boy."

The week after Ruth and Hettie returned from their "house call" to the ranch, Will Haywood delivered a new plow, courtesy of Lucas Gray. The generosity didn't stop. Next came a dozen setting hens and enough lumber and wire to expand the chicken coop and to fence in a good-sized chicken yard. A few days later a milk cow arrived.

"This has to stop," Ruth said. "It's . . . absurd. What will people think?"

"I don't know that Lucas cares much what people think," Hettie said, "and if we protest, he will likely take it as a personal challenge and send over a well-drilling crew or something equally ridiculous. As soon as he's back to full strength, he'll be too busy running the ranch to think so much about us. I think it's best to ignore it—beyond saying thank you." She shrugged. "I wasn't able to contribute anything at all to the homestead at first. It's a very strange way to do it, but at least I can feel like I've done my share now."

"I suppose you're right about Lucas. Trying to get that man to listen to reason would probably be a waste of time. I declare, I never met anyone so hardheaded. The man must have rocks for brains."

Hettie laughed softly. "Maybe that's where he got the name for Graystone Ranch."

The well-drilling crew arrived the following week.

It wasn't long before Caroline realized that Zita was beginning to worry about her. Oh, she didn't say anything directly, but increasingly, Caroline would look up to see the older woman watching her with a look of concern. Once or twice, Zita referenced how unusually quiet Caroline seemed and asked if she was feeling unwell. She made comments about how she had thought she was too old to be of use to anyone, and now, with the ladies of Four Corners, she had found a new purpose and how privileged she felt when the ladies shared their personal problems and asked for her opinions or prayers.

While Caroline knew Zita was both a wonderful listener and a faithful woman of prayer, and while she had grown to love her as a second mother, she didn't think expounding on what Lowell Day had tried to do was the kind of thing Zita should hear. What good would it do to talk about it? The thing to do was to forget—and be vigilant. She was trying, but as soon as she managed to stop thinking about what had happened in the livery, other ghosts haunted her thoughts. She worried about Mama and Daddy and longed to know how they were.

Was the plantation house still standing after the war? She didn't know if Daddy would survive the loss of Mulberry Plantation. Most often, however, the thing that intruded on Caroline's thought life was the man with dark hair and blue eyes and a sweet redheaded daughter.

Matthew had not been to Four Corners since that day in May when he'd nailed the final shingle onto the roof. Sometimes, Caroline's longing to see him was so powerful it frightened her, but she kept telling herself that Matthew needed time with Linney. He needed to be about building a life for her. He was not a subject Caroline should entertain, even if he did have the most beautiful blue eyes and the strongest hands, even if she did sometimes feel literally weak in the knees when he helped her down from a wagon. Matthew Ransom was not meant for her. She was here in Nebraska to rescue *herself*. Matthew had other things to occupy his energies—not the least of which was fixing whatever it was between him and Lucas Gray.

*Lucas Gray.* Was that man not a caution. That day at the ranch when he'd warned her about Lowell Day, he'd seemed like a different person. He hadn't flirted once the entire time they talked. Even more strange than the change in Lucas himself was the fact that he'd asked about Matthew, bringing up the name and then backing away, almost as if he needed to know something but couldn't quite ask the real question.

It seemed that whatever Caroline thought about these days, she was confused. She couldn't quite convince herself to forget Lowell Day. Lucas Gray seemed to be a different man from the one she'd met on the train. And after seeming to find her attractive, Matthew had retreated.

On better days, Caroline could laugh at the idea of Caroline Jamison *not* being surrounded by men declaring their undying love. On other days, she jumped at odd noises and imagined Lowell Day lurking behind the barn. All of this and more circled through Caroline's mind as she hauled water to keep the trees alive, and shelled peas and pulled carrots, and watched her once-perfect hands disintegrate into the hands of a woman who worked for her supper.

Perhaps a drive to town would help clear her mind. She certainly wasn't finding any answers watering trees or pulling green beans. And, try as she might, the promise that she just might run into Matthew and the knowledge that she would at least get to see Linney, who would likely talk about Matthew, got Caroline into the buggy with the rest of the ladies.

Sally was the first to react to the changes in Plum Grove with a low whistle and her usual "Well, ain't this somethin'."

"How could it have changed so much in only a few weeks?" Caroline wondered aloud.

"Look at that." Zita pointed to a *Grand Opening* banner hung above the door of the newly completed combination photography studio and dressmaker. The frames for three more buildings along Main had been erected since the last time the ladies were in Plum Grove. Otto Ermisch was adding on to the livery.

"Are those *houses?*" Ruth pointed to half a dozen small buildings in various stages of construction on the prairie a short distance north of Main Street.

*Is Matthew building them?* "I declare." Caroline shook her head. "Can you believe it? There's hardly room to hitch a team on Main."

Ruth swung the carriage alongside the outdoor stairway leading up to the Haywoods' living quarters and hitched Calico to the stair rail.

As the ladies rounded the corner toward the mercantile's front door, Ella pointed toward the open wagon across the way with the hotel name emblazoned on the side. "Do you suppose they meet every train with that thing? I wonder if that's hurting the Immigrant House business."

"Who's to say?" Zita said. "But I don't imagine *that's* helping the mercantile much." She pointed to the store across Main advertising *Special Prices* that would *Beat All Competitors.*

"Well, now," Sally piped up. "That's just rude. There ain't any competition but the Haywoods. It ain't friendly to start a business by attackin' the neighbors. I wonder what Martha thinks of it."

Martha thought the newcomers were interlopers, they soon found out. High and mighty. They looked out for themselves over and above the community. When Will asked them to contribute to the village fund for community promotion, they nearly tossed him out of the store on his ear. "Nearly tossed him *out,*" Martha repeated. "Can you imagine?" She shook her head. "When I think of all my William's done for this county. For the way he's worked all these years—" She snapped the length of flannel in her hands for emphasis before smoothing it on the counter. "How many yards did you say?"

"Ten," Sally answered. "I got to get a head start making some warm petticoats for all of us."

Linney came in the front door, and after offering an enthusiastic greeting to the ladies, she glanced Martha's way and shook her head.

"Let's hear it," Martha said.

"Lots of business. And that flannel." She nodded at the striped piece the ladies were buying. "It's a nickel a yard cheaper over there."

"Cheaper quality, though," Martha said.

"I'm sorry, but it's not. I sneaked a peek at the paper label. It's from the same mill as that." Linney pointed to the bolt lying on the counter.

Martha shook her head. "The Immigrant House is full, the dining hall is doing a booming business, and look—" She gestured around her store, empty save for the ladies of Four Corners. "Something has to change. I just don't know what."

"They won't last long," Linney said. "They can't." She glanced at Caroline. "They aren't even *nice.* It's all about the price over there. You should have heard the way they treated some of the German ladies." Linney smirked. "As if *shouting* would make someone who doesn't speak

English understand you." She smiled at Martha. "Just be patient. Soon enough folks will realize who's friendly when they come through the door and who takes the time to make people feel *welcome.*"

The ladies all agreed. "You'll always have our business."

"You're warmhearted and you make strangers feel welcome," Zita said with a nod.

"Several of us were near to demanding return tickets when we first arrived," Caroline offered. "We stayed in Plum Grove mostly because of you."

"And here I thought it was Hamilton Drake's promises and that spring snowfall." Martha laughed, although it was obvious she appreciated the kind words. "Speaking of Hamilton Drake, you'll love this. He went back to St. Louis intending to bring more brides west, but all he got was a bride of his own. Helen said that James got the telegram last week. He's married and working for his wife's family."

"Working at what?" Sally asked.

"Something down on the levee. Can you imagine?"

"All I got to say is his wife better check his pockets to make sure he isn't selling dances with those steamboat girls on the side." Sally crossed to the fabric shelf and ran her hand over a length of double pink calico, even as she returned to the topic of how Martha's being so nice was one of the things that she'd always remember about her first impressions of Plum Grove.

"Well, thank you." Martha folded the length of flannel and then wrapped it with paper. Suddenly she looked up, her smile widening. "That's it, Sally! Thank you! That's what we'll do!" Newly energized, she grabbed a piece of paper and began to write furiously. "I'll take out half a page in the *Pioneer*—I wonder how much they're charging for that—and Bill Toady can play—and we'll put it right out front—a dance floor—right in the street—" She kept writing as she talked, and finally she held up a small version of a poster. "What do you think?"

HAYWOOD MERCANTILE
WELCOMES YOU TO PLUM GROVE WITH
MORE THAN FAIR PRICES
COME ONE, COME ALL TO THE
INDEPENDENCE DAY WELCOME DANCE
JULY 4, 1871
DANCE TILL YOUR FEET DROP OFF
FREE REFRESHMENTS TO ALL OUR NEW FRIENDS
COURTESY OF HAYWOOD MERCANTILE
THE FIRST, THE BEST, AND THE LAST DRY GOODS STORE
A SETTLER WILL EVER NEED
YOU AREN'T JUST A CUSTOMER—YOU'RE A FRIEND
AT THE
HAYWOOD MERCANTILE

Martha pointed with her pencil as she spoke. "Now, if the paper can just put a drawing down in this corner of something ladies like—say, high-button shoes—and something over here for the men—maybe a hat—don't you think that'll just set it off beautifully? We'll bake up some nice cakes . . . and Mavis said there's a fellow staying at the Immigrant House who plays the accordion. And another who's really good on a mouth harp. We'll get a jump on what anyone else might want to do for the Fourth."

Martha paused. "It can be a new tradition . . . Haywood Mercantile and Independence Day. It's perfect." As Linney began to wrap up the other things the ladies had stacked on the counter, Martha flipped through a stack of mail sitting in the "post office" on the back shelf.

"Could you . . . would you mind giving this to Jeb Cooper? I hear he's been doing a lot of work on your place lately."

"Not so much," Ella said.

"But we could stop by on our way home," Ruth offered. "It's not that far out of the way."

"Thank you. I know he'd appreciate it. He gets a letter every week or so—addressed with such beautiful script. And—" Martha reached below the counter and pulled out a beautifully embossed leather-bound book. "This came with the last letter. Someone made a mess of the package. I'll rewrap it if you can deliver it."

Ruth gazed down at the Four Corners shopping list and said, "Go ahead and wrap it. We're finished for this trip."

"But you didn't get your coffee yet. Or the cinnamon. And what about—"

"The rest will have to wait."

"But . . . why?" Martha asked.

"Don't worry." Ruth was quick to reassure her. "We aren't headed across the street. We just need to be careful. We can do without the rest for now."

"Let me show you something." Martha reached for her ledger book and, opening it to a new page, turned it around and held it up for all to see. "You see this says *Four Corners* at the top." She pointed to the credit balance. "You'll also see that you can get whatever you need today."

"But-but," Ella sputtered. "That's—"

"That," Martha said, "is Lucas Gray's way of thanking Ruth and Hettie for saving his life." She lowered her voice. "And his note said to make sure he's notified when it's down to twenty dollars. Which I take to mean you will all have a running credit here."

Ruth and Hettie exchanged glances. "He won't listen," Ruth said.

"Rocks for brains." Hettie shook her head.

Caroline lingered in the mercantile while the others headed to the dining hall for lunch. She wasn't hungry, and while she wasn't exactly hiding, if she stayed and helped Martha so that Linney could have lunch with the others, she would not only have a chance for a nice visit with Martha but also avoid running into anyone who was, according to Linney, working on the newest building on the other side of Main today. Someone she was already thinking about entirely too much. Someone who probably didn't want to see her anyway.

"Not that I need help," Martha said as the ladies exited, "but I'm pleased as can be to have a chance to catch up on Four Corners news."

Caroline recited the garden news, the livestock news, the weather news, and the news that, according to Hettie, Lucas Gray's leg was going to be fine. When Martha thanked the good Lord for that miracle, Caroline nodded agreement. They were standing by the counter when Martha reached over and grasped Caroline's hand and gave it a squeeze. "You can talk to me, you know. About anything."

Surprised when tears gathered so quickly, Caroline squeezed back. "Thank you," she said. "But there's really nothin' anybody can do."

"I can—and will—pray for you, dear. And that's not nothing." After a moment Martha said, "He does care for you, you know. And Linney flat-out adores you. Give him time, Caroline."

She sighed. "Am I that obvious?"

"No, but I've been watching. And listening. Linney talks about you all the time. And when she talks about you, Matthew enjoys listening. He's drawn to you, but he's going to be careful about it. That's wise. Just give him time, dear."

"Well, I'm just gonna take a look," Sally said. "I can re-tie the string." She'd been guessing at what kind of book Elizabeth Jorgenson, whose name appeared on the return address of the letter, would be sending Mr. Cooper for what felt like hours, and Ella wished she would hush.

"Here, Ella," Sally said, when she'd finally picked the knot open and untied the book. "You read it."

Ella handed the book to Caroline without a word. "I don't think it's right to read a man's mail."

"We ain't readin' his mail," Sally protested. "We're just lookin' at the book."

"*Sonnets From the Portuguese*," Caroline read aloud. "Elizabeth Barrett Browning." She ran her gloved hand over the tooled cover. "I *love* this book." She opened it. "Here, listen.

> *"If thou must love me, let it be for nought*
> *Except for love's sake only. Do not say*
> *'I love her for her smile—her look—her way*
> *Of speaking gently,—for a trick of thought*
> *That falls in well with mine, and certes brought*
> *A sense of pleasant ease on such a day'—*
> *For these things in themselves, Belovèd, may*
> *Be changed, or change for thee,—and love, so wrought,*
> *May be unwrought so. Neither love me for*
> *Thine own dear pity's wiping my cheeks dry,—*
> *A creature might forget to weep, who bore*
> *Thy comfort long, and lose thy love thereby!*
> *But love me for love's sake, that evermore*
> *Thou mayst love on, through love's eternity."*

"Sounds like Mr. Cooper's thinkin' about courtin'," Sally said.

For the rest of the way to Jeb Cooper's, the topic of conversation was not one that Ella enjoyed.

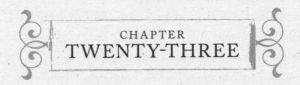

## CHAPTER
# TWENTY-THREE

*Unless thy law had been my delights,*
*I should then have perished in mine affliction.*

PSALM 119:92

Ella thought Jeb must have heard their carriage coming across the prairie, because as soon as Ruth brought them to a stop, he ducked out the front door of his soddy with a smile on his face. "Just the people I need to see," he said, and came to help the ladies down.

Sally held out the book and the letter. "Martha thought maybe you'd be comin' back to our place. Which you ain't. But here's your mail, anyway."

Jeb looked down at the envelope, read the name, and smiled. "Thank you. I've been looking forward to getting this. Actually, coming back to Four Corners was what I wanted to talk to you about." He proceeded to outline their need for a fruit cellar and an adequate barn, and his need for what Ella thought amounted to an entirely new wardrobe, which Sally was more than willing to make. Before long, it was agreed. Jeb Cooper would dig a fruit cellar and put in a barn at Four Corners.

"Don't you have your own work to do?" Ella blurted it out before thinking, then thought it sounded rude. "What I mean is—we don't want a neighbor's own place suffering because he helps us."

"Well, now that you mention it I can't come your way for a couple of weeks yet. Ransom and I have a project to work on together first.

In fact, with your permission, I'll see if he might want to come with me when I do make it out your way."

"Linney was bragging on how busy Matthew is with building projects in Plum Grove," Caroline said.

"But we'd love to have both of you." Mama winked at Caroline.

"We could use a bigger chicken coop, too," Sally said. "One that will keep the varmints out better. Mr. Gray sent lumber and wire for it, but we ain't had time to use it yet."

Ella glowered at Sally. "I told you I would handle that."

"I know," Sally agreed. "And you will. Just as soon as you plant that twenty acres of corn and map out the four pieces of ground and run fence around one to keep cattle in and—"

"All right," Ella said. "You made your point. But the idea was for us ladies to homestead. Not to lounge about while hired hands do all the real work."

"I'd say you've already proven your disdain for 'lounging about,' Mrs. Barton," Jeb said. "There's a little cave back up behind the house here where I've been keeping things cool. Ransom's coming out to help me build a spring house. We could think about doing the same for you. If what I have in mind works the way I envision it, it could make your lives easier." He smiled at Ella. "You don't have any objection to letting a man make life a little easier for you, I hope."

Of course Ella did not. As they drove away, Jeb Cooper's singing carried on the wind. And the ladies would not let Ella be.

By the time their soddy was in sight, Ella had had enough. "Now that you've all had your fun, it's time to hush. What you're thinking is ridiculous, and I don't want to listen to any more of it."

"Who says we're thinking anything?" Sally teased. "Just because a man orders a book of love poetry in the mail—and offers to come back to our place and do work that will likely take him most of the summer—and just because he talks to *you* about it and teases about a man making life easier for a woman—why, there's no reason to think anything of that. He's just being nice. I'm sure that's all it is."

Caroline took up where Sally had left off. "She's right, of course," she said. "Not one bit of it has a thing to do with the way Mr. Cooper seemed to always find a way to work with Ella when the soddy was going up. It was purely coincidence. Absolutely. Not a doubt about it. Nothin' but a li'l ole coincidence."

Ella waved a hand in the air. Still the women didn't stop teasing. Frustration became anger. Anger evolved into hurt. Finally, when they pulled up in the yard, Ella was the first to jump out of the carriage. She grabbed a stack of the packages from the mercantile and headed inside. Let someone else unhitch Calico tonight. But no one did. Instead, they followed her like a bunch of clucking hens pecking at the same bug. And then the strangest thing happened. Instead of hearing her friends teasing her, Ella heard Milton's voice. *What man in his right mind would come into your bed, you cow.*

Dear Mama must have read her expression. She left off teasing. Her voice was gentle when she said, "We're only having a little fun. We love you, Ella. We want you to be happy."

"Then leave . . . me . . . alone." Her voice broke, and Ella fled out the back door. By the time she reached the carriage, she was sobbing so hard she could barely see to unharness the little roan mare in the fading light. She was fumbling with a buckle when Caroline's hand slipped beneath hers and took over the task.

"I'm so sorry, Ella. No one meant to hurt you." She handed over a clean hanky.

"It doesn't matter."

"It *does* matter. We should have known—"

"—but you don't. You don't know anything." Ella walked around to unbuckle the harness on the mare's off side. Surprised by the anger she felt, she let the words fly. "You with your tiny waist and your beautiful smile . . . with Lucas Gray and Matthew Ransom coming to blows over—" She broke off. Shook her head.

"I like you, Caroline. I really do. I didn't think I would or could, but you aren't what I expected. You work hard and you haven't asked to be coddled at all. So I believe you mean well, but the truth is, you don't know *anything* about what it's like for a woman like me." She felt thoroughly humiliated when she couldn't keep from crying.

It was quiet for a few minutes, and then Caroline said, "Well, honey, that just goes to show that even as smart and capable as you are—and you are both of those and so much more—even you can be wrong about some things." She paused. "You know, I'd love it if just once a man would actually look at my *eyes* when we're first introduced."

Ella frowned. She hadn't thought about that. That would be awful.

"I was almost raped in town. Before we moved out here."

The words came out so quietly that Ella wasn't sure she'd heard right. Her hand stopped in midair between two harness buckles. "*What* did you just say?"

Caroline kept her head down as she fiddled with a bit of harness. "That night I went after Jackson in the fog. Remember Sally had that funny story when we got back about how I'd climbed up on a haystack and refused to come down because I saw a rat in the barn?" She looked away. "Well, there was a rat in the barn all right. A two-legged one."

"Dear Lord." Ella reached for Caroline's hand and squeezed it.

Caroline squeezed back. "I know that doesn't mean I understand exactly how you feel, but I'm not completely ignorant, either." She took a deep breath. "We have more in common than you think. We'd both like to be loved for who we are *inside*."

"And we'd both like to take a swing at a certain species of male," Ella said with a bitter laugh.

While Caroline unwove the reins from the traces, Ella finished undoing the harness. Finally, she was able to speak without a wavering voice. "Why would Jeb Cooper be reading love poetry? Who's Elizabeth Jorgenson? And why do I even care? I don't want him to know I care. I don't want *anyone* to know. It's embarrassing."

"Everyone wants to be loved. That's nothing to be embarrassed about."

As Ella prepared to lead the little mare away, Caroline said, "By the way, Lucas Gray and Matthew Ransom aren't fighting over me. Apparently there's years of hard feelings between them. Even if I am attracted to Matthew—and I am, Lord knows I am—I shouldn't be stepping into his life right now. When I was at the ranch and Mr. Gray started asking questions about Matthew, I told him just that. I've got to keep my distance."

"You talked about all of this with Lucas Gray?"

Caroline shook her head. "No. That was a very little part of it. Mostly Mr. Gray wanted to warn me about Lowell Day." She paused. "I didn't tell him the warning was a bit late."

"So the shotgun over the door is about more than protecting the chickens."

"I sincerely hope not. On the other hand, a lady has to be prepared to rescue herself now and then." Caroline turned to go.

Ella called after her. "Thank you, Caroline."

"For what? Teasin' you to the point-a tears?"

"For being my friend."

Caroline dipped into a little curtsey. "It is my distinct hon-uh, Miz Bah-ton." She turned and went toward the house.

As Ella worked to rub down the little mare, she thought about Caroline and how she used her accent at will, as if she liked to hide behind it. *Now, ain't that somethin'.* They all had their places to hide. Ruth hid behind high-necked dark-colored dresses and a stern manner. Sally hid out in the open, using her frank conversation and almost bawdy humor to keep people at a distance. Hettie was hiding behind half-truths and, Ella suspected, an outright lie or two. Caroline hid behind what people assumed about southern belles. *And you, Ella, what do you hide behind?* She knew the answer, of course. She hid behind the never-ending, exhausting cycle of work it was going to require to make Four Corners a success. She hid behind the belief that her life could be better without a man.

*Everyone wants to be loved,* Caroline had said. Of course it was true. The question was, how did a woman ever know when professed love wasn't just another way for a rat to hide?

"You don't really care whether you have a spring house or not, do you?" Matthew swiped at the sweat on his forehead, then sat back on his haunches.

"Why would you say such a thing?" Jeb frowned. "Improvements are what a man does to his property."

"But you aren't planting. You aren't building a new house. Don't get me wrong, the place looks wonderful. But it's basically the same. Except for this spring house."

"This place already has everything I need," Jeb said. "And as for the spring house, I'll likely be grateful for that when there's five feet of snow banked up along the way to the cave back there." He nodded toward the rise in the distance where Matthew had, long ago, tunneled back into the earth to create a primitive larder.

The spring house was a small structure beside the windmill. When the windmill turned, it pumped water out of the ground and into a pipe. Cold water flowed through the pipe and then into the spring house, flooding first a shallow trough where crocks of butter and milk could sit, and then a deeper vat where all kinds of things could be stored in huge round crocks constantly being bathed in cold well water.

"It's good practice for the one we'll be putting up over at Four Corners next week."

"Sure you don't want to dig a fruit cellar here, too?" Matthew smiled. "For practice, of course."

Jeb grinned. "I've heard about your building skills. I think we can probably handle digging a rectangular hole in the ground without too much practice."

Matthew nodded. But he still didn't understand how Jeb was going to get through the winter with no crops to sell and no livestock to slaughter.

With a sigh, Jeb sat back. "All right," he said. "I'll confess."

"You aren't going to tell me you're on the run from the law and you're going to disappear this winter, are you?"

Cooper laughed. "No—to the part about being on the run from the law, but yes to the part about being on the run and disappearing this winter. But it's not what you think." He took a deep breath. Scratched his neck. "Let's have us a cup of coffee." He got up then and led the way inside, through the room full of books and into the front room.

A letter lay on the kitchen table. It was addressed in a fine script. Matthew noted it was from a lady. "Ah," he said. "You're headed back east this winter to get a wife." That made sense. A spring house was a thing a woman would want. It was the next thing he'd been going to do for Katie . . . before the world stopped. He'd thought Cooper might be warming up to Mrs. Barton. Apparently not.

"What?" Cooper looked at the letter and then, as he ground coffee, laughed out loud. "No. By disappearing I meant that I'm looking forward to being snowbound here." He gestured around them, then pointed toward the book room. "I can't think of anything better than having an excuse to spend time with my 'friends' on these shelves. Unless"—he smiled—"it would be building something for a neighbor."

He went about making coffee, talking as he worked. "Speaking of holing up with a good book, you were going to come and read a little, as I recall."

"Ah, yes," Matthew said. "The book with all the answers." He stood up and went to the doorway, peering at the bookshelves. "Which one would that be?"

"This one."

Matthew turned back around. Sighed. Cooper was pouring coffee. His Bible lay open on the kitchen table. "Now, before you run screaming out of the house, I should probably tell you the truth about who I am."

"You're a preacher."

Cooper looked surprised. Frowned. "Oh, my goodness . . . no. Definitely not." He sat down and took a sip of coffee. "First off, I'm not what my family expected. Like I told you when we hauled all those books in here, I'm from a family of teachers. College professors. A long line of them actually, going all the way back to the founding of Harvard in 1650. So you can imagine that when I took to working with my hands . . . well. Let us just say the family was not pleased."

He gazed through the window for a moment. "Funny thing about Harvard. It was founded as an institution to train pastors. That was my family's second choice for me. But I didn't want that, either. So. In my youthful stubbornness, I patterned myself after a distant uncle and took up blacksmithing, and, as it turned out, I was very good at it. Some called me an artist."

"Looking at that fence around Katie's grave, I'd say they were right."

"Yes, well. Others would say that when I lost my hand in the war, that was God's way of punishing me for being rebellious and refusing my intended path."

"But you didn't think that way."

"Honestly, Matthew, I didn't know how to think. All the hours I'd spent reading philosophy and theology and every other 'ology' known to man, and when this happened"—he held up his stump—"I didn't have one single answer to the questions that mattered."

"But this"—Matthew tapped on the Bible—"answered them all." He didn't try to remove the sarcasm from his tone.

"Did I say I had all the answers?" Jeb shook his head. "No. If you think I said I have all the answers, you misunderstood. I don't. I do, however, believe, from the soles of my worn-out boots to the top of

my gigantic frame, that the only answers that matter are right here."
He laid his massive hand on the open book. "We all have to find our
own way, Matthew. For me it came after a long winter reading this
book. Mostly the story of a man named Job, and yes, I see the irony
of that, given my name." He took a deep breath. "Job convinced me
that losing my hand wasn't punishment for something I'd done. It also
convinced me that I'll never—this side of eternity—have answers to
all my questions, but that God doesn't mind my asking them, and he
really only requires one thing of me."

"Which is—?"

Jeb laughed. "Well, you aren't going to like it." He clamped his
hand over his mouth.

"Which is?"

Jeb repeated the gesture, then took his hand away. "Putting my
hand over my mouth and listening." He tapped the Bible's open pages.
"It's in there. You can read it for yourself if you want to."

What Matthew wanted was to stop being afraid that the demons
he'd seemingly outrun were going to catch up with him. He wanted
Linney to be happy and, if possible, proud of him. He wanted not to
spend the rest of his life alone. He also wanted to have the kind of
peace Jeb Cooper exuded. He wanted to sing . . . not out loud, but in
his soul.

"As to the spring house," Jeb said quietly. "I'd be happy to build
the rest of it all by my lonesome, if you'd be willing to see if there's
any answers in there for you." He nodded at the Bible.

"What about all those other books?"

Jeb shook his head. "There's pure delight in that room. But this
book is the only one a man really *needs*."

Not only was he not angry, Matthew realized, he was also curious.
What did he have to lose? Cooper had no real stake in whether Matthew read that book or not, whether he believed it or not, whether he
found his way in life or not.

"I should tell you the rest of my story," Jeb said. "Just so you don't learn it from someone else someday and think I was dishonest."

Matthew half wondered if Cooper was about to confess to some terrible crime after all.

Jeb picked up the letter, opened it, and handed Matthew the bank draft written for more money than Matthew would earn in a year. "Elizabeth Jorgenson is my sister," Jeb said. "She sends me one of those every other month—along with whatever books I've asked her to buy for me. The money comes from a combination of our parents' estate and a few things I've invented over the years that most of the blacksmiths in America seem to think make them more productive."

"You're telling me you're rich."

Jeb shrugged. "I'm telling you why I don't need to plant or harvest to live out here. But I like helping folks, and I like the peace and quiet." He nodded toward the back of the house. "I have an idea for a system that might water a garden while cooling a spring house. If it works, I'll patent it." He smiled. "And, yes, I was hoping to lure you out here so maybe you'd read God's book and see if it might have a word or two that could get you through the rest of your life."

By the light of the summer moon, Matthew Ransom opened the gate to Katie's grave and sat down. For a long while, he didn't say a word, just sat with his back to the iron fence and listened to coyotes and the creaking of the windmill and the faint splashing and trickling as cold well water made its way up out of the ground and into the newly erected spring house.

Jeb had said something that week as they worked together about "living water," but he'd waited until tonight to direct Matthew to a passage in the Bible that started with the words "Ho, every one that thirsteth," and went on to invite a man to incline his ear and go to God so that his soul could live. In recent days Matthew had realized that if he could get past his own emotions long enough to pay attention, the Bible indicated that God really did want to be sought and called upon. He didn't just sit up above everything and point his finger when a man failed.

The prophet recorded God saying, "For my thoughts are not your thoughts, neither are your ways my ways." Matthew could appreciate that. A loving God probably wouldn't have gone off in a rage and done anything so reckless as to accidentally kill someone he loved. When Matthew wondered about it aloud, Jeb agreed that he didn't think the concepts of "accidents" and "God" meshed.

The Bible promised a lot. It said a person could "go out with joy and be led forth with peace." That spoke to a longing inside of Matthew that he had been ignoring ever since Katie died. He'd been drowning in anger and bitterness and guilt since then.

Jeb said that guilt might be the last thing to go. "Katie—" Matthew started at the sound of his own voice in the night. When had he begun talking to Katie instead of thinking about God? Somehow, though, it felt right and so he kept it up. "Oh, Katie." And he began to cry. "I . . . I'm . . . so . . . *sorry*." It was like a dam burst inside him. He had so much to be sorry about. He'd failed her. Brought her out here and then gone off and left her alone so much, and slapped the few requests she made away like so many bothersome gnats. He hadn't listened at all to what might be important to her.

"I didn't listen and it had to feel like I didn't care what you felt or thought. That wasn't it, Katie-girl. I was just . . . so . . . stupid." He hung his head. "Even if you did run to Lucas, who could have blamed you? But I'm sorry for that, too. Sorry for not believing you and for getting angry. Sorry for taking the chances I did. For—" He broke off for a few minutes. Waited to calm down before he said more.

"I didn't mean for that to happen. It wasn't murder. But I'm guilty and oh . . . Katie . . . God . . . can you forgive me . . . please?"

He went forward onto his hands and knees then and leaned across the grave and wept some more. At some point in his weeping he realized he wasn't talking to Katie anymore. Instead, he was talking mostly to God again. Asking forgiveness. And finally breathing, actually breathing and feeling almost whole for the first time since the moment when, thrown out of a runaway wagon, he had crawled through the spring grass and embraced his wife's lifeless body.

Matthew spent almost the entire night inside the fence at Katie's grave. He wept and prayed and talked to Katie and to God, and as the eastern sky began to grow pale in a promise of dawn, he had finally poured it all out. He felt as if he'd been wrestling with some of those demons all night. Maybe he had. He'd never know for sure. But he knew one thing. The Matthew Ransom who closed the gate on Katie's grave as the new day dawned was not the same Matthew Ransom who'd opened it the night before.

*My son, if sinners entice thee, consent thou not....*
*For their feet run to evil....*

PROVERBS 1:10, 16

Rumpled clothes and a face creased with dirt. An oversized hat sporting a dark ring of sweat around the crown. Boots with spurs. Sunburned hands. Ruth rose from where she'd been helping Sally select medium-sized cucumbers for a new batch of pickles. "Hello, stranger," she said to the cowboy, then glanced at Sally. "Is it just my imagination or does this cowboy bear an amazing resemblance to my son, Jackson?"

"Oh, Ma." Jackson flung himself down out of the saddle and administered a fierce hug. "We're on our way back to the ranch," he said, with a glance in the direction of his partner. "But Pete said I should make sure it's still okay to stay on."

Pete nodded. "Took us longer than I expected to cover the canyon territory. Figured you'd be worried about him."

"There's still branding to do, Ma. I want to stay on with the boys." Jackson leaned close and muttered, "Please, Mother. They just quit calling me *Jacqueline*. If I don't finish the job, they'll never let me live it down."

Pete shifted in the saddle. "Might be you'd want to ride up next week and see your cowboy bulldogging and branding."

"I can't imagine you'd want a bunch of ladies in the way when you've got so much yet to do," Ruth said.

Pete grinned Sally's way, then looked back at Ruth. "Well, ma'am.

The fact is the boys would probably love an audience. Especially one as pretty as you all—if you don't mind my saying so."

"Well, in that case," Ruth said, "we'll see if we can't oblige." She gave Jackson another hug. "Can you stay long enough for us to feed you?"

Jackson looked at Pete. With a slight shake of his head, Pete said, "Best be hitting the trail." He nodded Jackson's way. "You go on now and say hello to the other ladies. Just make it quick."

As Jackson retreated toward the house, Sally said, "You boys have been gone so long I bet you don't know about the new mercantile in Plum Grove. The Haywoods decided to have a big doin's for the Fourth of July. Even a dance."

Pete nodded. "The boys always head into town for the Fourth. We draw straws, and the short straws stay home to tend the place—and usually feel right sorry for theirselves."

"The foreman doesn't have to draw straws, does he?"

"Are you askin' me for a dance, Mrs. Grant?"

"Well . . . what if I am?"

"What if I want more than just one?"

Sally's face turned nearly as red as her hair. "Well, that depends." "On what?"

"On how often you stomp on my toes during the first one."

Pete grinned. "Well, I guess we'll just have to wait and see, won't we?"

Jackson returned and, after another quick hug, climbed aboard Sam. Pete touched the brim of his hat. "I'll tell the boss to be expectin' company." He grinned at Sally. "And start practicing my do-si-do."

Jackson chirruped to Sam, and together he and Pete rode away.

"That boy is growin' up faster than the big bluestem up on the hill," Sally said.

Indeed he was. Ruth's eyes misted over at the thought.

"I'm so sorry." Hettie clutched her stomach and gave Ruth a private, knowing look as they entered the soddy with Caroline after morning chores. "I'd like to see Jackson bulldogging and branding and whatever else he said he was going to do. Really, I would. But I just . . . I just don't think I should leave with so much to do in the garden."

"I don't mind staying behind, either," Caroline said. "Someone needs to be here to tend the livestock and the chickens. Y'all go ahead. Hettie and I will manage just fine."

Zita spoke from where she stood at the kitchen stove mixing up flapjack batter while Ella and Sally set the table. "I can stay, too." She nodded at Ella. "You go on with Ruth and Sally." She shook her finger at Sally. "Just see that you behave around that cowboy."

"Don't worry, I will," Sally promised. "I'm savin' my best stuff for the Fourth of July dance."

"You've got a good vantage point from up there."

Ruth looked back to see Lucas limping toward the buggy she'd drawn up to the corral.

"It was Pete's idea."

Lucas hauled himself up beside her as he asked, "So what do you think of your little boy now, Mama?"

"He's a completely different young man. Just as you predicted, he's much more confident, and amazingly unafraid."

"Oh, I think he's still afraid." Lucas nodded to where Jackson stood in the middle of the corral trying to rope a calf for about the eighth time. "But he's learned to go ahead and do what needs to be done in spite of it."

"Then I'd say he's learning the real meaning of bravery."

"Just like his mama did." Lucas leaned back in the buggy seat and stretched. "Wah Lo's missed having a lady around the place," he said.

"He's been grumpier than usual ever since you and Mrs. Raines left us. How is Hettie? I'm sorry to see she didn't come along."

"Caroline and Zita stayed with her. I'm afraid Hettie's not very well. She's having trouble keeping anything down. And she was already so thin."

"When's the baby expected?" At Ruth's look of surprise, Lucas smiled. "Wah Lo doesn't keep things from me."

"Christmas, she says."

"You might ask if he has anything besides the tea he sent home with you before."

"Thank you. I will."

Jackson finally got a rope around the calf. The animal bolted and nearly dragged him onto his face, but while the cowboys standing around the corral whooped and hollered encouragement, he stiffened both legs and held on until he'd regained control. Finally, he managed to bring the calf down. The watching cowboys cheered and threw their hats in the air while another wrangler applied the brand. Jackson looked her way. Ruth waved and applauded.

"Not exactly what you had in mind for the boy, is it? Ranching, I mean."

"I've been thinking about just that," Ruth said, "ever since he and Pete stopped by at Four Corners. What I *really* had in mind was for him to be happy. I didn't expect it to happen this soon. Or this way. But what was it I heard Pete say the other day? 'If it ain't broke, don't fix it.'"

Lucas laughed. "Good for you."

"The only thing I'm worried about now is that he'll be bored silly when he comes back to Four Corners. We've got a little more in the way of livestock to tend—thanks to a certain rancher who won't listen when he's told what to do—but Four Corners is a far cry from a working ranch."

"Well, that's one of the reasons I climbed up here beside you, ma'am. What would you say to my giving the boy a start on a small herd? Say, a half dozen cows due to calve in the spring. There's good grazing on part of your place. They'd do fine. Eventually Jackson could keep the difference between the market price and what he'd owe me for his start. I'd like to make it a gift, but I'm thinking you'd throw a fit. Besides, if it's a gift, then he doesn't learn just how hard it can be for a man to keep himself alive, let alone support a family out here. If things go well, he wouldn't have to depend on his ma's selling her place to give him a future."

He glanced at her and shrugged. "Who knows? Nebraska could grow on you. You might decide you don't want to sell out and move on."

"I don't suppose that while you're helping Jackson learn about life, those cows grazing on Four Corners might possibly take up with a few stragglers from the Graystone Ranch?"

Lucas chuckled. "The possibility had crossed my mind. But only *after* the idea popped up of getting Jackson a little start of his own." He paused. "If I'm overstepping, I'll back down. But I like Jackson, and I probably won't ever have a chance to help my own son—"

"I don't know why not," Ruth said. "You're still a young man. Heavens, you could have a *dozen* sons in as many years."

Gray cleared his throat. "Well, ma'am, the last time I checked, that kind of thing required a wife."

*Keep it light. Tread carefully.* "The last time *I* checked you didn't seem to have any difficulty attracting ladies. The only reason Caroline didn't come is she didn't want to leave Zita and Hettie alone. And don't forget that I was on that train and have been witness to your charms."

"Yeah, well—" He shook his head. "Nearly killing myself showing off made me realize that my 'charms' weren't nearly as charming as I used to think." He paused. "In fact, I've changed my mind about a lot of things since that night. Being completely unable to control the future is a sobering thing for a peacock."

"I hate to tell you this, Lucas, but you've never been able to control the future."

He chuckled. "Ah, but now I readily acknowledge the fact. As to the rest, it took thirty-one years, but I think I've finally matured to the point where I realize that love-at-first-sizzle can end badly. In fact, it probably isn't real love at all."

Ruth glanced at him. He was looking straight ahead, his thoughts obviously elsewhere. Was he regretting the way things had begun between him and Caroline and wishing she were here . . . or thinking about the woman he'd called out to in his feverish dreams? She cleared her throat. "I'll have to speak with Ella and the others about the cattle, but I can't imagine anyone will object. We've talked about running cattle on one quarter, but with Jackson over here, there wasn't anyone to keep track of them, and there's no fence up yet—" She sighed. "There's always so much to do."

"I don't want the idea of Graystone cattle grazing your land to be an issue. If you have any hesitation about that at all, then never mind about any other cattle besides Jackson's. How about you ladies talk it over and you can let me know . . . maybe at the dance on the Fourth? You might even reserve a dance or two—assuming, of course, you don't mind a partner with a limp."

Her heart thumped. He wanted to dance with her? *To talk business.* She nodded. "I suppose I can put up with a limp. For the sake of business."

"Good. And as long as you're in the mood to say yes, is there any chance you'd walk over to Hannibal's corral with me right now? I want to test a theory."

Ruth frowned. "I've seen quite enough of Hannibal *and* his handiwork. And didn't you just tell me you've learned your lesson when it comes to showing off? Only a fool would try to ride that creature after what he did to you."

"Who said anything about trying to ride him?" Lucas shook his head. "No, you're right on that score. Hannibal is going to live out his days entertaining the ladies and being generally spoiled. But he's still got a bad attitude about life, and the last time you were here—well . . . please. Indulge me." He slid to the ground and held out his hand.

Ruth let him help her down. "I'm warning you. At the first sign of his charging the fence, I'm hightailing it in the other direction."

"Fair enough."

Together they walked through the swirling dust and away from the activity in the branding corral. "Clyde Day couldn't do a thing with him. I stepped in and put an end to his more . . . intense methods. But—" Lucas stopped. "There. See that?"

"See what?" Ruth frowned. "He isn't doing anything."

"Oh, but he is," Lucas said. "He was causing a ruckus until just now. Now he's watching *you.*"

Ruth shuddered and stepped back—inadvertently into Lucas. He put his hand at her waist. "Don't be afraid." He was standing so close she could feel the warmth of his breath on her neck. She began to blush like a schoolgirl. "Take a step forward," Lucas said. "I'm right here. I won't let anything happen."

She stepped forward. The horse turned his head to one side. She took another step. He put his head down. Then he stepped forward.

"Here," Lucas said, his hand still at her waist. "Stop right here." They were a few feet from the fence. Hannibal watched. "Say something to him."

"What should I say?"

"Try 'hello,'" Lucas teased.

"Well, hello, you worthless bit of horseflesh," Ruth said. "I personally think the man behind me should be feeding you to the coyotes after what you did to him, but—" Hannibal's head came up. His ears came forward. He took another step. And whickered.

"Keep talking," Lucas said.

Some of the cowboys at the next corral over had turned their way to watch what was happening. What *was* happening? "Yes. Well, as I was saying, I personally think you should have been coyote food long ago after the fit you threw that nearly killed my friend. There's no accounting for your beha—"

Hannibal tossed his head and pawed the ground. Next he walked to the fence, bobbed his head up and down and lifted his upper lip to show his teeth.

"If you are honestly thinking of taking a bite out of me, I do not approve. I don't even know why we're standing here, but—" Clyde Day came around the other side of the corral. Hannibal snorted, lurched away from the fence, and as he headed away, kicked the air with both hind feet. But then he stopped when he got across the corral and turned back around, again clearly watching Ruth.

"Well, I'll be—" Lucas kept his hand at her waist even as he chuckled.

"What you'll *be*, Mr. Gray, is sorry if you don't tell me what's going on." Ruth stepped away from him. "I don't appreciate being used as bait."

"You aren't bait, woman. You're . . . reassurance. Hannibal likes you. Not just you, probably. Probably all women. I've heard of things like this before—a horse that has a distinct preference for a certain kind of companion. Stable mates range from goats to—I heard about a racehorse that took a liking to a rabbit once. The owner actually built a warren in the horse's stall."

"I will admit that it does seem he calms down when he sees me, but—it has to be a coincidence. Doesn't it?"

"There's only one way to find out." He reached in his pocket and handed her a lump of sugar.

"Oh no. I'm not putting my hand anywhere near that creature."

"Why not? From the other side of a corral fence, no horse can do much damage compared to . . . oh, say . . . an Apache war party chasing someone. Or a rattlesnake striking at a general."

Ruth glowered toward the corral where Jackson was, at that moment, branding a bawling calf. She would speak to him later about telling stories behind her back.

She lifted her chin. "Fine." She spoke to the horse again. "It seems Mr. Gray believes you have taken a liking to me. That's impossible, of course, but I've this lump of sugar. And if you want it—" Ruth held out her hand. Hannibal came to the center of the corral. "You're going to have to do better than that," she said. The horse tossed his head. "Oh no. I'm not coming in there. You have to come to me." The horse did it. He walked to the edge of the corral and thrust his head over the top rail. He snorted. And pawed. "If you're planning murder," Ruth said, "you need to know that my friend here has a gun. I'm not certain he'll use it if it comes to a choice between you and me, but—"

"Hey." Lucas's voice sounded in her ear. "That's not funny."

"Well, the horse did cost you a lot of money."

"Just offer him the sugar, Ruth. See what happens."

What happened was . . . not much. Ruth opened her hand and Hannibal lipped the sugar cube off her palm, sucking on it not unlike a child savoring his favorite candy. "So," Ruth said, "this ridiculous man seems to think you like me. What do you say?"

Hannibal tossed his head, although it appeared to Ruth to be more of a nod.

She stepped forward. The soft muzzle touched her palm. She felt warm breath, and then slowly she put her hand alongside the jaw and stroked, very carefully. "Well," she said, "I suppose I should apologize for that comment about the coyotes."

"You should apologize for the comment about me choosing him over you, too," Lucas groused.

"A lady never apologizes for telling what she believes to be the truth, Lucas."

"You," he said, and tugged on a curl at the nape of her neck, "are treading very close to hurting my feelings."

Ruth snorted. "I believe you're man enough to handle it, Mr. Gray. And no, I will not move to the ranch to improve Hannibal's mood." She meant it as a joke, but then she realized what she'd said and could feel her cheeks burning with embarrassment. Muttering something about going to find Ella and Sally so they could watch Jackson in the other corral, she hurried away.

Caroline woke with a start. What a strange dream. Linney and she were picking wildflowers together in a field more like the meadow at Mulberry Plantation than anything here in the west. Just as Caroline added a brilliant orange poppy to her bouquet, Linney called out to her pa. Caroline looked up, and there was Matthew, just visible on the horizon, loping toward them astride Patch. He rode straight to where Linney and Caroline waited, then dismounted and, putting one arm around Linney, reached out to Caroline and— Patch snorted. Caroline jerked awake. A snort. In her dream . . . or not?

She lay in the dark, listening, then lifted her head to peer into the center room, lighted by the lamp they always left burning on the window ledge. Because Hettie wasn't feeling well, she'd stayed downstairs this evening, sleeping in Ruth's bed while Zita kept watch from Ella's. But there was no sign of movement coming from that bedroom.

As a shadow played across the whitewashed wall above Zita's cot, Caroline caught her breath. *There it was again. A muffled . . . something.* Taking a slow, deep breath, Caroline suddenly felt like she was strangling. *Peppermint. Dear Lord . . . no.*

Slowly, ever so slowly, she rolled to the edge of her cot and reached for the Winchester lying on the hard-packed earthen floor next to her bed. She'd just sat up with the rifle in hand when a man appeared in the doorway. "If I were you," she said, "I'd rethink my plan."

"Now, why would I want to do that, sweetheart?"

*Dear Lord in heaven, help me.* Her voice wavered as she said, "Because if you take one more step I'm going to pull this trigger."

The figure looming in the doorway hesitated, and so did Caroline. It was only a second, but their plan worked. The stranger looming in the doorway had distracted Caroline just long enough for Lowell Day to launch himself through her bedroom window.

*Watch ye, stand fast in the faith,*
*quit you like men, be strong.*

1 Corinthians 16:13

The moon was high and the evening breeze warm with the scent of wildflowers when Calico finally clip-clopped over the rise and headed down the slope for home. Sally was in midsentence lamenting that she hadn't had nearly enough time to "charm the socks off that foreman of Mr. Gray's," when Ella put her hand on Ruth's shoulder.

"Pull up," she said. "Something's wrong down there." Ruth complied and the buggy came to a standstill. Calico tossed her head and stomped a protest. "The lamps," Ella said, nodding toward the house.

"What about the lamps?" Sally asked. "We always leave a lamp burning."

"*A* lamp," Ella said. "Not all of them." Calico whickered. "Ruth. Can you get down and keep her quiet? I don't want them to know we're nearly home."

" 'Them'? Who . . . 'them'?" Ruth gestured toward the house. "They probably felt a little lonely and wanted some extra light. Remember how we all felt those first nights in the Immigrant House when the coyotes were howling?"

"But we're used to coyotes now."

Just then, the front door opened. More light spilled out of the house, but no one appeared in the doorway.

"I don't like it," Ella said.

"It does look a little strange," Sally agreed.

Ella cleared her throat. "Caroline didn't want me to say anything, but . . ."

"She told you about Lowell Day," Sally said.

"Yes. And that Mr. Gray had suggested she be a little more vigilant for a while because Day has disappeared."

"What on earth are you two talking about?" Ruth asked.

Sally filled her in, finishing with, "But Lowell Day's long gone from Dawson County. Caroline and me made it clear we'd tell Mr. Gray if he didn't *stay* gone."

"But Lucas has been . . . incapacitated," Ruth said. "What if Day heard about it somehow?" Her voice wavered. "What do you think we should do, Ella?"

"Can we tie Calico up somehow? Leave the buggy out of sight and walk down?"

"You mean sneak down there. With Sally's gun. Right?"

"Yes. That's exactly what I mean." Ella took a deep breath. "If someone were watching and waiting for just the perfect time . . . it's probably nothing. But I don't see where there's any harm in taking precautions."

"Tell us what to do," Sally said.

"Let's climb down from the carriage. We'll lead Calico and take a wide berth around so we can see the back of the house before we decide what to do."

"That's good," Ruth said with a nod. "Let's go."

Several minutes later the three ladies were looking down on the house . . . and two strange horses tied out back.

"Now what?" Sally said.

"I'll walk down toward the back," Ruth offered, "and untie those horses. I can keep the buggy whip with me for a weapon."

Sally held the gun out to Ella. "Take this. You'll look more . . .

intimidating. It's got a real easy trigger, so be careful. I'll pick up a piece of kindling for a weapon when we walk by the woodpile."

"So the two of us go in the back," Ruth said. "And Ella goes in front. With that." She pointed at the gun.

Ella nodded. "As soon as you spook those horses, we all charge in." She forced a soft laugh. "If Mama and the others are sound asleep, we'll never live this down."

As Ella moved down the slope toward the house, she watched Ruth and Sally's progress out of the corner of her eye. She still couldn't see anything inside that front door. The wind wasn't strong enough to blow it open like that—was it? Maybe those horses belonged to a couple of newcomers looking for homesteads. Maybe they'd just stopped by and been invited to stay the night before continuing on their way. Folks out here did that kind of thing often enough. *But who leaves their horses saddled overnight?* Ella closed her eyes for a second. *Please, God . . . let Mama be all right. I'll never ask you for another thing if only Mama is all right.*

Sally and Ruth had reached the corral. Ruth tied Calico to the gate. She took the buggy whip from its stanchion, and together, she and Sally moved toward the house. Ella slipped along the front of the house, pausing at the bedroom window and peering around the corner. Nothing in the room. Just the blazing oil lamp in the window. No clear view into the next room.

Slipping past the window, Ella grasped the gun with both hands, sidestepping along the front of the house until she was standing with her back against the front door. She could hear grunts . . . was that a moan? *Please, God . . . please . . .*

"Yah! Git on! Yah!"

The second Sally and Ruth's voices called out, Ella stepped through the door, planted her feet, and pointed the gun at . . . *Lowell Day.* She didn't know the other one. Stringy yellow hair. Pale eyes glittering above a gag made from a strip of yellow calico.

Ella lowered the gun. Across the room from her, Sally and Ruth lowered wood and buggy whip. They all stared in disbelief at the scene before them—two men tied to chairs, Hettie and Caroline—the latter with a huge pistol in one hand—seated on either side of Mama, who was perched on the edge of her rocker with Caroline's Winchester across her lap.

"Finally!" Mama said, and, jumping up, handed the rifle to Sally. "I thought you'd *never* get home!" She gestured at Ella. "I think you can put the gun down now. They aren't going anywhere." As she spoke, Caroline and Hettie got up, too. Caroline laid the gun she'd been holding on the kitchen table, while Hettie slid the chairs back into place.

Sally found her voice first and nodded at Lowell Day. "Is he . . . dead?"

"I don't think so. He was breathing fine when we tied him up." Mama shook her head. "They had it all worked out. This one"—Mama pointed to the yellow-haired man—"crept in through the door. And the second Caroline aimed her shotgun at him, the other one planned to come flying in through the window." Mama shook her head again. "What they didn't expect was an old lady with a frying pan." She reenacted clocking Day's partner.

"He's lucky I knocked him out, because he barely missed getting shot when Caroline pulled that trigger. But then the other one came through the window and tackled Caroline. I was worried for a minute, but Hettie came to the rescue with the other pistol." Mama beamed at Hettie. "I didn't know you could sound so determined, Hettie." She nodded at Ella. "But she did. You should have heard her. 'Let go of her this instant or I will put a hole in you the size of Texas' is what she said. Can you imagine our little Hettie saying such a thing?! Even so, I wasn't sure we could handle him—" She pointed at Day. "So I knocked him out, too."

"Oh, Mama." Ella laid the gun she'd been holding atop the

sewing machine and swiped at the tears of relief spilling down her cheeks.

Mama sounded defensive. "We had two of them to tie up, Ella. We couldn't take any chances."

Lowell Day's eyes flickered open, and Mama shook her finger in his face. "You should be ashamed of yourself! Trying to manhandle defenseless women!" She shook her head and spoke to Ella. "He's a bad one. But him—" She pointed at the yellow-haired stranger. "I think he's just misguided. He came to while we were tying him up, and he was very good about doing just what he was told."

"The hardest thing," Mama continued, "was getting that one"—she pointed at Lowell Day—"into the chair when he was still unconscious. Did you know that an unconscious man is as limp as a rag? They just flop around every which way."

"Where'd you get enough rope to do that?" Ella nodded at the men, tied to two chairs and wrapped with more rope than she knew they had on the place.

"That was my idea," Caroline said. "Cowboys ride with lariats."

Mama nodded. "And it's a good thing Caroline thought of it. We wouldn't have had enough otherwise."

"And the front door? Why'd you leave it open that way?" Ruth asked.

Mama beamed at Hettie and Caroline. "I told you that was a good way to let them know something was amiss." She pointed at the two men. "We were afraid there might be more of them out there waiting for the rest of you to get back. That's why we kept the guns ready and waited for you to come home. If there'd been more varmints on the loose, we could have threatened to shoot their friends if they didn't stay back."

"Did they say what they wanted?" Ella asked.

Sally kicked Day's boot as she said, "He wanted his guns back. Ain't that right, you slitherin', yellow-bellied, rat-faced, yellow-toothed, sour-smellin'—" She broke off. Then, with a little smile, she said, "You ain't even worth cussin' at."

Ella and the other ladies of Four Corners certainly hadn't come to Nebraska planning to become famous, but they were anyway. It happened one Sunday morning in June, when the six of them drove the two criminals seated in the back of their wagon into Plum Grove. That, in and of itself, would have made them the topic of many a conversation. But the way they did it gave the editor of the *Pioneer* fodder for quite a news story. Gagged with strips of a woman's yellow apron. Tied to kitchen chairs with their own lariats. And guarded by three armed ladies. One shotgun, two pistols. It was like nothing Plum Grove had ever seen before, nor would likely ever see again.

As Ella drove the wagon up Main Street, people stopped whatever they were doing and stared. The town grew quiet. The unnatural quiet drew others out onto the street. By the time Ella pulled the wagon up outside the Haywood Mercantile, just about every soul in the growing town had gathered to watch what would happen. Among those souls were Jeb Cooper and Matthew Ransom. Both men loped alongside the wagon as Ella drove up Main. Will Haywood, the Village Board chairman, who would act on the matter in absence of a proper sheriff and a jail, came out of the mercantile.

And then a wonderful thing happened to Ella Barton, and it was much better than fame. Jeb Cooper reached out both arms and said, "Let me help you down, Ella."

*Don't let go.* That was Caroline's first thought when it was her turn for Matthew to help her down from the back of the wagon. He'd gone first to Zita . . . and then he and Jeb helped the others down. When

Caroline laid her shotgun aside and took Matthew's hand, she began to tremble. The ladies of Four Corners might have rescued themselves, but oh, it was good to be in town, where they could get some help. Where something besides her shotgun and a bit of rope would stand between her and Lowell Day. Where Matthew—should he take a notion to do so—could hold her. And he did. Just for a moment before Will Haywood commandeered the now-empty dining hall for a courtroom.

Will asked the ladies to sit down and write out formal complaints. When Sally said she "didn't write so good," Will offered to write for her. And so it began. The ladies gathered around a table writing, Sally at another table speaking in a low voice while Will Haywood wrote, and the two criminals still tied to chairs with Matthew Ransom and Jeb Cooper stationed at the door.

After what seemed like half the morning, with each member of the Village Board reading over the ladies' written statements and preparing to take down testimony from Lowell Day and his partner, Charlie Obermeyer—one of the board members recognized him and was able to provide his name—Will apologized for having to ask them to stay, but he thought it best for the men to have to face their accusers when they said their piece.

The minute Charlie's gag came off, he began to jabber. "I wasn't there when Day tried to hurt that lady"—he nodded at Caroline—"I had nothin' to do with—"

"Shut your trap." Day struggled against the ropes and nearly tipped his chair over with the effort.

Matthew grabbed Day's chair and jerked him several feet away from Charlie, then stood between them.

Charlie spoke again. "I ain't gonna hang. I didn't do nothing to hang for. We didn't steal anything. I'll tell you everything. It was him. It was all his idea."

Day snarled, but he stayed put. His eyes roamed the room, landing on Caroline and making her shudder. Sally reached for her hand. She took it, but found herself wishing it was Matthew's. When she looked his way, he was watching her. She couldn't interpret his expression exactly, but she felt better all the same.

Will didn't know what the courts would decide, but he and another armed citizen were going to take Lowell Day and Charlie Obermeyer to the nearest jail a day's ride to the east. "My guess is neither one of 'em will see the light of day for a good while to come" was all he could say.

Caroline wasn't convinced that Will's assurances were quite enough to remedy her nerves and her nightmares. But then Zita said something profound. Not that Zita realized it was profound. That was the way with her. As they all watched the wagon taking the criminals to jail disappear into the distance, the little woman said, "Let's see if we can get Martha to make fresh coffee. There's no reason to give those two snakes any more power over our days than they've already had." She looked up at the blue sky and, taking a deep breath, said, "It is *such* a beautiful day."

Caroline thought about that for a very long time. It seemed like just another instance of Zita being cute and clever, but Caroline finally decided there was real wisdom behind it. After all, if a body let people from the past ruin today, didn't it do just what Zita said—give snakes more power than they deserved? In a sense, it let them win. Caroline thought back to the old man—her very own father-in-law—scratching at her bedroom door. To Lowell Day's hands groping her body in the barn. She would always shudder at the bad memories, but even as she acknowledged that truth, she was deciding that Caroline Jamison's life was not something to be handed over to men like that—that every moment she let them run through her memories was a moment she could have been enjoying life.

Starting right now, she was going to do everything she could to stop giving evil men from her past power over her present. As she sipped coffee with her friends, Caroline managed a smile.

"Mama, I've told you this before. Hanging pictures on the walls doesn't turn a barn into a fancy parlor." Ella reached up to pull the red ribbon out of her hair. "I don't really even want to go. After what Jeb said they're saying about us in town—"

Jeb and Matthew had been camped at Four Corners for the better part of the past week while they dug the fruit cellar. Jeb was trying to talk the ladies into a spring house, too. He had ideas for somehow making a spring house water the garden, and while Ella was intrigued by the man's ingenuity, she couldn't help but wonder what Elizabeth Jorgenson would think if she knew the man she wrote to every single week was spending more time helping women homesteaders than he was preparing his own place to welcome a wife. And surely that was Jeb's intention. Why else would a man be reading love poems like the ones in that book they'd delivered to his door?

"You leave that be!" Mama said, and slapped her hand away. "It's a *dance*, Ella. All the ladies will dress up." She twirled about in her new skirt. "It's what women do."

Ella caught a glimpse of Caroline and Sally just now coming through their door into the main room. Caroline was wearing her gold silk dress—complete with parasol. The matching hat shimmered against her dark curls. Sally looked like a redheaded blue bird in her dress as she waltzed across the floor. "I'm gonna dance that cowboy's boots off tonight!" She stopped in midstep and peered at Ruth. "No offense, but do you *have* to wear black? It's a celebration, not a funeral."

"It's my best dress." Ruth sounded offended.

"More's the pity." Sally shook her head. "I'm sorry, Ruth, but don't you think part of starting fresh out here might include putting off widow's weeds? Seems to me it'd be a nice surprise for Jackson when he rides in with them cowboys tonight. Why, it'd do him a world of good to see his mama celebratin' his homecoming that way."

Caroline had retreated into her bedroom while Sally was speaking. She reappeared in the doorway holding up a lavender-and-white-striped dress. "What about this?"

"It's lovely," Ruth agreed, "but it won't fit."

"Might be I could make it fit." Sally reached for the dress. "You're about the same height."

"There is no corset in the universe that will draw my waist up to match hers." Ruth pointed at Caroline.

"There's darts I can take out. It won't take but a minute." Sally was already opening her sewing basket and drawing out a tiny pair of scissors. "Be right back. I want the morning light." She stepped outside.

"You'll have to wear it now." Caroline smiled. "You don't want to hurt Sally's feelings."

"I don't have a bonnet," Ruth protested. "I'll look ridiculous in a lavender-and-white dress with a black bonnet."

Caroline disappeared back into her room and returned with a matching bonnet. "Any more excuses?"

Sally came back inside and handed Ruth the dress. "No darts. Try it on."

Matthew ran his hand along the edge of the notched piece of lumber. He'd hurried to give Martha what she wanted, but he wasn't happy with the results. Standing up to stretch, Matthew added the last board to the pile in his wagon and drove up to the mercantile to begin assembling the portable dance floor that Martha expected to be the talk of Plum Grove. It would take him and Will the better part of an hour to lay it out, and that was just the beginning. Martha wanted an arbor and a row of lanterns so the dancing could go on half the night if folks stayed. She expected they would.

Plum Grove's Main Street was no longer inhabited by jackrabbits and the occasional human. The grassy expanse had begun to give way to wagon ruts and a steady stream of wagons, buggies, and riders. On most days the air was filled with the sounds of hammers and saws as more buildings sprung up along Main, which was looking more like a real street every day. The town even smelled different. It used to be a man could step outside the mercantile and breathe in the pure air of unpopulated prairie. Now the air was just as likely to smell of grease from the dining hall kitchen—or manure.

Plum Grove wasn't the only thing changing. As he and Will laid out the dance floor and then raised the standards and created the arbor, Matthew enjoyed having people stop and admire his handiwork. He'd stopped wanting to avoid people. In fact, he liked visiting.

He wouldn't linger in the shadows tonight and grit his teeth and think of dancing with Linney as a debt he must pay. Tonight he would delight in Linea Delight Ransom. He smiled at the thought. Delight had been Katie's maiden name, but Matthew liked the other meaning, too. He did delight in his daughter. And while "delight" was probably too strong for his improved outlook on life at the moment, who knew but that the future might just hold other "delights," as well.

He wondered what Caroline would wear tonight. And what it would be like to dance with her. Guiding her around the dance floor and smiling down into those dark eyes of hers just might be another . . . delight. The thought stopped him in midstep as he carried a piece of lumber from wagon to dance floor. Not because of guilt. But because there wasn't any.

Of course, no one asked *her* to dance. Ella pretended she didn't care. Seated next to Mama up here on the boardwalk in front of Haywood Mercantile, she had a grand view of everything. She and Mama clapped their hands to the music as Bill Toady led the new musicians in reels and waltzes and jigs until the dancers were out of breath and begging for a break. The accordion player began a slow dance.

Linney and Martha were serving up a white cake so light someone quipped that they'd better hold it down lest it fly away. Ella stood up. "I'll get you some cake, Mama. And coffee?"

"I can get my own." Mama hopped up. Suddenly she leaned close. "There he is!" She pointed up the street to where Jeb Cooper had just come out of the livery. Reaching into her bag, she brought out a tiny perfume bottle, and before Ella knew what hit her, she'd been sprinkled with lavender water.

"Mama!" she scolded and waved her hands in the air. "Put that away."

Zita made a show of lifting her own chin, touching first here, then there with the tiny glass applicator before she tucked the little bottle back into her bag. "I'm going to see if Martha needs any help," she said, and gave Ella a little shove in the direction of Jeb Cooper.

Ella went for cake and ended up in a line that brought her face-to-face with Jeb as he stepped up behind her.

"Evening," he said. He glanced toward the front of the line. "Good cake?"

"So I hear."

"And coffee?"

"Yes." The little woman in front of Ella glanced back ... and up ... and looked away quickly.

Ella reached up to feel the red bow in her hair. She should never have worn this thing. It looked ridiculous. The woman in front of her was likely trying not to laugh. She spoke to Jeb. "I'm getting some for Mama. And me. We're sitting over there by the mercantile. Mr. Toady made an announcement earlier. He wants to start a town band."

"That's a wonderful idea."

"Do you play music as well as you sing?"

Jeb shook his head.

"Do you dance?" *Oh, Lord, just open up the earth and swallow me now. It sounds like I'm asking him to dance.*

Jeb bobbed his head from side to side. Noncommittal. He shrugged. "Only when I have to. Weddings and such."

*Ah. Weddings.* Of course he would be thinking of weddings these days. She gulped. "Well, have a nice evening, Mr. Cooper."

Jeb grinned. "You too, Mrs. Barton." He dropped out of line and went to speak with Matthew Ransom.

"That's a bear of a man," the little lady in front of her said.

"Who? Jeb? Oh yes," Ella stammered. "I suppose so."

"Is he a friend of yours?"

"Oh no . . . no." Ella shook her head. "Mr. Cooper was part of the crew who helped when my friends and I built our house."

The woman's eyes grew large. "You're one of those women from Four Crosses, aren't you?"

"Four *Corners.*"

"Yes, that's it. And you brought those cattle rustlers into town tied to your kitchen chairs." The woman beamed. "Please. Tell me your name."

"Ella. Ella Barton."

"Mrs. Barton . . . you're my hero."

And so the evening went. The conversation kept flowing. The music was lively. All in all, everything was just grand. Ella remained on her boardwalk perch with Mama and observed the festivities. She saw Sally waltz with Pete Mills, and Ruth dance with Jackson, who'd ridden in with the cowboys from the Graystone Ranch and looked more grown-up than ever. Matthew guided Caroline out onto the floor, and they were so beautiful together they made Mama sigh. Husbands and wives, friends and neighbors laughed and clapped and enjoyed life under the prairie sky.

The sun set; the stars came out. The dining hall served a buffet supper, and the mercantile did a brisk business. And all the while, Ella smiled and joked and pretended she didn't mind that Jeb Cooper was essentially ignoring her.

What made it even worse was that Jeb did dance. With Mavis Morris, of all people. He was terrible at it, but somehow Mavis had gotten him out there on the dance floor. He stumbled and lost count and finally gave up, just when Ella was about to slip around back and wait in the buggy.

Mama clutched her arm. "There's something wrong with Hettie," she said, and sprang up to weave her way through the crowd.

Ella followed. Together they made their way to Hettie's side. She didn't seem to notice them. She was staring at the passengers climbing down from the specially outfitted wagon the new hotel sent to meet every train.

"What is it, dear?" Mama said, and reached to take Hettie's hand.

Hettie didn't answer, merely stared openmouthed at the man limping toward them from the hotel. He looked significantly older than Hettie, but no less amazed. He stumbled as he crossed the street, regained his balance, and frowned as he looked from Hettie to Zita to Ella and back to Hettie.

Finally, Hettie reacted. Clasping Zita's hand, she ducked behind Ella. That simple act transformed Ella from onlooker to protector, a role Ella accepted willingly. For once, she was grateful for her imposing size. She took a step forward, not saying anything, just taking up her station.

"Please," the man said, and motioned for Ella to step aside. But she could sense Hettie behind her. She could almost feel her trembling.

"State your business, sir. You've upset my friend."

The man cleared his throat. "Gates," he said. "Dr. Forrest Gates."

"I see. And your business in Plum Grove?"

"Business? I could ask you the same thing, madam."

"You could, but you didn't. You've upset my friend. So I ask again. Please state your business."

The man thought for a moment. "My business is with the lady standing behind you. As I said before, I'm Dr. Gates. Forrest Gates. And Hettie is my wife."

*And be ye kind one to another, tenderhearted, forgiving one another,*
*even as God for Christ's sake hath forgiven you.*

EPHESIANS 4:32

Is what he's saying true?" Zita asked. "Is this man your husband?"

From where she stood half-hidden behind Ella, Hettie answered, "Y-yes." Ella stepped aside then, and Hettie felt herself curl inward. Her head went down, her shoulders rounded. This must be what it felt like to be an animal caught in a trap.

"I've been looking everywhere for you," Forrest said. "Hettie . . . I . . . I'm so sorry. When I got to Denver and Aunt Cora said she hadn't heard from you—"

"Y-you've been to Denver?"

"I've been everywhere I knew to go." He brushed his palm across his forehead. "Oh, Hettie . . . I thought I'd lost you. When I thought I'd lost you—"

He took a step forward. Hettie took a step back. Closer to Ella.

"You need to stay over there," Ella said.

"And you need to stay out of the business between a man and his wife."

"Hey!" Zita pointed at him. "We don't know you, but we do know Hettie—"

"—apparently not very well if you didn't know she was married." Forrest took another step toward them, only to come face-to-face with

Jeb Cooper, who spread one hand across his chest and propelled him backward three steps while warning him to calm down. Hettie took a deep breath and stepped out from Ella's shadow.

Ella took her arm. "You need to talk to us," she said. "Now."

"Over there." Hettie tipped her head toward the darkened storefronts on the opposite side of Main.

"I don't know what you're afraid of, Hettie," Forrest said. "I've never laid a hand on you and I never would. I love you. I want—" His voice broke. "I just want you to come home."

Just the mention of the word brought back the searing memory of that house and the last time they'd been in it together. Hettie could see it as if it had just happened yesterday. The black crepe on the door . . . the chairs lining the parlor . . . and that small casket. She took a breath and failed to stifle the sob. "I'll *never* go back there."

Forrest took a deep, shuddering breath and bowed his head. "All right. I can understand that. I haven't been able to stay there, either. We can go anywhere. Anywhere you say. Just . . . oh . . . I'm so glad I finally found you."

She felt herself sway and for a brief moment thought she might faint, but Ella grabbed her on one side and Zita on the other, and together they walked her to the edge of the boardwalk and made her sit down.

"I'll get you a glass of water," Zita said, and bustled off.

Hettie waited in uncomfortable silence, not knowing what to say, what to do. She wanted to order Forrest to get away from her, to leave her alone, to go away and never come back again. If it weren't for the new life growing inside her, that's exactly what she would have done just now. She had no intention of ever going back to Forrest, but the baby made a difference. Taking a deep breath, she stood up.

"I want you to stay away from me," she said as calmly as she could. "Yes, you've found me, and I can't deny you're my husband. That means I have to decide what to do. But I cannot do this tonight. I just can't." She leaned into Ella. "Please, Ella. Please . . . can we go home?"

She sensed rather than saw whatever it was that passed between Ella and Jeb Cooper. But when Ella put her arm around Hettie's shoulders and led her away, Hettie felt confident that whatever else might happen, Forrest would not bother her again tonight. He wouldn't try to follow her home; he wouldn't try to force her to talk to him. For that, she thanked God and Jeb Cooper.

Jeb and Matthew came back to work at Four Corners. They put the roof on the fruit cellar and installed a door. They laid in stone steps and put up shelves. At times, Ruth found herself wishing she could go down into that cellar, to cool off and have some time alone to sort out her feelings. Because of the blistering heat and the never-ending work, no one noticed that Ruth wasn't herself, and she was grateful. The truth was so laughably immature she would have had to lie.

Just because Lucas Gray had bared his soul to her a few times; just because Ruth had finally realized that Caroline wasn't the least bit interested in Lucas but was falling in love with Matthew; just because Lucas had put his hand at her waist and blathered on about how he'd changed and realized that "first-sight sizzle" wasn't real love; none of that meant that Lucas was interested in Ruth Dow as anything but Jackson's mother and a good friend. It was embarrassing to feel like her middle-aged heart had been broken. It was ridiculous the way she reacted when Jackson told this story or that about his time on the ranch. At times Ruth almost held her breath, waiting for the boy to mention Lucas. Then when he did, she felt foolish for the way her heart lurched . . . for the way she savored thoughts of Lucas . . . and the way she loved hearing how much Jackson admired him.

Tonight, thoughts of Lucas kept Ruth awake as her mind wandered through the tangle of reasons why having allowed herself to be attracted to him was so ridiculous. Thank goodness he had no idea how she felt. She reached under her pillow for the note he'd sent with

Jackson—the note Jackson had forgotten to give her until very late the night of the Fourth.

*I have some pressing matters I have to attend to before I can make it into Plum Grove. If they aren't handled by the Fourth, I hope you'll forgive me for not showing up. Please send word about the cattle with Pete. Your friend . . . Lucas.*

He was her *friend*, and thank God for that. After four hours of mental anguish, Ruth gathered up her blanket and pillow, crept outside, and *did* go down the stairs to the still-empty fruit cellar. The room was cool and dark and blessedly private. Spreading out her comforter, Ruth sat down and, burying her face in her pillow, cried and cried and cried. She'd worn a new dress for him. She was such a fool. Finally, she fell into an exhausted sleep.

Ella did her best to give Hettie time, but when several days came and went and still she'd said nothing about the husband waiting at the hotel in town, she nearly forced the issue, but Mama told her to wait.

"How long? I don't think Dr. Gates is going to just sit at that hotel forever."

Mama shrugged. "Maybe he'll wait longer than you think. By now he's probably heard that his wife is staying with those crazy women out at Four Corners. I doubt he wants to be the next man hauled into town tied to a kitchen chair. I suspect he'll wait at least a few more days."

Mama was right. There was no word from Dr. Gates, and after supper on Monday, Hettie was finally ready to talk. She asked Jackson to give them privacy, and once he'd gone outside, she took a deep breath and said, "Y-you all know my husband is—was—" She broke off. "My husband *is* a physician."

"You ain't a widow?" Sally blurted out.

Hettie looked at Ella. "You didn't tell them what happened in town?"

"It wasn't my place," Ella said. "Everyone was ready to leave anyway. I just said you weren't feeling well and we needed to get you home."

Hettie looked at Ruth, glanced around the table, then back at Ruth. "And you haven't told . . . the rest."

"Of course not. I gave you my word." She pressed her lips together and looked away.

"You ain't a widow," Sally repeated.

Hettie shook her head. "No." She gulped. Glanced around the table again. "And I . . . I'm . . ." She took a deep breath. "I'm pregnant." There was a collective gasp, then silence.

"I know." Hettie sounded miserable. "I told Ruth about the baby out at the ranch, but I let her think . . . I let her think what you all thought . . . about my husband. And then Ella and Zita met Forrest, so they knew I wasn't a widow, but I didn't tell them about the baby."

Sally stared at Ella and Zita. "You knew she ain't a widow?" She glanced at Caroline. "Guess you and me is the only ones that didn't know nothin'." She shook her head, then sat quietly, chewing on her bottom lip and frowning.

Hettie apologized. "I . . . I'm sorry. I tried not to lie. Exactly. I just . . . I just had to let you all think . . . for a while . . ." She looked Ella's way. Pleading, Ella thought.

"Do you want me to tell what I know?" When Hettie nodded, Ella spoke up. "Most of you didn't see the hotel wagon bring the passengers over from the depot."

"I saw it," Sally said. "I just didn't pay much attention."

Ella nodded. "Yes. Well. One of the passengers was Dr. Forrest Gates."

"Raines is my m-maiden name," Hettie said.

"Apparently Dr. Gates has been looking for Hettie with some degree of dedication ever since she left St. Louis."

"That's why you were so interested in watching the trains come and go," Caroline said with a little frown.

Hettie nodded. "But Forrest h-hasn't been looking for me all these months. H-he's only been looking since . . . since he sobered up."

"Ah," Ella said. "I didn't know that part." Hettie motioned for her to continue. "Dr. Raines said he'd already taken the train to Denver, expecting to find Hettie at her aunt's home there. When the aunt hadn't heard from her—"

"Aunt Cora?" Ruth broke in.

"Yes. I didn't write her because I didn't want her to know where I was. In case Forrest asked about me. She needed to be able to say she hadn't heard from me."

"So when you told me you were pregnant at the ranch, and when you said your aunt had 'strong opinions' about things, that wasn't about your being pregnant at all. What you really meant was that she would have insisted you return to your husband—who is very much alive." Ruth's tone wasn't exactly accusing, but it wasn't sympathetic, either.

Hettie nodded. "But, of course, Aunt Cora couldn't tell Forrest anything. So he started retracing his steps, stopping in every town between Denver and home, asking questions. Over in Cayote he heard about a lady doctor who was new in Plum Grove and who'd tended a rancher with a broken leg. S-so he came here. Hoping, he says." She still sounded miserable. "I really am sorry." She looked at Ruth. "What I told you at the ranch was true. I *had* bought a ticket all the way to California. I never even meant to stop in Nebraska. But then . . . you were all so nice." Her voice wavered and she fell silent.

"So now you're going back to your husband," Ruth said.

"No!" Hettie fiddled with her glasses. "I can't. Not now. Not ever."

Caroline asked, "Does he know about the baby?"

Hettie shook her head.

"A man deserves to know he has a child," Ruth said.

"Forrest doesn't. He drank. He drank every day."

"Did he hit you when he was drunk?" Sally spoke up. "Because if he hit you, he don't deserve nothin'."

"No . . . that's not it. Forrest was never violent. Ever."

"All right," Sally said. "But a drunk don't deserve a kid, either."

"But what if he's stopped drinking?" Mama asked gently.

"It doesn't matter," Hettie insisted. "We had a child. A boy." Tears began to slide down her cheeks. "H-his name was Oliver. We named him for my father. He . . . he's gone. Dead." Her voice was barely a whisper. "And Forrest is to blame."

While the ladies sat in stunned silence, Hettie struggled to regain her composure. Finally, Ruth took a deep breath and reached over and took Hettie's hand. "It's going to be all right. I told you that at the ranch and nothing has changed. You shouldn't have lied to us, but you were afraid." Ruth exchanged glances with the others. "We all know what it's like to be afraid." She squeezed Hettie's hand. "And we're still your friends. We're still going to help if we can. But you have to help *us* understand. You have to tell us everything."

Hettie took a deep breath. When Mama set a glass of water in front of her, she took a sip. "Forrest started taking Oliver along with him on calls when Oliver was only six years old. Barely old enough to know anything. Of course he liked being with his father, but . . . he was too young. I told Forrest he was too young, but he just wouldn't listen." She paused.

"Forrest arrived at a house one night—a confinement, except it was just supposed to be a routine visit. There and back, Forrest said. The baby wasn't due for weeks yet. But suddenly he was involved in a difficult case. He couldn't leave. He gave Oliver a book, but . . . you know how boys are." Hettie took in a deep, sobbing breath. "N-no one even realized he'd left the house." She shuddered. For a few minutes she cried quietly. Finally, she swiped at her eyes and blew her nose.

"Th-the nearest they could figure was Oliver was reaching for the dipper hanging on the side of the bucket and—" She broke off and closed her eyes. While the tears streamed down her cheeks, she managed to say, "That well was nearly two hundred feet deep." She spoke through fresh tears. "I *begged* him not to take Oliver with him that day. But he wouldn't listen. He had to have his little buddy along." Her voice was bitter. "His little buddy."

Handkerchiefs swiped at tears all around the table. Sally finally broke the silence. "Men have turned into drunks over a lot less than that," she said. "He musta been hurtin' something terrible."

"I don't know what I'd do if something happened to Jackson," Ruth murmured. "One thing is certain. You've been through the worst loss a woman could ever face."

Mama reached over and took Hettie's hand. "I can't tell you what to do. But I will pray God's comfort. For you both."

Hettie took a deep breath. "Thank you," she said. "Thank you."

Her hands caked with grime, her back aching, Caroline swiped at the sweat pouring down her face as she knelt to pick green beans. *Laws o'massey,* it was hot today. She couldn't wait for Sally to finish the green calico dress she'd cut out just a few days ago. A dress that allowed for twenty-three inches of waist. Caroline would forgo her corset in favor of breathing.

She glanced toward the house, mindful of Sally's furious pace on the treadle sewing machine. Hettie was taking a nap, although how that woman could sleep when it was this hot, Caroline didn't know. They were going to have to can beans tomorrow, and that would be a caution in this heat. What she wouldn't give for a glass of cold buttermilk right now.

A fly buzzed past. Caroline waved it away. Feeling a little dizzy, she worked to the end of the row, then sat back for a moment to catch her breath. Her throat parched, she stood up and wobbled her way toward the well. All she could think of now was a drink of cool water. When she finally got to the well and a stream of cold water burst from the pump head, she leaned down, welcoming the sensation of the frigid water dousing her dark hair. She straightened back up just as a scowling Matthew Ransom headed in her direction.

"I thought you were going to faint before you got to the house," he said. "You can't work in the sun without a bonnet on a day like today, Caroline. You'll kill yourself."

She ignored the scolding. "Did you find how that varmint is gettin' at Sally's hens?"

"I did. Patched it. He won't be a problem at least for a while."

"Well, I got almost all the beans picked. That'll be a nice surprise for everybody when they get back from Jeb's."

"Certainly better than the surprise of finding you fainted from sunstroke." He strode toward her then and, taking her hand, led her to the bench by the back door. Ordering her to sit down, he took a clean kerchief out of his pocket, went back to the pump, wet it with cold water, and brought it back. "Put this to the back of your neck," he said, then got a quart jar from inside and filled it. "Drink," he said. "All of it. I'll finish picking the beans. You catch your breath."

A few minutes later, he strode back, a basket filled with fresh-picked beans beneath one arm. "Set them by the well if you don't mind," Caroline said. "I want to have them all rinsed and snapped before sundown. But I've got a few other things to do before I get back to the beans."

A new kind of heat set her heart to pounding when he smiled at her. "I could be convinced to linger and help a lady."

Caroline forced a little laugh. "Be careful what you offer, Mr. Ransom. You might live to regret saying you'll help."

"Try me."

"Well, now, let's see . . . milk the cow, churn the butter, hem my new dress, knead bread . . . oh, and if y'all don't mind, Jackson was just saying how he'd like his mother's hundred sixty acres fenced before Lucas Gray brings his cattle over."

Matthew frowned. "Luke's giving Jackson some cattle?"

"Not giving. Just getting him started. They've got it arranged somehow."

"I see."

"Now, I know you don't like Mr. Gray," Caroline said. "But if you'd seen how excited Jackson is about those cattle—and besides, Ruth says Mr. Gray has changed."

"Do tell."

Caroline patted her neck with the cool cloth. "I'm just tellin' you what Ruth said, Matthew. Don't get all riled up because I spoke the name. I don't want any part of whatever it is between you and Lucas Gray, and I already told him as much, and now I'm telling you."

Matthew sat down beside her. Taking in a deep breath, he said, "I'd like to make it your business. If you're willing to hear me out."

The way he looked at her made Caroline's heart thud. "I . . . I don't know what you mean."

He reached for her hand. "I think I'm falling in love with you, Caroline."

It felt like someone had knocked the air clean out of her.

The reaction wasn't exactly what he'd hoped. The minute he said, "I think I'm falling in love with you," Caroline gasped and snatched her hand away. It only made him long to pull her into his arms, but he didn't have the right. If he was ever going to have the right—or so much as a chance—he had to tell her everything.

He spent the next few minutes talking and thanking heaven she didn't tell him to hush and get off her land. He told her everything: how he'd met Katie; how he'd cut in when she was dancing with Luke; how she'd chosen him over Luke; how he'd brought her out here and then failed her; how his anger and his jealousy had ruined everything; and how he'd spent the last few years since she died.

"And so," he said, and swallowed, "when I plowed into Luke that day at the mercantile, it wasn't for anything Luke ever did. It was because I'd spent years blaming him for the mess I'd made of my life. All those years of festering anger were in that one punch, and I threw it because Luke dared to smile at Linney." He let out a breath. Caroline hadn't moved. What did that mean? There was no way to know. He kept talking.

"You said Ruth thinks Luke has changed. Well . . . so have I." He told her what he'd learned from reading Jeb Cooper's Bible. "I'm still not sure how to articulate what happened that day, but I do know I'm different. I haven't tried to put it into words until just now. But it's . . . it's like something rotten's been scooped out of me." He turned toward her. "Does any of this make any sense at all to you?" He couldn't see her eyes because she wouldn't look at him. But he could see tears spilling down her cheeks.

"I thought you might get mad. I didn't expect you to cry."

She cleared her throat. "Have you told any of this to Mr. Gray? About changing and feeling rotten before and things being different now? Have you said you're *sorry?*"

Matthew shook his head. "I wouldn't know where to start."

Caroline got to her feet. "You start the same way you did with me just now. Oh, you don't say the love part." She blushed. "But, Matthew . . . you and I—" She shook her head. "Everything *isn't* clean and new. Not until you make it right with Lucas Gray. You have to know that. You have to talk to him. You at least have to try."

"You're right." He swallowed. "Do you think once I've done that—"

"You've got to do what's right just because it's right. Not because of me." She cleared her throat. "I've been married to a coward, Matthew. I don't know if I want to marry again, but one thing is sure. I will never knowingly walk into the space between two men who don't have the courage to step over their egos and fix something worth fixing." Tears gathered in her eyes again. "When I married Basil, my family disowned me. I thought they'd forgive me someday. I was so sure they would."

Her voice wavered. Fresh tears spilled down her cheeks. "Maybe they would have, if all three of my beautiful, intelligent brothers hadn't died in the war."

How Matthew longed to reach out to her. But he didn't.

She sniffed and took a deep breath. "I've got no family in my life, Matthew. These ladies here at Four Corners are my family now. Having my first family disown me—that was my doing, and I have to live with it. But you have a chance to get your family back. To my mind, that is a treasure worth fighting for."

She paused. "I'll handle the churning and milking and such," she said. "I think you've got more important things to tend to, don't you?"

When he nodded, she laid one palm against his cheek. He closed his eyes, hoping there would be more, but there wasn't. There was, however, reason to hope. "You be careful on your way to the ranch. We've been talking about having a harvest dance out here at Four Corners, and I have a particular fondness for waltzing beneath the stars with men who make my tender li'l Tennessee heart pound."

*Now faith is the substance of things hoped for,*
*the evidence of things not seen.*

HEBREWS 11:1

S-so," Hettie said. "I know it's not what you want. But it's the best I can do right now." She'd agreed to come into town and talk, but now, as she sat back in her chair at the dining hall table and waited for Forrest to respond, her resolve wavered about what she was proposing. Zita said God would reward obedience, but Hettie wasn't sure of that, either. Linney Ransom stopped by and poured coffee into their half-empty mugs. Neither of them had eaten a thing. They handed over their plates.

After an eternity of contemplating the cup of coffee before him, Forrest let out a long, slow breath. "All right, Hettie. If that's what you want."

A family came in the front door, their child skipping alongside them jabbering in what Hettie thought might be Swedish . . . she wasn't sure. She only knew the child was about Oliver's age, and the sight of him tore at her heart. She swallowed. "I don't *know* what I want. I just know what I *don't* want. I *don't* want to ever see that house again. And I *don't* want to leave my friends." The family sat down, and Linney hurried over to them with a bright smile. "And I don't want to feel this way forever. Zita says I won't. She says I should have faith that things can be better between us." She glanced at Forrest and then away. "Zita says I should give us time, and she's one of the wisest people I've ever known. I think I should listen to her."

Forrest closed his eyes for a moment and sighed before saying, "But you aren't willing to listen to *me*. To believe I'm telling you the truth when I say the drinking is done."

"I *did* listen. I just . . . I can't go off with you and be all alone again if you . . . if something happens. I need my friends. I need their support."

"It's asking a lot to expect me to battle all those women and what they're telling you to do. Not that they aren't fine women. That's not what I mean. But they exert a formidable influence on you."

Hettie pushed her spectacles up on her nose. "You don't have to battle them. You should be grateful for them. They're the ones who came up with what I'm proposing."

Forrest picked up the napkin he'd had spread across his lap. Folding it, he laid it on the table. "All right, Hettie. I'll leave first thing in the morning. I'll take care of everything. Just get me a list of anything you want from the house." He reached across the table and laid his hand atop hers. "And promise me you'll still be here when I get back."

"I'm not going anywhere." Hettie blinked the tears away.

It was a week before Matthew caught up with Luke, not because the rancher was hard to find, but because . . . well . . . because Matthew had to talk to Jeb about things and then plan a speech and practice it and . . . because for all his talk to Caroline about how he felt clean and new, he still dreaded facing Luke, who would likely toss Matthew off the ranch. Maybe plant his own fist on Matthew's jaw. And then what? What would Caroline do when Matthew reported that he'd collected enough courage to go ask for forgiveness, but Luke wasn't willing to give it?

Jeb Cooper said that all God expected of a man was for that man to do his part. To be obedient and leave the results with God, since a man couldn't control results anyway. It was called living by faith, Jeb said, and Matthew understood the concept, but acting on it was one of the hardest things he'd ever done.

Jeb agreed. "It's called living by faith," he said, "not sight."

When Matthew rode into the green valley that comprised the heart of the Graystone Ranch, Luke was standing in the middle of a corral lunging the same gray stallion Matthew had watched him unload back in April. His heart pounded just like it had back then. Only now it wasn't hate that caused the reaction. Now it was just plain nerves. At least there weren't a lot of other wranglers about. Matthew was grateful for that. He hadn't planned on even dismounting—at least until he saw how Luke was going to react to what he had to say, but the stallion didn't seem to like the idea of Patch getting too close, so Matthew retreated to the big barn, dismounting and hitching Patch before returning to where Luke waited. He'd stopped lunging the horse and reeled him in.

"Mrs. Dow said your leg healed up pretty well." *Stupid*. Not what he had planned to say at all. But looking Luke in the eye for the first time in years seemed to have erased his practiced speech.

Luke nodded. "Thanks to both of them—Ruth and Hettie." He stroked the stallion's neck. "No thanks to me and my cursed pride."

Matthew glanced around. "Things look good."

"Could be better. That late spring snow didn't help with calving."

"Ruth's son. He thinks a lot of you. He likes Pete, too. But he talks about you more."

Luke shrugged. "Did you ride all this way to tell me that Jackson Dow likes me?" He rubbed his jaw. "Or did you want another chance at knocking me clean to heaven—or hell, where I likely deserve to go."

Matthew shook his head. "I don't want to knock you anywhere. I want—" *Why is this so hard?* He nodded at the stallion. "He's a beauty. Reminds me of Silver."

"Silver was a good horse."

"Well, he would have been. If I'd listened to you. But I didn't. I was too bullheaded to listen. About a lot of things. And then when he turned up lame I blamed you." Sweat trickled down his back. "I've blamed you for a lot of things that weren't your fault. Things I should own up to. More important things than that horse I ruined." His voice wavered. He stopped talking.

Luke reached up to unsnap the lead from the stallion's halter. The horse gave a little snort and danced away. Still, Luke remained in the center of the small corral. "I didn't betray you with Katie, Matthew. I did love her. I did want her. And I did beg her to stay with me that day. But she didn't. She loved *you*. I was wrong to act on my feelings. I was wrong, and if I could take back what I said to her that day—and to you—I'd do it."

He looked down at the ground. Took his hat off, brushed his forearm across his forehead, and put it back on. "I was wrong and I'm sorry. Of course saying that after all this time isn't enough." He gestured around him. "You may not believe it, but I'd give everything you can see and more to fix things for you. But money can't fix the really important things." He broke off. "Can you do it, Matthew? Can you forgive me?"

"I came to say I'm sorry," Matthew blurted out. Surprise shone in Luke's eyes.

"All these years I've blamed you. It wasn't your fault. None of it. I wouldn't see it. It's taken me all this time to see it true." He took a deep breath. "So I came out here to ask you to forgive me." He held out his hand. It felt like the hand stayed out there for years. In reality, it was just the seconds it took for Luke to cross the corral and grasp it.

"Done," he said.

Matthew nodded. "Done."

Awkward silence reigned for a few seconds. Finally, Matthew said he'd be getting on his way. He turned to go.

"Matthew." When he turned back, Luke nodded toward Patch. "That horse know anything about driving cattle?"

"Not a thing. Why?"

"Well, I promised Jackson five cows. I haven't gotten them to him and—well, I thought maybe you could help me drive them that way when I have the time to deliver them."

Matthew's heart sank. He'd seen Lucas talking to Caroline that first day. Of course he hadn't known it was Caroline then . . . but she'd been there in the mercantile, too. What if it wasn't Linney that Luke was following? What if it was Caroline? *History repeating itself. Would God let that happen?* The rock returned to his gut.

Luke cleared his throat. "I suppose I should confess there's a little more to my interest in Four Corners than taking cattle to Jackson."

Here it came. Matthew steeled himself to hear it.

"The truth is . . . I'd like to call on Ruth."

Sometimes Ella wished that Jeb Cooper wasn't quite so smart. Every time the windmill creaked and sent water through Jeb's system of pipes toward the garden, it made her think of him and how much she was dreading meeting his bride. Jeb Cooper had gone back east to get the woman who was sending him those letters. At least that was what Ella concluded when he said he'd be gone for a while and didn't explain himself any more than that. Not that he owed her an explanation.

Even Martha Haywood thought that's where he went. As postmistress to the area, Martha saw everyone's mail, and when Ella was in town on Saturday, Martha didn't have a letter from Elizabeth Jorgenson and thought that was odd since Jeb usually got a letter nearly every week from her. And then Mavis Morris came in hinting and asking if they knew where Jeb Cooper was going on the train yesterday all dressed to the nines.

Ella came back home, and as she and the other ladies worked to put up their garden produce, she hoped on hope that Elizabeth Jorgenson knew how to work hard, because if their well was deep enough to supply a reliable amount of water, that woman was going to have a good garden—just like the ladies at Four Corners. She was *that woman* in Ella's mind. She could not bring herself to think in terms of *Elizabeth Cooper*.

They were into canning season now, spending hours a day over the hot stove processing tomatoes and beans, carrots and beets. They filled gallon crocks with brine, and Mama showed them how to make pickles. They shredded small mountains of cabbage and added crocks of sauerkraut to the larder. No longer did the fruit cellar smell like earth. Now it smelled of vinegar and spice.

Jackson located chokecherries and buffalo berries, elderberries and plums. They gathered baskets of ripe fruit. Even Hettie went along to gather wild fruit, now past the early weeks of her pregnancy and feeling better. The ladies spent long hours in the kitchen making jam and jelly and drying fruit for winter pies.

Still there was no sign of Jeb Cooper. No sign of Matthew Ransom, either. Ella thought Caroline seemed almost as distracted as she felt. But she didn't bring it up. Still, she wondered if once again, she and Caroline, the unlikeliest candidates for such a thing, shared similar concerns about certain things.

Sometimes, Ruth thought, emotions were like a horsefly. Just when you thought you'd banished it from the kitchen, here it came buzzing back. *If only there was a flyswatter that could kill stubborn, stupid, illogical . . . hope.* She'd been doing so well. She hadn't thought about Lucas for several days. At least not very often. In fact, she had convinced herself that she would rarely think of Lucas at all if it weren't for Jackson's wondering aloud about when the Graystone cattle would arrive. And now here they came, bawling their way across the prairie on the last Tuesday morning of July, driven by none other than the rancher himself, looking so handsome Ruth wanted to— She stopped in mid-thought at sight of the other wrangler. *Cattle driven by Lucas Gray and Matthew Ransom—together? But—that's impossible.*

"Will wonders never cease," Zita said from where she stood in the doorway.

"Well, ain't that somethin'," Sally echoed from the open window.

Ruth stood speechless, water bucket in hand, beside the seedling trees. Caroline, who'd been watering the seedlings at the opposite end of the house, set her bucket down and waited, shading her eyes with one hand. While the cattle scattered in the general direction of the cottonwood tree and the spring in the distance, Lucas rode up to Ruth.

"Good day, Mrs. Dow. I believe I promised your son some cattle." He grinned at Jackson, who'd come running from the direction of the barn. "Think you and Sam can manage to keep track of a dozen?"

"I don't know about me," Jackson said, "but I'm pretty sure Sam's up to the task."

Lucas laughed. "Well, you've learned one of the most important lessons in a cowboy's life. If you've got a good horse, listen to what he has to say."

Matthew rode up to Caroline and dismounted. Ruth didn't know what he was saying to her, but whatever it was, she seemed to like it.

"You'll stay for dinner, of course," Zita said.

The men said they would. Lucas dismounted. When he took off his hat, that same lock of hair fell over his forehead. Ruth wished for a flyswatter.

Somehow Ruth made it through dinner without knocking over a glass or spilling peas down her front. She remembered these feelings from those long-ago days when she was a reasonably attractive young woman invited to dinner by the much-sought-after cadet with the long name. Back then she'd been so nervous she could barely eat, and that's exactly how she felt now. How ridiculous for a grown woman—a widow and the mother of a half-grown son, no less—to feel this way.

She might not be wearing black anymore, but that didn't mean she should be harboring any notions about Lucas Gray.

Things went from the ridiculous to the absurd when Lucas asked if they could take a walk. Her heart began to hammer. She didn't wait for him to speak. Instead, she took up the topic she was certain he had in mind. "We are all fine with your cattle grazing on that section of our land this year, but I hope you've schooled Jackson in what he needs to know. None of us knows a thing about your longhorns."

"The cattle will be all right. That's not what I wanted to talk to you about." He kept walking. Ruth hurried to keep up. Finally, when they were farther from the house than she cared to wander as the sun went down, he stopped. "You did get the note I sent with Jackson?"

"I did."

"I wanted to tell you something first. I'll tell the others when we get back inside, but I didn't want to ruin a nice dinner with this news. Lowell Day's serving ten years in the penitentiary at Lincoln. Charlie only got three, but I honestly don't think he was ever a real threat to any of you. But mostly I wanted to say that I was really sorry to miss that dance. The trial took longer than I expected and then—"

"You went to the trial?"

He looked surprised that she'd ask. "Of course. I always knew I should keep an eye on Lowell. I only hired him because of Clyde. Clyde's a good man. I wanted to give his brother a chance." He shook his head. "In a way I feel responsible for what happened. Thank God it worked out as well as it did." He smiled a slow smile. "But just because I sent a note doesn't mean I don't owe you a special apology. It also doesn't mean I don't expect you to make good on the promise. Two dances at the very next hoedown."

Ruth crossed her arms over her body and took a little step back. "That isn't necessary. We were going to talk business. The business got attended to. That's what matters."

"I see." He didn't seem pleased, but he guided things away from the subject of dancing. "Well. Maybe we'll come back to that. You'll recall the note said I had things to attend to before I could come back into town. Things . . . plural?"

"I remember." *I memorized every word.*

"How much do you know about my . . . history . . . with Matthew?"

Ruth's hand went to her collar. "Enough to know it's none of my business."

"I appreciate your respecting a person's privacy. But I've reasons for wanting you to make it your business. Will you hear me out?" When she nodded, he began. "Matthew and I came out here together. We had a plan. . . ." He told her what Ruth presumed was everything. The whole tragic story. He didn't try to gloss over his own behavior. She could tell it was difficult for him to form the words, and yet he did, staring off toward the horizon as the setting sun painted his handsome face gold.

"I still can't believe we just managed a cattle drive together and didn't come to blows even once." He shook his head. "Maybe miracles do still happen from time to time." He smiled at her. "Maybe this is my year for miracles. After all, here I stand on two good legs."

Ruth didn't know what to say. Everything he'd just shared was horrible . . . and wonderful. Her mind was whirling so that she almost missed it when Lucas said something about yet more "business" between the two of them.

"I'm going to go for a third miracle." He lifted her chin. Met her gaze with those cool gray eyes . . . not so cool at the moment. "Would you be open to my calling on you from time to time?"

Ruth pulled away. Gently. She frowned. "You can't mean that."

"Why can't I mean it?"

"Well, because I'm old enough to be your—"

"Yes, ma'am." He nodded. "Thanks be to God you're old enough. I have made inquiries about you, Ruth Dow. You are exactly three years, two months, and fourteen days older than me. You're also smarter and braver and a heck of a lot more honorable. But you aren't very good at answering questions sometimes. So I repeat, may I call on you?"

"I don't . . . know." She looked toward the house. "I . . . I have Jackson to think of."

Lucas sighed. "All right. I can respect that. I thought you might react this way at first. Can't say that I blame you. But I'm not giving up, Ruth. As I told Jackson earlier, if you've got a good horse, listen to what he has to say."

"I fail to see what *that* has to do with this conversation."

"Hannibal liked you from the start. I should have listened to what he had to say a long while ago." He glanced toward the house and stepped back. "I have a long ride home in the dark, and I should get started. Are you sure you can't give me an answer tonight?"

Ruth managed a laugh. "After the long ride home I imagine one of you will come to your senses and regret this little speech."

"One of us?"

"You or that horse you listen to. But if, for some reason, you and Hannibal both fail in the common sense department, and if you really want to make calls that require hours in the saddle, then yes, you may call. Now, let's get back to the house before they send out a search party." As she and Lucas made their way back across the dew-soaked prairie toward the house, he took her hand.

Dear Lord in heaven above, she was going to need a bigger fly-swatter.

# CHAPTER
# TWENTY-EIGHT

*For God hath not given us the spirit of fear;*
*but of power, and of love, and of a sound mind.*

2 TIMOTHY 1:7

In the middle of August, Hettie told her friends that Forrest would be returning to Plum Grove the next week and opening an office in one of the new buildings on the town square. "So Plum Grove will have a real doctor." She smiled and went on to say that Forrest had sold the house in Missouri along with most of the contents and would store the few things she'd expressed some interest in keeping in the back at the clinic. "He's living in the upstairs apartment for now. It's . . . nice." She glanced at Caroline. "And he's hired Matthew to build a house on one of the city lots not far from the office."

"A double lot, actually," Caroline said.

"Ain't that a little pushy?" Sally asked.

Hettie shook her head. "No. It's not like that. Forrest has always had a good head for business. He said it's a good idea to invest in real estate here in town. At the rate things are going, he says a house that costs a few hundred dollars today could be worth a few thousand someday."

"Too bad I ain't got a few hundred dollars," Sally murmured.

August was such a long month. Especially for a woman missing a man who'd gone back east to marry and communicated very little ever since. "All I know," Martha said when Ella expressed concern one day over the hay that was going to go to waste over at Jeb Cooper's, "is that Jeb telegraphed Will to say Elizabeth was ill, and he was going to be delayed. So Will telegraphed back and said he'd see to the haying."

It was nice, the way the folks in Dawson County took care of one another. Ella didn't let on that it hurt her not to be invited to the haying. After all, she'd promised Jeb she'd help with haying as payment for his cutting all that sod this past spring. When she talked to Will about it and offered to move Jeb's livestock over to Four Corners until Jeb got back, she got yet another surprise.

"Well, that's real nice of you," Will replied, "and I'm sure that will mean a lot to Jeb, but you don't need to worry. Frank Darby took the livestock. Jeb gave him a real good price, too."

"He *sold* them?"

Will nodded. "Said that given Elizabeth's health, he didn't know when he'd be able to get back, so it seemed the best thing to do for the time being."

In mid-September Hettie decided that Zita and Ruth and God—although not in that order exactly—were right, and that while it was likely going to be the hardest thing she'd ever done, it was time to talk with Forrest about the future. She rode into town with the ladies, walking to the clinic while the others shopped. When she opened the front door, a little bell rang. It made her jump.

"I'll be right out," Forrest called from the back room. "Just have a seat."

Hettie sat on one of the oak chairs arranged along the wall in the waiting room, clasping her hands in her lap.

"Hettie." He smiled. "What brings you to town on a weekday?"

"Sally ran out of thread. Both Caroline and Ruth seemed to think it was an emergency." She smiled. "Although personally I think they both wanted an excuse to come to town. Caroline walked over to see the progress on our—on the house. Ruth's up at the mercantile visiting with Martha Haywood."

"Caroline and Mr. Ransom seem to be . . . close," he said.

Hettie nodded. "Do you mind if I pull down the shade and put out the closed sign—just for a few minutes?"

Forrest did it for her, then sat down in the chair next to hers.

"Everyone is saying nice things about the new doctor. Nancy Darby seems to have finally been convinced that *you* are the one to attend her confinement . . . not me."

"Well, it's nice to be trusted."

Hettie looked at him over the top of her glasses. She smoothed her palm over her abdomen. The baby kicked. "People always did think you had a nice manner. I'd forgotten that. I'd forgotten a lot of the good things. It all got buried under . . . the rest."

"I will never forgive myself for what I've put you through, Hettie. Never."

"No." She held up a hand. "Don't. That's not why I'm here." She cleared her throat. "If it was up to me, I would have run away and kept running. I'd still be running. But for whatever reason, I met up with those ladies on that train and I ended up here. In the middle of nowhere." She took a deep breath. "I'm glad that happened. I'm glad I didn't run farther. And . . . I finally think I'm glad you found me."

She gulped. "You keep saying that you want a chance to prove yourself. I think I've always wanted to give you that chance, but I've been afraid. Sometimes a person like me needs a little . . . kick—" She smiled as the baby responded appropriately. "A little kick to move them past the fear. I'm still afraid, but I'm being kicked." She took her husband's hand and pressed it to her abdomen. "I'm surprised you haven't noticed, but I've only just begun to have to loosen things.

I don't suppose it's really all that obvious. And you've never been all that observant about—"The baby kicked again.

Forrest jerked his hand away, and a whole host of emotions passed across his face. The last one brought tears. He slid to the floor before her and buried his face in her lap and wept. She stroked his dark hair. She was still afraid. But she was also still in love.

It was a beginning.

Martha made quite a show of things. "A letter? For you? Well, now . . . let me see . . ." She pretended to search and then feigned surprise. "Well, would you look at that. There *is* a letter addressed to Mrs. Dow."

Ruth just shook her head and tucked it in her bag. Lucas was nothing if not creative. She'd only seen him once since he'd asked to call, but that didn't mean she felt abandoned. Apparently he'd ridden into Plum Grove not long after bringing the cattle to Four Corners, and either the long hours in the saddle had addled his brain or he really was one of the most charming men she had ever known.

It had begun on the first Saturday in August. *I intend to call, although you may not see me as often as I hope we'd both like. We're having to keep special watches out because of the danger of fire right now, and I can't leave the boys and go hightailing it off on social calls. Please check with Martha every Saturday when you come to town. I've spent a long and very enjoyable day today planning a little something to keep you from forgetting me, but Martha knows to hold back so there's one for every week. The first "something" is this note, and a request that you make sure to read this week's edition of the Pioneer.*

It had taken Ruth a few minutes to find it, but amongst the columns of ads inviting people to buy six hemmed handkerchiefs for twenty-five cents at the Haywood Mercantile and subscribe to the *Pioneer* for two dollars a year, right below the mention of Graystone

Ranch having shipped a carload of "the best beef in the nation" to markets in the east she saw a curious notice. It caught Ruth's eye because of the line drawing of an elephant. All it said was *Hannibal sends greetings to RD.*

The next Saturday, Lucas's note directed Ruth across the street to the Portrait Gallery. Mr. Lucas Gray had left her a cabinet photo. He'd posed in a suit—Ruth didn't know he owned one—and looked . . . wonderful. It wasn't until she got back to Four Corners and took the photograph out by lamplight after everyone else had turned in that she noticed he'd scratched a note on the back. *Hannibal says that someone is missing from this photo. I quite agree.*

After that, the notes grew longer. *Wah Lo asked after Mrs. Gates today. Pete's hoping for a chance to dance with Sally again before too long. The boys are already planning all kinds of devilment at Jackson's expense during spring roundup next year. It means they like him, by the way.* The danger of prairie fires remained high. Lucas said not to worry and ended with another reference to the stallion. *Hannibal doesn't seem nearly as concerned about the need for rain as the rest of us. He seems to be single-minded in his missing you.*

"Aren't you going to read today's?" Martha asked.

Ruth started and blushed. She was getting a reputation for being distracted these days, and that would not do. "No. I thought I'd wait until . . ." She didn't want to admit that she wanted to wait until she was alone. But that was it.

"There's a package, but you're supposed to read the note first." Martha smiled. "I'm doing my best not to be nosy, Ruth, but I don't mind saying that as the weeks go by, it's getting more and more difficult."

Ruth only smiled. She opened the letter. *I hope you aren't getting bored yet. When you read this I will likely be gone to the cedar canyons north of here cutting fence posts. We've renewed all the firebreaks, and I'd like to get more fence run before winter sets in.*

*I don't mind telling you that many of the neighbors are bemoaning the influx of homesteaders because of what it means in terms of losing open range. I also don't mind telling you that I rather like the idea of homesteaders. Martha has a little gift. I hope you will take it in the spirit it is meant. I know it may shock you, but I beg you to consider. I wish I could see your face when Martha brings it out. I can almost hear you scolding me. I don't mind. Hannibal offers no words of wisdom today. He turns away and sulks.*

He'd jotted a postscript. *I imagine either Matthew or Jeb has explained how to make a fireguard, but just to be sure, I'm reminding you to see that it's done. Try to keep a wagon loaded with empty barrels parked by the well and throw every empty feed sack you've got in the back with the barrels. We can talk more about such precautions the next time we're together. About more than prairie fires, I hope.*

The idea that Lucas had gone to such lengths to arm them against fire made her feel at once valued . . . and afraid. When she asked Martha about Lucas's concerns, the older woman explained. "It's a danger every spring and every fall. We're just one big field of wild grass out here, and when frost kills off the green and the roots dry out—" Martha cupped her hands together and pantomimed a small explosion.

"How do they start?"

"Lightning. Hunters. Indians, sometimes." She leaned over and pointed to Lucas's note. "But if you do what he says, you'll be prepared." She smiled. "I'm not saying the danger isn't real. I'm saying there's no reason to stay up nights worrying. It's like anything else in life. We do what we can to prepare and then trust God."

She turned around and reached for a bolt of red cloth set apart from the others. "Now. As to Lucas's gift." She unfurled the cloth. "I told him you wouldn't like it. He said to tell you that Hannibal would approve and so would he, although he thought Hannibal's opinion might carry more weight with you. I have no idea what that means, but he seemed to think you'd find it amusing."

Martha waited for Ruth to explain. Instead, she just shook her head. If he were here this instant, she would be scolding him. But he'd just grin, and she had no ability to resist that grin. She'd ask Sally to make her something for the Harvest Festival. If Lucas showed up, then she'd show him.

Ella had always thought hosting a Harvest Festival at Four Corners was a grand idea, and as time went on community enthusiasm built, and the event seemed to take on a life of its own. Caroline got Bill Toady to say he would come and play, and Bill said he'd do better than that and bring a seven-piece band. Of course, once the band was coming, it only made sense to borrow the Haywood Mercantile dance floor, and if they were hauling the dance floor out, Martha said they might as well put up an arbor, too, and she would decorate it in a harvest theme, and after all, wasn't it a good idea to have the lanterns in the event the "harvest moon" went behind some clouds?

When Jackson said something about that "feather-light white cake from the Plum Grove Dining Hall," Caroline said she'd see to it that he had more than he could eat. And then Sally joked about a cake-eating contest and that turned into a pie-eating contest.

Alice Bailey suggested an outdoor quilt show; the ladies could display their quilts draped over the sides of their wagons. When Caroline carried that suggestion home from town, Ruth mentioned that pumpkin orange was, after all, appropriate for the season.

It was as if the wind carried the news, and before the ladies of Four Corners quite knew what had happened, they were hosting an event that was akin to a county fair, complete with a quilting bee to begin at noon and ending with a dance that would likely last most of the night.

Wagonloads of neighbors began rolling in at midmorning on that clear September day, and by suppertime, not only had the ladies tied two comforters and quilted half of one of Caroline's pieced quilt tops, Dr. Gates had been called upon to put four stitches along Jackson's left cheek when he tried—and failed—to jump Sam over a fence. Ruth didn't know whether to scold him or encourage him to try again. She opted for the latter and cheered louder than anyone when Sam sailed over the fence successfully.

When the wranglers from Graystone Ranch began to arrive, it was only natural that someone had to earn bragging rights about having the fastest horse in the county, and so a race course was set up from the cottonwood tree up to the section line, across Cross Creek, and back again, the winning rider to be awarded a dance with the lady of his choice. When Sally Grant called out, "And it had better be me," everyone laughed.

Lucas Gray didn't race, even though everyone knew that if he did, that flashy chestnut gelding of his would win. Every time Ella saw him, Gray was either talking to Jackson or laughing with Ruth—who'd shocked everyone by wearing a new red dress for the event. She looked ten years younger in it. In fact, Ruth was looking younger in general these days. Mostly because she was smiling more, Ella thought. Mama said it was more than that, that Ruth was falling in love again.

All in all, Ella had a wonderful day. She moved from one group to the next, welcoming people onto the place and answering more questions than she cared to about the "night you all hog-tied two desperadoes in the kitchen." She loved watching Mama flit around and retell her version of "the desperado story," and she didn't even mind the idea of hosting a dance, because Jeb wouldn't be there to not dance with her.

Everything was grand until, along about sunset, Jeb Cooper's wagon appeared coming over the rise, and there she was. Elizabeth. She looked more like a queen than a homesteader's wife. The closer the wagon got, and the more Ella could see of the woman's elegant green traveling suit complete with matching parasol, the more Ella's head hurt. When Jeb reached up and, with a loving smile and a little laugh, lifted Elizabeth to the earth, Ella decided the headache was just too much. She must lie down and rest.

Thank goodness the community's babies were sleeping in the opposite end of the house. When she slipped into her bedroom and lay down, no one was the wiser. Until someone came in the back door. Footsteps hurried across the floor and paused at the open door to her room. Ella closed her eyes.

"Ella! What do you think you are doing?! Jeb Cooper's back. He's asking for you."

"I'm resting, Mama. I have a headache."

"Don't be ridiculous. You don't get headaches."

"Well, I have one tonight. Please, Mama. Go back to the party. Offer Jeb and his wife my congratulations and tell him I'll see them in church on Sunday."

"What are you talking about?" Mama came to stand at her bedside.

"Elizabeth. Mrs. Cooper. I'll meet her on Sunday."

"You aren't making any sense."

Ella sat up. "You don't have to spare my feelings, Mama. I've known Jeb was going to get married since we delivered that fancy letter and that book of poems weeks ago. So—"

"Jeb Cooper is *not* married." Mama put her hands on her hips. "I declare, Ella, sometimes you are as dumb as a board when it comes to men."

"Mama! I saw her. Elizabeth. Sitting beside him."

"Well, of course you did." Mama sighed. "Now, get up and get outside. Jeb's asking for you. He wants his *sister* to meet you."

Elizabeth Jorgenson née Cooper was nearly as tall as her brother. She was, Ella decided, probably the most intelligent woman on the earth, but she also appeared to be one of the nicest. It took no time at all for the Four Corners ladies to invite Elizabeth for lunch on Sunday, and Elizabeth didn't wasn't any time in retrieving a blanket out of the wagon bed of her brother's wagon and thrusting it into his arms with a meaningful nod in Ella's direction.

Jeb smoothed the blanket over his arm and came to Ella. "Can we . . . talk?"

He led her up the rise away from the house. When they turned around, Ella was struck by how beautiful she thought her place looked tonight. *Thank you, God.*

"I missed you," Jeb said.

"And we missed you. I don't mind telling you I was a little hurt that you didn't ask me to mind the livestock. That's what neighbors are for, you know. They watch out for each other. You didn't have to sell them."

"Actually, it makes things simpler." He spread the blanket and asked her to sit with him. Ella sat. Jeb talked. Her mouth fell open more than once. She could not picture Jeb Cooper in a fancy house. "I didn't fit at home with all the professors," he said, "because I like to be outside working with my hands. And I'll never quite fit out here because I don't really want to be a homesteader, at least not in the conventional sense." He chuckled. "I like to read too much." He shrugged. "I'm a misfit."

*Just like me.*

He shifted on the blanket so he could see her face in the moonlight. "I like you, Ella, and I'd like to be your friend. And friends deserve explanations. I'm sorry I haven't done a better job of that. I honestly didn't think— I never meant to hurt you. I should have explained more."

"I thought you'd gone east to get married. I thought Elizabeth was your wife."

Jeb began to chuckle, and then he laughed. "You thought I was getting a woman? In the *East?*" He shook his head. "Why would I want to do that when I already live right by one of the best women on the earth?"

Ella had nothing to say. Nothing at all. But even as her heart pounded, her eyes looked over at what she and her friends had created from empty prairie, and she didn't think she could give it up. If that was where Jeb was headed . . . what would she do? What would she say? There was still so much to do, and it wasn't about the fence or the buildings or the livestock or the crops nearly as much as it was about Ella Barton knowing. Knowing that what she'd been saying all along was true. She didn't *need* a man. Oh, she might *want* one. But she didn't need one.

"So." Jeb spoke again. "Here's what I've been thinking." He nodded toward the homestead. "You have a dream down there. And you have a nightmare to forget. I don't want to stand in the way of either one of those things taking their natural course." He looked her way, the moonlight showing enough for her to tell he was smiling. "But I *do* want to be here when you decide you're ready for a new dream. Would you be all right with that?"

Ella felt a tear slip out of the corner of one eye and slide down her cheek. It must have glistened in the moonlight. Jeb reached up and wiped it away with a calloused thumb. She caught his hand and held it next to her face so he could feel her nod. "Yes," she said. "Oh . . . yes."

CHAPTER
# TWENTY-NINE

*And I will restore to you*
*the years that the locust hath eaten. . . .*

Joel 2:25

The next morning, the ladies of Four Corners stood in a row between the soddy's front door and the buggy. Someone joked about Hettie's "running the gauntlet" as she made her way down the row, hugging each of them from Ella to Zita, past Sally and Jackson, and then finally to the carriage, where Ruth and Caroline waited to drive her into town. She hugged them all once . . . and then again . . . and then everyone laughed. Nervous laughter. Laughter laced with tears. The kind of laughter that said, *We are so proud of you . . . we want you to be happy . . . we're hoping on hope ever.*

"All right, y'all," Caroline finally said. "We'll never get her to town at this rate. And I allow as to how Dr. Gates is expecting us before midnight." More nervous laughter, and then Hettie climbed up beside Caroline and they drove away, past the field of pumpkins and squash lying atop the earth like so many orange moons. The thought of orange would forever make Caroline smile.

People had been very complimentary of Alice Bailey's creation using the orange remnants Martha had put on sale. But they'd been positively astounded when Mrs. Peterson unfurled hers. She called it "Prairie Stars." No fewer than eighty stars—Caroline had counted them—glowed across the surface of a black quilt, and after sundown when the black faded into the shadows and the lamplight brushed across the surface of that quilt, it truly was as if stars twinkled in the night.

Alice Bailey was not pleased. The ladies were already wondering what she would create for the next Harvest Festival.

*Next year* . . . As she gathered her shawl about her against the autumn chill, Caroline wondered what her first winter in Nebraska would bring. What would it be like out at Four Corners when bitter winds blew and snow fell for days? Sometimes she thought Will Haywood's storytelling talent included a morbid taste for disaster. For a while he'd concentrated on "long red tongues of fire" licking up the dry grass. Lately, though, he'd switched to blizzards, advising the ladies to tie a guide rope between the house and the barn, the house and the fruit cellar, the house and the well.

Caroline couldn't imagine winds so high and snow so deep a person could get lost between their own house and barn, but Matthew agreed with everything Will said. He'd helped Ella with a fireguard, plowing the sod up in two concentric circles a few rods apart all around the Four Corners house, then set fire to the undisturbed grass in between. When Ruth mentioned Lucas Gray's note about barrels by the well, Matthew said that was a good idea, too.

As for being ready for winter, Matthew thought the ladies were, what with the mountain of buffalo chips for fuel and the larder full of garden produce. "You can always bring the team into the house," he said, and laughed when Ruth looked horrified by the idea.

"Well, if that's what it takes to keep Red and the girls safe," Sally said when the idea came up, "you'uns had best get used to the idea." She grinned. "In fact, now that we don't need Hettie's loft no more, maybe—"

"No!" everyone shouted in chorus.

"Aw, I was just foolin'." Sally grinned. "But mind, I won't be foolin' if it comes to keepin' 'em from freezin' to death."

"What?" Hettie asked when Caroline chuckled to herself.

"Oh, I was just remembering Sally's threat to bring the hens in the house if we get a blizzard." When Hettie didn't smile, Caroline realized the poor thing still had a white-knuckled grip on her carpetbag. She reached over to squeeze her hand. "It's gonna be all right."

"I know." Hettie didn't sound convinced.

"Dr. Gates has been brave enough to put down the bottle and follow you and risk everything all over again. I'd say life with a man like that is worth rescuing."

Hettie nodded. "You're right."

"What is it Zita always tells us . . . forget what's behind and press on with hope." Caroline pulled her shawl closer.

"I'm doing my best," Hettie said. "Wait until you see the cradle Matthew's loaning us for the baby. It's a work of art." She loosened her grip on the carpetbag and took a deep breath. "I hope it's a girl."

Matthew ran his hand over the cradle's smooth finish and then stood back to admire the soft luster he'd brought back to the surface of the wood. With the tip of his toe, he set it in motion. "Well," he said, "what do you think?"

"It's perfect." Linney unfolded the simple baby quilt Martha had helped her make and laid it atop the red-and-white-striped feather tick.

Together, they carried the cradle out the back of Matthew's carpentry shop, across the dry prairie, and toward the newly completed house waiting in the distance. "You all right?" he asked. "Say something if you need a rest."

"I don't need a rest, Pa"—Linney rolled her eyes—"and if we don't hurry, they'll beat us to the house." She jiggled the cradle. "Giddyup!"

With a chuckle, Matthew moved into a slow lope. Dr. Gates was waiting for them on the porch, his hands braced on the railing, his eyes fixed on the horizon. Motioning for them to follow him inside, he led the way to the back bedroom. They set the cradle in the corner and stepped back.

"Well," Matthew said to Linney, "what do you think? Can your pa build a decent house or not?"

Back out in the hall, Linney ran her hand over the carved newel-post.

"You're welcome to see the upstairs, too," Dr. Gates said. "There's two more rooms up there. I just wanted to keep things convenient for Hettie by using the main floor for right now."

"You're sure you don't mind?" Linney gazed up the stairs.

"Not a bit. Your pa builds fine houses. Take a look."

Matthew followed her upstairs. On the landing above he decided he couldn't wait any longer to ask the question again. "So. What do you think?"

"It's wonderful."

He gestured from one room to the other. "Which room do you like best?"

Linney didn't hesitate. "The one with the window seat."

"All right. The one with the window seat it is." When Linney looked confused, he said, "I'm building ours next." He grabbed her hand and walked her toward the front of the house. Pointing out the window, he said, "Right there. I got my last check for that final pile of pelts a few days ago. So it's official. Town Lot Number Ninety-three belongs to Matthew Ransom."

If he'd known how much joy a man could give just by buying a square of Plum Grove dirt, maybe he would have done this long ago. On the other hand, as Linney let out a squeal and grabbed his neck and he swung her around, Matthew realized that this was exactly the right moment for him to be doing this. Any earlier, and it would have been out of guilt. Now it was for all the right reasons, and for just the right future, if he had anything to say about it.

"There's something else about the house," he said as he set Linney down. "Something very important. And I don't want you to answer me right now. I want you to think about it. All right?"

Linney nodded. Matthew took a deep breath. "What would you think of our sharing that new house with someone? I haven't said anything about it to anyone else. So if you—"

Linney's eyes grew large, and she blurted out, "It's Caroline, isn't it! You want to ask Caroline to marry you! Oh, Pa!" Once again, she flung her arms around him and gave him a hug. "It'll be wonderful. We can plant flowers together and cook together and make quilts together and—"

While Linney was going on and on about what she and Caroline could do together, Matthew was watching the buggy headed toward them across the prairie. His heart began to hammer. He looked back at his daughter. "Well, before you make all those plans, don't you think we'd better find out if she'll say yes?"

"She'll say yes."

"You sound very sure."

"I am."

"And how can you be so sure?"

"Oh, Pa." Linney shook her head. "Did you pay *any* attention when you two were waltzing at the Harvest Dance?"

Well, now that he thought about it . . . he had.

Linney and Ruth had hurried over to the mercantile—the latter to get what Caroline supposed was yet another one of Lucas Gray's missives, and Linney apparently worried that Martha would be upset with her for being gone so long. Hettie and Forrest had gone over to the clinic to discuss what furniture should be moved into their new parlor, and here Caroline stood with Matthew on the front porch of a house so lovely it made her heart ache. "It's so beautiful," she said. "You should be very proud."

Matthew shrugged. "I think I might try a different shape on the porch finials next time. On the other hand, it'd be nice to build with brick. Will said the new courthouse is going to be brick. That would definitely make for a warmer house. Of course, I'm no bricklayer, but I could do more with the railings and the trim inside if—" He broke off. "Which would you want? If you were choosing?"

"Oh, I don't suppose that'd matter much," Caroline said. Her heart began to beat a little faster. "A fancy house isn't what's important." Her accent was getting worse. She took a deep breath. "I mean, the fancy brick house in St. Louis wasn't worth anything compared to how I feel about the Four Corners soddy."

Matthew nodded. He tilted his head and looked down at her. "Well, I'm thinking brick would be the way to go someday. But I'm not sure I want to wait until I can afford brick. And Linney's already approved of what I'd like to do. Which is"—he put his hands at her waist and drew her close—"to see you in every house I live in from the day you marry me until the day I die." He leaned down and kissed the side of her neck. She shivered and pulled him closer. "Marry me," he said, and kissed her neck again, then worked his way up to her jawline . . . the tip of her chin . . . and then he stopped and looked into her eyes again. "Marry me *soon*." He kissed her lips.

She said yes.

"What do you mean he's *gone*?" Ruth looked down at Sally, who'd just come out of the soddy as they drove up from town.

"He rode up practically in tears, and by the time he finished tellin' us what was goin' on he *was* in tears. Said the cattle was sick and he's afraid it's Texas Fever and two were already down and he was goin' to Lucas to see what to do about it. He didn't even step off the horse, Ruth. Just lit out."

Ruth looked toward the north. *That boy*. When she got her hands on him he was going to get a talking to the likes of which he would never forget. She sighed.

"I'll ride with ya if you want to go after him—and I expect you will." Sally grinned. "Just give me time to get my new dress on."

Ruth hesitated. It was asking a lot of Calico to head out on a twenty-mile journey when she'd already done as much or more going to Plum Grove and back today. And Jackson might be rash, but the truth was he knew the way to the ranch very well, Sam was a good pony, and she'd never hear the end of it if she chased after him like a hysterical mother.

Lucas already said the boys were planning some sort of initiation rite for him at the spring roundup. She could just imagine the merciless teasing he'd get about his mama following him everywhere if she drove up there yet tonight. What was it that Lucas had said once ... something about outfitting her with boots and a hat and letting her trail after him? She shook her head. "No. Just because Jackson's being headstrong doesn't mean you and I have to go charging across the prairie like two mother hens."

"You sure?" Sally seemed disappointed. " 'Cause I could be ready in a whip-snap-minute." She grinned. "And ain't it sorta nice to have an excuse to see ... folks?"

*Not if he's going to tease me mercilessly about being an overprotective mother.*

No, the more Ruth thought about it, the more it seemed right to stay put. Almost impossibly difficult, but right. Lucas already called Jackson a "young man," not a "boy." Ruth supposed she should let him be a young man in this case. His cattle were sick. He needed help. And he'd gone after it. She had to admit she liked very much the idea that Jackson's first thought was to go to Lucas for help. With a sigh, she climbed down from the buggy. And then she remembered. "Caroline has some news. . . ."

She might have said all the right things in broad daylight, but now that the sun had gone down, and Jackson was "out there somewhere," Ruth couldn't sleep. He'd started for the ranch early enough in the day to have already arrived. He might even have run into one of the crews putting up fence. He knew the way. There was nothing to worry over. Still, in the night Ruth wished there was such a thing as an invisible telegraph wire that could send her a message. With a sigh, she turned over in bed. The moon was high now, the night so still she could hear the windmill creaking. Sometimes the rhythmic sound was comforting. Tonight was not one of those nights. She gave up.

Zita was sleeping up in the loft now, and so Ruth padded into the living area, lit a lamp, and sat down at the table with her Bible. She opened it and took out the cabinet photo of Lucas. It made her smile. She was flat-out, all-in, head-over-heels in love with that man. God was good. So very good.

Laying the photo aside, she stood up and walked to the front door and tiptoed outside. And that's when she saw the fire. Not actual flames . . . but a red sky . . . the very kind of sky Will Haywood said signaled something they called a head fire . . . the kind of fire that raced across the prairie for miles, jumping creeks and lapping up everything in its wake . . . *sometimes even outracing the fastest horse.* Clutching at the door, Ruth barely stifled a scream, but she couldn't scream because she couldn't breathe.

Backing against the sod bricks that formed the front of the house, Ruth stared at the horizon, her hand at her heart. *You will not faint. If you faint, you'll be of no use to your son. Don't faint. Get back inside. Get dressed. Get . . . going. GO. GO. GO.*

None of the women sleeping in the house behind her would knowingly let her race straight toward a fire. They'd tie *her* to a kitchen chair if they had to. *They mustn't know. You have to go . . . but they mustn't know.*

As she made her way trembling across what they had started calling the parlor and caught sight of Lucas's cabinet photo, Ruth whirled back about and looked toward the north. *Don't think about it. Don't think. Just do.* She turned down the lamp and tiptoed into her room. Pulling yesterday's dress off the hook by the door, she collected stockings and shoes off the floor and crept outside and toward the barn.

She dressed in the barn, barely managing to button the row of tiny buttons marching up the front of the red calico dress. Creeping about like a horse thief, she backed Calico between the traces, wishing she could trust herself to simply jump astride the little mare bareback, knowing that would be the height of this night's foolish decisions. But she had to do this. If— *No. Do not think IF. Do the next thing. Buckle the harness. Check it again. Bring your nightgown so you can wrap the mare's head if you get caught in the— If you need it.*

As quietly as she could, Ruth led Calico and the buggy away from the barn, past the house, wincing with every turn of the squeaking wheel, watching for movement in the house, knowing that if anyone called out, she'd only hurry away faster. *Please don't let them hear. Let them sleep. Let me go.*

She'd crossed the firebreak before she dared climb aboard and take up the reins. Finally, she urged Calico into a lope. The hardest thing was not to crack the whip and set the mare to running. But she knew better. They had a long journey ahead, and she needed the mare to make it every step of the way. As the moon shone down on Four Corners, Ruth headed north toward the red sky.

*. . . Weeping may endure for a night,*
*but joy cometh in the morning.*

PSALM 30:5

This was nothing like that other desperate drive north to tend an injured rancher last spring. She'd been a different woman back then. A woman whose life centered on one thing in the future—getting her son an education. Lucas Gray had been little more than another human being who needed help she could give. That Ruth Dow was doing her duty like a good soldier's wife should. This Ruth Dow was not only a desperate mother but also a woman in love. A woman so terrified that as the buggy wheeled across the hills, she began to weep. *Pay attention to the mare. Drive carefully. Here. Stop and let her drink. Yes, that's it. Get a drink yourself.*

If she pulled outside of herself and let Ruth Dow, the soldier's wife, narrate the night . . . tell her what to do . . . if all she had to do was obey the voice in her head . . . then she would be all right. Snippets of things Zita had said over the months also came to mind. Things about hoping and God's everlasting arms. Things about God being a shelter. A high tower. A solid rock. *The* solid rock. What was it Jeb Cooper always sang? It was absurd to sing along this desperate journey, but if it kept her from panicking— Ruth sang, "On Christ the solid Rock I stand. All other ground is sinking sand."

Long before Ruth could smell the smoke, Calico stopped, tossed her head, and tried to turn back. "I'm sorry." The buggy whip came out. "We can't turn back. I can't let you—" Ruth won the battle. The mare didn't like it, but she kept going.

The first time a deer ran past, Ruth didn't think much about it. A grunt, a flash, and the creature was past them before she realized what it was. But then came another and another. And then antelope. Antelope were shy. Flighty. In fact, until now all Ruth had seen of antelope was a flash of white as they lifted their tails and darted away far in the distance.

Calico stopped again. This time she would not be moved. She trembled. Suddenly the horse took off again, and it took all of Ruth's skill to keep her from bolting. Ruth could smell it now. *If I can smell it, what must it be like for the horse?*

She saw the first injured animal at dawn. A stag, one side of its coat singed, the flesh beneath it darkened. And then . . . oh, then . . . blackened earth as far as she could see. Calico whinnied when her hooves first touched the burnt prairie. Again, she stopped. This time, she refused to move until Ruth laid the whip on.

"I'm so sorry, Calico . . . so sorry . . . but we have to keep going. We have to keep going." When the mare finally moved, it was more sideways than forward. Fearing the buggy would overturn, Ruth kept at it with the whip until finally they were headed north again . . . always north.

The first time she saw a dead bird she didn't realize she was look-ing at a charred carcass. *The flames can catch up with a running horse.* She began to cry again. Unable to form words, she said God's name over and over and over again. Calico trotted on.

*Stop and rest or you'll kill the horse.* Knowing it to be true didn't mean she could do it. Everything in her screamed against it, but somehow Ruth listened to the inner voice, and when they came to the place where she thought Pete had stopped that long-ago night when they'd dashed toward an injured Lucas Gray, she pulled up and let Calico drink. Soaking her nightgown in the cool water, she wrapped it over the horse's nose, entwining it through the bridle, hoping it would somehow obliterate at least some of the stench and keep the mare going.

*Keep her going. Keep me going. Let me find Jackson. Let him be all right.* As she climbed back aboard the buggy, Ruth forced herself to envision Jackson and Lucas laughing at her ridiculous race through the night. *Yes, Lord. Let it be nothing more than an anecdote in some future pioneer's memoir. Let them laugh at the stupid woman, so foolish to head into a fire when all the while her son and the man she loved were sitting on the front porch of a ranch house drinking coffee. Foolish woman. Panicked when there was no need.*

Again, Calico stopped. Ruth raised the buggy whip. But she didn't use it. Terrified as she was, the little mare had done it. Brought Ruth right where she wanted to be . . . through miles of scorched grass . . . along the trail and up the last hill to where the Graystone Ranch buildings had nestled in a green valley like an emerald set atop a bit of tan velvet.

Ruth dropped the buggy whip and climbed down. Trembling, she stumbled down the rise toward what had once been one of the prettiest places in the sandhills. It was gone. All of it. No cattle. No bunkhouse. No corrals. No horses. No barn. Nothing but charred remnants and black earth.

She didn't know how long she stumbled about what was left of the place, from where the barn had once stood to the corral where Jackson had learned to ride and then back to the house. Her throat so parched she couldn't scream, her last ounce of strength spent, Ruth fell to her knees. Curling onto one side, she lay on the burnt grass and wept.

Calico brought her back to her senses, snuffling at her hair and whickering. *Water.* The horse would have to find her own. For now, at least, Ruth would lie here beneath the wicked blue sky. How dare the sun rise on the earth as if nothing had happened? As if life should go on.

How dare . . . Calico whickered again. "Go away," Ruth croaked, but the horse was insistent, lipping her shoulder, and when still she did not respond, grasping a lock of her hair in its teeth and tugging.

Frowning, Ruth opened her eyes. Not Calico. Not a little roan mare, but a great gray— *Hannibal. Of course. They would have opened all the gates and stalls and sent the livestock and cattle ahead of the fire, hoping some would survive.* Hannibal had survived and come back home.

Ruth staggered to her feet. The stallion snuffled at her dress and snorted. She looked down at the filthy red dress and more tears flowed. The stallion stayed close. She buried her face in his mane and sobbed until she had no more tears. And then Hannibal lifted his head and gave an odd little grunt.

"What is it? What do you see?"

Two riders. No . . . three . . . maybe five . . . she didn't know. She didn't care. The only ones who mattered were the first two, because as they came closer and her eyes focused, Ruth saw a boy on a buckskin pony and a man astride a chestnut gelding.

Hannibal snorted and danced away. Lucas held back so that Jackson reached her first. "Oh, Ma," he muttered. "I didn't think. I just had to get help. There wasn't any fire and then there was, but I was closer to the ranch by then, so I gave Sam his head. I didn't know Sam could run so fast. When I got here Lucas and me and the boys we tore out for a rocky canyon." He pointed east. "Lucas set a backfire and we just launched ourselves down into that canyon, Ma. I heard the fire go by. The roar . . . but we made it."

As she listened to him jabber, Ruth closed her eyes and thanked God for ears to hear her son's voice . . . surely one of the sweetest sounds on earth.

*A leader of men.* That's what people had said about General George Dow, and now, as Ruth watched Lucas react to the devastation around him, she saw the same qualities. He'd set aside what this all meant for him personally, and was operating at a level that his men—wranglers—needed. He made decisions quickly, and it wasn't long before Pete and a dozen of "the boys" had headed for Frank Darby's ranch. Lucas was fairly certain the line of fire wouldn't have gotten that far, in which case Darby would be able to resupply the men, enabling them to get to rounding up whatever cattle might have survived.

As the men discussed rounding up cattle, Ruth and Jackson helped Wah Lo rummage along the edge of the buildings. Finally, with a shout of triumph, Wah Lo lifted a blackened pot out of the debris. Together he and Jackson rigged a way to haul fresh water up out of the well. They began to water the horses.

In an amazingly short amount of time, there was a plan for resurrecting the ranch. Three wranglers were assigned to head into Plum Grove for tents—Lucas gave a wry smile as he instructed the men making that supply run to tell Will Haywood his "operating cash" had been inside the rolltop desk in the parlor. Will would need to extend credit.

Finally, just as Ruth handed off a bucket of water to Jackson, Lucas came to where they stood and, taking her hand, asked Jackson if he minded "if I had a word with your mother."

Jackson looked from Ruth to Lucas and back again. Something seemed to pass between boy and man before Jackson smiled. "Of course not," he said, and went back to watering the horses with Wah Lo. Taking Ruth's hand, Lucas led her away.

"I'm so sorry," she said, gesturing toward the ruins of the house. "Everything you've worked so hard for—"

Lucas waved the comment away. "When I saw Jackson come tearing into the yard—when he told me he'd just left without telling you—I knew. I knew what you'd do. And there was nothing I could do. You were headed straight into a lake of fire and I couldn't stop—" His voice broke.

They were a few rods away from the men working the ruins of the ranch now, and he pulled her close. Taking a long, ragged breath, he croaked, "Dear God in heaven, woman. If I'd lost you—" He stopped talking with words . . . and didn't let go until the boys started hooting their approval and applauding. Glancing their way, Ruth saw one of them nudge Jackson, who was grinning for all he was worth.

Loosening his grip a bit, Lucas looked down at her. "Promise me you will never do anything that reckless—anything that foolish—again."

She smiled up at him. "I don't think I can promise *never* to be reckless or foolish again, Lucas."

He cocked his head. Questioning. "And that's because . . . ?"

"Because I need to be able to say yes when you propose."

He laughed out loud and bent to kiss her again. This time, when the boys hooted and applauded, he looked over. Without releasing Ruth, he called out, "Nobody told you to give up on catching the horse."

Indeed, Hannibal had spent the last several hours eluding any attempt to lasso him. It seemed obvious he wasn't going to bolt and run off, but then again he wasn't in the mood to be captured, either.

"Oh, for heaven's sake," Ruth said. Slipping out of Lucas's arms, she went to the chestnut gelding and pulled down Lucas's lariat and headed to where Hannibal danced, just out of reach of anyone's rope. At the sight of her, the stallion stood still. His ears came forward.

"I don't think they should feed you to the coyotes anymore, you two-bit bag of wind," she said, walking toward him as she talked. "But I really do think you should acquire an entirely new set of manners." She held out the lariat. "I'd appreciate it if you'd behave yourself so these men could get something done. They've a ranch to rebuild." She held the noose open with both hands. Hannibal lifted his head and put it through. As the boys stood openmouthed, Lucas walked up, put his arm around her waist, and pulled her close.

"And that, boys," he said to them, "is how it's done."

Hope On ◆ Hope Ever

# ATTRACTIVE WIDOWS

I was sitting at a desk at the Nebraska State Historical Society Archives researching a quilt documentation book when that headline caught my eye. "Another cargo of war widows arrived . . ." As questions like *how* and *why* and *what if* flew through my mind, I knew that I was on my way to a new adventure with imaginary friends who would eventually populate my next novel. When further research revealed that hundreds of single women successfully homesteaded in the west, Sally and Ruth and Caroline and Ella and Hettie became more and more real to me, and I couldn't let them go.

*Five* women's stories in one book? I'd never tried that before. Could I do it? Truth be told, there were times during the writing of *Sixteen Brides* when I felt more like I was wrestling a behemoth than telling a story. If you enjoyed reading about the women we came to call the "Fav-Five," the credit goes to Ann Parrish and the other Bethany House editors who unselfishly gave of their time to help me win the wrestling match with the "biggest" story I've ever attempted.

Thank you, Bethany House Publishers, for continuing to believe in my work and support it. Thank you, Ann. Your friendship and editing expertise are among the best of God's blessings to me. Thanks to Marge Caldwell and Brooke Reinhard for reading the early editions and pointing out flaws, and to the Kansas Eight who brainstorm and answer middle-of-the-night panicked emails with love and support and, best of all, faithful prayer. Thanks also to the women of Nebraska's Dawson County Historical Society who helped me unearth "the real story" behind my imaginary tale. (Errors in the history are mine, not theirs.) Thank *you*, dear reader, for allowing me a novelist's license to adjust a few—just a few, mind you—details and dates.

God has a way of yanking me into the unknown and bringing me to the end of myself for the express purpose of drawing me closer to him. Not surprisingly, that's what he does with the women of the Ladies Emigration Society in *Sixteen Brides*. Thank you for making time to head west with them. I hope you found joy in the journey.

Grace and peace to you and yours,
Stephanie

# Stephanie Grace Whitson

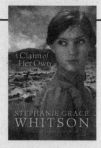

When Mattie O'Keefe arrives in Deadwood, South Dakota, she finds the future she hoped for shattered. Determined to claim a fresh start, Mattie soon must decide where true riches lie— and what's worth dying for.

*A Claim of Her Own*

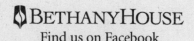